Love's Lessons to Laurel

RITA JONES

HOPE

DENVER, COLORADO

Published by:

HOPE

DENVER, COLORADO

Visit www.loveslessonstolaurel.com

ISBN: 978-0-69289-721-8

First printing 2017

Cover design and production by Gary A. Rosenberg
www.thebookcouple.com

Printed in the United States of America

"To get to the core of God at his greatest,
one must first get into himself at the core of his least."
—MEISTER ECKHARDT

"My thoughts are always in truth. For lo!
Myself has become the truth."
—BUDDHA

"Eternal Happiness belongs to the wise
who perceive Him within themselves."
—THE VEDAS

"The kingdom of God is not coming with signs to be
observed; nor will they say, 'Lo, here it is!' or 'There!'
for behold, the kingdom of God is within you."
—JESUS CHRIST

"He who knows his own self, knows God."
—MOHAMMED

This book is dedicated to:

My grandparents, parents, friends,
teachers, spouses, and children—
we accomplish nothing alone.

C. R. S.—The Light who illuminates the dark.

Alcoholics Anonymous—Who lifted me
from the hollows of hell to the summit of serenity.

All those who believe in God but have found
that religion has left them unfulfilled.

Contents

Acknowledgments

I sincerely wish to thank Jennifer Read Hawthorne, who doesn't edit works of fiction. Why she agreed to work on this novel still baffles me. However, the book would not be its best without her outstanding editorial skills.

And God said, "Let there be light," and there was light.
God saw that the light was good, and He separated the
light from the darkness. God called the light "day,"
and the darkness He called "night." And there was
evening, and there was morning—the first day.

—GENESIS 1:3–5

Palo Alto, California
Stanford University Medical Center, 2015

It was three o'clock in the morning as I stood in the waiting room next to the cardiac transplant unit. I had been here night and day for over six weeks while my mother awaited a new heart. Yesterday around noon, it had happened. An eighteen-year-old young man due to graduate high school in three weeks was driving his truck on I-25, outside of Casper, Wyoming. A strong wind blew a semi rig on its side, and the teenager struck the back of it straight on. He was airlifted to Denver, where brain death was confirmed, and we were quickly notified that the transplant would proceed as soon as the heart arrived.

Mom went into surgery at seven o'clock, and surgeons removed a heart that had barely functioned since her third and last heart attack. She hadn't gotten out of the operating room until around two thirty in the morning. I had briefly seen her in intensive care, but the transplant team was too busy setting up her postoperative monitoring to allow me extended visiting.

Shortly after she entered the ICU, a tall man wearing a surgical hat and gown walked toward me as I sat in the waiting room. A crumpled surgical mask hung around his neck, along with a set of special glasses fitted with two-inch magnifying loops. Perspiration had soaked halfway down his scrub top, and a two-day stubble shaded his face. I did my best to clean up, but my ragged hair sprouted everywhere and crying had converted my mascara into a pen-and-ink sketch of the Mississippi Delta. I tried to hide this fact, but the best I could do was cover it by putting on my reading glasses.

Up until now, Mom and I had not met the lead surgeon because the internal medicine heart team had provided her care until a suitable organ was found. The cardiothoracic fellow had taken us through the preoperative consents. Now, the lead surgeon sat down beside me and firmly clasped my right hand with both of his. Instantly, I understood that two of the world's most gifted hands were supporting mine.

The man before me had done four years of undergraduate school and four years of medical school. But those were just warm-up courses. Medical school was followed by a five-year surgical residency and two years of a cardiothoracic fellowship.

On top of all that, he had earned a PhD, which was printed after the MD on his identification badge. On my mental checklist, that amounted to about seventeen years of post–high school education. Probably, the man knew what he was doing.

"Miss Jones?" he asked. "Are you Mrs. Montgomery's daughter?" I nodded and asked him to call me Rita. "I'm Omar Gynsin, and I headed the team that did your mother's transplant. There were no difficulties, and I'm happy to say there was no leakage around any of the surgical anastomoses—uh, I should say, connections. The heart was an outstanding tissue match for your mom, and provided she does well over the next twenty-four hours . . ." He suddenly paused and looked at me intently for several seconds before he went on. "I'm sorry, Miss Jones—I mean Rita. I'm going on thirty-five hours straight and my energy is starting to fade. My point is, the next day is critical, and after that period, the prognosis rapidly improves. Here is my card. If you have any concerns that the nurses or fellows cannot address, you may call me day or night at that number. If I'm in surgery, I'll return your call as soon as I'm finished."

When he stood up to leave, I took off my glasses and couldn't stop myself from giving him a big hug. As I looked up, I saw his blue eyes sparkle, and I sensed he was a man who gave every challenge his best effort. He didn't like to lose. To me, that meant more than seventeen years of training. I knew Mom was in the best hands. He smiled, gently patted my shoulder, and turned to walk away.

His profile reminded me of a young man I'd dated and loved during high school and college. But there was no confusing the two. I hadn't seen Denny since 1988, when I had volunteered at a homeless shelter and he wandered in, shaking and intoxicated. Over the next three days, I visited him in the shelter as his mind grew less foggy, but he never did recognize me. On the fourth day, he was back on the streets.

Thinking about him still made me sad, for perhaps I was to blame. If he was still alive, it was only by the grace of God. From past experience, I was sure God had a particular fondness for Denny. But tonight, I couldn't let memories of an extinguished flame ruin Mom's good news. Besides, something astounding was about to happen.

I asked an orderly if there was a window facing east where I could look out over the city. He directed me to an empty patient's room, where I took a seat and waited for four o'clock to come around. During this hour, most normal people were asleep and the electrical grid used the least power. That was not a secret. The secret involved a highly classified project that would occur at precisely four o'clock, when all electrical power in Northern California would cease for one second before coming back online. Every home, business, bank—even McDonald's—would go dark.

While at first this didn't seem like such a big deal, a planned power outage affecting twenty-five million people had never occurred until last year, when it was tested three times in preparation for tonight. This kind of information in the hands of cyber-criminals could seriously cripple the American economy—especially when battery-powered laptops and tablets needed only microseconds to steal millions of dollars.

But even that was minor compared to how history would remember this moment. My mother had done many behind-the-scenes consultations for the federal government. She was privy to top-secret information and knew that because of my work, I also had a high security clearance. Prior to surgery, she told me what to look for and said, "Honey, if today is my last day, I'll leave this world knowing that man finally bottled the sun."

She was right. In this early morning, fifty miles east of San Francisco, hundreds of physicists would turn their attention to the 192-laser array at the huge Lawrence-Livermore National Ignition Facility. Each laser would take small amounts of electrical power and amplify that energy eight hundred thousand times. When every laser fired simultaneously, 192 points of directed ultraviolet light would uniformly focus 500 trillion watts on a small gold canister holding a supercooled, spherical, deuterium-tritium pellet. Enough energy to fuel a country one thousand times the size of the United States would strip the electrons off the surface of this hydrogen isotope pellet and increase its core temperature to 80 million degrees Fahrenheit.

At the same moment, pressure forces three times greater than those found in the core of the sun would evenly collapse the hydrogen sphere to one thirty-fifth its original size, where aftercoming shock waves would compress it even further. The coulomb forces that normally caused two positive protons to repel each other would be greatly overwhelmed, and the two protons would push together and fuse. Once the core was ignited, it would continuously yield Helium-4 and vast amounts of clean energy on a scale not previously imagined. Unlike the thousands of earlier tests, which had verified the fusion reactor's reliability, tonight the facility would not shut down. When the lights came back on, man's dream of harnessing the sun's power would be accomplished for all to see but few to realize. Northern California would continue thriving using only fusion power!

With ninety seconds to go, I stood up and looked out the window. I'd left the door to the patient room open. The lights in the hall were dim, but a small amount of glare was reflected in the window. As the seconds drew down, I noticed in the glare that a figure was approaching. The closer he came, I realized it was the surgeon I had talked to only minutes ago. Fear mounted as I assumed Mom had taken a turn for the worst.

When Dr. Gynsin stood a foot away, he asked softly, "Rita, did you use to go by the name Laurel Montgomery?"

I was stunned. No one had called me by that name for years, and very few even remembered it. Because forty years had passed since I had graduated from high school, my appearance had significantly changed. Only those who knew me well could have associated that old name with me. I thought about falsely answering his question, until I remembered that I had trusted him to put a new heart in my mother. Why shouldn't I be completely honest with him? I hadn't changed my name because of anything illegal. I answered, "It's been a long time. But yes, I used to go by the name Laurel Montgomery."

He moved closer as he took off his surgical hat and removed the mask around his neck. I tried to recognize him, and at the moment I saw the scar on his nose, he pulled me close and kissed me with passion I hadn't felt in years. All my feelings from the 1970s quickly flooded my thoughts, and long-repressed emotions made themselves known. Somehow, Denny Jensen was holding and kissing me just as he had done so long ago. How the drunk I had taken care of so many years ago had become a cardiac surgeon—and had just operated on my mother—was beyond coincidence.

As the lights outside vanished and came back on, only one common denominator linked tonight's two miracles: Iris Wimple! And she was a story no one would ever forget.

CHAPTER 1

Autumn 1971

Life in Sutter, Oregon, approached perfection. Surrounded by forest pines and situated next to a beautiful lake, Sutter was so quiet and lovely that it was hard to believe Portland was only thirty-five miles away. It was autumn, and northwestern fall colors painted our quaint community. Mount Hood's summer snow had melted, creating a myriad of streams crisscrossing the town.

Main Street had Penney's, Montgomery Ward, and every other essential shop except Fred's Auto Garage, which took up half a block directly behind the Dairy Queen. Every road was two-lane, and heavy traffic consisted of three or more cars. Since the police handled few crimes, jaywalking qualified as a federal offense, and a bar fight was reason to call out the whole force.

Life-changing controversies rarely if ever disrupted the peace in our small town. So no one could have known that a religious storm was about to circle over and descend upon Sutter. The eye of the storm would be a teenager named Laurel Montgomery. That's me.

For those of you who don't remember the early seventies, let me take you back for a moment. There was no computer smaller than a house, cell phones didn't exist, and a "text" was a book needed for class. Every household owned a large car, and with gas at thirty-six cents a gallon, filling the tank didn't mean declaring bankruptcy. The Dow Jones hovered around nine hundred, and the 1970 United States census estimated the population at 200 million.

Television changed when the long-running *Ed Sullivan Show* ended. Daring satire stretched the limits of TV censorship when *All in the Family* hit the airwaves. Mature audiences couldn't get enough, and the modern sitcom came to stay. Archie, Edith, Meathead, and Gloria made Americans realize that old, accepted ideas needed to be reexamined.

After the Apollo 13 crew turned a near disaster into a triumph of human ingenuity, television documented the majestic glory of the most powerful machines ever built when the crews of Apollo 14 and 15 returned to walk once again on the moon. People born before the flight at Kitty Hawk watched those crews escape Earth's atmosphere at over 25,000 miles per hour, gazing on that achievement and knowing they'd witnessed man's evolution from the horse to the heavens.

California sentenced Charles Manson in the Tate-LaBianca murders, and three months later, President Nixon announced his plans to visit China in 1972.

My life, however, was carefree, with few responsibilities. Summer disappeared quickly, and school started the day after Labor Day.

I was fourteen years old, and every day the world appeared more complex. Four weeks after starting ninth grade, six out of my seven teachers began assigning homework. Except for finding the time, completing assignments didn't demand much; a few pencils, some notebooks, and occasionally a ruler would smartly outfit a student for the entire year. School was my life; I reveled in clubs and took part in sports. While politics wasn't my strong point, as a member of the student council, I enjoyed looking for ways to improve school life.

I found that advancing from eighth to ninth grade brought increased responsibility and a strong craving for boys. As with many young girls, puberty had started when I was twelve. Until now, it hadn't raised any difficult questions.

I lived at home with my mother, Marie, and my dog, Otis. Dad left when I was an infant, so I remembered nothing about him. All I knew was that he didn't stay in contact or pay child support. Mom was an attorney working in a law firm that specialized in negotiating mergers between international corporations. I didn't know it then, but throughout the world, Mom had a reputation as one of the finest corporate lawyers in mergers and acquisitions. Her work often meant travel, meaning I had to share the household responsibilities.

Mom was an outstanding parent. She loved me and provided both of us with good meals and a comfortable home. Fulfilling her many responsibilities wouldn't be easy for a single mother today, let alone in 1971. My education was her top priority.

When Mom looked relaxed, I felt comfortable bringing up difficult topics. Mom, on the other hand, didn't do well with intimate questions. Men and sex, for example, were subjects Mom tried to avoid. Like on the day I asked about a phrase I'd heard at the mall: "Mom, what's a blow job?"

Mom started blushing, swallowed hard, and signaled for me to wait as she poured a whiskey. Returning to her desk, she said, "Laurel Montgomery! You shouldn't be using those words. It's a term describing intimate communication couples share when expressing their love for each other. You'll understand when you're in love and married."

I persisted. "But, Mom, what is it? What do you do exactly?" Being an attorney, Mom preferred asking questions, not answering them. When she didn't immediately respond, I used a legal tactic and tried rephrasing the question. "Don't you want me to learn this stuff so I can be a great wife? Doesn't someone have to teach the lessons?" The more I asked, the more she pleaded the fifth. Pouring another whiskey and searching for words, she looked relieved when the phone rang. I momentarily put the subject aside as I lifted the receiver.

It was my best friend, Joann. Joann and I met when we were six. She was blond, and at fourteen, had a sleek body that attracted many young men. While I was shy and reserved, she was outgoing and gregarious. She would ignore a warning if adventure lurked beyond the horizon. Growing up together, we had learned to sense each other's thoughts and predict each other's actions. While Joann sometimes pushed the boundaries of acceptable behavior—like rafting near the edge of a waterfall—she recognized my ability to keep us afloat on the rare occasions when our raft went over the edge. We made a solid team.

In warm weather, Joann and I liked to hike. September in Oregon is a sight to behold. The colors of nature's palette unfold in a masterpiece of exquisiteness. The reds, yellows, and greens begin turning deciduous trees into living rainbows. Temperatures stay near seventy, and for several weeks, the rain ceases.

The small lake next to Sutter had a six-mile trail following the shore. We usually walked this trail, often taking a picnic. The smell of the pines and the variety of wildlife always provided adventure. Besides raccoons and squirrels, we occasionally saw a deer and, rarely, an otter.

Answering the phone, I said, "Hello? Hey, Joann, what do you want to do this weekend? There's a new movie at the Rialto called *Love Story*. The film's a year old, but it just hit Sutter. It's rated M for mature and only costs a quarter." Of course, we weren't allowed to see R-rated films, and we weren't old enough to sneak in.

Joann replied, "It's supposed to be sunny, and the boys are planning a project near the lake. Rumor is, Bill Arnold and Kevin Stone are building a tree house just off the trail. I know their tree house could use a woman's touch. Seeing boys beats any movie."

"Well, I guess we could," I said, quickly thinking through the possible bad results. Finally, I said, "Sure. That's fine. By the way, do you think the boys know what a blow job is? It involves men and possibly blowing in their ear, but I'm not sure. I asked Mom, but she won't even talk about it."

"Laurel, I don't have a clue. You're pretty smart. If you're stumped, Bill and Kevin wouldn't know. They're handsome, but dumb. Look up the word *stupid* and you'll find their class pictures. Let me ask Tim."

I heard a distant discussion as Joann conferred with her brother. Tim was eighteen and graduating next May. As siblings, they got along well; Tim was always advising Joann—and by extension, me—in the ways of the world.

I heard a loud yell, "No way, Tim. Are you kidding? And guys like this? That's crazy." Joann picked up the phone.

"You won't believe this," as she described the act in vivid detail. "Tim said if we ever gave a blow job without a guy wearing a rubber, we'd get pregnant."

Unbelievable! I'd never do that, and I couldn't understand why married couples did it either. Surely gallons of Listerine would be necessary after finishing. But how could women get pregnant by swallowing sperm? I knew from biology this wasn't right. Maybe Mom was correct: I'd understand when the time was right.

We gossiped for another hour and fine-tuned our plans for Saturday, deciding to take our swimsuits in case the lake was warm. I couldn't foresee that our autumn hike would highlight my last tranquil day, nor did I hear the thunder in the distance.

Friday morning dawned. As was the case with most students, this was my favorite day. Tonight, Sutter was hosting a high school football game—but first, I had tests in algebra and world history. I never understood why we studied these courses. Adults I knew rarely used algebra or history. But my complaining didn't help. On the track to high school graduation, these subjects were just two more compulsory hurdles.

The class I hated most was home economics. For numerous archaic reasons, the school felt obligated to teach young women how to care for home and family. In the seventies, if women weren't stay-at-home mothers, they usually worked as secretaries, teachers, or nurses. There were few women professionals. My life plan didn't involve home economics. I couldn't sew or cook, and I despised cleaning. Above all, I loathed doing laundry.

When school ended, Mrs. Gallagher, our home economics teacher, went to the teachers' lounge to smoke. In the coming week, she was planning to test us on the proper use of a washer and dryer. Because I despised laundry, I decided to speak for every woman who hated cleaning clothes. I'd seen my granddad repair a washer. I didn't remember every detail, but I knew washers needed a rubber belt to rotate the drum.

Joann was coming down the hall. I grabbed her and said, "Come in here; I need your help."

"I have swimming practice," she said, resisting.

"This won't take long. Come on!" I dragged her into the classroom. We pulled the washers out, and I opened the back panel covering the motor. The drive belt ran from the motor to a flywheel mounted on the carriage drum. I knew this belt rotated the drum and washed the clothes. Without the belt, no agitation or spin drying could occur.

"Quit playing with your hair and get me a butcher knife."

"A butcher knife? Laurel, what are you doing?"

"Hurry! Mrs. Gallagher will be back soon." Joann ran over to the kitchen counter and returned with a meat cleaver. I glared at her.

"What am I going to do with a cleaver?" I asked.

"It's the sharpest tool I could find." She was right. The cleaver sliced the belts in under ten seconds. I closed the panels, and we pushed the washers back in place.

As we were leaving, Mrs. Gallagher appeared. "Hello, ladies. I'm sorry I wasn't here. Did you need help?"

Looking guilty, Joann struggled for words. I piped up, "Mrs. Gallagher, Joann was wondering—well, you know—if there were any after-school projects she could do to raise her grade. I said you were a compassionate teacher and could help. Joann's thinking of becoming a home economics teacher," I lied.

Joann suddenly seemed on the verge of spitting nails. Mrs. Gallagher replied, "Joann, I'm so glad you enjoy my class. Of course I'll help you. I usually don't teach knitting until tenth grade, but you have long fingers and could be a great knitter. Starting Monday, show up a half hour early. If you knit a scarf by Christmas, I'll raise your grade one letter."

"Thanks, Mrs. Gallagher," Joann replied, hissing through clenched teeth. "I love getting up early. It keeps me from missing breakfast." She paused momentarily. "But you know, Mrs. Gallagher, Laurel has always wanted to learn knitting. Can she join me? Look at her excitement!" My mouth dropped open. Joann rarely thought this fast.

"That's a great idea. She's right, Laurel. You don't have the home economics aptitude; Joann does. Your grade could also improve. Join Joann, and next year, you'll be ahead of your classmates. Have a great weekend, and study for Tuesday's laundry test. I planned on giving it Monday, but the machines are making funny noises. It's been a while, so the appliance man will take a look. Bye-bye, girls."

As we exited Mrs. Gallagher's room, Joann pulled my hair. I sensed she wasn't happy. "I'm going to kill you after I beat you to a pulp. I hate home economics. Knitting excites me as much as dating Mike Beckwith."

"Gee, Joann, he'd be fine if he'd bathe and stop picking his nose."

"You know what I mean. We'll be the laughingstock of the ninth-grade girls, and what's worse, we're still taking the laundry test. If anybody finds out we cut those belts, we'll be knitting until high school graduation."

As Joann left for swimming practice, I pondered what had happened. I decided that wherever life took me, knitting might be useful. I imagined knitting in my rocking chair while Walter Cronkite asked, "Madame President, how does your administration plan to stop the war in Vietnam?"

I liked the image I saw. Someday our country would elect a woman president. A female's perspective on policy might be the cure for the Good Ol' Boys' Club. In modern times, Indira Gandhi and Golda Meir were the only women leading a country. I thought a woman president was way overdue.

"Well, Walter," I would say as I knit one, pearled one, "let me tell you my plans."

Walking home from school, my only concern was what to wear for tonight's game. Sutter was a safe and friendly town. The population barely exceeded five thousand people. Many had advanced degrees and commuted to Portland, so they could enjoy Sutter's small-town atmosphere.

Portland's West Coast location attracted people of many nationalities, bringing diversity to the community. Residents living in Sutter traveled throughout the world. As a teen, I didn't realize how lucky I was to experience various cultures. Sutter didn't have the prejudices running rampant in many big cities.

Or at least that's what I thought. Within days, I would learn how wrong I was.

CHAPTER 2

A Trade:
China for Iris Wimple

It was 3:30 Friday afternoon when my mother walked through the front door and sat at the dining room table sorting the mail. Seeing her home so early surprised me. Friday was her busiest day, and usually, she wasn't home before seven. Thankfully I wasn't doing anything wrong. I put down my books and wandered toward the kitchen.

"Hey, Mom, why are you home so early?" I asked.

She said, "Well, Laurel, I have good news—or bad news, depending on your point of view. I'm leaving for China on Sunday. President Nixon has opened communications with the Chinese, and the business opportunities for American companies are endless if mutual terms can be reached. I'm going to China in hopes of closing the gaps and reaching an agreement."

Brilliant words graced my tongue, "But Mom, you don't speak Chinese, and you hate Chinese food."

"Honey, I'll be with people who speak Chinese, and I'll survive if I don't think about what I'm eating."

"But, Mom, what will I do about Otis, and who's going to look after me?" Of course, I already took care of Otis, and being a teenager, I didn't want my friends thinking I depended on my mom.

"Unfortunately, I'll be gone almost six weeks." Six weeks! God, what an eternity. Her business trips were never that long. Then it dawned on me: I'd have the run of the house for six weeks! I imagined slumber parties, games, listening to Bobby Sherman records—the opportunities were endless.

"Well, I guess if you have to go, let's not put it off; get your bags and I'll help you pack. I'll look after the house, take care of Otis, and pick up the mail. If you sign some checks, I can pay the bills." Secretly, I saw a check or two improving my bank balance. "What do you say?"

"Well, honey, I trust you, but at fourteen, you're still too young to stay alone. I've asked Mrs. Wimple to stay with you while I'm away."

My glorious adult-free vacation quickly faded into the sunset. Mrs. Wimple had last looked after me when I was eleven. "I don't need a babysitter. I'm in my teens. You know I can stay alone; I've done it before! Please, Mom? Please? I'll clean my room and weed the garden. I can even paint the fence—and, you know, all that stuff. Come on, Mom!" I begged.

"No, Laurel, I've made up my mind. Mrs. Wimple is coming over Sunday, and that's that."

"Maybe I could stay with Joann?" I persisted. "They've always welcomed me. I can even take Otis. He behaves as long as Mr. Van Skok closes his underwear drawer and the cat stays in the basement."

"Laurel, I've never been gone this long. It's an imposition to stay with the Van Skoks for six weeks. If I have to stay longer, I don't want any bad feelings. They're good friends, so let's keep it that way."

"Gee, Mom. Do you have to go?" Guilt was all I had left. "I'm your firstborn child. How can you abandon me?"

"Laurel, you're my only child. It's times like this I'm glad there's only you. Assuming I successfully complete this agreement, I can pay off our home, buy a new car, and put away money so you can attend college. I'll miss you, but meeting future goals means we have to sacrifice today. Remember, no one owes us a living. Hard work provided everything we own. You're fourteen, and I felt I could leave you here. Am I wrong?"

I didn't know what to say. I'd been trying to prove I was mature, and now she was using my words against me—an old lawyer ploy. Reluctantly, I said, "No, Mom, you're right. It's just—I haven't had time to digest all this."

"You're right, honey, you haven't. I'm sorry this trip came up quickly, but it's an event I can't control. You and Mrs. Wimple get along, and you're one of her favorite young women. I'm leaving her the paperwork to make any serious decisions during my absence. She will consider your wishes, but remember, the final decision is hers. Do you understand?"

"Yes, Mom."

I had a long history with Iris Wimple. Iris was a wonderful woman who'd lived in Sutter many years. She'd looked after me numerous times when my mother was away on business. Iris volunteered at hospitals and the Red Cross. When she wasn't volunteering, she baked for sick and elderly people. She was also an excellent gardener. The flowers around her 1,200-square-foot home were stunning. She often gave roses to folks who needed cheering up.

How Iris earned a living, no one knew. Social Security seemed the most likely source. To my astonishment, she couldn't drive, and she was the only person I knew who didn't own a TV.

If Iris had an oddity, it was her uncoordinated wardrobe. Her blouse might be purple and her slacks orange. She thought nothing of wearing a multicolored scarf, a blue Parisian hat, and a set of Tony Lama cowboy boots. While it was the seventies and bright fashions ruled the day, Iris took color to a new level. She had dressed this way long before the seventies, so she fit in well with the times.

I looked beyond her dress and saw her radiance. Her positive and outgoing personality made Iris a joy to be around. She never yelled or reprimanded me harshly. When she wanted my behavior to change, she explained her reasons. Avoiding difficult issues and manipulating were not her style. After considering Iris's unique personality, the thought of spending six weeks with her became more exciting.

Maybe she'd know what a blow job was.

CHAPTER 3

The Cost of a Magnificent Win

I grabbed dinner and ran to the football game.

When the pioneers founded Sutter, they preserved the trees. So when they built the football field, loggers spent four weeks clearing ten forested acres, and construction teams spent months removing stumps and leveling the terrain. The trees that remained around the field were high enough to make it invisible from fifty feet outside the school perimeter. When the sun went below the horizon, it created a red background that silhouetted the dark evergreens.

This night, fall permeated the air. The atmosphere appeared perfect for football. Sutter was playing Beaverton. The two schools had been rivals for years, and three games into the season, neither team had lost. Sutter had a great squad—the best in years. Our senior quarterback, Brett Moore, was tall and handsome, with a cannon for an arm. His skills had steadily improved over the previous three years, and he was a candidate for All-American. A solid core of seniors and two juniors completed the team. They worked well together and despised losing. The whole town predicted a state championship.

I saw Joann talking to Cindy Summers. Like Joann, Cindy was outgoing—but they had nothing else in common. Cindy was popular and loved to attract boys. Her mother allowed her to use makeup, and she always had the newest clothes. In physical education, Cindy stuffed her bra. With enhanced breasts and miniskirts, she caused boys to trip over their tongues.

Among the girls, the bet was six to one that Cindy's virginity would sail into the sunset before Thanksgiving—if it hadn't already left port. She bragged about French kissing sixteen-year-old Greg Donovan, and it was only a matter of time before Cindy would explore the backseat of Greg's car.

Joann broke away from Cindy when she saw me, and we went over to our friends Jill Kennedy and Tanice Shepard, who were sitting nearby.

The game started at seven o'clock. Beaverton got the ball first and marched down the field without any trouble. Our defense seemed disoriented, and Beaverton scored quickly.

Now it was Sutter's turn to receive. The kick sailed to the 15-yard line, and Shagg Mobley was immediately tackled. Brett Moore, our quarterback, lined up and threw a pass to Ed Pennington, whom the announcer called a tight end. Joann said to me, "I'm not familiar with the tight end, but I love the sound of it. He has the cutest butt!" We started giggling.

Tanice piped up, "It's better when the tight end goes deep and uses illegal hands. Can you imagine being the quarterback and putting your hands on those butts? I'd like to start at quarterback just one game—only I'd get so distracted, we'd lose!" All of us laughed hysterically.

Busy gossiping, we missed Brett throwing a 60-yard touchdown pass. People started stomping on the bleachers and yelling, "Sutter's good, Sutter's great, Sutter High will win the state!"

The crisp autumn air cooled as the game progressed. A slight wind blew up, and the temperature dropped into the fifties. At halftime, the cheerleaders changed from skirts to pants. Tied at seventeen, neither team controlled the game. The marching band played "Fight on, Sutter" while we bought Cokes and flirted with boys.

Rodney Talley and Ralph Schumacher were sitting directly behind us. Denny Jensen sat next to them, assembling a gadget he'd removed from his backpack. From their twisted smirks, I knew they were planning something shady. I watched as Rodney and Ralph climbed on top of the broadcasting booth and Denny handed them a box full of wires. "Hey, Denny, what are you guys doing?" I asked.

Denny blushed and replied, "Hi, Laurel, how are you? We're, uh, uh, fixing a light on the broadcast booth. It went dark when the crowd stomped on the bleachers."

"I don't see any bulbs going up that ladder." Rodney and Ralph had reputations for trouble, but not Denny. Usually, he was quiet and avoided social contact. "Tell me the truth or I'll call the cops."

Denny smiled and said, "OK, Laurel. This is a huge game, so Rodney and Ralph are preparing some victory fireworks."

Joann interrupted, "You idiots understand Sutter might not win? The game is close, and our defense looks like they're on strike. They're only missing protest signs."

"Sutter can't lose to Beaverton—they gotta win," said Denny. "We've been working on this for a week. We've got bottle rockets from last July, and we bought some M-80 firecrackers. They're hard to find since they stopped making them in 1966. One M-80 equals a quarter stick of dynamite. I wired them to a battery igniter. It's on the roof of the broadcasting booth, and from here I can see when to fire."

"If you hurt somebody, I'll kick your asses," Tanice interjected. "You know, there's a good reason they quit making M-80s."

"No, no. We placed the pyrotechnics fifty yards from the crowd and away from playing children."

Tanice pointed out, "Rodney and Ralph *are* children. Putting their brains together rivals a first-grader. Add their lack of common sense to the fact they're studying for degrees in delinquency, and this plan spells disaster."

"Trust me, Tanice. We know what we're doing. I know a little about electronics, and I'm all about keeping the public safe."

I liked Denny. We lived a mile apart and had attended first grade together. During elementary school, we'd walked to school together, usually discussing daily events. Unlike Rodney and Ralph, it was possible Denny knew what he was doing.

Denny was shy, with a few odd twists I couldn't define. Seemingly smart, he'd earned a reputation for not applying himself. Nonetheless, I sensed something within him most people hadn't seen. He had a geeky Clark Kent appearance, with a pocket protector and occasional heavy glasses. His blond hair was clean but disheveled. Although small for fourteen, Denny was cute—at least I thought so.

As the second half started, Denny continued directing Rodney and Ralph. Whatever the score at the end of the game, fireworks were going to fly.

The kickoff to Sutter was high and long. Eric Olefsky, a thin kid with the speed of a jaguar, caught the football and headed toward the sideline. The defense chased after him with outstretched hands, and as a flash mob converged on Eric, he disappeared from view. It appeared the defense had tackled him, but a microsecond later, a stick man sprang from the pile, holding the football and heading for a touchdown. He ran with the speed of a rocket.

As he zipped past our section, the cheerleaders began jumping—so much so that they encroached on Eric's path. He hit the girls with enough momentum that pom-poms and megaphones went flying. Our cheering squad had accomplished what Beaverton's defense could not: they had brought Eric Olefsky to a halt. Dazed, Eric didn't mind that he hadn't scored. He was ecstatic as cheerleaders kissed and hugged him.

Two plays later, Brett moved the ball to Beaverton's 10-yard line. On third and seven, Brett handed off to our running back, Randy Farley, who ran around the right side. The gap closed fast as the defense clung to Randy's waist. He turned left, dragging defenders, cocked his arm, and threw the ball to Brett, who was running toward the end zone. Reaching full speed, Brett caught the ball and scored a touchdown.

In 1971, minimally padded goalposts—shaped like the letter H—stood on the goal line. If the defense didn't stop you, the goalposts might. When Brett, still running, turned toward the crowd lifting the ball in celebration, he hit the goalpost at full speed. The sound of the impact rang like a bell.

The crowd rose as Brett collapsed. As teammates circled around, he showed no movement. Coaches and team members ran onto the field. Dr. Klonniger, who always attended the football games, hurried to help. Coaches started CPR while the broadcast booth announcer called for an ambulance.

In those days, our town didn't have an emergency 911 phone system, so Wilford Whitehall was Sutter's mortician and ambulance driver. He drank heavily but avoided criticism when folks considered his job. He was always reliable when a serious injury occurred, and he never blew the siren unless someone was critically injured.

Within minutes, Wilford drove the ambulance down the field and securely loaded Brett and Doc Klonniger. Chest compressions had stopped, so no one knew if Brett was alive or dead. The ambulance sped off, leaving us to ponder Brett Moore's fate and Sutter's football season. That night, the siren blew.

The crowd remained standing as place kicker Tory Gomez came in and added the extra point. The team ran to the sideline, trying to regroup before the kickoff.

Beaverton didn't get a first down and had to punt. Now Charlie Donovan, Sutter's freshman backup quarterback, would run the offense. Coach Bulgrin never started a ninth grader, but tonight he had no choice. To reassure the team, Charlie needed to instill confidence and move the ball. He crouched behind the center and took the snap—immediately fumbling the ball. The Beaverton safety picked it up and ran untouched for six points.

The crowd's remaining morale faded away. To tie the game, Beaverton needed the extra point. Both teams lined up, with Sutter placing its tallest players in the middle. Every defensive player focused on blocking this kick. The holder—the guy holding the football for the kicker—signaled for the snap. The kicker ran forward, his leg moving in a graceful arc—but to everyone's surprise, no ball left his foot. The holder ran around the defensive, going for two points.

As he crossed the goal line, Beaverton's fans became ecstatic. The conversion put Beaverton ahead one point. The demoralized Sutter team sauntered to the sideline. Ninety seconds remained. The odds of winning were scant.

In the minds of fourteen-year-old girls, certain subjects mattered: boys came first, with popularity, clothes, and music a close second. Tonight we'd lost our gorgeous quarterback, and now we were losing the game. Our lives revolved around Sutter's football team. A loss meant a lifetime of hardship—at least until Monday. We sat there, eagerly awaiting the final showdown.

Again, the kickoff came to Eric Olefsky. Anticipating Eric's urge to run toward the cheerleaders, assistant coach Wall screamed for him to run along the opposite sideline. Eric changed course and reached the Sutter 40 before running out of bounds. We had great field position.

Two more plays put Sutter at the 31-yard line. The clock stopped at twenty seconds. I'd never been to church, but I figured a prayer couldn't hurt. "God, please let Sutter win. If not, please let Brett have a minor brain injury, so he asks me out." I hoped that covered it.

Randy called time-out. Charlie trotted to the sideline to confer with the coach. The atmosphere was electric. Fans shouted continuously. The cheerleaders were getting laryngitis but jumping to new heights. Charlie went back to the huddle shaking his head. Whatever the call, he wasn't happy. The team huddled, and Charlie's hand gestured like an orchestra conductor.

The huddle broke. Silence. Charlie positioned his hands under the center and shouted the cadence. An instant before the snap, I noticed movement above me. Rodney had tripped and ignited the fireworks. As the ball snapped, simultaneous explosions rocked the night. Bottle rockets shot across the field, and a tall pine began tipping toward the goal line. It seemed that Ralph had placed too many M-80s at the tree's base.

Eric Olefsky ran across the field shouting, "I'm open! I'm open!" The defense concentrated on Eric while Sutter's smallest and fastest player, Jimmy Dover, sprinted down the field. Charlie heaved the ball. The pass was perfect. Jimmy never broke stride as the ball landed between his numbers. He was going to score!

Well, maybe.

The tree behind the goal line was falling and picking up speed. Even though it was Oregon, where logging was king, I'd never witnessed a falling tree. I estimated this tree would cross the goal line about the same moment as Jimmy Dover. The clock reached 00:00. Everyone froze, watching the pine and Jimmy share a dance with death. The tree was seven feet from the ground when Jimmy launched vertically, leaping for his life.

Several seconds passed. Expectant and worried, the crowd was silent; no one moved. Dust swirled while fireworks continued to explode. Another minute elapsed, until the dust and smoke lifted, revealing a shoeless football player standing atop a two-foot-diameter log—holding the ball high. Jimmy had survived!

The referee signaled *Touchdown!* as Sutter players ran from the bench and hoisted Jimmy above their shoulders. Bloodied, and missing his shoes, Jimmy Dover, for one shining moment, was king of the world.

Today, a piece of that tree rests in the high school's trophy case, next to Jimmy's cleats. The tree's impact had driven the cleats six inches below ground level. Why Jimmy's feet weren't in those cleats was anybody's guess.

The Log Bowl, as it became known, is still a focal point in Sutter history. Today, events are spoken of as having happened before or after the Log Bowl.

Four hundred people attended the game. Forty years later, five thousand people claim they saw it in person.

CHAPTER 4

Boys and Beavers

The excitement died down around ten o'clock. We walked to French's Fry, a diner loved by all the students. Holly and Irv French, who owned the place, were generous student supporters. If you didn't have a dime for a Coke, Holly would give you one and say, "Pay me next time." Students paid their debts because peer pressure became unbearable if they didn't. If you'd broken up after "going steady" for a week or failed a test, Irv offered a fifty-cent banana split for a quarter.

That night, we sat outside despite the chill. As we ate our fries and drank our root beer floats, we overheard seniors saying Brett Moore had a severe head injury. Dr. Klonniger had transferred him to the University of Oregon Hospital in Portland. We felt bad. Brett was different from other jocks. Most seniors avoided junior high students, but Brett found time to stop and talk. In summer, he earned money mowing lawns. He enjoyed physical labor, and his work was excellent. Mom had hired him to mow our lawn for the last three years.

After talking at the diner, Joann, Tanice, and I walked to my home before saying good-bye and going separate ways.

Mom was still up. "Hi, honey. What was the final score?"

"Mom, didn't you listen on the radio? Sutter won an incredible game! I can't believe you didn't tune in because of work." I described the action and told Mom what she had missed.

"Sounds like a great time," she said. "I hope Brett recovers. I can't imagine how worried his parents are. If I were remaining in town, I'd offer to help. I'll ask Iris to do some baking. She always knows how to cheer folks up. What are your plans for tomorrow?"

"Joann and I are going to hike around the lake and have a picnic." I omitted the swimming part. Mother couldn't swim and would never let me get in the lake without adult supervision. In past times, adult supervision meant parents staying on shore, drinking beer, and playing gin rummy while I swam, so I thought supervision was different from paying attention. In Mom's mind, they were equal.

"Tomorrow night, I'm taking you to dinner and a movie. It's our last night together for several weeks, so be home by four o'clock. That gives you time to get ready."

"Right, Mom. Love you. See you in the morning." I went to bed, worried about the next few days.

I awoke to a ringing doorbell. Mom should have answered it, but she didn't. I slumbered out of bed, put on my robe, and wandered downstairs. Looking out the window, I saw Joann staring in. Why was she here early? I opened the door.

"Laurel, you're not dressed. It's time to go!"

"But it's only seven thirty or eight in the morning! What's your rush?"

"No, Laurel, it's ten thirty. We're already late. I got behind fixing my hair, so we need to move faster. Start dressing. I want to track down the boys and decorate their tree house."

"OK, give me a few minutes." I hurried upstairs, dressed quickly, and grabbed my swimsuit. Then I ran back down and searched the kitchen. Mom had left a note saying she was at the office finalizing arrangements for China. She'd packed me a lunch and reminded me to be home by four. I grabbed my hat and we bolted out the door.

"Have you heard any more about Brett?" I asked.

"Today, the radio reported they took him to surgery during the night for bleeding around his brain. He's listed as critical and in intensive care. I hope he pulls through. It's a bummer for Sutter's team. Their chances of reaching state just dropped through the floor. Last night's game is probably the highlight for the year."

"Do you know if they caught the guys?" I asked.

"Well, the radio stated that falling trees are acts of nature. The town is still excited, but nobody wonders who set off the fireworks. The guys are fine if they lie low several weeks. They'd never outrun the cops; they're too stupid. You're not reporting them, are you?" she asked, looking concerned.

"No way. Their secret's safe with me."

When we arrived, the crystal clear lake was uncharacteristically calm. Trees were reflected in the lake's mirror, and only the water skippers caused ripples. The pine trees were forest green, and the willows were yellow-brown, accented by a faint autumn whisper of fallen red leaves. Sounds echoed from birds migrating south, while human noise was remarkably absent. Few perfect days occur throughout our lives, but this day promised to be one of them.

We started hiking with hidden thoughts of flirting with the boys. As we walked, we discussed songs climbing the charts. "Have you heard that new song by the Bee Gees, 'How Can You Mend a Broken Heart'?" I asked. "If I ever have money, I'm going to Woolworth's to buy the single. Their love songs make men sound good enough to marry. Next Saturday, they'll be on *Bandstand,* and we can watch if you want to come over."

"I might," Joann said. "Tim doesn't know it, but I've been listening to his records. He's got Cher's *Gypsies, Tramps & Thieves* and that song by Rod Stewart, 'Maggie May.' I like them but not enough to buy them. If I'm buying music, I want John Lennon's album *Imagine.* The title song is the greatest hit I've ever heard. It reminds me of Simon and Garfunkel's 'Bridge Over Troubled Water.' When we're older, those two songs will still be popular."

"Gee, I haven't heard them, except for the Cher. Mom lets me listen to the radio when I'm not studying and the TV isn't on. Our car is a '63, so we don't have an eight-track player. Can you believe it? That's one reason I like your parents' new Ford LTD. The eight-track player and air-conditioning are neat. How'd you get your mother to spring a buck ninety-nine for the Carpenters' album *Close to You*? The record's worth it, but my mom's stingy. 'We've Only Just Begun' is a groovy song, and listening through your car speakers makes it ten times better. They'll never improve on how good the music sounds. Eight-tracks are the best invention since the skateboard."

"I don't know, technology never stops. In a few years, they'll have a computer as small as a house. It's simply a matter of time, money, and labor," Joann stated with certainty.

"Yeah, well, it's not happening anytime soon. I heard the computer at the University of Oregon occupies half a football field. Maybe when we're seventy, a computer will fit in a garage."

We'd walked a third of the trail before spotting a tree house hidden twenty yards off the path. We didn't spot any boys, but there were signs; they weren't far off. A baloney sandwich sat near the base of the tree with a bottle of pop and the October 1971 issue of *Playboy.* A naked centerfold stared at us. The photo sensually depicted her in a right-profile pose, showing the outline of her butt and her breasts. The photo exuded sexuality.

"Look at this woman, will ya? Her boobs aren't that big. By next year, we'll have her beat," I said, secretly wishing I'd be right.

Joanne replied, "I don't ever see myself looking like her. She has a tiger tattooed on her butt, so I'll bet she's a tramp. Have you ever seen boobs that perky? I haven't. They look like flesh-painted funnels with the tips trimmed. Girls in the locker room don't look like that. And why would you put a tattoo on your ass? Only sailors get tattoos, and I guarantee, she's not in the navy."

Just then, we heard rustling in the bushes.

"God, I needed that piss," stated a squeaky voice.

"Yeah, me too," said a deeper voice. "I drank so much Coke, I could have out-peed a moose. You know, standing by the stream, my dick's so long I could tell you how cold the water temperature was."

Squeaky bragged, "Well, mine's so long I could tell you—how deep it was."

Suddenly, Bill and Kevin walked out of the brush. Denny Jensen followed quietly.

We stepped from behind the tree, making our presence known. "Hey, guys, we heard voices and wondered who was here," I volunteered. The boys looked guilty, pondering whether they needed to hide something. Breathing sighs of relief, they relaxed—until Kevin spotted the *Playboy*.

"Laurel. Joann. Gosh, we weren't, like, uh—expecting any girls, uh, women, uh, to be like, well, uh, comin' around. Did you girls leave this?" he asked, picking up the *Playboy*. "Or, uh, did the wind blow it in?" There wasn't a breeze blowing for miles.

"No, not ours," Joann piped up. "Probably drug here by raccoons. You know how they rummage through the trash. It's incredible what they find, isn't it? We'll take it and throw it away, since you guys don't read this stuff, right?"

There was mumbling as Bill whispered to Kevin, "That's my dad's. It needs to be home before he is."

"Sure, girls, go ahead—toss it. We never read those kinds of magazines. You're probably right about the raccoons," Kevin said. Bill stood cringing, worried about how to replace it. "Did you come around to see our tree house?"

"We didn't know about your tree house," I fibbed. "We were hiking and heard the noise, so we thought we'd investigate. I'm not surprised seeing you and Bill, but after last night, I figured Denny would stay out of sight."

Denny replied, "Hey, you aren't going to say anything, are you? There wasn't much damage, though that tree blocked a beautiful view of the parking lot. Ralph placed the charges a little close. With over a hundred M-80s, it's hard to predict the explosive force." Denny sounded as if he used dynamite every day.

"Denny, that tree was 150 years old. Rodney and Ralph couldn't roll down a car window, let alone place explosive charges," Joann countered. "The blast excavated an elephant-sized hole. Now you're here with these two, dreaming up more idiot schemes."

"Listen, Joann, the reason I'm here is because Bill and Kevin wanted electricity in their tree house. I was nervous staying home, so I decided to come help."

Not seeing any power lines, I said, "Denny, there's no electrical lines—unless, of course, you plan to tap into a current bush," I joked. Joann started giggling.

Denny, not amused, replied, "You're just in time to see my idea work. Come with me." Denny led us behind the tree to a small creek, where he'd diverted the water into a deep, wide, hand-dug pit. A waterfall flowed over a rock dam at the opposite end of the pit. A bicycle wheel rim holding twenty-four evenly spaced cups rested at the waterfall's base, collecting the tumbling water and swiftly turning the wheel. The wheel hub was attached to the electromagnetic coil of a vacuum motor. Wires from the motor ran to the poles of a car battery.

Bill climbed into the tree house. "Hit it, Bill!" Denny yelled. In moments, Bill held a glowing bulb out the window. Once more, I suspected people underestimated Denny. I remembered the proverb "Still waters run deep." With Denny, no one had ever looked below the surface.

"Denny, that's incredible. What else are you planning?" I asked.

"Well, the guys want phone service. A buried phone cable lies seventy-five feet away. There are six houses around here, all connected to that party line. Another addition shouldn't bother anyone. I just need a phone cable and an old phone." With Denny's ingenuity, Kevin and Bill would probably have heat, indoor plumbing, and phone service by November.

We ate lunch with the guys and decided to finish our hike. We started hiking at a brisk pace. The temperature reached eighty, but the humidity stayed low. Ducks glided along one by one, leaving V-shaped ripples behind them. The ripples headed toward a willow patch guarding an inlet. Near the inlet's peak, a stream flowed over moss-colored rock and cascaded into the lake. During the summer, this was a popular swimming hole. The water was chest deep, with a shore masquerading as a beach. Secluded by pine trees, teenagers loved swimming here.

"Laurel, let's swim," Joann said. "We've got time."

"OK, I'll get changed."

"Laurel, we have the swimming hole to ourselves. Ditch the suit; we'll skinny-dip," Joann proclaimed.

Being cautious, I replied, "What if somebody comes along and sees us—it's illegal."

"Listen, Laurel, the boys are at their tree house. No one's around, and whoever wanted to swim would already be here."

Joann's argument convinced me. Exposing my body was difficult. Puberty brought daily changes, and I feared comments in the locker room. Skinny-dipping took my fears to a new height. "You'd better be right, Joann, or I'll never forgive you."

We put our clothes on a rock and ran into the water. The chill bit my skin, and there was tingling in places I hadn't felt before. But after a few minutes, our bodies adjusted and the fun began. Joann started splashing me, and I returned the gesture. Dunking her seemed appropriate, so I jumped on her back and pulled her under. This went on for fifteen minutes, then we stopped to rest.

Inspecting my skin, I remarked, "Getting sunburned isn't part of my plan. We didn't bring lotion, so we shouldn't swim long," I advised.

"Laurel!" Joann exclaimed with authority, "Everybody knows you can't sunburn in the fall. It happens in summer when the sun's overhead. Nobody gets sunburned in late September." Joann was wrong, but she sounded as if she'd studied sunburns for many years.

"Yeah, Joann, but most people I know don't swim naked in September. Plus, we might sunburn in sensitive places. It makes me cringe and cross my legs."

Just then, something moved in the water. Twenty feet away and paddling toward the willows, it looked large. Within seconds, we heard movement on the shore. Wading toward the willows, we searched for whatever had made the sound. The water plants were dense, so it took several minutes before we found the carcass of a dead beaver. Someone had shot the animal, but not recently. Feeling sad, we knew it wasn't the carcass that had made the noise. Whatever it was had disappeared.

We had started swimming again when we heard the sound a second time. There, on the shore, were two baby beavers.

"Look, Joann," I shouted. "They're kits. I'll bet the dead beaver's their mother. They're born in late spring, so they're probably several months old. Do you think they have a father?"

"No, Laurel, like Jesus, these are immaculate-conception beavers! Of course they have a father! What did you think?"

"Jeez, Joann, I'm not stupid. If the father isn't helping them, we'll have to take them home," I asserted.

"We don't have a clue about raising beavers. I say we leave the Cheetos and check on them tomorrow. If they're worse, we'll do something. Besides, if word gets out we're raising beavers, the teasing won't stop. I can hear the guys asking, 'Hey, ladies, can we pet your beavers?'"

What would be wrong with letting them pet a beaver? I wondered. "People pet Otis. Why couldn't guys pet my beaver?" I inquired in a serious tone.

"Laurel, we need to talk sometime about how naïve you are. Until we do, if someone asks to pet your beaver, just say no, OK?"

"Well, of course I'll say no. Until these animals have rabies shots, I'm not letting anyone close."

"God, Laurel, I swear!" Joann said, shaking her head. "Come on, let's get our clothes. We'll come back and bring something more nutritious. I doubt they eat butterscotch pudding, and that's our only snack."

We swam five more minutes, then waded to shore—where we quickly discovered that our clothes were gone. "Didn't we put our clothes on that rock over there?" I pointed. My stomach started sinking.

"Yup, that's where they were," Joann replied. "I'm guessing the boys hid them. Let's go look."

"Joann, I'm embarrassed. What will we do if we can't find our clothes? We're a half-mile from the trailhead, and the last hundred yards are wide open. How'd you convince me to do this?"

We searched twenty minutes with no luck. Worse, there wasn't anything we could use for clothes. We sat on the rock, pondering the worst-case scenario. I decided the tree house offered the only chance to find makeshift clothing. "Let's hike to the tree house. There's probably something there we can use," I suggested.

"It's a mile back, and it'll be dark in two hours. I say we run for it and try to avoid arrest for indecent exposure. If we're late, the whole town will start looking for us. Do you want our naked asses plastered in *The Sutter Sentinel*?"

We heard a cough close by. We scurried behind the rock and peeked out. Denny Jensen was carrying our clothes.

"Hey, Laurel! Joann!" Denny yelled. "I know you're here. I heard you. Your clothes were on the trail. I think Kevin and Bill probably swiped them when they headed home. If you want 'em, come get 'em'!"

Joann hollered back, "Denny, bring those clothes toward the rock until I say stop, then leave. You probably swiped them to begin with. I'm going to kick your butt when I catch you! Now bring us the clothes." Denny approached the rock, getting within five feet, when Joann said, "That's enough. Drop em' right there." Denny did what she ordered. "Now disappear," Joann said.

Denny retreated up the trail as we grabbed our clothes and dressed behind the willows. Relieved, we walked to the main trail and found Denny standing there, waiting.

"I bet you enjoyed the peep show. I hope you liked our performance, because you're going die when I've got more energy," Joann threatened.

"Look, you two, I didn't steal your clothes," Denny replied. "Bill and Kevin went home to play baseball. I stayed behind tuning the waterwheel. I was walking the trail when I saw your clothes near the path to the swimming hole. I recognized your blouses, so I figured you were here somewhere. Do you skinny-dip often? Could I join you? I love swimming," he said, as though he routinely swam with naked women.

I interrupted, "No, Denny we rarely skinny-dip, and when we do, you're not invited. Were you spying on us before you handed over our clothes?" I asked.

"Gee, Laurel, what do you think I am, a prevert or something? I'd never spy on you," Denny responded.

"It's *pervert*, not *prevert*," Joann corrected. "We know you'd watch us because you're a guy. Mom says guys own a brain and penis but have just enough blood to use one or the other."

Denny reflected, "Well, I've never thought much about that. Scientifically speaking, the heart pumps five liters of blood; a guy should be able to pee and think simultaneously. Let's see . . . the bladder, brain, and penis would need about fifteen hundred milliliters a minute. Gosh, Joann, at first glance I'm not seeing a problem. Working together produces efficiency."

"Denny," Joann responded, "I didn't think anyone was as naïve as Laurel. You two belong together. God, I can't believe it!"

"Well?" Denny said, looking at me. "She says we're made for each other. The junior high homecoming dance is Saturday. Want to go?" Secretly excited, I gave Joann a look that said, *See what you got me into?*

Denny had surprised me by asking me out. I liked him but had never dated. In my mind, dating led to marriage and marriage led to kids. I didn't need any kids right now. "Gee, Denny," I stalled. "I've got to ask Mom. Are you planning any funny stuff?" I queried.

Denny replied, "Well, I don't know much comedy, but I'm happy to learn. Flip Wilson's my favorite—especially when he plays Geraldine. Tell me what jokes you like, and I'll work on some funny stuff."

Joann looked at both of us in disbelief.

Denny's answer wasn't what I'd expected, but at least he was honest. "I'll check with Mom and give you a call."

We started hiking again, and I realized how memorable the day had become. Was it the scenery, the boys, the skinny-dipping, or perhaps the thought that I could never re-create this perfect day? The setting sun would leave only my recollections. I had lived this day to the fullest, and thinking about Brett Moore, I recognized for the first time that I should try living every day to the fullest. My future was finite, and the pleasure I received from life depended a great deal on the passion I put into it.

"Denny, I've thought about it: we're going to the dance!"

CHAPTER 5

Mom's Advice for a First Date

Mother and I went to Stuart Anderson's Black Angus restaurant for dinner. Beef tenderloin cost six dollars, so I planned to order the rib eye until Mom said, "Laurel, indulge yourself. I'm not sure when I'll be back, so let's splurge. I'm having lobster, myself. Order your favorite entrée."

Mom didn't have to tell me twice. "I'm having shrimp cocktail, filet mignon, a baked potato, and chocolate mousse for dessert. If dinner's too expensive, I'll pay the extra."

"Dear, it's fine. Did you and Joann have a good hike today?" Mom asked, as she sipped her martini.

I recounted the basic facts, omitting details about the *Playboy* and skinny-dipping. I told Mom about Denny's waterwheel as I considered approaching her about my date. Remembering Mother's reaction when I brought up oral sex, I took a subtle and reassuring approach. "Mom, Denny invited me to the homecoming dance. I told him I'd go. I know that worries you, but I'll emphasize, 'On our first date, you can't pet my beaver or expect a blow job.' He'll probably say, 'Hey, that's fine Laurel—maybe the next date.' That should ease your mind, right, Mom?"

Mother took a long drink of her martini. "Laurel, where are you hearing this slang? Do not call Denny and tell him what you just said. You can attend the dance, but setting intimate behavior rules won't fly with Mrs. Jensen. She'll lead a lynch mob to our front door. My headaches and your character will surely suffer. Promise me, Laurel, if you hear more slang words, don't ask Iris. The poor woman is old, and I doubt she can adequately address these subjects. She'd have a stroke."

"I don't know, Mom. Iris is smart. There's whiskey to calm her nerves, and she drinks as much as most men. Plus, she might have a different perspective. Any details you miss, Iris probably knows."

"Laurel, don't get smart! Do as I tell you, or you'll catch hell when I return. If I have to return to straighten you out, you'll think jail sounds good! Do you understand?"

"Yes, Mother," I replied.

"Speaking of Iris, I talked to her today. We discussed your chores and Otis. There's money to cover incidentals, and she knows where it is. Is there anything you want me to discuss with her?"

I couldn't think of anything. "No, Mom. We get along, and I'm sure she'll have us baking pies or volunteering. It'll be good to see her again. She's almost eighty, but I saw her riding a bike a few months ago—she hardly acts her age. Last time she visited, oil leaked from the lawn mower. She disassembled the engine, got a new part, and fixed the mower. Most women can't start one, let alone fix it."

At that moment, our appetizers arrived, so we stopped talking and started eating. Like the hike, our evening proved to be memorable. After dinner, we went to see *Summer of '42*. Jennifer O'Neill was the most beautiful woman I'd ever seen, and I fell in love with Gary Grimes. Romance movies had never provoked these feelings before. Deep down, I imagined Gary escorting me to the homecoming dance, kissing as Sinatra sang "Strangers in the Night." It seemed Mom felt the same emotions: when the movie ended, we were both sobbing uncontrollably.

We got home at eleven thirty. The day had brought many new experiences, and I felt exhausted. Tomorrow was Sunday, and I could sleep in. Mother wasn't leaving until two o'clock. I said goodnight and went to bed thinking about where my life would lead.

I didn't foresee tomorrow starting a three-week odyssey that would change my world.

CHAPTER 6

Giant Sequoias in a Wagon

I awoke at 10:30. Mom's bags sat by the front door. The goal of this trip was drafting a trade agreement between the United States and China. If successful, China's vast markets would open to American industry. The deadline for completing the negotiations was January 1972. President Nixon was planning a summit meeting with Chairman Mao in February, so only four months remained.

In 1971, air transportation was an expensive way to travel. Passengers dressed in their finest clothes for even the shortest of flights. Having diplomatic status, Mom dressed for the occasion. She wore a navy blue dress with a formfitting bodice and full-length sleeves. White lace circled the collar, complemented by white borders around the hem and cuffs. A three-inch turquoise stripe, centered vertically, ran from the collar to the hem, with evenly spaced navy blue buttons accenting the stripe. She wore two-inch blue heels with a matching handbag.

She looked magnificent.

Worried about men asking Mom out, I said, "Mother, you look stunning. Your dress is beautiful, but it will be uncomfortable after flying eleven hours. You probably shouldn't wear it often—especially around single men."

"Yes, honey, it's rather formal. The State Department advised us on clothes selection and Chinese customs. This is the first time in decades the United States has sought diplomatic relations with China. How we dress and what we say will undergo intense scrutiny. Until we truly understand our Chinese hosts, it's better to behave formally. They're good lessons, Laurel. Courtesy helps define integrity and makes a lasting impression. These are many important customs I've had to learn while practicing international law. Someday, I'll tell you more, but Iris should be arriving any second."

"Gee, Mom, why so early? Your flight doesn't take off until four o'clock. I didn't think you were leaving until two."

"That's our departure time, honey. We're having a brief meeting first to ensure we've thoroughly prepared."

Pointing out the window, she said, "Look, here comes Iris, now."

Iris couldn't be missed. She wore a flowered Hawaiian muumuu expressing every color in the visible spectrum. A beat-up straw hat and tennis shoes finished her ensemble. Behind her she pulled a Radio Flyer wagon containing a huge suitcase and an eight-foot plant. Mother said, "Let's go and give her a hand." We hurried out the door as Iris came up the sidewalk, smiling from ear to ear.

Arms wide, Iris called, "Come here, give me a hug!" We both stepped forward and got a heartfelt embrace. For a woman her age, she had powerful arms. Her hug made me feel secure and that all would be well while Mother was gone.

"Look at you, Laurel. My, you've grown! It's been a while since you and I have talked. I look forward to spending time with you and hearing about your life." She turned to Mom, "Marie, how are you? What a historic journey you're going on. Your team is the true builders of next year's landmark summit; however, the politicians will take the credit."

Iris's words made me gasp; Mom was shaping a date with destiny. She had more diplomatic credentials than I realized.

Mom said, "Laurel, bring in Iris's plant and bag and we'll talk for a few minutes."

The suitcase didn't appear heavy—until I wrestled it through the door into the guest room. The plant came in through the garage and soon rested in the living room. "Honey, that's just fine. I'm nursing this giant sequoia back to health. It's a gift to you and your mother. It looks bad, but I'm cautiously optimistic."

Did she say "giant sequoia"? I'd seen these trees—they were at least a hundred feet tall, with trunks the diameter of a carousel. I couldn't recall any residential property with a giant sequoia. Grasping the fact that sequoias took hundreds of years to reach maturity, I imagined this tree transplanted outside and consuming the entire front yard—or worse, falling on the house. But I saw no reason to argue with Iris—she had a way with nature. Over the coming weeks, I might convince her that a sequoia would thrive better at the city park.

Mom and Iris finished the checklist. When Mother's ride arrived, my face had withered from too many good-bye kisses. Her boss loaded the luggage as I received more affection. Then the van drove away with

Mother waving like a maniac. I was sorry she was leaving, but for me, this was the beginning of a big adventure. If I played my cards right, I could live almost independently. In the past, Iris had only helped if I asked, and she never set strict rules. (Although within a week, I'd learn that my judgment of human nature needed fine-tuning!)

Heading back into the house, a voice called from the kitchen, "Dear, what's the plan for today? I've mixed meat loaf for dinner, and I'm going to bake kosher pies for the synagogue."

I didn't know Iris was Jewish. Unsure how to respond, I inquired, "Iris, did you become a member of the synagogue. Are you Jewish?"

"Well, not officially, dear. The pies are for Avram Kirshbaum's bar mitzvah. Avram has studied the Torah since he turned twelve. Now he's your age. His family asked me to bake the pies. I cared for Avram over six years, so it's an honor to do it."

Thinking back to Iris's question, I responded, "Well, Iris, I'd like to walk to the lake. Yesterday we found some baby beavers. Their mother was dead, so I want to make sure they're OK. I'll take food, but I'm not sure what beavers eat. Yesterday we left Cheetos, but I'm guessing *National Geographic* says that isn't their normal diet. Want to come?"

"Sure, the walk would do me good. If we can find them, we'll do what we can and avoid interfering. Do you know what they eat, Laurel?"

I didn't have any idea. Trees seemed likely. Perhaps a fish or two? I'd never heard of beavers banding together to take down a deer, but who knew?

"No, how about you?" I replied.

"Well, honey, here's what I know. The North American beaver's species name is *Castor canadensis.* They live five to ten years in the wild and typically weigh forty to sixty pounds. They mate for life and are thirty to fifty inches long. They eat trees, mainly cottonwood, dogwood, and any tree that helps build a dam. Beavers also eat willows and most herbaceous plants. Families reach up to ten, but the average is six. Juveniles stay with parents for up to two years. They're the largest rodent I know. There's more relevant information, Laurel, but those are the essentials."

Her "Sermon on the Beaver" caught me by surprise, but this was the modest mind of Iris Wimple. Like a cheetah ready to pounce, facts about bizarre subjects sprang from nowhere, catching most people off guard. Relieved I hadn't inquired about nuclear propulsion, I commented, "You sure know your beavers, Iris. Where did you learn these interesting facts?"

"Well, sweetheart, age allows you to gather some strange information. My biggest problem is memory. Today I can't even recite the entire Declaration of Independence by heart." Honestly, nobody I knew could quote this astounding document from memory.

"Gee, Iris, I only remember one phrase from the Declaration: 'When in the course of human events.' I think you do well in spite of your years," I said, trying to find a compliment.

"Well, Laurel, I urge you to read these American treasures and understand their impact," she said. "The Declaration and the Constitution lay the foundation of the greatest contribution ever made to accelerate human progress. I won't lecture, but understanding the value of freedom and the sacrifices necessary to keep it will put you light-years ahead of everyone else. Most people in America don't recognize the gift they've received."

The piecrusts finished baking, so we headed to the lake. Walking along the shore, I asked, "Iris, did you hear about the football game? Except for Brett Moore getting hurt, the game has to be one of Sutter's top five."

"Well, dear, as it so happens, I attended the game," she replied.

"I'm surprised," I said. "Have you been a football fan your entire life? With all the excitement, I didn't spot you."

Iris replied, "Normally, I'm not a fan, but Nubs Fritzmeyer is. We've been friends many years, and you know she's Sutter High's oldest living graduate. She's been a fan since Sutter first had a football team. Anyway, Nubs planned on driving, and you know how bad her vision is. Since it was dark, I decided to ride along in case she needed help."

Florence "Nubs" Fritzmeyer was a widowed ninety-two-year-old woman who, like Iris, had lived in Sutter for years. She and her husband, Leonard, had owned the local butcher shop. During summers, Florence helped Leonard handle the increased tourist business. According to gossip, she had gotten her right hand caught in the meat grinder, which explained why she had only one finger and part of one hand remaining. After the accident, people called her Nubs, and the nickname stuck.

"Iris, how does that work? She's blind and missing part of her hand. You don't drive at all. How could you possibly help?"

"That's easy. I simply tell Nubs when to make a turn. Occasionally, I offer advice on the speed limit and the color of the traffic light. She enjoys driving, and I'd hate to see them impound her car. She has no family, so it's the least I can do. Her only accident was backing into the outdoor dining tables at Godfrey's Bistro. No injuries occurred because Nubs backed through the restaurant fence at a turtle's pace and customers had time to move. She paid for everyone's meal, and Godfrey had her stay for dinner."

I knew to look both ways before crossing the street, but it had never occurred to me that dining outdoors could be a traffic hazard.

Iris commented, "It was a misfortune about the Moore boy. Today's *Sentinel* stated he was in critical condition and may not survive. I feel so sorry for him and his family. I'll take a meal to them later this week. Could you believe the tree falling during the fireworks? What an odd coincidence. The paper stated the police have launched a search for the culprits. There will probably be jail time for whoever was responsible. You didn't see anything, did you?"

I hesitated. "It was a blur, Iris. The excitement kept me from seeing exactly what happened. It was a miracle Jimmy Dover came out alive." Iris's comment about jail conjured an image of Denny shackled to a wall in an orange jumpsuit. "Iris, do they lock kids up for as much time as adults?" I inquired.

"Usually not; kids often get leniency. However, I expect the punishment will be paying for cleanup and possibly a fine. Usually, the judge tries to teach kids a lesson and not impose the sentence he'd give a hardened criminal."

When I got home, I'd check my bank balance and see if I could keep Denny out of jail until after the dance.

Eventually, we came to the inlet where Joann and I had spotted the beavers. We found the carcass of the mother but didn't see the kits. Finally, we heard splashing and walked toward the willows. There, in the reeds, sat two small beavers chewing on fallen tree branches. "There they are, Iris. What do you think?" Secretly, I hoped she'd bring them home so we could care for them.

"Well," she replied, "these babies look well. They're active and have good appetites. Honey, there's an old saying, 'The sworn enemy of good is better.' Beavers thrive best in their natural environment. If we remove these fellows and take them home, they won't be better off. Our goals, while noble, would imprint human dependence on such young kits.

Anyway, if they came home, I'd worry about them chowing down my sequoia. The tree already has problems, so a beaver infestation wouldn't help." Iris had a point. "Let's come back tomorrow and check on them."

We arrived home at five thirty. I started my homework while Iris cooked dinner. Within an hour, we were eating savory meat loaf, home-grown corn on the cob, and potatoes. It was fantastic. I noticed a single piece of bread all buttered up. "Iris, how come you buttered just one piece of bread; aren't you having any?"

"Dear, this meal is informal. My buttered corn trick isn't suitable for any meal except casual dinners with close friends. Take the buttered bread in your hand and roll your corncob in it. It causes the least mess when buttering corn. It's good for about six ears."

As usual, Iris was right. How did one woman know so much? Beavers, giant sequoias, philosophy, corn, and pie! Was there any subject she hadn't mastered?

I decided I'd challenge her with a question she couldn't possibly answer. I told her our world history class was in the middle of studying religion's impact on history. I said, "Iris, you know many facts. Can you define God?"

The minute I asked, I realized that explaining this subject might take the entire evening. Mom had begged me to not ask Iris difficult questions. I should have followed her advice.

Iris didn't answer immediately. She carefully considered her response. "Well, Laurel, your question is either difficult or simple. The answer depends on the experience of the person you ask. Let me think about it and see if I can answer in a way that makes sense. Besides, you have to finish your homework before Sunday night television."

I offered to wash dishes before starting my homework. Like many families, we didn't have a dishwasher. Mom wanted one but thought they were too expensive. So, usually, she made dinner and I washed dishes. But Iris excused me to go study. When I finished, we sat down and watched *The F.B.I,* followed by *Bonanza.* When Hoss and Little Joe Cartwright finished, it was ten o'clock.

Exhausted and ready for bed, I remembered tomorrow was the first day of knitting class. Setting my alarm, I reflected how comfortable I felt around Iris. I suspected the next few weeks would sail by too fast.

And they did—right into treacherous waters.

CHAPTER 7

Teachers of the Year

I woke up after 7:00 a.m. with cramps, signaling the start of my period. Most women don't treasure these days because they're a nuisance.

In 1971, periods were private matters. Americans embraced a stigma about menstruation, and the rule was strict: daughters talked to mothers, and sons talked to older sons or listened to Dad complain about Mom's mood, while drinking beer in the garage. Everyone knew that for seven days every month, women became raving lunatics and were best left alone. Had a tampon commercial appeared on TV, a network would have lost its license.

In the women's locker room, misinformation always floated around. For two years I believed girls couldn't concentrate during our periods because the blood loss affected our brains. For many young girls, absence from school was common at the onset of bleeding.

Classes didn't start until 8:30, so I'd have time to grab a bowl of Captain Crunch. To my surprise, Iris had prepared eggs and bacon. "Good morning dear. How did you sleep?"

"Good, Iris. After the weekend, I feel rested. My homework's finished, and I'm caught up." I dug into breakfast and savored the excellent food. After I finished, while grabbing my backpack, I said, "I'm headed to school. Today, Joann and I start knitting class so we can receive extra credit in home economics." Avoiding the details about why we were starting knitting, I added, "I hope it's not difficult. Knitting wasn't something I planned to learn, but Joann needed extra credit and wanted company. So I said sure."

"Laurel, it's wonderful you're so sympathetic. I know Joann recognizes your sacrifice. Here's your lunch: meat loaf sandwich, chips, an apple, three cookies, and a cream soda." Man, Iris packed a great lunch. Such outstanding food was raising my standards. When Mom returned, I'd offer advice on how to make a better school meal. No more store-bought deli subs—I wanted home-cooked, honest-to-goodness food.

"Have a wonderful day, Laurel. I'll see you after school." I hugged Iris good-bye and was out the door.

Arriving at school, I went to Mrs. Gallagher's room. She was talking to the appliance repair man. "Yeah, here's your problem, Lois. These cheap Taiwan bastard belts just snapped. There's so much shit comin' from Asia, I can't see why Nixon talks about importin' more. I'll put on some damn fine American belts, which'll last 'til hell freezes over."

Just then he turned and saw me. "Oh, 'scuse me, miss. I didn't hear you come in. I apologize for my cussin'. It's a damn bitch to stop." He headed out to his truck as Joann entered.

We spent the next half hour learning the definitions of knitting terms. During that time, the repairman fixed the washing machines as he smoked half a pack of Camels.

Despite my reluctance, I grasped the essentials of knitting and left thinking it was a craft I might use. Joann, however, wasn't fully appreciating our knitting lessons. I sensed this when I found a knitting needle sticking through my sandwich.

I had seven 50-minute classes during the school day. I enjoyed having a different teacher for each subject. The different personalities added flair—although they occasionally challenged my patience. I considered myself tolerant, but an hour with some teachers produced agony.

This year, that teacher was Mr. Schonbacher. He grew up in Germany and immigrated to the States after World War II. He spoke with a Bavarian accent at a slow pace. It took several tries to make us understand each lesson. If I were rich, I'd have offered a bounty for the cretin who hired Mr. Schonbacher to teach English. "Schtudents, zee preeposition-aal phrase ziz anything zee duck can dooo to zee cloud. For inschtance, zee duck can fly 'to' zee cloud, 'from' zee cloud, 'by' zee cloud, 'into' zee cloud, egcetera, egcetera, egcetera. Achtung, paay a-tenshon boyz and zee girlz. Vee is trying to learn zee English here. If you vant to schpeak and write as vell as I do, put some verk into it, people."

Fortunately his class started immediately after lunch. If I got to class early, I could grab a cherished desk near the back wall. These seats were popular because Mr. Schonbacher never figured out that students slept better by resting their heads against a wall.

Today, my first class was algebra. Mr. Olson was the math teacher. Every student spoke of Mr. Olson in flattering terms. Originally an architectural engineer, he had helped design many New York skyscrapers. His passion, however, was teaching. He had no family, but he had arrived in Sutter with his best friend, Don Caster. Sutter Junior High had recruited Mr. Olson, but the bonus was his roommate, Don, a renowned chef. Don opened Sutter's first gourmet restaurant, The Roasted Pear. I'd never dined there, but reviews rated the food as outstanding.

Mr. Olson and Don were strong supporters of Sutter's many charities. They'd shared a home for twenty years so they could split expenses; at least that was the story in 1971. Mr. Olson was a strict teacher who wasn't afraid to enforce discipline.

In the seventies, school discipline was more creative than today. Teachers often inflicted corporal punishment if it was necessary. In shop class the boys rose to new levels, with a novel idea that would let them sign Coach Langley's inlaid oak paddle and enjoy the notoriety of that rite of passage.

Marv Langley had played linebacker for the Chicago Bears. Now in his sixties, he often smoked a pipe during shop class. The boys had cleaned out his pipe and stuffed it with gunpowder, walnut sawdust, and, finally, tobacco. When Marv lit a farmer's match, he ignited the explosive mixture—the blast surprised everyone. Besides blowing the end off Marv's pipe, the blast burned his nose, removed his eyebrows, and inflicted a permanent receding hairline. Saying Mr. Langley didn't appreciate the humor was an understatement. He paddled each boy, twice daily, for a week. The incident set a precedent. From that day, teachers felt free to conjure up punitive variations that left students with lasting impressions—although the fear of the unknown created among students was usually worse than the punishments.

My next class was world history. Walking in, I noticed my favorite teacher, Penfield Wright, grading papers. Mr. Wright was a daunting man. He stood over six feet tall, and, having the muscular body of an athlete, he never had to ask for discipline. He had retired from the Marine Corps after thirty years of service. He had fought in World War II, Korea, and Vietnam, finishing his distinguished career at the Pentagon. During his time in uniform, Mr. Wright had earned his bachelor's and master's degrees in education.

As expected of a marine, his dress defined perfection. Straight vertical creases started at mid-shoulder and descended to the beltline, accenting his blue shirts. Mr. Wright's bow tie was symmetrical on each side of the button line. Spit-polished shoes radiated a blinding high gloss, underlining a black suit. His hands were manicured, and his teeth were ivory white. A sign on his desk proclaimed: "Penfield X. Wright—Your Tax Dollars at Work."

Considering his strict background, he was a wonderful teacher. As we adapted to his teaching style, it became obvious how much he loved kids. Mr. Wright's enthusiasm for bringing history alive was remarkable. Over the years, he had dressed as Genghis Khan, Charlemagne, and Thomas Jefferson, using their words to describe the times. He often arranged for local people to display their private historical artifacts in class, allowing enthusiasts to share their vast knowledge, describing how the items they'd collected were used to fill the needs of the day.

These demonstrations made history come alive. I never had to memorize dates or documents because Mr. Wright preferred we understand history by knowing the prevailing thoughts of the time. He stressed how thoughts became actions, and actions determined the way history unfolded. "People, in this class, I want you to take history's greatest ideas and build on those foundations. More importantly, thoroughly remember the bad ideas—and don't repeat them."

Another characteristic made Mr. Wright notable: he was the only African-American man in town. No one gave it much thought. Well-known and liked, Penfield Wright had distinguished himself in the military and in education. I can't say I never heard racial slurs spoken in Sutter; years passed before those disappeared. And I'm sure Mr. Wright and his family dealt with degrading behavior. So perhaps his greatest accomplishment was refusing to let discrimination block his path to success. Sutter's population considered Mr. Wright a testament to the resilience of the human spirit.

In recent classes, we'd been studying religion's impact on the modern world, and today we were having a special event. Mr. Wright told us thousands of religions had influenced history after the dawn of civilization, emphasizing that some of history's good ideas—and many of its bad ones—were due to specific religious beliefs. Our curriculum would allow time to focus on five major faiths: Hinduism, Buddhism, Judaism, Christianity (Catholicism and Protestantism), and Islam.

Mr. Wright stressed that he was a devout Catholic. Father of nine children and an altar boy at St. Mary's Most Precious Blood, he often performed charity work for the church. He explained that his bias toward

Catholicism wouldn't allow him to fairly review the other religions. So for the first time at our school, he'd invited a Buddhist monk from Portland, Sutter's Lutheran minister, and a Muslim leader to address our class. Other spiritual leaders attending would be Rabbi Edelstein of Beth Israel Synagogue, Father Blevins from St. Mary's, and a Hindu faith leader who lived in Salem, Oregon.

World history alternated with science class in two-hour blocks. One day, we'd have two hours of history, and the next day, two hours of science—which allowed us to finish longer science experiments. Each leader would have fifteen minutes to describe his religion. Mr. Wright asked the leaders to touch on their religions' founding principles, testaments, and rituals. He specifically cautioned them to inform about, rather than promote, their religions.

Mitch Hardisty sat across from me. He lived on a ranch and only came to town to attend school. He dressed in a red Western-cut shirt, Levis, and cowboy boots. "Laurel, I ain't much interested in this God stuff," he said. "It's goin' to be two long, hellacious hours. Ya got any chewin' tobacco handy? I left mine in ma locker."

School rules were difficult to figure out. It was OK to use chewing tobacco in school, but a student smoking cigarettes was quickly expelled. We couldn't chew gum in class, but if students were diabetic or had the doctor's permission, they could eat during class. Chewing tobacco didn't require permission from your doctor or your parents; Mitch always had a wad between his cheek and gum. Since he was under sixteen, his dad bought it for him. The family reasoned that chewing tobacco would keep Mitch from smoking. Mitch also kept Budweiser in his thermos bottle. Teachers seemed amazed at the amount of cream soda Mitch drank over lunch break.

Every week he gave me more tin tobacco holders to keep handy in case he ran out. Since we shared five of seven classes, this worked well. "Yes, Mitch, I've got a pack right here in my purse," I answered.

"Goddamn, Laurel! You're a lifesaver. Ya know we're castratin' bulls this next weekend. Would ya like to help? We'll ride some horses and do some cow milkin' as well. You'd enjoy it."

In twenty-four hours, I'd gotten invitations for two dates. Why was I appealing to boys? I didn't have a clue. However, I couldn't imagine pulling on a bull's testicles while someone else removed them, so I answered, "I'd love to Mitch, but I can't. My mother's out of town, and I've accepted an invitation to the dance next Saturday. Thanks for the offer. Maybe some other time."

"You're damned tootin', Laurel. We're doin' more castratin' come spring. I'll let you know plenty early," Mitch responded.

I could hardly wait.

CHAPTER 8

The Question

Our first speaker was Reverend Willard Pole. Reverend Pole was a bald, portly man with a ruddy face and a waddle in his walk. Loved by his congregation, he'd led Sutter's Lutheran church for many years.

Reverend Pole's only son, James, had died in the beginning of the Vietnam War. Drafted in 1964, James had taken leave from medical school to serve his country. He'd died rescuing three wounded men, including a medic. Having successfully recovered the first two soldiers, Jim Pole had headed back to retrieve the corpsman—and stepped on a land mine.

After James's death, Reverend Pole started drinking, which caused occasional problems. But folks in Sutter recognized the good deeds Reverend Pole did, and while the emotional pain he endured wasn't a reason to drink, those who had known James understood and forgave his father. Somehow, we knew that the toll of war far exceeded the reasons for fighting it.

The reverend put on his spectacles, adjusted his jacket, and began, "Good morning, students. If you'll follow me, let's start with the Pledge of Allegiance." We stood and covered our hearts with our right hands, and when we finished the pledge, we sat down.

Reverend Pole continued, "I'm thrilled Mr. Wright asked us to speak. I'm Willard Pole from the Lutheran Church. Kids, Mr. Wright's invitation is a gift I hope you'll remember. Ask yourselves this question: if six men with different faiths can sit here peacefully discussing modern issues, why can't governments achieve the same goal? The answer, my friends, is education.

"Each person is unique. Individual distinction fulfills our lives and keeps us from dying of boredom. We each have skills and thoughts that move the world forward. Restricting ourselves to one way of thinking inhibits progress. Learn tolerance and patience. Try to see another person's perspective and use what you learn today to say, 'I disagree with this person, but our differences aren't worth fighting over. Let's find a way to compromise.' Many people throughout history have died because they questioned the prevailing faith. God and I both had sons who died while demonstrating that the only justification for that supreme sacrifice is saving your fellow man.

"Now let's move ahead. Father Blevins and I are both Christians. To discuss the differences between our faiths, I've asked Father Blevins to help. Father, please come join me."

The class clapped as Father Blevins approached the podium. James Blevins had been Sutter's priest for the last fourteen years. In college, Father Blevins had played linebacker for Notre Dame. He loved gardening and baseball; in honor of the funds he helped raise, our Little League field bears his name. Every summer, Father Blevins umpired twice a week. In the few games I attended, I never saw anybody dispute his calls. Standing six feet seven inches tall, he rarely had critics.

Jim Blevins and Iris had been friends for many years. He often sought her advice on the growth and care of roses. Sutter's less fortunate families who faced funeral expenses often received beautiful flowers without knowing who the donor was.

Like Reverend Pole, Father Blevins had a large congregation. Most people didn't know that Father Blevins, Reverend Pole, Rabbi Edelstein, and the police chief played poker on Tuesday nights. Clearly, gambling wasn't an issue for the faiths represented today.

Father Blevins towered over everyone as he got ready to speak. He adjusted his collar, took a deep breath, and said, "Good morning, students. Like Reverend Pole, I'm thankful for this opportunity to discuss my faith. I fondly remember the free spirit of being young.

"Let me encourage you to immerse yourselves in learning about the splendors of God's world. Experience the creativity and variety lying within and around you. Don't marry too young or have kids before you're ready. I guarantee that the time will soon come when the responsibilities of jobs and perhaps even being parents will dominate your life.

"What you learn in school can lead to wise decisions and the ability to justify your choices. Your quality of life rests on the foundation of all your previous decisions, so don't hesitate to ask for help. Taking the time to advance your education after graduation will make your life better— don't pass up that opportunity.

"Let's begin, shall we? Here's a brief history of Christianity. Protestants, like Reverend Pole, and Catholics, like me, both believe in God.

Both religions follow the principle that Jesus is the Son of God and His mother was the Virgin Mary. Catholics believe Mary was without sin; Protestants disagree. But both faiths agree that God sacrificed His only son as payment for the sins of man.

"After Jesus died on the cross, His followers removed His body, anointed it, and placed it in a tomb. Today, Good Friday pays respect to the day of crucifixion. Three days later, his disciple Mary Magdalene and the Virgin Mary opened the tomb and found it empty. Over the next forty days, Jesus appeared on multiple occasions, confirming He'd risen from the dead. On the fortieth day, Jesus ascended into Heaven. The miracle of the Resurrection is the foundation of Christianity, and millions mark this miracle by celebrating Easter.

"Catholicism began after the death of Jesus, when His disciple Peter continued promoting the Gospel of Christ. Emperor Constantine gave Christianity a boost by declaring it the religion of the Roman Empire. Peter became the first pope of the Catholic Church. Over the next fourteen centuries, the church grew and seven sacraments became part of our faith. These include the Eucharist, or communion, where we re-create the Last Supper. We also baptize new members and practice confirmation, a rite in which Catholics—and some Protestants—reconfirm their baptism. In addition, we follow the sacraments of confession, the last rites, marriage, and holy orders. Holy orders constitute the sacrament of becoming a priest, and they come with great responsibility.

"Along with Protestants, we believe people reach Heaven only if they are without sin. Catholics achieve this by following the scriptures in the Holy Bible and taking part in church traditions like the sacraments, Holy Mass, and performing good deeds.

"Until 1518, the Catholic Church sold 'indulgences.' In return for a fee, a certificate signed by the pope granted the owner access to Heaven. Wealthy people could afford the indulgences and were often the only individuals receiving them. But in time, a monk named Martin Luther preached that you couldn't buy your way into Heaven—eternal life was a gift of God's grace, granted to anyone who believed Jesus died for their sins.

"Luther claimed that reading scripture and doing good deeds weren't enough to get into Heaven. Opposing indulgences, Luther's teachings proclaimed that one didn't have to be a priest to communicate with God. After protesting against the church, Luther was excommunicated by Pope Leo X in 1521. Freed from Catholic teachings, Luther started the Protestant Reformation. Today, the Presbyterian, Lutheran, and other prominent churches represent the Protestant faith. Reverend Pole, can you expand on my introduction?"

Mitch leaned over and whispered, "Laurel, do ya think I could buy me some indulgences from Father Blevins? I figure four outta do it for me, Dad, my brother Ron, and Uncle Red. Mom ain't done no sinnin'. At least nothin' like the rest of us. Wonder what he'd charge?"

I replied, "Gee, Mitch, I don't know. Why don't you ask him during the break?" Secretly, I could use one too—if not for me, certainly for Joann.

Reverend Pole continued the lecture. "Well, Father, in a short period, you covered much of Christianity. Brevity is a virtue. I hope you remember that when reciting Mass this Sunday." The class started giggling.

"I'll describe several more differences separating Protestants and Catholics. Protestants don't believe in the pope's authority, nor do we pray to the saints. In addition, we only believe in Heaven and Hell. Catholics believe in a third place called purgatory. After death, Catholics believe this is where a soul goes to receive God's final judgment. Priests and nuns also take lifetime vows of poverty, which is different from the vows taken by Protestant religious leaders. I try to help Father Blevins keep this vow every Tuesday night when we play cards.

"I'll stop there, because we've covered the basics. I know you have questions. Write them down, and we'll answer them after everyone speaks."

"Now I'd like to introduce Ekaraj Promsu, who will discuss the Hindu faith."

A thin dark-skinned man with black hair approached the podium with palms together. He wore white, baggy trousers with a long purple silk coat. His jacket was decorated with flower patterns and buttoned up the center.

I expected a rapid-fire staccato East Indian voice; the few East Indian people I'd met all talked that way. But surprising everyone, he spoke with a deep British accent, taking care to pronounce every syllable. "Thank you for welcoming me to history class. It's an honor having the opportunity to describe my faith, which is practiced by almost one billion people.

"My religious beliefs are quite different from those of Christians.

However, in one significant aspect, we share a common gift: each provides a path for parishioners to find peace and tranquility. If you give the idea some thought, our five basic emotions are sadness, anger, happiness, loneliness, and fear. We all experience them. No matter how hard the effort, we cannot avoid them. We need God daily, but we need Him most in difficult times.

"I am not here to convert you to Hinduism. A faith delivering a powerful message doesn't need salesmen. If you are searching for God, here are three conditions you should seek. First, find a god who is always dependable, who never fails to lessen your pain. Dependability is the reason your car shouldn't be your higher power—one day, it stops working. And believe me, the car always quits when it's most needed." Snickers could be heard throughout class.

He continued, "The second condition requires that God must be available at all times. Bad events happen at inconvenient hours. It does you no good if God is enjoying a coffee break when you need help. Finally, God must accept unlimited problems. The Almighty shouldn't tell you that His quota is full, so you're on your own.

"Keep these conditions in mind as I outline my faith. Unlike Christianity, we do not use the Bible. Instead, we treasure the ancient *Vedas* as our doctrine. This holy teaching has no beginning or end. Should the universe vanish, the Vedas continue.

"We call our god *Brahman*. Brahman has no physical form. We describe this Essence as the unchanging reality among and beyond us. Hindus believe Brahman's spirit is limitless—an eternal, steady constant throughout time. We can't see or hear Brahman, but finding His nature entails seeking the deepest knowledge about ourselves.

"In Hinduism, we search for truth and strive for dharma. *Dharma* is the path that supports the positive, or if you prefer, the correct order of the universe.

"We spend our lives discovering the truth and trying to make the world a better place. On this journey we use many personal gods called *devas*, who are extensions of Brahman.

"There are a few more points I think are important. We believe the soul is immortal. When a person's soul leaves the body, it enters another. We call this cycle *transmigration*. If a person has done something wrong in a previous life, he must pay the penalty in the next life. This cycle repeats until our good devotions and actions release the soul from this life-and-death cycle. These actions unite the soul with Brahman, and we discover our true self.

"Thank you for letting me speak with you. I wish you serenity, peace, and happiness."

We clapped, as Mr. Wright got up. "People, let's take a break, and then we'll hear from our other distinguished lecturers. If you have urgent questions, our speakers are available during the break."

I headed for the door as Mitch made a beeline for Father Blevins. Reaching the hall, I saw that Tanice had Denny pinned in a corner and was giving him an earful. I stayed out of sight but moved closer to hear the conversation.

"I just got out of the principal's office, Denny. You know, they found that igniter on top of the broadcast booth. The announcer didn't know who used it, but he remembered me sitting below the booth and told the principal I probably saw something. For fifteen minutes, Mr. Martin practically pulled out my fingernails trying to get me to talk."

"Gosh, Tanice, what did you tell him? You didn't squeal, did ya?"

"No, Denny. Despite the agony of repeated questioning, I didn't squeal. That's because I'd heard you plan on taking Laurel to the dance. I didn't want you jailed until after the dance. Laurel's sweet on you, and God only knows why. When will you pull your head out of your ass and start applying yourself? You might as well give your brain to science; you're not using it. If I hear you've treated Laurel badly, I'm going to kick your balls into your head so far you'll have to blow your nose to pee. Do you get it, Denny?" She grabbed his collar, repeating, "Well, do ya?"

"Gee, Tanice, settle down, will ya?" Denny replied. "I'd never think of doing anything bad to Laurel. She and I are good friends." Tanice put a fist in Denny's face and then strutted off. I knew she would carry out her threats. She had five brothers and had learned to sail her estrogen battleship through the sea of testosterone.

I quenched my thirst at the water fountain and headed back to class. What struck me was that somehow, despite their different philosophies, our guest religious leaders had learned to respect one another. What secret allowed them to avoid conflict? Rabbi Edelstein would provide a clue.

Mitch sat down and said to me, "Well, Laurel, that Father ain't sellin' no indulgences, but he said if I wanted to confess, he'd absolve me of my sins. I told him it'd take about a week. Course he'll wanna know about us

FFA boys steer ropin' them stoner hippies and bathin' 'em in the Holiday Inn pool. I bet them folks don't visit the town no more. I never seen so much dirt in my life."

Rabbi Edelstein stood up, interrupting Mitch's list of sins. "Students, I am delighted to be here. I agree with my colleagues. This is a rare opportunity to explore the major religions from men who study and practice them.

"Before I discuss Judaism, here's a useful tool for life: only change the one person you can—yourself. We can try making others see the world through our eyes, but we're not blessed with nearly enough power. People only change if they want to change. Forcing others to conform to your wishes usually encourages them to continue the same behavior out of spite. *Showing* people how our beliefs have improved our lives is more powerful than telling them. If they still don't get it, the second point is acceptance. Accepting and forgiving allows us to avoid conflicts. People we don't forgive inhabit our minds and never pay rent. This advice takes practice, and it's not easy. But if you start now, your life will enjoy much peace.

"OK. Let's talk about Judaism. How do we differ from Christians and Hindus? Our religion starts nearly thirteen hundred years before Jesus with an elderly man named Abraham. God made a contract with Abraham when Abraham was ninety, allowing him to become the Father of Many Nations. The symbol representing this contract is the rite of circumcision.

"A circumcision removes the foreskin covering the tip of the penis. I see the young men cringing; however, most of you are probably circumcised. If you're not circumcised, don't panic. There's no reason to have surgery unless you're converting to Judaism. Abraham circumcised himself with a knife, a technique I recommend avoiding."

Almost instantly, the girls started giggling and couldn't stop chattering. In contrast, the boys remained silent as they looked between their legs with pained expressions. During their next locker room visit, a visual examination to compare genitalia would take top priority.

Rabbi Edelstein continued. "To continue, Abraham had two sons named Ishmael and Isaac. Ishmael became the patriarch of the Arab people and a prophet of Islam. Isaac, Moses, and Abraham became founding Jewish patriarchs. I'm focusing on Judaism since you'll hear about Islam shortly.

"The Hebrew Holy Scripture is the Tanakh. Its teachings consist of three sections. The first section constitutes the Torah and is familiar to people outside Judaism. Carefully handwritten in Hebrew and rolled into a scroll, the Torah contains the first five books of the Old Testament: Genesis, Exodus, Leviticus, Numbers, and Deuteronomy.

"The second part of the Tanakh is the Nev'im, which concerns the eight prophets. The final section is the Ketuvim, which deals with important Hebrew writings. We also rely on one other essential text, the Talmud. It records thousands of opinions handed down from distinguished rabbis. The writings discuss Jewish laws, customs, and other important matters.

"Christians and Jews differ in several other respects. Jews believe there's one god, but we don't believe Jesus came from the Immaculate Conception or rose from the dead. In Judaism, Jesus isn't the Savior, nor do we believe that Jesus died for our sins. Jews achieve a bond with God by doing what's moral. Salvation isn't our goal; our endeavor is to fully live life while giving maximum service to God. We value education, charity, and serving God; Jews strive to achieve all three.

"One more thing: you see I'm wearing a skullcap, called a *yarmulke*. I do this to show atonement to God. Men wear the cap, along with a prayer shawl, while worshiping in the synagogue. Women cover their heads, as do the children. Jewish society values young people, but they aren't considered full members of the community until girls reach twelve and boys reach thirteen.

"Well, that offers a brief summary of the Jewish faith. You're welcome to visit our synagogue, but you likely won't understand the service unless you know Hebrew. If there are questions, I'll be happy to answer them briefly."

The class clapped, and Susan Small raised her hand. Mr. Wright asked, "Yes, Susan, what would you like to know?"

At that moment, looking perplexed, she wondered, "I'm confused about the significant points of these religions. I thought I was Presbyterian, but listening to these guys, I might be a Jew or a Muslim. Rabbi Edelstein, I have roots in all three, because Abraham fathered all the founders. Is it possible I'm an Arab?"

Mr. Wright replied, "Susan, it's possible but unlikely. I'm sure you're not an Arab, although your family could still practice Islam. Expecting your confusion, our guests made handouts, and when class finishes, everyone will get a copy. Let me suggest you confirm with your parents which faith you belong to. This sound advice goes for each of you. Understanding your faith demands devotion and study. As you mature, it's possible your concept of God may change and guide you to a different faith. If you haven't done so, or if you're not sure, ask for help to find your starting point.

"OK, people, let's keep moving. Our next speaker is Hermat Ruhi. He's the leader of the Islamic faith in Portland."

Mr. Ruhi wore a white robe with a blue woven vest. On top of his head was a yellow, brimless cap. In a serious tone, and speaking as if our survival hinged on embracing every word, Mr. Ruhi began. "Students, today is the first time I've spoken in history class. I praise Mr. Wright for letting me explain the Islamic faith, which is unlike the religions already discussed. People practicing Islam are called Muslims. It's estimated more than one billion Muslims practice Islam.

"Our religion began around 610 AD. Our revered prophets are Adam, Noah, Abraham, Moses, Ishmael, and Jesus. We value the wisdom of Jesus and we believe in the Immaculate Conception, but we don't believe Jesus is the Savior or that he rose from the dead.

"We have one god, called Allah. We believe Allah is a Divine Being, neither male nor female, and the one true god. Supreme, eternal, and pure, Allah passes judgment on every human. The duty of every Muslim is to follow Allah's divine will and commandments. So that our people could better understand this, Allah sent the prophet Muhammad to deliver his revelations. Allah gave Mohammad the first of many revelations when he was forty. The wisdom given in these principles helped Muhammad unite the Islamic nations. Muslims believe Muhammad is the last true prophet sent to mankind.

"Our Scriptures are contained in the Quran, a book we believe contains the true words of God. Islam asserts that Christianity and Judaism changed biblical manuscripts by altering the Torah, the Psalms, and the Gospels. Islam summarizes this belief in the Tahrif. The sacred writings outlined in this document are the source of many religious conflicts. Young people like you must advance man's thinking to reach a peaceful resolution letting all faiths coexist. Despite past and present attempts, this goal still eludes us."

Reverend Pole and Rabbi Edelstein were shaking their heads in clear disagreement with Mr. Ruhi as he described the Tahrif. Apparently, our

Muslim speaker had touched a raw nerve and took a few moments to carefully consider his next words.

In a soft tone, he continued. "There are five pillars of Islam, considered essential duties for true believers. The pillars consist of a pilgrimage to Mecca and belief in the Shahada, a creed pronouncing our belief in the oneness of Allah. In addition, we give alms, or charity, to the poor, and we confirm Muhammad as the Prophet by facing east and praying five times each day. The final pillar is Ramadan, which is a daily twelve-hour fast lasting one month. It honors Allah for revealing the Qur'an.

"Our followers believe in the afterlife, which we call Paradise. Muslims reach Paradise by doing good deeds and achieving the Five Pillars. The Islamic faith involves much more, but this short outline provides a summary of the religion. However you choose to believe, and wherever the future takes you, always set aside time for helping others. You didn't reach this point without many helping hands. May Allah bless you all as your journey continues. Thank you."

We clapped and began whispering, as our next speaker gathered his notes.

Elle Dutton sat behind me. History was the only class we shared. I knew Elle was intelligent but self-absorbed. She believed most of her classmates weren't worth her time. Her father, Norman, was a dentist, and her mother, Amelia, had been runner-up in the 1957 Miss America Pageant. The family oozed money, often bragging about their wealth.

She leaned forward and whispered, "Laurel, do these religions make sense to you? The men seem smart, but bright people are usually Presbyterians! You know Sutter's important people worship at the Presbyterian Church. Reverend Jaswell has stated numerous times how his congregation gives him so much moral material to work with. Obviously, he feels we beat other churches hands down. You should join us. Since your mother's a lawyer, you'd fit right in."

I turned and faced Elle. "Gee, Elle, it's hard deciding because there are so many choices. Protestant churches are like different brands of gas. Each sounds like the best, but they smell identical and transport you to the same place. Anyway, what makes the Presbyterian Church special? Is it because your parents donated for the Dutton Garden outside the rectory? I mean, your family's name is everywhere on that church. If you ever decided you believed differently from the Presbyterians, would you transfer to another church or stay where you are just to socialize with important people? These guys are encouraging us to brownnose God, not the town leaders."

Elle took a deep breath and blurted out, "Fine, Laurel, keep being selfish and see where that gets you. I'm helping the Presbyterian women auction jewelry to raise money for folks living in Warren Trailer Park!" I couldn't argue.

Our final speaker stood and centered himself. He was of Asian descent—a small, dark-skinned man who walked calmly but purposefully. His clothing consisted of a crimson robe draped over his left shoulder. His right shoulder remained bare, and he was completely bald. He wore simple sandals.

In broken, Mandarin-accented English, he spoke softly. "Students, like the other learned men, I am pleased to be here. My name is Chen-Tao Hoen. I'm a Buddhist monk. Choosing what to tell you about Buddhism is a difficult task. My faith has no relation to the religions already discussed, nor do we offer any opinion on Christianity, Judaism, or Islam. What I'll summarize today takes years of study for devout Buddhists. My goal is to keep my talk simple so you better understand a religion foreign to most Americans.

"Our faith started around 563 B.C. in Nepal with the birth of Siddhartha Gautama, a prince born to royalty. Despite his material wealth, the young prince believed he lacked an essential piece necessary to fulfill life. Finding this missing piece became his goal; at age twenty-nine, he traveled among his subjects for the first time.

"During the journey, he discovered people suffering from severe mental and physical pain. He decided to give up his royal holdings and become a beggar. During his time abroad, he studied religious teachings, and over time, he achieved a deep meditative consciousness. However, Siddhartha still wasn't fulfilled. He abstained from worldly pleasures, but even this denied him serenity. Continuing the long search, he discovered an idea called the Middle Way. The term simply means moderation in all areas of life. Siddhartha vowed to sit beneath a *bodhi* tree until he discovered the truth and gained contentment. After forty-nine days of meditation, he became enlightened. Thus the Hindu word for Enlightened One is *Buddha*.

"Enlightenment is the foundation of Buddhism and consists of what we call the Four Noble Truths. Along with meditation, following the Four Noble Truths helps us reach the state of nirvana. Mr. Wright tells me the class has heard of *nirvana* but may not know its true meaning. It means 'removing greed, hatred, and ignorance.'

"To explain the Four Noble Truths, I would like to describe the key idea of the dukkha. *Dukkha* means suffering and is the first noble truth. We can suffer from problems inherited from our parents, as well as from not getting things we want and receiving things we don't want. We also suffer when we don't allow or accept change.

"The second noble truth explains the first noble truth in more detail by discussing the origin of dukkha, or how our pain arises. It may be difficult to imagine this at your age, but suffering begins from disturbed emotions. People preoccupied with themselves can't understand the motives, emotions, or nature of the world around them. In craving pleasurable experiences, our minds focus on getting goods we don't need and ridding ourselves of problems we don't want. Avoiding these painful emotions becomes our greatest obsession.

"The third noble truth ends dukkha—the suffering. We gain the ability to understand and heal the emotions causing our minds great unhappiness. For Buddhists, this is life's fulfillment.

"The last noble truth is the Eightfold Path all Buddhists walk, leading to alleviation of dukkha. The path consists of correct thought, livelihood, effort, mindfulness, concentration, understanding, speech, and action. These eight ideas, when practiced together, bring about serenity and peace.

"Buddhism does not have a god. We believe our lives are a continual cycle of birth, suffering, pain, death, and rebirth, which we call *samsara*. We guide the samsara cycle with our thoughts and actions, combined with the words we speak. The general term for these qualities is *karma*, which refers to good or bad deeds. In Buddhism, it influences our immediate and future lives. To gain nirvana, we must break the bad karma cycle and become enlightened.

"My last point concerns the Holy Scriptures, which consist of the Buddha's teachings. Called the *Tripitaka*, this book is a set of writings broken into three sections. Scholars compiled the *Tripitaka* after Buddha's death. Remember that *nirvana* means surmounting ignorance. Our goal as Buddhists is victory over mistaken beliefs within ourselves and the world we occupy. It's an exhaustive search for the truth.

"Like Catholics, Buddhism has both monks and nuns. Our spiritual leader is the Dalai Lama.

"I leave you with several final thoughts I hope will help. Each creature on this earth has natural instincts. To survive, every living entity intuitively answers five questions: can 'I' eat it? Can 'I' reproduce offspring with it? Will it hurt 'me'? Does it feel good to 'me'? And finally, should 'I' nurture it? You'll notice each question contains the words, 'I' or 'me.' 'I' and 'me' refer to the 'self.'

"The selfish answer only considers the well-being of the individual asking the questions; it doesn't consider how its response will affect others. Watch a young child and you'll notice his behavior revolves around fulfilling his own desires. Our primitive instincts provide for survival, but when natural instincts rage out of control, they create every sin and misery ever known. Uncontrolled instincts are the root of all evil. Examine world history this way and you will understand how past motives shaped today's civilization.

"Humans possess blessings far beyond those of other animals. We hold the gift of a higher brain, allowing us to apply logic and engage in abstract thought. As you mature, master these skills to rise above your instincts and serve others the best you can. Helping less fortunate people will provide you with happiness you've never imagined.

"Thank you very much. I am going to stop so there's time for questions. I know I've covered much, and without doubt, it's confusing. I invite you to visit our temple and ask questions. You are always welcome."

We applauded as he bowed and took his seat. To me, the revealing words of all six men had opened a door guarding the truth about the world. I had glimpsed philosophies that made me realize I needed to work on understanding myself. I didn't know which path to take, but each led these men to deep, perceptive views on human behavior and ways to comfort the soul. Their collective insight revealed wisdom seemingly inspired by something greater than themselves.

Mr. Wright got up. "What questions do you have?"

Donna Roberts spoke first. "Hindus and Buddhists believe in a cycle of life and death, as well as meditation and yoga. Are both faiths branches of an older religion, like Protestantism and Catholicism are branches of Christianity?"

The Hindu answered first. "No, we aren't divisions of the same religion. Hindus have a god, and Buddhists do not. This point is a major difference. Another difference is the Holy Scriptures each faith relies upon.

Our guide is the *Vedas;* for Buddhists, it's the *Tripitaka.* Buddhists equally cherish every living organism, while we revere the cow."

"Many Buddhists and Hindus live in India, but our faiths differ radically," added the Buddhist monk. "There are three branches of Buddhism. Some branches share more with Hinduism, but the most important similarity is the fact that both religions promote nonviolent, peaceful coexistence."

Holly Olson raised her hand with a question for the entire group. "Are all six of you married?" she asked. Reverend Pole nodded affirmatively.

Father Blevins spoke up. "Along with the vow of poverty, the Catholic church doesn't allow priests or nuns to marry. Our vows demand total devotion to God. Marriage and children violate this commitment. You probably think we're lonely, but I have many people in Sutter who've made me part of their families. It's a blessing."

The Muslim added, "My family was killed in the Arab-Israeli war, and I have not remarried. Our religion allows marriage to more than one woman, but this isn't legal in the United States. Because large families are costly, most Muslims marry only one wife."

Holly went on. "If Muslim men have many wives, can Muslim women have multiple husbands? Don't you think women deserve equal rights?"

Reacting as if challenged, the Muslim replied, "No, young lady, women do not deserve equal rights. Our religion doesn't allow multiple husbands and never will."

"Well," Holly said, "I think men dominate all your religions, and I doubt God put them in charge. Mom says, 'Men can't organize anything so if you want something done, ask a woman.'" The girls were clapping as Mr. Wright started to stand. Holly continued, "If the world wants less war, let women run the show. That's what I think!"

Mr. Wright quickly intervened. "Thank you, Holly, for your commentary and opinions." Wiping his brow, he said, "Unfortunately, we're out of time. Our speakers are staying in case you have more inquiries. Our next class isn't until Wednesday, so here's your assignment, which is due Friday.

"The summary I'm passing around provides a comparison sheet for the religions discussed today. Each speaker has generously given a copy of his holy scriptures to the school library. If you need references, ask the librarian.

"You've finished hearing six intelligent, spiritual men describe their faiths. Your assignment is to answer the following question: why do these men see God in substantially different ways—or do they? I realize the answer takes some speculation and research. There aren't right or wrong answers—only better and worse.

"Gentlemen, thank you for this marvelous discussion and your valuable time. Class dismissed."

We stood and clapped.

CHAPTER 9

Baloney and Liquor:
Help for the Homeless

The rest of the day was uneventful. I spent Mr. Schonbacher's English class trying to decide whether Mom and I were atheists or agnostics. If we believed God existed, which god was it?

Arriving home, I noticed the sequoia planted in the front yard. The garden hose poured water into the depressed soil surrounding the base of the tree. The sequoia still looked unhealthy, but getting the tree transplanted had helped its appearance. Iris's red wagon sat by the front door.

Walking into the house, I immediately noticed the silence. This concerned me, because Iris wasn't a spring chicken—she might be dead. Fear came over me as I went through a dead-person mental checklist. I'd have to call the mortician and possibly Father Blevins, since he and Iris were good friends. There was no need to call Mom, because if Iris was dead, I'd have the house alone for five weeks.

My fears vanished as I searched the house and couldn't find a body. Otis was in the backyard, not chewing on body parts, so I assumed Iris must be out.

In the kitchen, fifty wrapped sandwiches sat on the island. Next to the sandwiches were the same number of plastic medicine bottles, resembling my cough syrup. Each bottle contained a brown, unlabeled liquid. Experiencing a momentary lapse in judgment, I took the lid off the first bottle and drank several teaspoons.

Oh my God! My throat was on fire and I thought I was going to barf. The liquid was strong whiskey! Sitting by the sink was an empty half-gallon whiskey bottled labeled "W.L. WELLER CENTENNIAL—100 PROOF." What party was Iris planning?

Looking around, I noticed three smaller bottles were also empty. Then a revelation hit me: Iris was a closet drinker! Wandering around drunk, she had probably gone on a short errand and couldn't find her way home.

I decided to track her down, thinking what a great job she'd done of hiding her drinking problem. I'd never heard anyone mention it.

Looking at the kitchen, I realized her condition was serious. I called Joann, who answered on the first ring. "Joann, it's me. I need help finding Iris. There's empty whiskey bottles scattered throughout the kitchen. I know she's drunk and lost. Can you help me find her?"

"Calm down, Laurel," she responded. "Are you sure she's drunk? You know, she's engaged in strange behavior, but I've never heard about a drinking problem. Try to think where she'd go. She doesn't have a car, so she can't be far. I'll come over."

Ten minutes later, Joann was at my side. "Laurel, I think I know where she is. If I were a drinker, I'd go where they had liquor. Let's visit Blitzer's Lounge—it's closest. If she's not there, we'll go to Pickler's Liquor."

In 1971, bars didn't automatically expel minors. If you were seventeen and possessed good moral character, you might even buy a beer. Blitzer's owner, Larry McGrew, was one of the nicest people in Sutter.

Mayor Hugh Swan sat at the bar. Mr. McGrew said, "Hello, ladies, how can I help you? Need a soda, root beer float, something to eat? You look rushed; what's your hurry?"

I blurted out, "Larry, we're looking for Iris Wimple. We think she's drinking and figured she'd come here or maybe go to the liquor store. Have you seen her?"

"No, she hasn't been by. Mayor, have you seen Iris?"

Most people liked Mayor Swan. It was a widely known fact that the mayor spent little time working at City Hall—his primary office was Blitzer's Lounge. If you had city business, it was best to visit the mayor before two thirty. "No, Larry, I haven't seen Iris today," he said in slurred words. "But I doubt she's drunk. What makes you kids think she's been drinkin'?"

I told him about the convincing evidence. "Well, ladies, what you're sayin' makes sense. Is today Monday or Tuesday?" We told him it was Monday.

"It's likely Iris is at the liquor store. I expect she needs more whiskey for the homeless folks who've come to town. Word's out: Sutter's the place to live if you're on the street. Every Monday or Tuesday, Iris makes sandwiches and delivers 'em to people livin' along the stream. She also gives 'em stout whiskey to prevent the DTs. Have you girls heard of DTs?" We hadn't.

"When you stop drinkin', you get shaky and start to sweat. 'DTs' stands for *delirium tremens;* if you've been drinkin' a long time, ya hallucinate and get seizures that can kill ya. That's why she gives 'em the booze. Trust me, ladies, I've had experience dealin' with this crap. I know what I'm talkin' about."

Thanking the mayor for his drinking insights, we hurried over to Pickler's. When we arrived, Iris was standing at the counter with three bottles of bourbon. Acting guilty, she quickly bagged the liquor, and said, "Laurel! Joann! What a surprise!" She tried hiding the bags by blocking them.

I commented back. "You're surprised? What brings you to Pickler's?" I teased. "It looks like you're planning a party—probably Celebrate a Sequoia Day. You've bought enough liquor for a whole block!" I pointed out.

By then, Iris had gathered her thoughts. "Indeed I have!" she replied. "Help me load the liquor and haul it home. I'll have you two join me this evening. We're going to help the homeless. I believe serving the homeless makes us appreciate our own blessings. This experience will be one you won't forget."

As we walked home, Iris confirmed what the mayor had told us. She explained that during her younger years, while volunteering in a hospital, she had seen a homeless woman die from alcohol withdrawal. The woman was admitted with pneumonia but had lied about how much she drank. Her pneumonia improved, but she died three days later because of seizures. It had made a lasting impression on Iris and made her vow to help others dying from alcoholism.

Arriving home, Iris had Joann call her mother and get permission to stay for dinner. We filled the remaining prescription bottles and packed two boxes. Then we dined on a great dinner of pot roast, rice, broccoli, and fruit salad.

While we ate, I told them about history class. Eventually, I related Mr. Wright's assignment. "I can't begin to imagine a good answer. Today made me realize how little I know about people and religion."

Iris replied, "Honey, your words show you're becoming wise."

I looked at Joann. She looked at me. "I'm not sure I understand, Iris."

"It's simple, ladies. When people mature and achieve a good education, they believe they're brilliant. Life moves on, and most folks realize there's so much they don't know. Admitting what you don't know and asking others for help demonstrates humility and brings wisdom.

Tonight, you'll learn that humility means helping people who will never, in any manner, repay you."

Joann and I helped Iris wash the dishes. Iris needed to call Nubs, so Joann and I wandered into the living room.

Joann said, "Boy, Iris keeps busy. I've never seen so much spunk in a person her age. And man, can she cook. I don't know what we're getting into, but I'm certain we haven't done it before. Before Iris is ready, let's think about what we're wearing to the dance. You know, Denny's bragging about taking you to the dance. He boasts like he's the world's best fisherman who just caught the biggest fish in the ocean. Whatever possessed you to say yes?"

Thinking back to Tanice cornering Denny, I replied, "Well, I like him, and I'm sure he's a gentleman. There's more to him; I just haven't figured it out. He's a nerd and he hates formal sports, but he plays football better than anyone on the junior varsity. If Denny applies himself, he'll be the rose sprouting in the pigpen. And no, I don't know what I'm going to wear."

Iris came out of the kitchen. "OK, kids, Nubs Fritzmeyer is on her way. She'll pull into the driveway so we can load the car. I suggest you go outside and clear the front yard. Nubs has trouble with driveways. When you see her Cadillac, wave her down because she'll never see the address."

"Right, Iris." I grabbed Joann and we scoped out the yard. Our two-car attached garage sheltered one car and faced the street. The driveway was sixteen feet wide, but whether Nubs could drive up the middle was anyone's guess. It was also trash night, so I moved the trash can away from the driveway.

Within minutes, a Cadillac came lumbering down the street, swerving from side to side. Two of the neighbor's garbage cans achieved flight, and I grabbed a red rag and hurried into the street. Nubs slowed down and stopped. The window rolled down.

A bent-over, osteoporotic lady sat hugging the steering wheel. She wore a hat with a veil covering her face. I wondered how Nubs even saw over the dashboard. "Hi there, sweetie," she said. "Can you direct me to the Montgomery home? I'm looking for Iris Wimple."

"Well, Mrs. Fritzmeyer, you're at the right place. I'm Laurel Montgomery. Pull in the driveway and we'll load your car." She pulled forward a bit, then backed up, cranking the wheel hard to achieve a right angle to the street. I could see she was preparing to make a run straight up the driveway.

I dived to safety as the Cadillac set a speed record racing up our driveway. Joann stood plastered against the garage door, spread-eagled and wide-eyed. My friend was about to become a permanent part of our home when Nubs veered right, forcing the car to leave the driveway and cruise along the front of our home. She stopped two feet from the front steps, her car parallel to the house.

I got up, noting my grass-stained pants as Iris said, "Laurel that was thoughtful of you to have Nubs pull up to the front door. It makes loading much easier. Come on, Joann. Why are you looking pale? "

Joann walked over, still shaking. I remarked, "The good news is wherever we're headed, we're inside the car. It'll be safer than being on the street." Joann gave me the same look I'd seen after volunteering her for extra home economics credit.

"If that's the good news, Laurel, I don't know if I'll live through the bad news."

I reminded her, "Think of it as one of those exciting adventures you talked about a few minutes ago."

We loaded the car while Iris hopped into the front passenger seat. Even though the Cadillac was older, it came equipped with seat belts. Getting in back, we strapped ourselves in, expecting more than a leisurely evening drive. After driving several blocks, it appeared Nubs did much better driving forward than in reverse. Even so, approaching drivers who recognized her car pulled over, giving Nubs plenty of room to pass. She didn't stop at traffic lights. If another car sat waiting at the intersection, Nubs honked and went around. Obviously, she considered stop signs as suggestions rather than commands.

Despite the thrill ride, we survived crossing the town's narrowest bridge and parked by the stream. It was dusk as we exited the car, reciting a prayer of thanks. The sun backlit the clouds and created a gorgeous pinkish-orange sunset. We unloaded the boxes, the wagon, and Mrs. Fritzmeyer—who was nimble for ninety-two.

In single file, we hiked down the path to the stream. Liquor bottles and litter along the way suggested this was a well-traveled trail. When we reached the stream, we walked 150 yards before coming upon several men and one woman, huddled around a fire. They were dressed in dirty clothing, each of their garments showing many tears and iron-on patches. Every person had foil pie plates and Styrofoam cups. Utensils consisted of plastic forks and knives. A big pot sat on a grate over the fire; it looked as if black beans was the main course. As we walked up, the people stood and came to greet us.

They started by hugging Nubs and Iris and then came over to Joann and me. As the first man embraced me, I experienced the worst smell of my life. I couldn't believe the stench; he clearly hadn't bathed in weeks. I learned later he spent his time searching through trash cans. His beard was over a foot long and matted with food particles. I thought of the leftovers I'd just set outside in the trash. They'd provide this man with food for three days.

Joann looked paralyzed with fear for the second time that day. Iris noticed as well and hurried to comfort her. "Joann, this is Arnold. He's a wonderful man who's had bad luck; don't be afraid. Help me unload the sandwiches and pass them around."

As I met each of the nine people, I began to understand what poverty meant. Their valued possessions included their clothes and a cardboard box shelter. They had no cars, no family, no job, and little hope. Nowhere did I see a reason to continue living. Yet despite existing in squalor, some still held a spark in their eye.

The sandwiches and liquor were riches of gastronomic gold. Iris provided one sandwich a day for a week and a daily liquor supply for each homeless person. The sandwiches were chilled by sealing them in plastic bags and placing them in the stream. Rocks held the bags in place.

Greeting each person, we finished handing out the goods. One poor soul lay passed out under the bridge with his half-full liquor bottle, so we set the sandwiches and whiskey by his side. When we talked to the homeless folks, they all revealed a riches-to-rags story.

Joann became more relaxed and decided to help Nubs cut Arnold's hair. After fetching water from the stream, she warmed the bucket over the fire. Arnold sat on a rock while they shampooed his hair, cut it, and massaged his scalp. They also cleaned and trimmed his beard, making him feel like a new man. Four other stream settlers received the same grooming.

The only woman living with the group was Elizabeth. She hadn't tended to her hair in weeks. Getting my hair done was a simple pleasure I took for granted. But for Elizabeth, it restored dignity and self-respect not measurable in dollars.

Joann finished brushing Elizabeth's hair and applied some makeup. Iris added the finishing touch with some faux jewelry. Elizabeth came to life when she looked in the hand mirror. Her inner beauty radiated, projecting a smile from ear to ear. The men all took notice.

When we decided to stay longer, they found a chair for Nubs while the rest of us sat around the fire. A man named Ed spoke for the first time. "Iris, Nubs, you young ladies, I want ya to know how much this means to us. We can't ever repay ya. We're livin' here because of poor decisions, and we probably deserve the trouble we got. I can't speak for the rest, but for years I drank, stole, cheated, and lied. I left my family, lost my job, and robbed a bank. Did seven years. I just got out of jail a year ago. It fills my heart knowin' someone cares. In prison, I joined Alcoholics Anonymous, so at least I'm sober. Right now, AA and you people is about all I got goin' for me."

Joann asked, "How do you keep such a positive attitude?"

"Young lady, what's your name?" He asked.

"Joann."

"Well, Joann, I'm a wealthy man." I could see Joann tilt her head in a puzzled look.

"I'm sure you're a thinkin', 'He must be crazy; he ain't got nothin' of value.' And when it comes to material stuff, you'd be right. I learned the hard way: true wealth has nothin' to do with money. Life's most valuable possessions are self-confidence, self-respect, health, sobriety, and integrity. You can't buy that shit at Sears!

"I can't buy me no love or respect from another person, and I can't buy no happiness. Findin' these treasures meant lookin' inside myself. My whole life I used everyone and everything ta make me happy. I drank, chased me some women, and got hooked on them damned drugs. If I had money, I gambled.

"Gettin' locked up forced me to stop these outside fixes. With help, I started realizin' that spiritual riches always comforted me, no matter how bad the daily grind. Lookin' at Jimi Hendrix, he was the world's greatest guitar player and blessed with money. Yet at twenty-seven, he went and died of a drug overdose. Somehow, despite money and drugs, he couldn't find him no happiness.

"I don't plan on stayin' here forever. I'm lookin' for a job and hope to study at night, eventually rebuildin' my life. If I hadn't faced my own demons and done my best to make 'em right, I couldn't a made 'er this far. You may think livin' here's bad, but I assure you, it don't come close to livin' in prison. Someone's always sufferin' more than me. Truth is, among all men, I'm richly blessed."

CHAPTER 10

Better Living through
Old Women Philosophers

When we arrived home, I felt chilled. I took a hot bath and did my English assignment. I finished quicker than expected, so I joined Iris, who was watching *Rowan and Martin's Laugh-In*. I liked their suggestive humor—although Mom thought their jokes were too mature for me; when she was home, I never watched it. After *Rowan and Martin* came the *Doris Day Show*. As it started, Iris asked me how I planned to answer Mr. Wright's question.

"Well, I'm not sure. Thinking about it, this question would challenge a grown-up: I think it's too complex for freshmen. What's your opinion?"

"Well, it's a difficult question for anyone. But I'll tell you, age isn't a crutch you can lean on much longer. Whether you accept it or not, you've reached the age where the questions get harder and answers come in multiple-choice instead of Yes or No. Mr. Wright wouldn't have given you the assignment if he didn't feel you were capable of handling it. I'm glad he assigned it.

"Last night you asked, 'What defines God?' I think you were trying to confound me." I couldn't believe Iris had figured it out. "Whatever your reason, the table is turned—your history teacher has now asked you the same question. You'll see how elusive the answer is. It's just a suggestion, but before you respond, consider the question: does God even exist? If a supreme intellect doesn't exist, why answer who God is or why men differ on how they understand him. God either is or He isn't. There is no halfway."

"Gee, Iris, how do I discover if God's out there when I don't know what I'm looking for?" I asked.

Iris replied, "Well, long ago I asked the same question."

Somehow, I knew she had.

"Until last night when you asked, it had been years since I thought about the answer. Proving God exists is a difficult task. Philosophers have debated this question for six thousand years. We certainly won't settle the issue tonight. However, I'll share my perspective, which is probably wrong. Let me ask you, Laurel: what's your definition of God?"

I didn't have a clue. "Well, uh, gee, uh—I guess something greater than me in every respect. You know? Smarter, bigger, kinder, more physically fit, has more money—stuff like that. How's that sound?"

"It's a good start," she replied. "Keep going."

I thought for a moment. "I guess God is someone we pray to. Perhaps He's a king, except I can't imagine God wearing a crown. Maybe He's the king of the universe?" I speculated.

Iris responded, "I think you're on the right track. I believe God is a vast entity, perfect in every way and worthy of my respect and love. God is the Powerful Force binding the universe: a Force existing throughout time and without boundaries. Most important to me, God constantly does what is morally right—God is eternally good. Do you like that definition, my dear?"

"That's good Iris," I replied. "But why define God at all? Doesn't that restrict Him in some way? God might be greater than any one person can imagine. He may not approve of humans defining Him," I stated.

"I think you're right, Laurel. However, if we're arguing a case for God, you and I must agree on specifically what God is. If I asked you to go to Mort's Grocery and bring home a watermelon, it would be important for both of us to agree on what defines a watermelon. If you'd never seen such a melon, I'd be wise to describe its characteristics so you'd bring home the correct vegetable. I wouldn't need to describe every trait, but both of us should see the same mental picture. Doesn't that make sense?"

I nodded my head in agreement, wondering where this conversation was headed—and why Iris had called watermelon a vegetable!

"It's close to bedtime, so there's only time to discuss one of several arguments. The first idea comes from the study of our universe. Would you agree we both exist?" On the surface, her proposition seemed sound, so I agreed cautiously.

"Then if you and I exist, let's go a step further. Would you concede that there must be a legitimate process of how real objects came to be? We may not understand the technique, but if the building blocks exist and the requirements are met, a specific method must exist to create them." Again, I nodded—knowing the hard part was still to come.

Iris went on, "No one debated the existence of the stars or the universe. So it was a scientific shock when Catholic priest and astronomer Monsignor Georges Lemaître proposed that from the black void of nothing, the universe exploded into existence. Years later, another astronomer, Edwin Hubble, confirmed Lemaître's conclusion and discovered that the universe is continuously expanding. From absolutely nothing to filling the vastness of space . . . what process explains that, dear?"

That was all—the entire, difficult story? I'd expected a long-winded lecture involving multiple twists and turns. Couldn't Iris find a better answer? Aliens came to mind. Stuff like this always occurred on *Star Trek*—why not in everyday life?

I imagined Mr. Spock with test tubes, mixing different-colored fluids and reporting to Captain Kirk, "Captain, Mr. Sulu has committed an unfortunate error. He has destroyed part of the universe by accidentally detonating the antimatter torpedo pod. However, with help from Dr. McCoy, I have synthesized a new-universe formula, which I believe will work. It's based on work done by the Heatonian Badger Beasts from the Lorentz Nebula. The formula is risky, Jim, but the odds are 4,967 to 1 that our creation, logically, cannot be worse than the world that previously existed."

"Bones, what do you think?" asked Captain Kirk. "Can Spock make it work?"

"Blast it, Jim, you've got to be kidding!" shouted Dr. McCoy. "You're leaving a new universe in the hands of a pointy-eared Vulcan who has the world's lousiest haircut? Jim, I hope you don't have high expectations. I'm headed off to have some Romulan ale while Spock plays God. Join me when you can."

"Thanks, Bones. Spock, go ahead and do it!"

Popping back to reality, I stated firmly, "Well, Iris, I think aliens might be the reason the universe exists."

"Now, dear, if that's true, who created the aliens? Do you believe they just appeared out of empty space?"

"No, probably not," I replied. "Honestly, I'm guessing. I don't have any idea," I conceded.

"Laurel, are you sure you don't know? Perhaps you know and simply find the answer beyond belief. Let's stop there. It's getting late, and you've had a busy day. Tomorrow will bring new challenges. Think about our conversation, and if you want, we'll talk more in the morning."

I felt exhausted—more mentally than physically. I couldn't remember a day when so many difficult ideas had occurred so close together. The worst part was that none of them had easy answers. I said goodnight to Iris and wandered upstairs. Otis was in bed, waiting.

I dozed off wondering what these ideas meant. Deep down, I speculated what it might be like to dance with Denny Jensen.

CHAPTER 11

Iris and Archery: Catching Men with Sage Advice and an Arrow

Morning arrived in record time as I woke up with Otis giving me a tongue bath. I felt better than yesterday morning, so I dressed and headed down to breakfast. Iris wore her hairnet and a multicolored bathrobe. Her morning clothes bottomed out with Bugs Bunny slippers. She had prepared waffles and a fresh fruit dish. As usual, breakfast was delicious.

"Iris, this fruit tastes great. What's makes it tangy?" I wondered out loud.

"It's marinated in brandy, dear," she replied. I had to remember this recipe for my birthday party—my friends would love it. I reached for a second helping and decided to ask for dating advice. "Iris, what do you know about dating?"

"Well, sweetheart, it's been years since I've dated, but I'll do my best. What, specifically, would you like to know?" she inquired.

"I've got a date Saturday night with Denny Jensen." She nodded her head. "I've never been on a date, and I don't know what to do or say. How do you talk to a man?" I queried.

"Well, it's only a guess, but Denny probably invited you because he likes the beautiful young woman you've become. However, it's more than physical. The way you think, the way you talk, and how you act likely influenced his choice. I'd advise you to act normal and treat Denny like a close friend. Thank him for inviting you, and if he dresses well, compliment him. Men love hearing how handsome and strong they look. But don't overdo it. At the end of the evening, if you enjoyed yourself, tell him so and thank him for a great time."

"That's great, Iris," I countered, "but I'm sort of attracted to him. Do you think I should tell him? And what if he wants to kiss me? How do you kiss a guy?"

"Honey, as strange as it sounds, you'll know whether to tell Denny you're fond of him. You'll also know if a kiss seems right. As I recall, if the time, the place, and the moment are right, events fall into place as they're supposed to. Romance unfolds on its own clock. You're at the right age to experience these feelings. You don't need coaching. Does that help?"

I felt relieved. One of Iris's great qualities was that she never judged people. My questions didn't surprise her, nor did she embarrass me. "It does help. If I have more questions, can I ask you later?"

"Of course, dear. I'll be honest, I'm better discussing God than men. On the topic of men, I doubt even God has a clue."

I headed to school. The gossip among the freshman girls was that Brett Moore had awakened from his coma. No one knew much more, but believing someday he might be available boosted feminine morale.

Joann and I finished knitting and sailed through morning classes— until PE. I felt good, so I suited up. Volleyball was my favorite sport, and I played the game well. Our gymnasium had upper and lower levels. The lower level was for varsity basketball. The upper floor overlooked the basketball arena and had areas designed for wrestling and volleyball. If someone ran laps, they'd run the perimeter of the gym, which eventually took them past the volleyball court.

Today, the lower level was set up for indoor archery. Stacked hay bales formed a wall under one basket. Ten archery targets waited for aspiring Robin Hoods to nail a bull's-eye. Mr. Knoller had placed the archery equipment on a cart and parked it near the hay bales.

Jack Knoller was our wrestling coach, and at age fifty-five, he was in excellent shape. Only five feet three inches tall, he didn't look intimidating. However, students clearly knew Mr. Knoller had won four national wrestling championships during his college years. In 104 matches, he remained undefeated.

The girls gathered on the upper balcony, waiting for Mrs. Yorker to arrive. Mary Anne Kramer and I leaned over the rail observing Mr. Knoller organizing the boys. As usual, the guys were goofing around and teasing the class idiot. Whether class idiots are born stupid or they just act stupid, no one knows—but stupid is the key.

Our idiot was Brent Fuller. Brent was one of eleven kids. We concluded that he pulled stunts at school because he got little attention at home.

Mr. Knoller had lined up ten boys twenty-five yards from the targets. Brent was the third archer. Mr. Knoller stood behind the boys as they each shot three arrows. Then he ordered the bows put down and went forward to jot down scores. Looking at Brent's target, he said, "Fuller, this is damn good. I'd like to see more shots just like these."

To our astonishment, Brent picked up his bow and loaded an arrow. He aimed and got ready to shoot. Mr. Knoller had momentarily stood up; he saw Brent and realized what he'd said. There was nothing he could do but duck. The arrow hit the bull's-eye, two inches above Jack Knoller's head. "How's that, Mr. Knoller?" Brent asked, excitedly. "Want to see another bull's-eye? Move to the side a little, will ya? Your head's blockin' my target."

Jack Knoller stood up, fuming. Mary Anne looked at me and calmly asked, "What are the odds Brent will be alive in five minutes?" I was too stunned to answer. Mr. Knoller was sprinting toward Brent. But we knew our classmate was fast. If your behavior outrages critics, running is a valuable skill.

Brent made the 100-yard dash in less than eleven seconds. He ran up the steps toward the volleyball net, with Mr. Knoller right behind. Now, our PE outfits were ultra-short and left nothing to the imagination. Brent made the mistake of turning his head to ogle our feminine assets and clotheslined himself on the volleyball net. He was lying unconscious on the cement floor when our instructor, Mrs. Yorker arrived. Jack Knoller stood above Brent and said, "Serves him right. When he wakes up he'll be fine. There wasn't any brain to damage." Mr. Knoller walked away leaving Mrs. Yorker to awaken Brent with smelling salts and take him to the school nurse.

When PE finished, it was time for lunch. While eating, I had an idea about how to answer Mr. Wright's question, but it would require Mr. Wright's permission since it would involve a demonstration. I went to see him after classes finished.

When I walked into the classroom, Mr. Wright rose to a perfect, straight stance. "Laurel, what brings you here after school?" he asked.

"Well, Mr. Wright, I've been thinking about how to answer the question you assigned yesterday. I have my answer and I wonder if it meets your expectations. If it's not allowed, that's fine, but it's a novel idea."

"I'm open to new ideas, especially if they give a good answer. Tell me what you're thinking."

I told Mr. Wright my plan. He pondered my proposal several seconds and said, "That's a most intriguing idea, one that provides thorough insight into a difficult question. We have two hours this Friday. The first hour we'll listen to your presentation. The class should enjoy your answer: it will make them think and avoid a boring lecture. Do you need help?" he asked. I gathered my belongings, assuring Mr. Wright I had plenty of help.

I left his classroom feeling incredibly high. He was good at making students feel special. Years later, I still remember his class with great fondness. I hope someday I'll see him again to tell him how much he impacted my life.

When I got home, it was no surprise Iris was in the kitchen baking.

"Hi, dear. How was school?" she wanted to know.

"It was good, Iris. I had an idea about my history assignment, and I wondered if you would help. You're perfect for what I have planned."

"Honey, since I'm retired, free time abounds, and it's good to keep mentally and physically active. We're in good shape if your project involves baking. How can I help?"

I told her my plan and how she could help. "That's an excellent idea; I'm proud of you. I'll make the chocolates, but for the other items, we'll visit the Goodwill store tomorrow. After school should work fine."

"Why not today, Iris?" I asked.

"Dear, we're having dinner sooner than usual. Father Blevins called. The police chief bowed out of tonight's poker game, so they asked me to join them. Normally, I'd have said no, but you're able to look after yourself. I won't be later than eleven. If you have problems, call me at St. Mary's."

"Iris, I didn't know you played poker, let alone with those religious card sharks. They might be spiritual leaders, but I've heard they're merciless when money's involved. Are you sure about what you're doing?" I questioned.

"No, Laurel, I'm not proficient at poker. And you're right; they're quite vicious. But I've played with them before and picked up several tips. Reverend Pole is the trickiest of the bunch. Last time, I noticed he taps his left hand when he's bluffing. Rabbi Edelstein has reading glasses that reflect like mirrors: I can read the cards on his lenses. Father Blevins has a good poker hand if his index fingers paint an imaginary cross on his nose. I plan on using these tips to my advantage."

"Iris, that sounds like cheating!" I said.

"Well, suppose you're in an elevator and you overhear one person quietly telling another they buried money in a certain location. Using this information, you find it and realize this money was stolen during a recent robbery. You turn in the money, they arrest the thieves, and you collect a $10,000 reward. Is that cheating? I argue it's fair! You're using freely provided information to improve the common good."

"So, Iris, if I'm correct, tonight you consider yourself to be 'improving the common good'—am I right?"

"Yes, honey, you've summed it up beautifully. What an incredibly bright young woman you've become. Poker is like God. Just as God either exists or doesn't exist, poker is about winning or losing. There's no halfway. So tonight, the common good equals winning. That's the purpose of fun games. If they aren't about winning, why play?

"Laurel, success in life means working to win. If you're successful, you plan and use your talents to make a better life. You succeed by solving problems others can't. The challenge is not trampling people's dreams as you build your own. Above all, never brag about your achievements. Share your success with those who aren't as lucky, and stay quiet about your actions. Good deeds don't need your voice to speak for them. Tonight, charity will benefit. I plan to head over and pick their righteous pockets for every last penny! Tomorrow, we'll give it to Goodwill. Don't wait up," she concluded.

We ate dinner and soon Iris headed out the door, dressed in a Superman sweatshirt, a blue silk scarf, and Levis. On top of her head was a Dodgers baseball cap. If her special tips didn't work, the outfit stood a chance of distracting everyone.

I sat at the table finishing my homework. An envelope addressed "To Laurel" was propped against the napkin holder. Opening the letter, I found a note from Iris. It began:

> Laurel, I'm sorry I'm not there to explain this argument. I thought you might have extra time, so here's another line of reasoning supporting the existence of God. It's involved, but think about it and we'll talk later.

The evening was young, so I decided to continue reading and discover if her argument made sense. The note went on:

Once again, it's important to define terms. Certainly, you have some idea of what morals are, but it's best to be specific. For this argument, the word "moral" describes an issue people believe is good or bad. This belief occurs independently of our laws and the laws of different cultures. An example would be the mass extermination of the Jews during World War II. Nazi doctrine said Jews were responsible for the world's problems, so hiding a Jew was punishable by death. Italy followed Nazi propaganda and sent their Jewish population to Germany. Most Germans and Italians obeyed this doctrine, but some did not. They risked their lives hiding Jews because, despite the law, it was morally right to do so.

Two categories of morals exist: subjective and objective. Subjective morals concern the priority people give to an issue. For instance, many feel it's important to provide all homeless people with shelter and food. That goal may not be reached quickly—and perhaps never—but it's worthy of people's time and effort. Other goals command a higher priority, so society addresses those first. People not vaccinated against polio might spread a disease, for example, causing many others to suffer lifelong paralysis.

In contrast, objective morals exist regardless of what people believe. Cultures throughout the world accept the fundamental truth that killing and stealing are criminal acts. Without these universal truths, laws wouldn't exist and chaos would result. Most people violating the law know their actions are wrong. These laws are so important, society gives certain people the power to enforce them. Authorities such as the police and the military exist to restore order from chaos. When these agencies violate the law, who holds authority over them—the president? If so, who ensures the president is made accountable? Climbing the moral ladder, the logical conclusion becomes: only an authority who enforces perfect justice qualifies as the ultimate judge. If there were no Supreme Authority imposing the universal laws that govern our world, we'd all do as we pleased. Because people accept and follow these laws, the argument goes as follows:

1. If there's no God, there are no objective morals.

2. However, objective morals exist.

3. Therefore, God exists.

So, Laurel, that's the moral argument for God's existence. Let me know your thoughts.

Unconditional love,
Iris

Finishing the letter, I concluded this line of reasoning added to the cosmology argument. I still saw confusing gaps requiring an explanation, but my belief in God formed a firmer foundation. What caught my attention were the words *Unconditional love*. I'd always felt close to Iris. Whenever Mom traveled, Iris never said no. She cooked, cleaned, and helped with homework. Above all, she made me feel as though no one else mattered. She couldn't replace Mom, but occasionally, as with answering my dating questions, she had the upper hand.

Mom said she unconditionally loved me. She'd vowed to sacrifice her life for me if necessary. From Mom's serious tone, I knew she meant it. Did Iris's words mean the same as Mom's? Iris had never intentionally deceived others to cause harm. I knew, deep down, her words expressed what she felt.

The Buddhist monk had mentioned our primitive brain. He hadn't said which part of the brain's anatomy stored love and permitted sacrificing your life for another. The monk had discussed survival instincts and nurturing the young, but most animals forgot their offspring once they parted ways.

Based on the information I had, most humans held the special gift of love. It seemed the power of our spirit allowed us the ability to override the survival instinct, to sacrifice our lives for unconditional love. This love existed for spouses, children, and most honorably, for service men and women defending their country. What a powerful gift—and yet I had no explanation why it existed. Unconditional love seemed sufficient to prove God exists. Unless science could logically explain where it originated, I'd stick with God.

I wanted to call St. Mary's and report my revelation. Then I remembered how serious these folks played poker. "Hard core" and "dog-eat-dog" were tame words for this group. Interrupting a cutthroat card game to converse about God would be a sin not easily forgiven. Unless you were seriously ill or needed the last rites, it was better to let the gladiatorial bluffing continue.

CHAPTER 12

Better Loving through Science

I finished my math over the next hour and then decided to call my friends to check the latest gossip. I started with Denny. He wasn't a regular on my phone circuit, but I liked flirting and wanted to hear his voice. Mrs. Jensen answered the phone.

"Oh, hello, Laurel. He's in the basement working on a project. He finished his homework, and I haven't seen him since supper. Let me call him. Dennnney," I heard her yell. A few seconds passed. "He's on his way up. I hear you two have a date on Saturday. I'm surprised Denny got the courage to ask. When it comes to girls, his shyness reaches a new level. I wondered if he liked boys more than girls. I hope you'll show Denny how much fun girls can be. He needs more social skills, and it sounds like you're the perfect girl to help. Here he comes now. Bye-bye."

Me? How could I make Denny like girls more? I was sure he didn't like boys. Besides, why would boys show interest in boys? I'd never heard of such crazy behavior.

"Hey, Laurel, it's me, Denny," came the voice on the phone.

"Yes, I recognized your voice," I responded. "I called to discuss the plans for Saturday night."

"Well, I haven't thought about it much. Come on over and we'll decide. I'll show you my workshop. Mom just made fresh glazed doughnuts."

The invitation surprised me. I wanted to see Denny, but I wasn't sure about leaving home. I'd fed Otis and finished my homework. Calling my friends took priority, but hey—this was a guy. "OK, Denny, I'll come over, but I have to be home by nine. Iris is playing poker and I want to be here when she comes home."

"Hey, not a problem. I didn't know Mrs. Wimple was at your house. Your mom must be out of town. How long is Iris staying with you?" he asked.

"Well, at least a month. Mom's in China," I replied.

"Cool. Boy, Laurel, you have it good. Iris is the best. Come on over. I look forward to seeing you."

I went to the fridge. It sounded as if Denny liked to eat, so I thought I'd take him a big piece of peach pie. After all, Mrs. Jensen had asked me to demonstrate how women could have a positive impact on a man. Feeding Denny was a good start.

The Jensens lived a mile from my house. The evening was cool and quiet, and riding a bike would shorten the trip. I rode down Main Street, where the stores had closed for the evening—even the supermarket closed at seven. A large line formed at the movie theater.

I continued to Denny's and parked in front of his house. I rang the doorbell, and soon there stood Denny wearing a Beatles T-shirt, blue jeans, and a lab jacket covered in different-colored stains.

"Hey, Laurel, come on in. I'll show you my workshop, and then we'll make plans for Saturday night. I'm eager to see what ideas you've got. I don't know how to dance, so I was hoping you could teach me."

"Gee, Denny, I've only watched dancing on *American Bandstand*. Even then, I've never danced with someone. We might figure out a few steps by trial and error. Show me your work area, and we'll go from there."

We went down to the basement. I expected a small table with some tools and books. What I saw was beyond imagination. Filling two-thirds of the basement, an industrial-grade laboratory greeted my eyes. The lab was equipped with beakers, chemicals, and Bunsen burners. Arm-length glass columns displaying graduated markers stood on end. The workbench had a box labeled "Voltmeter," which Denny had attached to a car battery. A flat plate the size of a record album sat under a bright light suspended from the ceiling. Two wires ran from the flat plate to the poles of the battery.

I wasn't sure what to say, and my disbelief was obvious. Finally, I asked, "Denny, is this your dad's lab?"

"No, Laurel, I built it myself. I'm convinced the future of electricity will rely on solar power. I'm working with cadmium and silicon solutions to find films that better convert sunlight into energy. The problem with current solar panels is their inability to efficiently convert sunlight to electricity. Considering the total amount of solar power hitting these panels, current technology only converts 10 to 12 percent into electricity. I'm trying to increase that percentage. Recently, I achieved almost 16 percent."

Still overwhelmed, I said, "Denny, this is remarkable. Where did you learn this stuff?"

Denny replied, "Do you remember when we did a science project last year?"

How could I forget? Rodney Talley's project had explained how cats formed hairballs. It was so disgusting that the judges refused to closely examine it. He automatically received a C. For Rodney, it was a dream come true—probably his best grade of the year.

Denny continued, "I became interested in solar panels after reading Dad's *Popular Mechanics.* I started experimenting a year ago."

"But where did you find this equipment?" I inquired. "This stuff looks expensive!"

"I read in the paper that a community college had finished installing new chemistry labs. I called and asked if they'd sell some of the equipment. They said if I removed all the old equipment, I could have whatever I wanted. I kept what I needed, repaired the rest, and sold them for a profit. I also shop estate sales, looking for items I can use or sell. Last week, I found some great buys at Opal Bernstein's auction. I'll resell them and buy chemicals and a ventilation hood. The chemistry and physics took time, but over the learning curve, my math skills improved. Currently, I'm studying second-order differential equations."

Differential equations didn't ring a bell, so I asked, "Do they teach those equations in high school? I've never heard of them. Do people know you're secretly using these equations in your lab?"

"No, except for Mom and Dad, you're the only other person who knows about the solar panels. Just so you know, differential equations aren't secret. They're taught during the second year of college. I plan to keep my work quiet until I produce something useful. Everybody believes I don't apply myself, and they're right. I don't care about English, PE, or reading, but I do what's necessary to pass. With science, I'm probably better than people think."

What an understatement. Based on what I saw, Denny was smarter than any students in Sutter High. A subtle inkling began growing stronger. I decided to follow it. "Denny, may I ask you a personal question?"

"I don't know, Laurel—no one's ever asked me. What's the question?"

"I wonder how you feel when you get a B in class. Does it make you want to try harder?" I probed.

"Well, I don't know how it feels. Not to brag, but I've never gotten a B."

I knew it. I just knew it. Denny was a genius, but his shy reluctance to show people his skills led everyone to assume he was lazy. In truth, Denny used little effort to solve problems because they were easy. He didn't need to apply the same effort as other students. In 1971, no advanced placement classes existed; Denny solved this by creating his own.

Emotions flooded through me at my magnificent discovery. Immediately, I was happy and also a little smug. Denny had upheld my assumptions, and I now knew a secret few others knew. The girls loved Denny's good looks but had no idea about his intellect. If Denny's secret became known, he'd have girls galore.

I said, "Denny, you're not bragging. You told the truth. Just so you know, your secret's safe. I won't even tell Joann." Staying silent would be tough. I needed to tell someone. Maybe Iris.

"Thanks, Laurel. If people find out, I'll have to deal with the public, and I hate parties. That's one reason we need to make plans. I'm not sure how I'll do at the dance. Crowds scare me, and I'm terrible with small talk. It's hard to deal with big groups."

"Denny, you do great with the students at school," I responded. "The dance involves the same kids, with some music added in. The only difference is the fancy clothes. Besides, I'll help you. If you need to head outside, tell me. Let's have a code word. If you say it, I'll know you need a break."

"I never thought about it that way, Laurel. You're cool. I guess they are the same people. That puts the party in perspective. I like the word 'Cher,' like on *Sonny and Cher*. How's that?"

"Sure, that works. Do you have any other worries?" I asked.

"Well, I can't dance. We don't want to look like snakes trying to mate. Do you have any ideas?"

I remembered what I'd seen on *Bandstand*. That provided a good place to start. "Maybe I do. Let's play some records and practice. We'll see how it goes," I suggested.

We put on "Proud Mary." The tempo increased as we started spinning. Denny grabbed my hand, lifted his arm, and twirled me underneath him. We paused, facing each other with my hand still in his. He drew me closer, his arm around my waist, and we two-stepped for several seconds. Tina Turner's voice accelerated in an intense undulating rhythm.

Denny let go as we separated, beginning the Twist. Twisting back-to-back, front-to-front, and side-to-side, we danced in all the unoccupied space. I had such a good time, I didn't want the music to stop. When the tune ended, I felt breathless. Denny danced well. I sat down as Denny put on another record.

Slowly the volume increased. Denny quietly took my hand. As I stood up, he snuggled me next to him, putting both arms around my waist. The scent of his cologne contained whispers of lavender. The Carpenters sang "For All We Know" while we danced in unison. Denny raised his left hand, caressing the back of my head. For the first time, I noticed a scar on his nose and his gorgeous blond eyelashes. I gently touched Denny's face, reassuring myself this was real.

A tingling sensation swept through me like a warm wave skimming the ocean. Closing my eyes, I rested my head on his shoulder as we danced cheek to cheek. Vaguely distant were the lyrics, "Love, look at the two of us." First love held us in this moment.

Denny backed up as I lifted my head. Staring into his bottomless blue-green eyes, I could feel his warm breath brushing my cheek. Leaning forward, he softly pressed his lips to mine. I couldn't explain my unbridled craving, but I decided to go with it. Denny kissed me again, this time with increased desire. For the first time, I craved his touch. We separated for several moments—then, wanting more, I grabbed Denny by the collar and kissed him with newly discovered passion.

Kissing, like eating popcorn, was difficult to stop. Finally, feeling emotionally spent, I let go and sat down as Karen Carpenter's voice faded to "And love may grow for all we know." Neither of us spoke. We simply looked at each other. I'd never experienced such intense feelings, and Denny looked as though he'd crossed into uncharted territory.

Finally, he said, "Laurel, all I can say is thank you. That was—wow! I can't even describe it! I've never kissed a girl before, but I always hoped it would be you. It's a dream come true. I planned on finishing a solar panel tonight, but now I can't concentrate." His face knotted up. "You probably think I planned this."

"Denny, I know you didn't plan it. I called you, remember?"

"Hey, that's right," he seemed relieved. "I could never plan something this great! Let's go upstairs and have doughnuts and milk. I'm starved." He grabbed my hand, and soon we sat in the kitchen.

Mrs. Jensen greeted us. "Hey there, you two. Did you discover how to dance or just play music?"

I didn't want to lie, but telling her we went beyond discovering how to dance would invite more questions. "Yes, Mrs. Jenkins, we practiced several moves, but we still need more work." I winked at Denny. "Denny showed me his lab, and then we tried coordinating our footwork. He's a good dancer. Did you teach him?" I asked.

"Laurel, please call me Emma. When Denny was six, he started dance lessons and gymnastics. As he developed more interest in science, those pursuits fell by the wayside. But he's still talented."

I quizzically glanced at Denny. He'd told me he didn't know how to dance.

Sensing my confusion, he piped up. "Yeah, I was good at tap dance and ballet, but none of the modern stuff. Believe me, Laurel, I've never done what we practiced tonight. Past dance classes make it clear that continued work leads to great results. Don't you agree?" he asked.

A sixth sense told me what Denny wanted to practice. These feelings were so new I was at a loss for words. Then, caught by surprise, I started to sense remorse. Was I becoming a tramp like Cindy Summers? I wasn't stuffing my bra or applying makeup, but I'd just made out with a guy. What was worse, I had enjoyed it! Passion engulfed me, guiding my sleazy soul along the path of debauchery and lust. Guilt reigned supreme. What had I done?

As Emma served doughnuts and milk, Denny waited for a response. Finally, I said, "Well, Denny, let me get back to you. This week's schedule looks crazy. I have a big assignment for Mr. Wright, which needs at least a day."

"Well, sure, Laurel," he said. I could hear disappointment in his voice. "Or catch me at school. Whatever works. My schedule's open."

I finished the cookies, and Denny walked me to the door. We both stayed quiet. Clearly, love's barometer had ushered in a chill. In a rush to leave, I said, "Denny, thanks for the doughnuts and milk. I enjoyed meeting your mom and touring the lab." I knew Denny wanted a good-bye kiss, but I couldn't do it or even admit how much I adored him.

He looked at me and smiled. "Laurel, the milk and doughnuts were good, but they don't compare to the taste of your lips." He softly kissed me and said goodnight.

CHAPTER 13

The Art of Rejection Dating: Setting Up the Rejection

Riding home, I tried sorting out the evening. I think Denny was just plain excited, but excitement *and* fear held me hostage. Romance was black-and-white for most guys, but it wasn't so simple for girls.

I got home at 9:15 and decided to call Joann. I wanted to tell her everything but avoid the details. Offering sage advice on a lack of relevant facts was her specialty. She answered on the third ring.

"Hey, Joann, I thought I'd give you a call," I said.

"Well, it's about time. I tried calling earlier and no one answered—not even Iris. That's weird. Were you at the river feeding the homeless?"

"No, Iris is playing poker at the church, and I went over to Denny's house."

"Denny's house? It's great you have a first date, and I understand you have to start somewhere, but I don't see why you like him. He's lazy, and nearly everyone thinks he's a few pins short of a strikeout. Why were you at his house? For your own safety, I hope his parents were around."

"Yes, his parents were home. I called Denny to see what our plans were for Saturday. He invited me over. I'd finished my homework, so I went."

"God, Laurel, that's the oldest trick in the book. One redeeming fact is that you're brighter than Denny and can work your way out of trouble. I hope you made your plans and left. After Saturday night, you're free and clear."

"Well, yeah—I mean no—I mean, we made out in his basement." A rare moment of silence hung on the phone line.

Finally, I heard, "Mom, I need to run over to Laurel's and help her with a tough math problem. I'll be back in forty-five minutes." Ten minutes later the doorbell rang.

I opened the door, and there stood Joann, sucking for air.

"You, Laurel Montgomery, made out with Denny Jensen." I nodded. Joann hugged me tight, taking off her coat, wanting to hear every sordid detail.

"Denny is a genius, but I shouldn't have told you. Right now, his life is quiet. Denny likes it that way. If he makes a breakthrough in solar energy, his secret comes out. He's scared witless about publicity. I'm worried we don't know each other enough to kiss. I don't think Mom would approve. I need to cancel this date and become a nun."

"Laurel, let's recap. You're a popular and beautiful girl. This shy handsome guy, who behaves like a schmuck, asks you out after seeing you naked. You stumble onto the fact that he's brilliant and kisses like David Cassidy. An hour later you plan to break up? Don't forget the small detail that you've known him since grade school. Are you crazy?"

I reflected, "I wonder if Denny likes me because he's seen me naked or because he thinks I'm smart."

Joann softened her voice, saying, "To be honest, he probably 90 percent likes you for your hot body and 10 percent for your brains. The point is, Denny likes you because you're you. He's not after your wealth or your Beatles albums. Every guy and girl start somewhere. Mom says smart women rarely date dumb men. You're a smart woman for sure, Laurel. Don't botch it!"

"What I need to know, Joann, is who do smart men date? You conveniently left that part out."

"Well, that's more confusing. Mom never said anything until Alton Unrein divorced his wife, Louise. He's a physics professor in Portland who married one of his students. My mother says that smart men marry smart women. By age fifty, smart men want a divorce so they can remarry hot young babes called trophy wives. Usually, these women are incredibly stupid, but guys want what's between their legs instead of between their eyes."

"So, you're saying it's better dating Mitch Hardisty because his life centers on ranching and not education? Who do dumb men date?"

"Laurel, if a woman is smarter than a guy, he may not date her. It's an inferiority complex thing. Women, on the other hand, don't mind dating a smarter guy if he has the potential to be a good provider and father."

I sighed and said, "Now I'm more confused. It seems dating a dumber man is the best choice because I'd make the major decisions and

I wouldn't worry about him finding a trophy wife. I'm calling off this date." I headed for the phone to call Denny.

Joann's face was red. She shook her head. "Laurel, listen to me. I'm your best friend." I'd already dialed Denny's number and waited for the phone to ring. She continued, "You like this boy. He likes you and has for a long time." The phone now rang. "If you cancel this date, he'll be heartbroken and you'll regret it the rest of your life." The phone started its fourth ring, and I'd almost hung up when Denny answered the phone.

"Hello, Jensen home." Joann ran into the kitchen and listened on the second phone.

"Hey, Denny, it's Laurel. I called to tell you I can't attend the dance Saturday night because something came up." Silence occupied the line.

Denny's voice became quiet and surrendered. "Gee, Laurel, I hope tonight didn't change your mind about going."

I started to cry. "No, it's not that, Denny; you're too smart for me, and I don't want you leaving me for a trophy wife. Have a good night."

Hanging up the phone, I heard Joann yell, "God, my friend's an idiot!"

A second later, Joann burst into the living room. "Don't you realize what you've done? You led Denny on by kissing him. Now you've canceled a date because you can't deal with your emotions. When word gets out, you'll look like an ass. I'm calling Denny and inviting him to the dance." Joann ran out the front door, screaming, "I hope you catch cholera so I can avoid seeing you!"

In one hour, I'd lost my best friend and canceled a date with a young man I had always liked. Worse yet, we had only dated for seventy minutes. How had my evening wandered so far off course? The time was 10:15, and I felt emotionally empty.

If God existed, I hoped He'd lessen my difficulties. Then, in a manner never expected, using a method difficult to accept, God solved my problem, catching the town of Sutter by surprise.

CHAPTER 14

The Art of Rejection Dating: Motivation Using Threats

I didn't sleep well during the night. My conscience kept haunting me. When I finally fell asleep, it seemed only minutes before I heard a faint knock on my door. It was already seven o'clock. "Laurel dear, it's Iris. It's time to get up, dress, and come downstairs for breakfast."

I finished getting ready and went downstairs, where Iris percolated around the kitchen whistling "If I Were a Rich Man."

"Good morning, Laurel," she said.

"Hey, Iris, how was poker last night? Did you get out without mortgaging your house?"

"Yes, dear, I beat the pants off those three cardsharps. I won $57, and they didn't have any clue how I did it. I'll bet I'm not invited back to that poker game anytime soon. How was your evening, dear?"

"Well, you know, it was your basic boring evening. Did homework, talked to Joann, and read your argument on God," I lied.

"And what did you think of the moral argument?" she inquired.

"Well, I think it means our conscience always knows what's right even if we don't—and our knowledge of what's 'right' is God-given." I looked at my watch, realizing it was later than I'd thought. I stopped talking and started wolfing down my breakfast.

Iris smiled. "Yes, that's precisely correct, dear. You hit it right on the nose. Like all arguments, it's not foolproof, but it's a strong line of reasoning. We'll discuss it more later. When you get home this afternoon, we'll head down to the thrift store and get the items you need for your assignment. Have a great day at school."

School was uneventful, but it was all I could do to stay awake during classes. I looked forward to a big serving of apple pie à la mode when I got home. When I opened the door, however, I received a huge helping of Iris Wimple. Since breakfast, she'd surely doubled in height. She was scowling like a pit bull, and I knew burglars didn't deserve the treatment coming my way.

"Laurel Montgomery, park your behind on this sofa; we're having a talk." She'd never used this tone of voice. I had an inkling this didn't bode well for what was about to happen to me.

Iris went on, "Emma Jensen called today. She told me Denny didn't go to school. I suspect you know why." Opening my mouth, I started to explain, but Iris broke in, "He didn't go because you called off your date. Denny told his mother he was heartbroken. Laurel, tell me what the devil is going on? Did Denny hurt you or say something mean? Did he touch you inappropriately?"

I began crying and told her the story. I related how excitement and fear caused me to feel confused. I told her Joann and I talked about trophy wives and how I didn't want Denny leaving me for one of those, so I broke off our date!

Iris looked confused, which didn't occur often. "OK, let's forget about future trophy wives and focus on today. Do you like Denny—yes or no?"

"Yes, I like him a lot," I replied.

"Did you enjoy kissing him—yes or no?"

"Well, I guess so. I don't know. It was like nothing I've experienced before. It was scary."

"Laurel, let's talk about those feelings. You can't run from them. People who don't face their feelings often turn to liquor and drugs, trying to make emotional pain disappear. You must deal with why you're afraid of Denny. Tell me precisely what scares you."

"I'm not sure. I felt out of control. I kept thinking I wanted to be in his arms and stay there forever. That's not normal."

"Now you're making sense. What you feel are the stirrings of love. It's magnificent and terrifying when it first happens. But these feelings are normal. They haven't changed since the dawn of time. However, they're no reason to treat Denny so harshly. He feels sad because the girl he has a crush on told him he's not worth the effort. How would you feel, my dear?"

"Bad, I guess," I answered.

"There is no guessing, Laurel—you'd feel betrayed. Deep down you know it's true.

"Here's what's going to happen. You're going to go to Denny's, tell him you're sorry, and reaffirm you'll go with him to the dance."

"No way am I doing that. I can't. I'll die first. Besides, you said we'd go to the thrift store."

Iris calmly said, "You may go to the thrift store yourself, young lady. As for me, I'm having nothing to do with a young woman who knows everything about interacting with people."

She walked into the kitchen yelling, "You're responsible for your own dinner. Don't bother me unless you're bleeding to death. Even then, wait in line and take a ticket!"

Instantly, I felt demoralized.

At age fourteen, I thought my complications with Denny were the worst in the world. If she decided to call Mom, boy problems would pale in comparison. The words "grounded for a year" and "no phone calls" bubbled through my mind. A transfer to the Catholic school of St. Mary's would be a major change in my daily life.

Then a most horrible picture came to mind: Sister Sarah Agnes. Sister was the Wilt Chamberlain of nuns. At six feet seven inches tall and 280 pounds, she resembled a bulldozer dressed in a habit. Pondering this image for one-eighth of a second, I realized spending five hours with Denny would allow me to avoid reciting the entire Holy Bible from memory.

Riding my bike allowed me to reach his house in twelve minutes. Scared to death, I rang the doorbell, focusing on what I needed to say. The door opened an inch, and Denny looked out.

"What do you want, Laurel? I'm not feeling good today, so you should probably leave," he said in a sad tone.

"Look, Denny, I was wrong to cancel our date, and I'm so sorry. When we kissed, it caught me off guard. I want to be your date. If you say 'So long, bitch,' I won't blame you, but I'm not going with anyone else. Will you still take me?" I pleaded.

The door opened a little more. Denny spoke. "Here's my feelings, Laurel. I wasn't planning on going until Joann invited me." As he fully opened the door, I was astonished to see Joann standing inside. She smiled and deep down, I heard her silently saying, "See, I told you I'd do it."

"Hi, Laurel, how's your day?" she asked, grinning sadistically. "Since you couldn't make it, I asked Denny to the dance. It's a shame you can't go."

I was going to cover her in honey and stake her out near an ant colony.

Joann would likely back out, but before that happened, she planned to teach me humility. Unless . . .

Knowing my words might backfire, I lowered my head and spoke with remorse, "Joann, Denny—you're right. Denny, why I called off our date doesn't matter anymore. It's unfair of me asking Denny to decline your offer, Joann, so he and I can go as a couple. Denny, I sincerely apologize. Joann, I interrupted your time with Denny. Again, I'm very sorry. Mitch Hardisty mentioned he needed a date. If he can't go, I'll stay home."

I turned and walked toward the front door, saying, "You two have a great time. I look forward to seeing the pictures." I closed the door, but suddenly it stopped. Joann was pulling on the doorknob.

"Look, Laurel, I've reconsidered. I think Denny prefers going out with you. Besides, I'd have to cancel my date with Mark Landry. I'm not doing that."

I began smelling a rat. Turning around, I tackled Joann, forcing her to the floor. I sat on her chest.

"Joann, you set me up." A diabolical grin painted my face, and I started to giggle.

We both started laughing, until Denny interjected, "Man, this is great, I've never had two girls fighting over me. It's more fun than watching guys wrestle."

We both winked and said good-bye. Denny looked as if he'd found a little piece of heaven. I hollered at him as we left, "I'll call you tonight, but I'm not coming over."

I told Joann, "I'd love to kick your ass, but I have to get home and keep Iris from calling Mom."

"Yeah, Laurel, I'll bet you do."

When I got home, Iris was sitting on the couch reading *National Geographic.* She looked up and said, "Hello, dear, it's good to see you home. Did everything work out for the better?"

"Iris, you didn't call Mom, did you? I'm back in Denny's good graces, so getting Mom upset when everything's normal would cause unneeded emotional stress."

Iris looked up and said, "No, Laurel, I haven't talked to your Mom, nor do I plan to. Because of time limits and your refusal to follow my advice, I helped you recognize the results of your actions by using extreme measures. Denny's ego rested in your hands, and you had no reservation about inflicting a wound and leaving a permanent scar. I couldn't ignore that.

"Many people believe when something unpleasant happens, they're innocent victims, with no role in what occurred. Folks always influence their own lives, rarely seeing or owning up to their share. Only children are innocent victims. They're not old enough to understand their part and can't take responsibility. You're far beyond that stage, young lady!"

I simply said, "You're right, Iris. Let's go to the thrift store."

CHAPTER 15

Preparing for Undiscovered Problems

Iris and I grabbed the wagon and walked to Goodwill. We bought three queen-sized sheets, two floor spotlights with multicolored filters, and a cowboy hat. We added a rope, fireman's helmet, and Einstein wig, checking off the list as we went. Heading home, we visited Mort's Market and found three different air fresheners. This completed our mission.

At home, Iris baked two turkey potpies and served them with mashed potatoes. My upset stomach had miraculously improved after talking with Denny, and I was ravenous.

As we ate, Iris asked if we'd arranged dinner prior to the dance. I admitted we hadn't but planned on discussing it later. Iris then offered a suggestion that beat anything I had in mind. Most guys took their dates to dinner, but I owed Denny big-time. Despite my poor behavior, Iris offered to help me find my way out of the hole I'd dug.

After we finished the dishes, we wrote a script for my world history project. We had worked out the minor bugs when Iris asked, "Dear, can I tell you another argument for the existence of God? If not, we can watch TV or play cards."

"Sure, Iris, but first I need to call Denny and propose your idea."

"That's fine. I'll stay here so you have some privacy. If you have questions, let me know."

Soon Denny was on the line. "I want to apologize again for my behavior," I told him. "I like you a lot and would feel bad sitting alone Saturday night. Please forgive me. I can't wait to go to the dance with you."

"Laurel, if this helps, I was scared too. I blew it, and I figured you'd hate me forever," he remarked. "Iris called Joann and asked her to come cheer me up. When she arrived, we talked, and that's when she invited me to the dance. Iris was kind to think of me. She's a great woman."

Well, at least Denny thought so. My sweet, innocent nanny had royally set me up! I found it hard to believe Joann had had the balls to carry out her threat. I was right! She was a pawn in Iris Wimple's plotted chess match. I wanted revenge, but getting Denny back softened my anger.

"Right, Denny, Iris is wonderful. Just don't get on her bad side," I advised. "In fact, she has an idea for dinner before the dance and wondered what you'd think about it." I told him what Iris had suggested, and he instantly agreed. We made plans to meet Saturday evening at five thirty.

I headed back into the living room, where Iris was watching *The Carol Burnett Show.* "Well, dear, what did Denny think?" she inquired.

"Denny liked your idea, and we're on for five thirty. Are you certain you want to do it?"

"Yes, I do. This dance is important because memories of a first date are never forgotten, especially if you stimulate the senses. Food is a wonderful way to do that. Trust me, at my age, I'm happy to remember anything from long ago. I'm only sorry your mother isn't here. I'm not a good substitute for the wonderful woman who's raised you. She deserves to see her daughter become a young woman."

"Iris, it's best Mom isn't here. She faces dominating male attorneys every day. That never bothers her, but when it deals with me, discussing men isn't one of her strong points."

Iris gave me a hug and we sat down together. "Do you want to hear more philosophy about whether God exists?" she asked. I nodded affirmatively and she paused to think. "Laurel, do you like my banana cream pie?"

What a strange question, since she already knew the answer.

"You know I love your banana cream pie. It's the best dessert ever. You made one today. What's that have to do with God?" I asked.

She continued, "If you had a choice of imagining how my banana cream pie tastes or tasting a real slice, which one would you pick?"

"Gee, Iris, that's obvious: it's better to taste the pie," I said.

Iris continued, "Can we agree, then, if a virtuous truth exists in our thoughts, this truth is best when it exists in reality?" I saw no fault in her logic, so she continued. "Now remember how we discussed imagining God as the all-encompassing, perfect entity. In every category, God is supreme—or if you prefer, 'the best.' Do you still like that definition, dear, or should we change the meaning?"

"Yes, Iris, I agree. God's everywhere and all-powerful, but incredibly slow getting my imaginary pie out here," I stated. "I hope when it finally appears, there's ice cream on top!"

"OK, I'm almost finished. Here's the conclusion to the argument. Pay attention—it's tricky. You and I worked out a definition for God. We also said existing in reality is better than existing in thought. So logically, it follows God must exist in reality to be better than existing in thought. Only by actually existing, can God be 'the best.'"

"Wow, Iris! I see what you mean. It's a powerful line of reasoning that's not easy to appreciate. I'll understand it better with pie and ice cream. Those always help when I'm digesting difficult ideas."

Iris headed to the kitchen remarking, "Laurel, you're one incorrigible young woman. I teach you a brilliant argument supporting God's existence and you concentrate on dessert! This behavior follows your attempt to break a young man's heart. When your mother returns, she'll think I've unleashed your devil child. I'm inclined to agree, except it's more likely that the door from Barbie dolls to Ken dates has opened and you're stepping across the threshold. It's odd, but I sense that you and I will soon travel different directions," she said in a somber tone.

This wasn't a statement I expected. Was Iris sick, sad, or getting older? I needed to find out.

"Iris, you sound sad. Is something weighing on your mind—something you want to talk about? I can keep a secret, if that worries you. Can I do anything to help?" I asked.

"Dear, nothing is wrong. I hear your concern, but I didn't plan to worry you. In the last year, my age has caught up with me. I know in another year, the pastimes I enjoy today won't be possible. When you graduate, in all likelihood I won't be around, and it's gloomy. Being here now and seeing your curtain rise to adulthood means more than you can imagine. It saddens me to think I may never see where that path leads."

"But, Iris, you'll be here—I know you will. Everyone in Sutter loves you. Of all the graduation parties you've attended, you can't miss mine. That wouldn't be right!" I exclaimed. "Who'd make my favorite brandied fruit dish? Who'd bake the pies? No, ma'am, you're not leaving. You've been my second mom since I was little."

"Laurel, those are the sweetest words. You know I have no family. Now I'm old as the hills; the friends who I experienced life with are gone. I never married and have no brothers or sisters. Over the years I tried treating people like family. They kindly returned the love, and it's filled the void of not having my own. But there are special people who truly fulfill your life. During my life, Laurel, one of those people has been you."

Tears ran down Iris's cheeks and she reached for her handkerchief. When I went to hug her, I started sobbing. We embraced for the longest time. What could I say? Except for Mom, I didn't realize I was special to someone else. I'd never done anything earth-shattering. Was it possible Iris loved me because I was me?

"Iris," I asked, "what makes me so special? I can't think of any big accomplishment."

Through her tears, Iris responded, "Laurel, look at the small sequoia planted outside, then imagine this magnificent tree when it matures. Our little tree is special because we know the potential if we nurture it. The same idea applies to children. I've taken care of you since you were a baby. Looking at how you've matured, I see magnificent potential starting to blossom. Over my years, I've met many people, and I've learned to recognize people who have the skills necessary to change the world. You belong in that group, my dear. There's not a doubt. The fact that in a small way I've helped nurture you gives me great satisfaction. Simply know that regardless of where the future lies, I will always love you."

All I could do was hold her and cry. Unexpressed feelings passed between us, and something changed within me. I knew that one day soon, I'd have to take my place in the world to try and make it better. At least Iris felt the potential existed; personally, I couldn't see it. Her positive spirit would always rest within my heart. If I achieved what Iris felt I could, I'd need that spirit time and again.

It was only ten o'clock, but Iris and I had had an emotional, difficult day. We ate our ice cream and decided to turn in. Thursday would be busy. Everything needed to be ready for Friday's presentation.

As special as our evening had turned out, I felt uncertain when it ended. As I put my head on the pillow, I had no idea my last twenty-four peaceful hours had begun.

CHAPTER 16

The French Bring Culture to the Clan

The sun shone through my bedroom window, waking me from a deep sleep. The smell of bacon and eggs enticed me to go downstairs and eat, and I was soon enjoying smoked bacon and the world's best sourdough pancakes. Thankfully, Iris's brandied mixed fruit accompanied the main course.

While I ate, Iris loaded the wagon with props. On Friday, our rotating schedule would make history the first class of the day. This meant staying after school today to set up the room. I'd need help placing the props, so I went looking for Tanice; Joann had swimming practice.

When I found her, Tanice was talking to a girl I didn't know. This beautiful teenager had mature Asian features but blond hair that didn't quite fit. Her low-cut blouse revealed magnificent breasts and subtle cleavage.

"Hey, Laurel," Tanice hollered, "this is Utannah Donnay. She just transferred here from Paris and this is her first day. I just told her which boys are dickheads. You want to show her around?"

I introduced myself, wondering what would bring a French teen to Sutter. Anticipating my question, she replied with a hint of an accent, "My father works for the French consulate in San Francisco. France is interested in Oregon's lumber exports, and he's stationed in Portland to research the logging industry. My mother is French and Vietnamese and prefers a town with ethnic diversity. Sutter seemed right because it's close to Portland and mother loves the people there."

Utannah spoke French, English, and Vietnamese—a first for our junior high. The school had given her a schedule matching my rotation cycle, so I offered to orient her on the school's layout.

She wondered why I was pulling a loaded wagon. "Are wagons necessary for students to complete their assignments? When we asked about school supplies, they said nothing about a wagon. Should I go out and buy one?" she asked.

I thought about it. "No, probably not. Knowing our principal, he'd object to many students pulling wagons through the halls. However, if you chew tobacco, he's fine with that."

Since Tanice had karate after school, I convinced Utannah to stay and help. The day progressed smoothly, with the boys taking turns gawking at Utannah's cleavage and stunning good looks. Some "accidentally" ran into her head-on, apologizing profusely.

She remarked, "The boys here are so attentive. I feel welcomed."

I said, "Utannah, *feel* is the key word. The boys are 'copping a feel,' if you understand the term." She didn't, so I took her aside and explained.

Clearly embarrassed, she said, "French girls prefer this style of blouse. It's important to look feminine without appearing as an escort. Do these boys believe I'm an escort?"

Now I was confused. I felt sure *escort* was French for *model*.

"Utannah, this is the United States. If becoming an escort is your lifelong goal, start playing the part. Every month, *Ladies' Home Journal* features beautiful escorts. Maud Adams is on this month's cover. She's every man's dream and every woman's role model. When we get to home economics, ask Mrs. Gallagher for escort lessons. She has incredible knowledge about careers for women." Utannah looked puzzled as I continued talking. Eventually I said, "I've talked too much, considering it's your first day. I'll let you ask the questions."

Utannah smiled, "Laurel, I think you misunderstood. In France, an escort is a woman who sells sex for money. I had no idea your school offered classes."

"Jeez, Utannah, you're talking about sluts, not escorts. At least that's what they're called here. Going back to your question, no, you're not a slut. During math you'll meet Cindy Summers. Now Cindy's an honest-to-goodness, screw-me-anytime slut. If they made a bicycle seat with a penis, she'd be first in line. Try buttoning up your blouse and wearing a sweater. Then the boys won't be looking down your blouse," I reassured her. "Your good looks will still attract them, but I think these tips will cut down on the gazing."

When classes ended, we went to Mr. Wright's room, where I'd parked the wagon. Utannah tried to coax me into telling her about my presentation. I offered some details but stressed she'd have to wait until tomorrow. Considering the variety of items in the wagon, only a psychic could deduce the plan.

Mr. Wright wasn't at his desk. I decided his absence gave me permission to properly arrange my set. We tightly hung a rope six feet high across the classroom. We used clothespins to attach three sheets side by side along the rope. Then we cut two three-inch-diameter holes in the center of the middle sheet.

Next, we set up the floor lights behind the sheets and tested them, making sure Iris hadn't wasted sixty-seven cents. Then we carefully laid out the remaining props behind the sheets. The last task was dividing twenty-four students into three groups of eight.

I had pondered this dilemma the entire week. I didn't want to stereotype anybody, but each group needed a common theme. If I couldn't group students with similar backgrounds, this assignment would fail. Sutter had an eclectic population, and Mr. Wright and I had reached an agreement. I wrote down the sequence for students to enter the classroom.

The first group comprised kids living in rural areas. The second group held students residing in town, with parents who worked blue-collar jobs. The third group included kids considering college and white-collar professions; their parents practiced medicine or law, or worked as accountants and teachers.

I understood that these three profiles hinged on how families valued education as a means to success. My goal wasn't to degrade people based on their education, but to show how God makes His presence understandable to every group of people.

After we finished, Mr. Wright walked in. I introduced him to Utannah. He looked over my presentation, seeming pleased with it. He promised to lock the room so nothing would change overnight and to group the kids as I'd outlined when they showed up for class the next morning.

As Utannah and I left school, I asked, "Do you want to go to Rags to Riches with me? I need to buy a dress for the homecoming dance."

Looking interested, Utannah asked, "What's homecoming? Should I go to the dance?"

Being careful not to embarrass myself again, I answered, "In the United States, high schools have one football game every year where they invite all previous graduates to return. We celebrate with a parade and a dance. We start with a big bonfire, which is tomorrow night. We gather anything disposable that burns, pile it up, and set it on fire."

Utannah looked mystified. "That sounds like a wonderful tribute! I look forward to returning after I graduate. I'd love to visit the dress store now. I'll look for a dress in case I go to the dance."

"Sure, Utannah, you should definitely come," I said. "It's a little late to find a date, but anyway, it's better to come alone, dance with all the boys, and see who you like."

"That's a good idea. I may try to find a date anyway. Someone from out of town might be available. Let's go see the dress selection. I need some new clothes and I love to shop."

I reminded her, "You know, we don't have designer shops here; in Portland maybe, but not Sutter. The only 'designer' in Sutter is Pee-wee Newton, who paints and mows the football field. It's always a surprise since Pee-wee can't spell. Three weeks ago the fans found yellow fluorescent paint spelling 'SLUTTER HI' in each end zone."

"Did that cause trouble for Mr. Newton?" Utannah asked.

"No, not really. Pee-Wee's a wonderful man who helps students in auto mechanics. At halftime our principal, Mr. Martin, came on the field and sprayed the letter L there with green paint. Ignoring the mistake until the game finished would have attracted less attention."

When we reached the store, Utannah offered to help me pick my outfit. The top I chose was blue silk with ruffles around the base of the sleeves. A white cotton skirt ending above my knees accented my behind and upper legs. Blue shoes sporting two-inch heels complemented my dress. I thought I looked good, but Utannah sensed something was missing. She picked out a lacy gold scarf and white fishnet stockings.

I tried everything on, then stood in front of the mirror. Utannah instinctively rolled my hair behind my head in a vertical Twinkie. Hairpins appeared, holding my new coiffure in place. She unbuttoned the top two blouse buttons and covered my cleavage with the scarf. The image was suggestive but not seductive. When Utannah added a gold belt, the transformation was magical. The young woman standing in the mirror looked intelligent, sexy, and self-confident. I'd never looked this way!

"You look stunning," Utannah said. "A tailor couldn't do better. You'll be the girl running into hard pants as boys trip over their tongues."

Giggling, I pirouetted and gave Utannah a hug. "Utannah, you're a miracle worker. How can I repay you? Denny will go wild," I exclaimed. "You have a talent for fashion. I think you should make a career helping people look good."

Utannah smiled. "I'm pleased I could help. Matching a person's character with their wardrobe is something I enjoy. Unfortunately, I see nothing here that works for me, but I have a big wardrobe at home. Attending father's official gatherings demands formal dress. By Saturday, I'll have my outfit put together."

I offered to show Utannah more stores, but she declined, pointing out that her first day had been long. Thanking me for my help, she said she looked forward to tomorrow's presentation. We hugged each other and went our separate ways. I'd found a new friend who exuded a fresh touch of class.

Walking home, I felt deeply satisfied having discovered one of my hidden sides. I had spent $29.47 on my entire outfit, so I didn't have much left—just enough to hit French's Fry and order a root beer float. I hoped to run into some of my classmates, but only the high school kids were present.

Sitting alone, I overheard two girls say they'd spotted Donny Osmond near the school. This caught my attention. In 1971, Donny Osmond was every teen girl's crush. He had reached the top of the charts, with "Sweet and Innocent" at number seven and "Go Away Little Girl" the current number-one hit. If Donny was in town, I wanted his autograph. But nobody knew whether the rumor was true. I decided to ask the most knowledgeable source on Sutter gossip: one Iris Wimple.

As I reached the porch, the aroma of chocolate graced my nostrils. The scent of cocoa, vanilla, and caramel drew me to the kitchen. Standing among hundreds of decorated candies was a woman covered in chocolate. From head to toe, streaks of chocolate gave this woman the look of an Easter treat. Only the rabbit ears were missing. "Gee, Iris, I never knew making chocolates meant swimming in the pot," I jabbed.

"That's just hilarious, Laurel. Nubs came over and used the pressure cooker to quickly melt the caramels. Unfortunately, she didn't screw down the lid. That's why there's a hole in the ceiling and caramel dripping from the rafters." Sure enough, an eight-inch hole exposed the joists that supported the roof. "I'll see if Glenn Davis can come patch and paint before your mother returns." Then Iris spotted me eating my first chocolate. "And what do you think you're doing, young lady?" she asked.

"You know, Iris, since this is my project, I'm responsible for quality assurance. I must taste these candies to ensure my classmates don't get sick. You wouldn't want that, would you?"

Shaking her head, Iris replied, "You're so full of baloney you could open a butcher store. That's the lamest excuse I've ever heard for tasting my cooking. Help me clean up this mess and pack up the chocolates."

As we cleaned the kitchen, I asked, "Iris, have you heard rumors about Donny Osmond being in town? I'd like to meet him."

"Honestly, Laurel, I'm not familiar with Donny Osmond, but the *Sentinel* said some fellow with the same name was performing in Portland tomorrow night. I haven't heard that the Osmond boy was in Sutter. But I'll keep my eyes open."

After cleaning up, Iris was too tired to fix dinner, so we ordered a pizza. When we finished dinner, I went upstairs and did my homework. I reviewed the script for tomorrow's assignment and decided to call seven of my closest friends.

But Iris cornered me and said, "Laurel, before you surgically attach the phone to your ear, I have one last argument corroborating the existence of God. You may find yourself bombarded with questions after tomorrow's demonstration. This won't take long, and you'll feel armed with the answers. What do you say?"

I wasn't eager for more theology, but I reluctantly agreed. "OK, if it doesn't take long. I want to unwind before bedtime, and talking with friends helps." I went over and joined her on the couch.

Iris wasted no time. "Have you ever truly wanted something— perhaps dancing with this Osmond boy?" I admitted there were many experiences and items I didn't have currently that I hoped someday might appear. Iris went on, "Is it fair saying that in fulfilling those wants, only real possessions or experiences can satisfy your needs?"

"Yes, Iris. If I wanted a dance with Donny, using a cardboard cutout wouldn't do," I admitted.

"Perhaps you've not yet reached this point," she continued, "but have you ever experienced a difficult time where no experience or object could meet your needs—a time when you asked, *Is this all there is?*"

"Gosh, Iris, that hasn't happened yet. Should I expect it anytime soon?"

"Probably not," Iris replied, "but times will happen when nothing from the material world satisfies the emptiness that erodes your soul. Yet many people experience this feeling and recover. Obviously, if something real exists that restores you to wholeness, and it's not material, then it must be spiritual. Therefore, God exists."

"Wow, Iris, that's powerful. I can't remember Dad leaving, but I think Mom's had that emptiness for a long time. She never says much, but I'm certain it's there. Do you think God could help her?" I asked.

"Yes, Laurel, I believe God would help. The problem is, people won't admit there's a problem, nor will they ask for spiritual guidance. Individuals have to meet God halfway. Asking for help and listening carefully are only parts of the answer. The hardest part is complete surrender to a divine will. It's said when we pray, we ask God the question, and when we meditate, we receive the answer.

"Many folks feel God never answers their prayers, when in reality God answers but it isn't the answer they seek. Instead of surrendering and following God's advice, people adapt the answer to their desires and wonder why they keep getting bad results. If your claim about your mother is true, she simply has to ask God for help and follow His advice. Remember that you can suggest a spiritual approach after she returns, but unless your mother asks God for help, it won't happen. My experience suggests that until the pain of a problem outweighs the pain of the solution, people stay in the problem. Don't push too hard. If you believe in the ideas you've learned, practice them every day. Actions showing you're happy and serene will speak louder than words when it comes to your mother."

"I guess you're right. Boxers trash talk about how they're superior to their opponents, but until they win the fight, they're just spouting words. Thanks for all the discussions, Iris. I feel ready to handle whatever they ask tomorrow. If it's OK, I'm going to call some friends and go to bed. I love you, Iris. You're the best."

As I ran to the phone, I heard, "I love you too, dear. Prepare to stand in the ring and box because your fight's only ten hours away. I expect it will go the distance."

Coming from Iris, this was a strange comment. Was there a hidden meaning? In the morning, I would begin to know.

CHAPTER 17

God Rises above the Nerve Tonic

Friday started early. Rising at six thirty, I dressed in navy blue pants and a yellow blouse. Speaking to the entire history class required me to look presentable. Navy blue and yellow were the school colors anyway, and tonight's bonfire rally was the main event.

When I went downstairs Iris was dressed in what she called her "go to church" clothes. Studying her outfit, I hoped it was the Church for the Blind. Iris wore a white sweatshirt with three-inch multicolored dots. The blue pants had a yellow stripe down each side. She wore a purple hat vaguely resembling a portabella mushroom. Thankfully, her role at the presentation was behind the sheets—the part she played implied penitence and respect, and if anybody saw this outfit, they'd be laughing hysterically.

We headed for school after we finished breakfast. Iris had packed the wagon with what I assumed were chocolates. Stacked three layers high, there was no chance of starving to death en route to the school. The weather was chilly, but the sun shone bright. The weekend looked ready for a marvelous homecoming.

As we approached the school, Iris commented, "My heavens, I'm feeling young again. Do you know how long it's been since I attended junior high?"

Talk about a loaded question! I almost said, "Well, Lincoln must have been president," but I resisted and remarked, "I'm sure it's been some time."

"You've got that right, Laurel. I think you almost said something caustic. You're such a teen devil. I feel young just being around kids. Their parents probably feel exactly the opposite. Well, let's get started. There's much to complete before class starts."

Mrs. Gallagher had given permission to skip knitting class, so Iris and I started immediately. We carried the wagon upstairs and pulled it to class. Mr. Wright wasn't there, but he'd unlocked his room.

Iris said, "It's such a pleasure to attend class. I hope I see your teacher since I know him well. Three years ago we worked on the hurricane relief project. The Catholic Church sponsored the effort. Both of us volunteered and raised thousands in cash. Penny Wright's quite a man. No one had a better partner when it came to collecting donations. That man could sell furnaces to the Arabs. Well, Laurel, enough reminiscing. Let's get going so we're ready. I don't like last-minute scrambles."

Iris had just called Mr. Wright "Penny." Only an elderly woman could call a retired marine a female name and live to repeat it. If a student called Mr. Wright "Penny," he'd find himself bouncing off walls like a pinball headed for the next bumper.

We put a small table below the two holes in the center sheet. We placed twenty-four chocolates, each with a different filling, on the table. Iris retreated behind the sheets, put on the cowboy hat, and put her gloved hands through both holes. I turned off the lights and placed a green filter over the floor spotlights. Iris had sprayed the classroom with vanilla air freshener. Mr. Wright had requested a turntable from the AV department, and I'd brought three albums from home. I hadn't told Mr. Wright Iris was behind the sheets. This wasn't intentional—I'd just forgotten. But after hearing Iris describe their relationship, I felt good about my choice. They could talk after class.

It was still several minutes before class started, but Mr. Wright poked his head in and asked if I was ready. Anytime an assignment didn't involve sitting in class, kids eagerly awaited. Mr. Wright had successfully divided the adolescents into three groups of eight, and each student had received a piece of paper labeled "What is God?" Mr. Wright explained that they didn't have to believe in God, but they must assume that the unseen image behind the drapes was God.

The first group consisted of students from rural homes. To avoid guaranteed trouble while waiting, Mr. Wright sent the other two groups to study hall. He reassured students that the candy being offered was safe, but reminded them there were no seconds. Students were encouraged to write down any questions they had for "God," plus everything they experienced during their presentation.

I whispered, "Iris, are you set?"

"Yes, dear, I'm set. If this goes well, I'm expecting an Academy Award."

I stood behind the sheet by the spotlight so my shadow didn't project. I watched students' reactions through a small gap.

The first group slowly entered the classroom. During setup, I had stood in the same place to ensure the effects would capture their attention. Students smelled vanilla and saw green, backlit sheets with a cowboy shadow projected onto them. Roy Rogers sang "Happy Trails to You" on the record player.

As kids approached the sheet, gloved hands protruded and an index finger invited them forward. Each teenager stopped and gently touched the leather-lined hands. Upon feeling their touch, Iris gave each student a randomly chosen handmade chocolate. Anyone with a question handed it to Iris. She never spoke. The kids then had five minutes to observe and make notes.

The first group looked suspicious and seemed ready to leave. We didn't know why until Mr. Wright questioned them later. Many believed this was a test, with right or wrong answers. Others thought it was a prank, while one truly believed God sat behind the sheets. But eventually, they all filtered through, with most happy just to survive the ordeal. Plainly, for the rural crowd, even theatrical cameos of God struck fear into their souls.

When the room cleared, Iris donned the fire helmet and removed her gloves. She commented, "My, Laurel, I received two questions I'll have to compose inspiring, God-like answers to and jot down before another group arrives. That's a challenge, but I'll try." She picked up her pen and scribbled away.

I switched the spotlights to red filters. "You know, Iris, right now your shadow reminds me of Ann Landers melded with the Texaco Fire Chief. Good thing they're not seeing the real you—your red, ruddy face makes you look like you've been drinking."

She responded, "Well, to be honest, Laurel, I've had several nips of tonic to calm my nerves. I felt anxious, and whiskey provides a wonderful cure for fear. If you're uptight, dear, the flask is in my purse. Help yourself."

"Iris, are you kidding? They don't allow liquor or drinking on school property. It's bad enough you're drinking, but you're at least twenty-one. If someone discovers your flask, I'll be expelled. What's worse is you're portraying God. God doesn't drink!" I exclaimed.

"Dear, how do you know?" Iris rebutted. "No religion I'm aware of states that God doesn't imbibe. Sometimes believers don't drink, but surely God can handle His liquor," she proclaimed. "On that note, hand me my flask. God needs another snort."

I was aghast. "All right, but no more; embarrassment will haunt me forever if word leaks that God's drunk. It's not the message Mr. Wright wants to teach." I gave her the flask, and she took a long swig.

"Bring in my believers, Laurel. I'm ready to heal some souls."

Heal souls? How much "nerve tonic" had "God" drunk? I was sure Iris slurred several words and she still had to answer "Questions to God" in the next twenty minutes. Her answers, mixed with more "nerve tonic," might convince students that "God" needed an exorcism.

With only enough time to find my thermos of water, I returned and said, "Iris, drink this! You shouldn't become dehydrated."

She replied, "Honey, I'll do my best, but water tastes better with bourbon."

From the door, I heard Mr. Wright ask, "How's it going? Are you ready for round two?" Quickly, I grabbed the flask, poked my head out, and said, "I need two minutes, then bring them in." I hid the flask in my backpack and sprayed rose scent to hide the remaining traces of vanilla. I ducked back behind the sheet as students began to enter. I wanted the pace to move rapidly. If we waited too long, "God" might pass out.

This group of students lived in town and grew up in blue-collar homes. Only seven kids composed this bunch, since I was the eighth. When they entered, Tennessee Ernie Ford was singing "Sixteen Tons." The kids didn't loiter for long. A fireman's shadow could be seen against the red-light background. This image was clearly less daunting than the cowboy's, since students quickly formed a line.

A bare hand presented candy to everyone, and in return, Iris received one question. My classmates took a few notes, whispered a few comments, and soon headed out the door. Relieved no major incident had occurred, I reminded Iris, "Have some more water. It's hot sitting in front of those lights."

"Honey, I'm feeling good. At this rate I could continue all morning. Who's next?" she inquired.

I said, "It's time for Einstein. Get your wig while I place the blue filters and spray the room with orange fragrance." Clouding the air with citrus spray and preparing the spotlights, I noticed Iris acting more sober. I placed the used props in the wagon and quickly found six pies. "Iris, what are the pies for?" I asked.

"Laurel, I brought pie to serve during the question-and-answer session. Your classmates will be hungry, dear. Plates and forks are also in the wagon. Be sure and set them out before all the students come in."

Iris had fitted her wig and donned surgical gloves for our last cameo. Mr. Wright stuck his head in, and once again, I signaled we were ready. Standing behind the sheet, I marveled how much Iris resembled Einstein, right down to his pipe. His pipe? Einstein didn't smoke a pipe in class, at least not in this class!

Yet, here sat Iris Wimple puffing on a Calabash pipe. Visions of Mr. Martin's office flashed through my mind. Explaining Iris's disrespect for rules about smoking and alcohol would need creative answers. I'd consider excuses when class finished. If Iris smoked and drank here, Tuesday night poker was likely the devil's playground.

There wasn't time to dwell on Iris's habits. I started Pachelbel's *Canon in D Major,* and students from professional households trickled in. Blue pipe smoke created a slow tornado above the sheets as I watched the kids react. They seriously inspected and documented every detail.

Elle Dutton, the Presbyterian wonder child, exclaimed, "This is stupid. We know God looks like Jesus, not Einstein. There isn't even a Holy Cross or a Crown of Thorns! How am I supposed to imagine I'm seeing God? This is the dumbest assignment I've ever done."

Susan Small responded. "Elle, the point isn't to depict Jesus or Buddha or any other religious figure. I think it shows students that each person sees God differently."

Elle retorted, "Yeah, well, Jesus is the only God I know. In my opinion this is blasphemy. I'm not engaging in this pagan ritual! My dad's going to hear that the devil resides in this school." She walked out as kids shook their heads and continued through the line.

A surgically gloved hand gave out candy as the tobacco smoke blended with the orange aroma. Someone commented, "That's a weird smell. Do you suppose God's smoking orange peels?"

Another responded, "My parents' cigarettes don't smell like that. I'd be happier if they did. You know, we could ask God where He gets His tobacco."

"No, let's keep going. I had no idea God smoked. Did you?"

"No, but it makes God seem more human. I'm warming up to the idea—I could believe in God if He behaved like everybody else."

I started to feel like dog meat. My school legacy would remain forever tarnished by God's bad habits. Word would spread, and I'd spend years with Sister Mary Agnes learning what God really was. I hoped Joann would visit on occasions.

After five minutes, the third group finished. Mr. Wright turned on the lights, and I asked for several minutes to arrange dessert for everyone. Mr. Wright agreed and went to fetch Elle. Soon, every desk had pie and students wandered in for dessert. Thirty minutes remained for questions—but Iris hadn't finished writing a decent response to the five questions.

Once students were seated, I stepped from behind the curtain. Several clapped, probably wondering where I'd been.

"As you know, I'm Laurel. What you've seen is my answer to Mr. Wright's question, 'Why do many cultures see God in different ways?' I asked you to assume the image on the sheet was God. So I'd like you to tell your classmates what you experienced."

Terry Proxmire was part of the second group. His dad worked in sales. He was a great guy and well liked. "Terry, what did you notice?" I asked.

"Well, Laurel, God looked like a fireman. I smelled roses, and someone sang a song about 'owing their soul to the company store.' I ate a chocolate containing a strawberry filling—which, by the way, tasted great. The hands felt soft and looked a bit wrinkled."

"Could you see God's face or body?" I asked.

"Nope, I couldn't make out a face, but when God grasped my hand, I thought I smelled bourbon. Did the mayor play God?" he asked. The class started giggling.

Trying to avoid the topic of liquor, I replied, "You know, Terry, some candy may have had bourbon in it. About God's identity, is this your perception?"

I walked behind the sheets. Iris had heard the cues and put on the fire helmet. Her bare arms protruded through the slots as I switched on the red lights and Tennessee Ernie Ford. The lights turned off, and thirty seconds later, they came back on.

"Yes, Laurel, that's pretty much what I saw and heard."

Several other students disagreed. "That's not what we saw. God looked like Einstein."

Someone added, "No, God was a cowboy and whistled a tumbleweeds song. He also wore leather gloves. Not only that, it smelled like vanilla beans in here."

Soon everyone was arguing. It started getting out of control, so I hollered, "Quiet." Mr. Wright seemed impressed. "Let me show you another scenario."

Iris switched to the blue light while I sprayed orange scent. The lights dimmed as rubber gloves poked through the sheets as Einstein and Pachelbel sprang to life.

Then a voice said, "Yeah, that's it! Who else saw God presented this way? Raise your hand." Arms shot up from seven students.

Mr. Wright turned the lights on and I asked, "Will the seven classmates who experienced God like this tell the class what they tasted." All seven were surprised to learn they had each tasted different flavors. Eyes opened wide, and I sensed some class members saw the point of my presentation.

"OK, let me show you one more sketch." Again, the lights dimmed, and a cowboy's shadow bathed in green showed on the sheets. Leather gloves appeared, and "Tumbling Tumbleweeds" played in the background, with a vanilla smell wafting through the air. In thirty seconds the lights came on.

The entire class had now experienced all three scenes. I decided to stir up debate. "Which of these three scenes best depicts God?" I asked. "Do you feel a connection with one particular presentation? If so, how does your life relate to what you saw?"

It was quiet until the smallest boy in class, Gilbert Turner, slowly raised his hand. Gilbert sat in back and wore a brown sweater vest with a navy blue tie. His dad was an astrophysicist and his mother a social worker. He came from group three. Usually reserved, Gilbert said little but spoke volumes.

"Hey, Laurel," he said. "To sort this out, I'd honestly need more time. However, I think you arranged three different depictions of God to appeal to three diverse groups. Knowing my classmates, I believe the kids in each group have similar backgrounds. For me, Einstein's shadow hit home, and I think that was your purpose. For others, I'm sure the cowboy and fireman meant more."

Kathy Vendrowski interjected, "When we discussed our experiences, everybody insisted they were right. Each group argued their depiction of God was correct. It's like real life. The Middle East always fights over God. Now I'm starting to see your point."

I asked, "So again, which version is correct? Raise your hands if it's the cowboy." Eight hands went up. "Who believes it's the fireman?" Ten arms flew up. "Anyone agree that Einstein's shadow represents God's intelligence?" Six extremities flew into the air. "So," I continued, "some still disagree. To help you out, I'll reveal some details you're unaware of. The first is that each of you ate different-flavored candy. Second, and most important, the same person portrayed God in each scene. Knowing these details, what are your thoughts?"

Utannah sat in front and raised her hand. I nodded to her. "Well, Laurel, this is my first history class, but I think the theme is: there's one God who adapts to different cultures and recruits messengers each culture can trust. The messengers deliver God's words in a way specific societies understand. I believe the candy demonstrates that while many people believe in the same deity, God makes Himself personal to each individual."

"Utannah, you're exactly right," I congratulated her. "People see God differently because God becomes whatever a person needs Him to be. If God's purpose is providing lifelong direction and giving comfort during sad times, those goals are only achieved when we feel a close bond to God. This is why I believe people see the same God in many different ways."

I looked around the room. Mr. Wright looked pleased, and the students appeared impressed by my answer.

I went on, "We've received five questions for God. I'll read each question and the answer, but I'll omit the names. Please understand, these answers will differ from how your parents or church might answer. The first question comes from student A. It asks: 'Why are my parents getting divorced?'" Instantly, I regretted asking the question. Even Iris wouldn't know the answer to an impossible question.

I took a deep breath and continued. "God's reply is this:

Student A, I don't know why your parents are separating. There are different reasons parents divorce, but both parents have a part. What I can say is that you aren't one of those reasons. I am certain your parents both love you unconditionally. They'll always be there for you and offer support when you need them most. I sense you are lonely and afraid, so I encourage you to talk with friends, grandparents, and especially your parents. If all else fails, talk to me whenever you wish, and I will lessen your load."

Wow! Iris's answer sounded God-like, and considering she'd taken extra "nerve tonic," it wasn't a bad response.

I continued, "Student B asks: 'God, why do you let horrible events like war and poverty cause suffering around the world?'" For a second time, Iris received a tough question for anyone, let alone a drunken deity.

I cringed and read God's response:

"Student B, this inquiry is the most common question I receive. I'm sure you know there's a choice when Mr. Wright gives you an assignment. You can either complete it or cast it aside. Whatever choice you make, you must live with the result. This fact is true for every creature occupying the planet. I gave people the power of free will so they could decide what's best for them. Over the centuries I provided guidelines to help folks live a better life. War results from many people believing in, and carrying out, the wrong choice. Multiple wrong choices control the suffering most people experience.

Everyone suffers during their life. The amount they suffer depends on whether they have loving parents, safe shelter, and a good education. However, parents can only raise you to their level of skills and awareness. They cannot give what they do not have and do not know. So you can't use your parents as an excuse for not being successful. If you see a path other people have taken to achieve their goals, and your goals are the same as theirs, then be willing to work hard and follow in their footsteps.

If I programmed you like robots and took away your capacity to choose, I'd take away the vast amount of intuitive thinking that improves the world. The creativity of the human spirit and the satisfaction of improving the world exist only because of free choice. The founding fathers of the United States based our government on the principle of free will, and that's why the USA is the greatest nation on earth. Your Declaration of Independence guarantees only a chance to pursue happiness; it does not guarantee you'll achieve it. In summary: you can't experience the good, and fully understand it, unless you experience the bad. Work hard, ask for help, and find me if I'm needed. The happiness you seek comes not from objects you own but from the integrity of your character. Integrity, in turn, solely depends on the sum of good choices you make."

The classroom was so quiet you could hear a pin drop. Even Mr. Wright remained silent. Either Iris's answer contained depth and truth, or the class didn't understand her response. Her advice sounded profound to me. Since there was nothing I could add, I moved to question three.

"Our third question asks: 'God, how come no one can ever see you?'" I liked this question. The subject was straightforward and a common question for many people. God's answer was this:

"Student C, the reason many people can't see me is because they're looking in the wrong place. I exist within you and all living beings. Examine the miracle you are. You can speak, ride a bike, engage in abstract thought, and perform mathematics. Only in God do these remarkable abilities reside. Unlike any other creatures, humans uniquely hold this supreme understanding. Once you understand this, look around you. I am there as well. Tasting a tomato, freshly picked from the garden, you'll find the flavor divine. Holding a newborn and feeling the softness of its incredible skin—the touch is heavenly. Envision the extraordinary sunsets common to the Oregon coast and try creating one yourself. You'll never see if you don't look with the intention to find."

Was this Iris, or had divine inspiration embraced her? I looked around the sheet—her head rested on the desk, and she snored softly as she slept. I didn't sense the Almighty handing down revelations. However, once again, she had amazed me with her insight and wisdom. Currently, I worried about how she would get home. Glancing at my watch, only ten minutes remained, so I continued with question number four.

"Student D asks: 'God, how come people like Buddha, Muhammad, and Jesus have to tell everybody your message? Why can't you do it yourself?'" *Hmmm*, possibly this student had missed the point of the presentation. Nonetheless, I read the answer:

"Student D, there is a simple answer to your question. Some students walk to school. Some students take a bus or a car to class, while still others ride a bicycle. My point is: students arrive at school. Think of the great men you just mentioned as vehicles to deliver their people to me. Their messages are diverse, but their knowledge and wisdom bring people closer to God. Typically, I use people as my voice. On rare occasions, I appear and deliver the message myself, but as you might imagine, this causes a stir. I've found it works better if familiar messengers bring my words to the people."

Iris was snoring loudly, so I continued talking. "Does anyone have questions on the answers they've heard?" Complete silence followed. Normally during class, this group talked all the time. "Any questions at all?" I continued.

Mickey Gathers raised his hand. He rarely spoke, so this was a surprise. "Hey, Laurel, I wondered if Einstein's wig is for sale. You know, Halloween is coming up and I don't have a costume yet. I'll give you a buck if you'll sell it. If you add the pipe, I'll spring for an extra quarter."

Mickey's question wasn't what I expected, but it filled the void. "See me after class, Mickey, and we'll talk," I responded. "Now let's go to the final question. Student E asks: 'God, where do our souls go after we die?'"

Where did my friends dream up these questions? Typically, their inquiries had little insight; today, they were inspired. I didn't see how Iris could explain this one, but she'd done excellently so far. I read her answer:

"Student E, I will try explaining this in a way that makes sense. When water is poured onto a polished glass surface, droplets sitting close to each other quickly pull together. They form a larger pool of water, similar in shape to a small Frisbee. Only if a droplet sits a significant distance from this bigger pool does it avoid the static forces of attraction and remain a single drop. Like the drop sitting alone, I packaged a tiny part of my pool in you so I can experience your world. Born perfect and pure, you developed the traits making you the unique person I see today. Because I'm always with you, our bundled package lets you ask me for help whenever you wish. When the body dies, our blended spirit releases and reunites with the Holy Pool from which we came."

Unexpectedly, Elle Dutton raised her hand. Because she was upset at my demonstration, I assumed she'd stay quiet until class ended. Later, I realized my naïve assumption.

"Yes, Elle, what would you like to ask?" I invited.

Elle rose to her feet, and the results of summer finishing school showed themselves. Using her finest pronunciation, she expressed, "Laurel, the answers to these difficult questions are insightful and well-thought-out."

No need to argue there; I couldn't believe them myself.

She continued in a distinguished voice, "I do not believe you, or the person behind the sheets, has the intellectual capacity necessary to provide these beautiful philosophical answers in such a short period of time. Therefore, I assume you planted questions previously answered by theologians. It's possible you even copied them from college texts. What's your explanation, Laurel?" she demanded.

In front of the entire class, Elle had accused me of cheating! I was speechless. Looking to Mr. Wright, I expected he'd help, but his stern look suggested he took her accusations seriously and was considering the possibility of plagiarism. Meanwhile, my cynical brain found a response to this arrogant little bitch. The whole class waited for my response. Many thoughts crossed my mind; what came off my tongue surprises me even to this day.

"Elle, I rarely enter a pissing match with a skunk. However, for you, I'll make an exception. Your conclusion is possible. However, it's difficult seeing these accusations from your perspective because my head won't fit that far up my ass. So I firmly deny everything you've stated."

Elle started to speak, but I cut her off. Driving the wooden stake a bit deeper, I said, "I won't continue a battle of wits with an unarmed child."

The class clapped and soon chanted, "Go, Laurel! Go, Laurel!" Saying Elle got upset during the exchange would be an understatement. Her seething eyes and snarling lips made it clear she wanted my head skewered on her broom. Mr. Wright ran forward, holding Elle back before she could gather enough steam to tackle me. Secretly, I hoped he'd release her. She was smaller, and I knew I could land an uppercut if given the chance.

Mr. Wright hollered out, "Let's take a break, people." After the students left, he said, "Laurel, I'd like to see you after school. Right now, I'm taking Elle to the counselor's office so Mr. Dominick can make sure she's OK."

As Mr. Wright and Elle walked out, Utannah came over and offered to remove the sets. Out loud, I admitted my biggest problem was getting Iris home. Suddenly, from behind the curtain, a voice said, "Laurel, those were brutal words you said to that young woman. I suspect an apology is in order. I'll get home myself, thank you. Help me pack these items and transport them down the stairs. I'll be happy to assume responsibility from there."

I replied, "Iris, if you were awake, you heard Elle's words. I couldn't let her get away with false accusations. Since you didn't strike her with a lightning bolt, I had to say something."

Behaving like she'd never touched liquor, Iris replied, "We'll talk about it more after school. I need to hurry home and get ready for tomorrow's bar mitzvah. I'm proud of you and pleased at how the demonstration worked. Taking part in a school project brought back many memories."

Since the first hour had finished early, Utannah and I helped Iris down the stairs and out the correct door. We weren't trying to hide Iris, but strangely, no one saw her leave. When we returned to class, the remaining students wandered in as if nothing had ever occurred. Mr. Wright was ready to begin and asked who wanted to read their answers to the class.

Susan Small asked, "What happened to God? I have a question I thought of during the break."

Mr. Wright looked at me and pointed. Clearly, he wanted me to field this inquiry.

"Well, Susan, I only had one hour, and my hour ended," I said. For lack of a better reason, I added truthfully, "God left to prepare for a bar mitzvah."

Susan pressed, "Laurel, someone was behind those sheets. If he's a religious leader, the answers make sense. If you won't say, then it's possible that Elle was right. Otherwise, let me ask the students who wrote the questions. If they deny you planted the topic that works as well."

I said, "Here's the truth, Susan. The students' questions were personal. If your parents planned to divorce, would you want everybody to know? The person portraying God did their best to give a clear response to each question. The actor doesn't want folks hounding them for more insight or arguing over what 'God' said. For these important reasons, I won't reveal names. I assure you, the questions handed in by your fellow students occurred during the presentation. Only then did 'God' provide the answers."

Susan didn't appear happy with my answer, but I'd said all I planned on saying. Mr. Wright stepped in, asking several students to read their papers. My confrontation with Elle weighed heavily on my mind. Iris had warned me to expect controversy over my interpretation of God, but not the method I'd used to present it. I had no idea where things were headed. Plainly, Mr. Wright had more to say on the subject. Thankfully, the rest of history class was uneventful.

During lunch hour, the cafeteria was abuzz over my remarks to Elle. Because students thought she was pompous, I received many congratulations. My pride increased exponentially at Elle's expense. However, her absence, coupled with her parents' connections, made me wonder if these same kids would visit me in jail.

When my last class finished, I went to see Mr. Wright. He sat grading papers and listening to *Paul Harvey News.* As I walked in, he looked up, saying, "Hello, Laurel. Please come and sit down." I did as he asked but stayed silent, knowing anything I said could work against me. Mr. Wright went on, "Laurel, I want to say that your completed assignment was outstanding. Trying to top your answer to this difficult question will give future students a challenge. I'm giving you an A.

"I talked with the five students who presented the questions," he continued. "They confirmed each question was original. Whoever you chose to provide the answers, I compliment them on their scholarly and understandable responses. However, I wanted to see you because of your remarks to Elle." I started to squirm. Mr. Wright went on, "I know Elle has an attitude problem. I also know you're not the first student who's experienced her rudeness. What disappoints me is lowering your behavior to her level and shoving it down her throat."

"Look, Mr. Wright, I agree—I was wrong for swearing," I said. "But she raised doubts about my credibility. Since you didn't confront Elle, I felt compelled to do it myself. Calling me a liar when it's not true is something I won't tolerate."

"I understand, Laurel, but I think you owe her an apology. It may seem hard to swallow, but telling Elle you're sorry makes you the more mature person," he stressed. "Rarely do people find maturity in young adults but when they do, they never forget it. I promise you, if Elle doesn't soon realize the faults in her behavior, she'll pay a much higher price than she did today. Let her learn from bad experience."

Mr. Wright had a good point. If Elle returned to school, I'd track her down and tell her I was sorry. "OK, Mr. Wright, I see your point," I conceded. "I'll apologize."

"Good, Laurel. She's in the guidance counselor's office with her father, Dr. Dutton. I'll take you there and you can apologize."

For the fourth time this week, a trap I hadn't seen caught me by surprise. Following Mr. Wright downstairs, I thought about what to say. As an attorney, Mom advised her clients to say as little as possible. Right now, that seemed like a good idea.

Reaching the counselor's office, we found Elle and Dr. Norman Dutton waiting expectantly. Dr. Dutton was an imposing man. Standing over six feet tall and weighing at least two hundred pounds, he'd played running back at USC. By all accounts, the man was a wonderful dentist who had treated Sutter's citizens for over ten years. Based on the size of his hands, I couldn't believe he was a dentist—just one finger looked like a bratwurst. Mixed with my anxiety, the thought of him sticking a finger in my mouth made me gag.

With me threatening to vomit, everyone moved back as Mr. Wright asked, "Laurel, are you sick?"

The thought of vomiting on Elle and her dad brought visions of dodging an apology. However, throwing up would delay the unavoidable. "No, I'm good; just swallowed wrong," I stated.

Mr. Wright spoke up, "Elle, Dr. Dutton, Laurel has something she'd like to say to both of you."

I started eating humble pie and said, "Elle, I was wrong for cussing and saying such mean-spirited words. I understand how much they hurt, and I know my response made you look bad in front of the class. I offer you my apology and promise it won't happen again."

Elle and her father stared at me without a word. Finally, after thirty endless seconds, Elle hissed, "Laurel, I want you expelled from school. You've brought shame to me and my family. I don't ever plan on speaking to you again!" she shouted. "And if Mr. Wright hadn't insisted we study religion, this wouldn't have happened. He's as bad as you are," she said, pointing at Penfield Wright. "My dad also has something to say."

Dr. Dutton took a deep breath. "Laurel," he said, "I acknowledge your halfhearted apology, but it doesn't begin repairing the harm you've caused my baby girl. And you, Mr. Wright, had the nerve to violate the separation of church and state and invite non-Christian religious leaders to teach your class. I find both of your behaviors shameful. Therefore, I'm asking Principal Martin to petition the school board. Specifically, I'm asking the board to dismiss you and expel Ms. Montgomery. Restoring my daughter's integrity demands both of you must leave."

Well, there it was. Iris's smoking and drinking weren't the reasons for the complaint. No, I faced expulsion for answering a question and defending my answer. I looked at Mr. Wright in disbelief. His face appeared stern, and his eyes honed in on Dr. Dutton. He acted calm. In the movies, people looked this way when they'd made up their mind to shoot somebody. I waited for Mr. Wright to follow Marshall Dillon's example and blow father and daughter away in a hail of bullets.

Instead, he spoke quietly, "Dr. Dutton, you are a taxpayer in this school district. I'm sorry you disagree with my teaching methods. If you feel any teacher isn't using proper judgment, you have the right to approach the school board. But I must tell you, Ms. Montgomery's apology was sincere and adequately addressed your concerns. Your daughter played a role in what occurred, and she's admitted no responsibility. Both young ladies deserve the forgiveness we received during our formative years. As they mature, all young adults make mistakes. It's unfair to make Laurel pay such a heavy price for growing up. The blame is mine, and I take full responsibility. Please leave Laurel out of this. I wish you both a good day." Mr. Wright put his hand on my shoulder, and we turned and walked out.

Mr. Wright's actions humbled me. The Duttons couldn't deny his conviction for teaching or his confidence in defending his decisions. By example, he'd taught me how to deal with difficult people. At that moment, Penfield Wright became my lifelong hero. I still feared the future, but I knew Mr. Wright had my back. We would succeed or fail together.

CHAPTER 18

Housing the Homeless

Arriving home, I dropped my books and went to the kitchen looking for Iris. She was packing pies for tomorrow's bar mitzvah. "Hello, dear. How was the rest of your school day?"

I didn't know what Iris would remember, so I described my heated words to Elle and the possibility of suspension.

"My heavens, Laurel, I can't believe what happened! Mr. Wright called asking if you had arrived home. I said you weren't here, so he decided to speak with you on Monday and didn't leave a message. I assumed we'd left something behind. I had no idea what happened!" she exclaimed. "I'm sure you're upset. I know I would be."

I replied, "No, Iris, I'm not. Nothing happened except a threat. Unless some action occurs, I intend to enjoy this weekend. I'm happy about my grade and despite your 'nerve tonic,' I appreciate your help."

"Laurel, I apologize for my episode. It's been years since I've performed for many people. I hope you'll forgive me."

"Iris," I said, "you're forgiven as long as you're there if Elle's father files a complaint."

Iris shot me a determined gaze and spoke with a dominating voice I'd never heard. "Honey, I'm familiar with the Duttons. For twenty dollars, they appear to sponsor every community project, but they rarely contribute their time or effort. The entire family practices deception on a new level. I promise I'll support you should the need arise. Now, before it gets late, let's go find those beavers. We haven't checked on them for a while, and I want to make sure they're well."

We took a brisk walk to the lake and found the swimming hole. It wasn't long before we heard splashes among the reeds. I pushed the pussy willows aside—and there were both babies. They looked bigger, but one kit had a deep wound behind its neck.

Since Iris had more knowledge about beavers, I deferred to her. "What do you think, Iris?" I asked.

"Well, I hate to interfere with creatures thriving in their own habitat, but I think this one needs some help." Iris waded knee-deep into the swamp and grabbed both beavers, handing them to me. I had no idea what she planned to do with two beavers, so I assumed she had something in mind.

"Iris," I asked, "why did you rescue both of them?"

Without blinking, she responded, "These two babies have comforted each other from the day they were born. We must help the injured kit, so it's unfair leaving the other. We're taking them both."

Still perplexed, I said, "Yes, I understand. But where can we put them—in the bathtub? Besides, we don't have beaver food. I doubt they like Swanson frozen dinners."

"Don't worry, dear. The answers will come before we get home. These fellows won't survive cold weather without mother's milk. You have a bonfire to attend, so tonight I'll look after them."

When we got home, Iris took a hot shower and then called the local Gamble's store. The owner, Hal Maltby, knew Iris, and within a half hour, he arrived with a refrigerator box and a small inflatable pool, setting both in the living room. As Hal left, Iris was right behind him telling me to watch the beavers. All I heard was the word "*Woolworth's*."

In a flash she returned, towing the wagon loaded with bags of gerbil food. Iris tore newspapers into pieces while I found old dog cushions in the garage. We moved the box near the fireplace and lined it with a canvas tarp clipped to the sides with clothespins. I placed the pool inside, near one end of the box. The garden hose found its way through the front door, and soon the pool was partially filled with water. Cushions and newspaper lined the floor, and a big bowl of gerbil food sat next to the pool. The "Beaver Bed-and-Breakfast" was ready for boarders.

Iris took the healthy baby and placed him in the box. We needed better lighting to treat the wounded beaver, so we employed Mom's makeup mirror. Using antibiotic salve, Iris cleaned its wound while I fed the patient with a bottle. Holding these beavers for several hours didn't reveal anything distinguishing "guys" from "gals"—I wondered how to tell the difference. "Iris, how do you know if a beaver's a male or female?" I asked.

"Well, we don't know for sure. Discovering a beaver's sex is difficult, since their genitalia is hidden internally. Perhaps we should give them names that could belong to a male or female. What do you think about naming one Bobby and the other Jean?" she suggested.

"That's fine. But there's still no easy way to tell them apart. 'Jean' could possibly be a 'Gene.' So we'll start with one version, and if we have to change, we will," I commented.

"Well, now it's not too difficult. This beaver has a large, gaping wound occupying one-fifth of its lower neck; the other doesn't." Boy, did I feel stupid. Iris went on, "When the injured one heals, we'll probably see other characteristics telling them apart. For now, let's call the wounded beaver Bobby and the other Jean. Now, last I recall, that bonfire begins in an hour and a half. I made lasagna for dinner, as well as a green salad and tiramisu. That meal should keep you satisfied for several hours. Wash your hands and come to the table."

As usual, dinner was delicious. Ready to leave, I said enthusiastically, "Iris, dinner was great! I love you."

She countered with, "The reason dinner was great is because I dined with you! Don't be out past midnight, and have a good time."

CHAPTER 19

A Blaze for the Ages
Demands the Finest of Fuels

Being a small town, Sutter had only one public junior high and one high school. The two schools were located a block apart, and between campuses was an open area where they held the yearly bonfire. The goal every year was to build a fire bigger than the previous year's.

High school students were rounding up anything disposable and flammable. Oregon had one of the world's largest logging industries, so normally this wasn't difficult. However, the loggers near Sutter were on strike, making leftover wood products almost nonexistent.

Since necessity is the mother of innovation, several of the football players decided to visit Ordner's Exotic Furnishings. This company made stunning wood furniture using local materials and rare woods found throughout the world. Wealthy people waited months to receive custom-designed, collectible, inlaid furniture. The factory stocked multiple exotic woods, sitting in bins until ready for use.

Milt Ordner was a Renaissance man. He loved fine wines, fine cars, and fine art. From the outside, his home looked large but modest. But the inside was an artistic masterpiece. Ceilings displayed painted murals. Renoirs and Monets hung throughout his home. Gold-plated fixtures adorned each bathroom. Best of all, the basement had a bowling alley next to a 10,000-bottle wine cellar. Milt's daughter was a senior, so he was happy to supply scrap wood for this year's bonfire.

When the boys went to see Milt, his men had just loaded a truck with furniture headed for the dump. The pieces contained blemishes and didn't meet customer specifications, so he was discarding them. The boys could have the defective furniture, he said, if they would unload Milt's truck and remove the furniture from the property. It took five trips in a Studebaker truck, but the boys achieved their goal.

I arrived at the bonfire as the sun was slipping below the horizon and the kids were chanting for heat. I'd never seen this much furniture stacked so high. The pile rose thirty feet and filled a tepee-sized rock circle that outlined the fire's perimeter. To guarantee a successful ignition, every item was sprayed with gasoline.

The moment arrived for a spectacular night of controlled arson. The cheerleaders started their routine while the firemen drank beer in the fire truck. Being a junior high student, I took my proper place in the back of the crowd. The temperature hovered in the forties, so I wore a knitted tam with mittens. I hadn't seen my schoolmates, but it wouldn't be long before they arrived.

As the senior class president held the torch to the pile, a warm breath caressed my earlobe, followed by soft lips kissing my neck. Shivers electrified my spine as I turned into Denny's arms. Staying silent, I put a mitten on each of his cheeks and sensuously kissed him. Whatever troubled the world became distant. Only the two of us existed. Speech wasn't necessary; gazing into each other's "windows to the soul" spoke volumes. I knew—I'd always known: Denny considered me his soul mate.

Finally, I spoke. "I hope you don't greet every girl like that." Smiling, he rubbed my shoulders, stoking my internal flame to rival the bonfire's.

This was the biggest bonfire in Sutter High history. Graduates from decades ago sat together, covered in blankets, while the younger crowd sang around the inferno. When it looked like the flames couldn't go higher, seniors added more furniture.

The crowd had just broken into the school's fight song when a big Cadillac pulled up behind the fire truck. A man jumped out and started arguing with the firemen. I motioned Denny to walk us closer and find out what was happening. Approaching the fire truck, we saw that Milt Ordner was the man yelling and gesturing. He shouted, "You're not listening. That's my money going up in smoke!"

Even when Milt's antics increased, the firemen didn't seem concerned. Irish fire chief Ryan McShane replied, "Milt, I've heard every word. Ya told da seniors to take da scrap furniture. An hour ago, ya realized one o' your workers had already taken da scrap to da dump. While he was at da dump, another worker was takin' da truck o' new custom furniture to da freight depot but stopped to help wit' a mill problem. He parked dat truck in da same location as da scrap truck. Da senior class is burnin' yer custom inlaid furniture. Now, Milt, does dat about sum up what yuv been tryin' to tell me?"

"You're goddamned right, Ryan! That's exactly what I'm telling you. Now put the son-of-a-bitchin' fire out so you can rescue my furniture."

"Milt, instead o' shootin' yer mouth off, come wit' me." The chief grabbed a fire hose, and with Milt, broke through the ring of people surrounding the fire. "Step aside! Step aside!" Ryan ordered. Both men stood at the front of the crowd. "Now, Milt, I'm goin' to shoot water on da fire while ya run in dere and git yer furniture. When yuv got 'er out, tell me and we'll all be happy," he stated.

"Ryan, you're fuckin' crazy. I can't get close to that fire. It's scorching and will stay that way for some time."

Chief McShane took a swig from the bottle in his pocket. "No shit, Milt. Da fire's hot, is it? Ya can't get close, can ya? But ya want me men riskin' der arses savin' furniture for some rich bitch in Delaware. Well, take dat idea and stuff it up yer own arse. Now come on over, Milt. Me and da boys will share a snort with ya, and ya can report da loss to yer insurance tomorrow. Tonight, enjoy watchin' yer daughter and dat hunderd-thousand-dollar glorious fire. In me twenty-tree years, it's da biggest bonfire I ever seen—and da seniors have ya to thank. Milt, be proud of what ya did for yer daughter's class."

I looked at Denny and said, "It's good we don't always know what goes on behind the scenes. A hundred thousand dollars is vanishing in smoke. Can you believe it? No matter what I do, I doubt I'll make a hundred thousand dollars in my entire life," I predicted.

Denny countered, "I'll bet Mr. Ordner never thought he'd be worth millions. A few weeks ago, *The Sutter Sentinel* described his story. He grew up Catholic with ten siblings. His first job was a paper route. From there, he worked his way up. The unbelievable fact is that he never received a high school diploma. Nobody's quite sure, but it's rumored he gave five million dollars to research after his wife died of a tumor. His whole life centered on her and his kids. I couldn't understand how any guy could feel that way—until recently. Maybe it's the way men become. I'm sure I'll find out," he reflected.

"Denny, the thing is: those questions lie in the future. Let's just enjoy tonight and tomorrow. I'm thrilled to spend time with you. Iris is outdoing herself to make our dinner a memorable occasion. She says first dates are only first once, so they should be special. I don't know what she's preparing, but she won't disappoint. When the fire dies, we should walk to French's Fry and have a burger and a shake. My friends haven't arrived, but they're supposed to be here. Perhaps we'll find them at the diner."

We stayed at the bonfire a little longer. Through the smoke I saw Joann and her date, Mark Landry. Joann had a green silk scarf holding her hair in a ponytail. She had never done that before. Utannah stood close by. We went and joined the junior high crowd. "Can you believe this fire?" I asked.

Mark replied, "This is only the second bonfire I've attended, but it's huge. It must be extraordinary because a moment ago, the fire chief threatened to put it out. If he tried to extinguish it, we'd be in the middle of a riot. Besides, I didn't see the fire harming anything."

Denny exited his reclusive personality, commenting, "The only valuable object that's burned is Milt Ordner's wallet. Next year, I doubt he'll give as much to support the school's spirit." We told everyone what occurred. Everyone was astounded at how much money had just vaporized in the flames.

Joann giggled, "Maybe Milt will donate when we're seniors. I hope he doesn't fire somebody since it's his fault he didn't inspect the load before it left."

"Yes," Utannah said knowingly, "but people in charge rarely take the blame, unless they have to, to stay in power. Someone else is the scapegoat. For French politicians, that's how it works. Fortunately for Americans, President Nixon isn't that kind of man. I overheard my father saying private diplomatic talks have started between the US and China. Henry Kissinger secretly flew to China last July, during his tour of Pakistan.

"French intelligence has confirmed the details. We're living here because France believes your president plans on traveling to China to set up US-Chinese diplomatic relations. If he succeeds, the Far East markets will open. France wants Father available to negotiate trade arrangements. President Nixon's foreign policy decisions will make him your most admired president."

I didn't think Mom's trip was a state secret. She'd never said I shouldn't tell people her location. However, the French considered the information to be sensitive. Could Mom's work involve more than the law? Was she a CIA agent? Her business took her around the world. An international business attorney provided the perfect cover. Private discussions and information, mixed with politics, produced huge profits.

Few people held her credentials on the topic of foreign governments. Her briefcase files were often marked "Secret."

As I considered the possibility, the more it made sense. I'd never found a poison-injecting pen or a high-heeled phone, but then I'd never looked. When I got home, I was taking another look around the house. I decided to stay quiet and not reveal any national secrets.

"Wow, Utannah. You know lots of important stuff," I remarked. "I hope everything works out for your country."

Joann was pulling on her sleeve. "Enough, already. I'm starvin' and I'll faint if I don't get nourishment soon." Pretending to wilt, she acted surprised when Mark caught and hugged her.

Mark commented, "God, Joann, you're withering as I speak. I'm not dancing with a twig, so we'd better fatten you up," he teased. "Right now I can still throw you over my shoulder." He grabbed Joann, flinging her over his right shoulder. Joking, Mark said, "I've seen you eat, Joann. After you finish at French's Fry, lifting you might break my shoulder."

Joann's head hung above Mark's waist. I saw an evil grin, but I didn't know what was coming. Mark's payback started with Joann's right hand wrapping around the left side of his body, poised like a pinching lobster claw. In moments, her hand grasped Mark's family jewels, applying ample pressure to convert nuts into diamonds. Mark was stunned and started moaning. I instantly learned guys are insanely protective of their testicles.

"Mark, I didn't understand what you said, hanging upside down. Could you repeat it?" Joann prodded.

Embarrassed, Mark painfully replied, "Sure, Joann, I meant that when a woman like you is in good shape, they get good nutrition, and people can't fling them around—because they can defend themselves, you know?"

Mark looked relieved as Joann released her grip and he set her down. "Good comeback, Mark," she said. "For a minute, your chances of singing soprano seemed real good. Now let's grab some food."

We walked to French's Fry and selected a table. Only Utannah didn't have a confirmed date. I wondered if she had any prospects. "Utannah, any luck finding a date? Since the dance is tomorrow, you might have to go stag," I reminded her.

Joann chimed in, sounding like an old pro. "Laurel's right. By yesterday, all the cutest boys had dates. Last year I attended the dances alone and danced with whoever I wanted. Afterward, I didn't have a dickhead guy to dump, so I had a great time."

Mark cleared his throat as a grimace etched his face. "Joann, did you call me a 'dickhead guy to dump'? Was I hearing you correctly?" Joann turned red as she realized Mark sought revenge for her threat to his dangling DNA dispenser. "If you feel this 'dickhead' inhibits your ability to run the pack, I'll set you free and ask Ms. Donnay to accompany me."

Joann didn't know Mark was kidding. Utannah, however, understood Mark's intent, put her arms around him, and peered into his eyes. She said, "I'll go Mark. When should I be ready?" Joann looked upset, not knowing what to do. Should she grovel or should she kill Mark? She hadn't been so speechless since I told her about kissing Denny.

Utannah continued playing the perfect harlot. Fortunately, Mark couldn't stop giggling, and the prank was over. Joann put everything together and knew only she hadn't gotten the joke. Never outgunned, Joann walked over to Mark and Utannah. She gently dislodged Utannah's hold on Mark and pushed her aside. Joann put her arms around Mark's waist, holding her lips close to his. Staring at him eye to eye, she said seductively, "A hunk like you should easily handle the needs of a woman who loves 'running the pack.' What about it, Mark? Can you meet my needs?"

She reached up with one hand, untied her ponytail scarf, and shook her head. Blond hair tumbled down her back. Joann wrapped the scarf around Mark's neck and pulled him closer for a long, passionate kiss. Then she pulled back and asked again, in a sultry tone, "Well, Mark, can you?"

While Mark thought he was good at catching women, he never knew Joann had swallowed him hook, line, and sinker. When the food came, the burger Mark had ordered sat on his plate while he waited to share more of Joann's red-hots.

The rest of us addressed Utannah's problem. She provided an update. "It's not disappointing if I don't have a date. However, I'm optimistic a new friend might escort me."

This invited other girls to play 20 Questions. "Is he good-looking? Is he older? Where does he live?" Joann and I needed details. Utannah, however, wouldn't budge because she'd either have a date or she wouldn't. In her mind, there was no need to discuss useless facts about an event that might or might not happen. It was eleven o'clock when we ran out of gossip, so it was time to head home. Utannah headed home to decide on her wardrobe while Mark offered to walk Joann home. They strolled down the sidewalk holding hands, but it reminded me of a girl walking her dog. Mark was going wherever Joann wanted to go. I reminded myself I'd never let a member of the opposite sex have so much influence over my life. How incredibly immature!

Denny and I said good-bye and headed home silently, holding hands. Just a week ago, I had felt my hike around the lake was the best day of my life. Right now, alone with Denny, hand in hand, I felt a calm and serenity I'd never experienced. Everything was perfect, and I never wanted it to end.

I asked, "Denny, why do you like science so much? Why not football or other competitive sports?"

He asked me to sit with him for a few minutes. Denny thought several seconds and said, "Have you heard of Vince Lombardi?" I nodded yes. Mom was a Packers fan, and I knew a lot about Coach Lombardi. When he died in September 1970, Mom was sad for a month. At the time, I didn't understand her heartache, but Denny was about to teach me the Lombardi rules.

Denny continued, "Lombardi is an American legend. If there's a single word that defines him, it's *passion.* Rarely could anyone outdo his passion for God and football—not always in that order. Lombardi's devotion embodied penitence to God, love of people, and finally, the commitment to win. My favorite Lombardi quote is, 'Gentlemen, we will chase perfection, and we will chase it relentlessly, knowing all the while we can never attain it. But along the way, we shall catch excellence. I am not remotely interested in just being good.'

"I've enjoyed science since I was seven. I can usually improve any gadget, but sometimes there's a scientist who improves it better. That's the person I want to beat. My goal isn't making an existing item better—it's creating a product that blows other ideas out of the race. That probably doesn't make sense, but for me, it works."

It made sense, but I had more questions. "I get what you're saying, but wouldn't competing against other players offer more fun? I mean, you could be good at football, basketball—and science. Talented students challenge themselves against the best, both on and off the field," I pointed out.

"You're right, Laurel, that's exactly what they do. Both games promote teamwork—and I don't work well with others. In the scheme of life, mental competition takes me further. Winning a football championship is a great moment for any guy, but imagine discovering something no other person knows. My thrill is the chase. When a guy has the talent to be a professional football player, the skill's wasted if he doesn't develop it. I'm blessed with an intellectual gift, and it's crazy squandering time on football when I should be developing that gift. Olympic athletes start young, attempting to be the best. I'm following the same philosophy. Besides, I'm only in ninth grade. There are three more years for me to play sports. What do you plan on doing?" Denny asked.

"Honestly, Denny, life is simple right now. All I know is I want to continue to learn. As I've said, it won't be long before I'll have to start behaving like an adult. Next summer I'm finding a job. Mom insists that I know I'm owed nothing and that possessions mean more when I've work for them. Now, I enjoy what life offers and live each day to the fullest. The last few days have revealed truths I never knew. You were my best surprise. A week ago, I'd never kissed a guy. Now I can't keep my lips off you. Why do you suppose that happens?" I asked.

"Laurel," Denny replied, "you're my first discovery with no logical, scientific explanation. I can't rationalize it. I can't decipher it. I've had feelings for you since fifth grade. I've tried making sense of them, but I can't. My feelings for you keep increasing and I don't understand why. Sound weird or what? Worse, I can't discuss it with my parents. They don't have a clue about dating. How they met each other and have stayed together baffles me. My folks only work, cook, and sleep. They never spend time alone, and I'm not sure they're still in love. What about your mom?" he asked.

"My mom's a poor source for anything dealing with men, dating, and babies. She's thrilled you asked me to the dance, but Iris is a better resource when it comes to guys. She knows facts about the strangest things. You won't believe this, but she's planted a sequoia in our front yard. She's also running a nursery for injured animals inside the house." Denny's eyebrows shot up. "Iris helped with my history assignment, and on Tuesdays, we feed the homeless. What's amazing is she's almost eighty."

Denny nodded his head and said, "You're lucky to have Mrs. Wimple. I don't know her well, but anybody that connected to nature can't be bad. I've heard nothing but good about Iris. Her talent at poker must be great. At the nursery, Dad saw Father Blevins, who said Iris cleaned their clocks Tuesday night. What's great is her open-mindedness on many issues. Elderly people rarely change their ways."

Denny looked at his watch. "Come on, Laurel, let's get you home. It's almost midnight and I don't want us in trouble so close to the dance."

I was home by twelve. At the front door we embraced and Denny kissed me on the cheek and said, "Goodnight." He receded down the dimly lit street, slowly melting into the moonlight. I wondered if we belonged together—or did his departure offer a preview of Denny departing our future, leaving me only fond memories of my first love?

CHAPTER 20

Neighborhood Logging Results in Finding the "Law Officer of the Year" and Saving a Life

Saturday morning. The anticipated climax of the week arrived quietly. It was eight o'clock when I stumbled out of bed and dressed. Downstairs, I didn't see Iris anywhere. Then it dawned on me she'd gone to the bar mitzvah. The ceremony didn't start until eleven, but Iris was nothing if not punctual.

I put Otis in the backyard, and then sat down for a bowl of cereal. The beavers also needed time outside, and since I didn't have a beaver leash, I needed a helping hand. I called Joann. "Hey, Joann, I called to see if you've recovered from your slutty behavior or if you planned on relapsing tonight."

"That's funny, Laurel, real funny. For a minute, I was sure Mark had dumped me for Utannah—she's a French Mata Hari. Trust me, if she's around tonight, the girls need to watch their boyfriends. I decided my only hope of overcoming her charms was seduction. I imagined myself as Raquel Welch in *1,000,000 Years B.C.,* and all my reservations vanished. God, don't tell anyone. They'll think I'm challenging Cindy Summers for Bimbo of the Year. The effect on Mark was unbelievable. We stopped and kissed six times just walking home! He's already called twice, saying he wanted to see me today. I like him, but only in spurts."

"Listen, Joann, it's your fault. You could have apologized for your comment. Now you'll probably pay by getting a tongue down your throat and dealing with wandering hands. You've tapped a testosterone tank, and from what I've experienced, it's not easy controlling the flow. But I'm getting away from the reason I called. Can you come over? I need some help, and Iris left a note suggesting I call you. I've got a problem that needs two people."

"Well, I might come, if you give me a clue. I'm dealing with my own problems. I'll come over and help with your problem if you promise to help me with Mark. Deal?"

I teased, "Sure, it's a deal, but I think you're trapped. Judging from Cindy, once you're a bimbo, you're always a bimbo. Come on over and we'll figure it out."

As I hung up the phone I heard the comment, "Little bitch." Joann didn't harbor resentments. She sounded angry, but curiosity would draw her over. She knew I had a good track record for solving difficulties we strayed into, so it wouldn't take long to patch up her wounded ego.

Seven minutes later I heard a knock. Joann fell through the door as I opened it. "Hey, Joann, what took you so long? Are you out of shape or just taking your time?" I said, harassing her.

"Listen, Laurel, this is serious. As I walked out the door, Mom was answering the phone. I heard her say, 'No, Mark, she just left. Can she call you back?' If Mark gets me cornered tonight, I'm dead. You should have said he was a sexual deviant. I wouldn't have invited him to the dance."

"Wait a minute," I said. "I thought Mark invited you. Now you're saying you invited him? Then you cranked his motor. It's not my fault!"

"Laurel, you're my best friend. You're supposed to sense bad problems and prevent me from getting in trouble." Joann stood in the living room two minutes before noticing something was different. Then it dawned on her. "Why is there a refrigerator box in your living room? Did you get a new fridge, or is Iris working on a project?"

"Well, I guess it's a project—a family project. I thought you'd fit right in. Come look, and you'll see why I need help."

Joann went and looked inside the box. The beavers had buried themselves in newspapers, with one tail visible. "Laurel, this may sound silly, but why is a swimming pool sitting there in a refrigerator box? And what's with the big black spatula? Has Iris gone bonkers, or am I missing something?"

"That's not a spatula!" I lifted the newspapers, revealing the beavers sleeping in a yin-yang arrangement. "They're why I need your help. They need exercise, and I can only handle one at a time."

Joann gave me a stern look. "You had to bring them home, didn't you? I'll bet Iris wasn't happy. Didn't we plan to leave them alone unless something happened?"

"Something did happen. Look at Bobby's neck and you'll see a wound. That's why we brought them home. He needed treatment. We couldn't take Bobby and leave Jean alone. They need companionship. Think about separating from Tim after living together your whole life."

Joann just looked at me. "I wouldn't mind if Tim suddenly disappeared. He found out about Mark and won't stop teasing me. If he falls in a hole, I'll be the first to start shoveling! Now tell me, why did you name these beavers Bobby and Jean? Are you planning to keep them? Please tell me you're not."

I responded, "No, we aren't keeping them as pets. We don't know if they're males or females, so we gave them names suitable for either sex."

"Gee, Laurel, let's turn one over and look." Joann reached down and grabbed a beaver, gently rolling it over. Looking at its belly, she pointed, "See, there's no equipment poking out, so this one's a female." Checking out the second beaver, she added, "Same here. There, Laurel, you have two females. Pick better names like Kathy and Kimberly. Now, I've solved your problem. Can we work on mine?"

"Joann, Iris says beaver genitalia are internal. They're not visible, so both could be male. Besides, finding out their sex isn't my problem. My problem is watching them while they're outside. Are you going to help or not?" I persisted.

Joann thought a moment. "I've got an idea. Have the Murdocks left for Arizona?" she asked. I nodded affirmatively. "Then let's go see if their pool's covered. If it's full, these guys can swim while we discuss my predicament."

Oren and Eunice Murdock were retired teachers who lived across the street. Our families often celebrated holidays together, as well as many outdoor gatherings. The Murdocks loved to garden and work on their home. They had won the Sutter's Best Landscaped Home award several times.

Oren and Eunice had a patio surrounding their pool. A waterslide curved between groves of aspen trees before dropping into the pool. They had left for their Scottsdale home, and they rarely returned before April. Surely, they wouldn't mind the beavers using the pool.

We gathered the kits and headed across the street. The pool was full and not yet covered. We sat on the patio and let the beavers swim. Their hyperactive behavior reminded me of clowns on amphetamines, but I guessed it was normal beaver behavior. While they played, Joann and I discussed her difficulties with Mark.

"OK, Joann, here's my advice. Are you eating with Mark before the dance?" I asked. She confirmed that his mother was preparing prime rib. "Then tell him what you told me. Make it clear you didn't understand that his scene with Utannah was a joke. Tell him you were inappropriate and apologize for giving the wrong impression. Let Mark know that you like him but you won't go steady or anything else. It's likely nothing will happen at his house. If Mark gets fresh later on, there's no choice but to slap him a good one. How's that idea?" I inquired.

"Gee, Laurel, that's harsh. He's fun to be with, and beating him silly might overdo it."

"I read *Ann Landers* every day. She says men can be aggressive when it comes to love. Sometimes, they're like an octopus feeling you out. You have to be firm," I reiterated. "Have you discussed this with your parents?" I asked.

"Are you kidding? If I told them, Mom would ground me for a week and Dad would get his shotgun and start hunting Mark. Considering the ways to handle it, that's worth avoiding. Now, if my date was Brett Moore, I'd play along. Some men are worth the risk.

"Not to change the subject, but I heard next week they're releasing Brett Moore from the hospital. Apparently, he suffered severe brain damage and has to undergo intense outpatient therapy. The bleeding around the brain was similar to a stroke. He's unable to walk and can't speak. It looks like Sutter's lost their best quarterback and a great guy."

I started to reply, "Considering his collision, he's lucky to . . ." Just then we heard a rustling, followed by a loud crack. My mouth stood open as an aspen tree toppled into the pool. "God, Joann, I hope the beavers are OK!" I cried. "Strip off your clothes so we can rescue them!" I'd already undressed and was preparing to dive in when a hand grabbed my shoulder.

"Laurel, are you crazy? The beavers aren't in the pool. They're in the new aspen grove." Another tree toppled as she spoke. As I ran half naked into the trees, Joann sported a wicked smile and I could see her smirk when she said, "It's a guess, mind you, but I think Bobby and Jean are recovering rapidly."

"Joann!" I hollered. "Get in here before there's firewood for the entire neighborhood."

She ran over and joined me. Bobby and Jean sat in the middle of the grove chewing a divot into the third tree. Only halfway through, they seemed forlorn when we interrupted their fun.

I sighed, "Well, Joann, got any other ideas? The Murdocks planted these trees a month ago. There'll be hell to pay if someone notices and calls Scottsdale," I predicted.

"You're right," Joann agreed. "No one's going to notice. Listen to this," she offered. As we returned to the house with two worn-out beavers, she filled me in on how we could replace the trees with a visit to the nursery. We'd take Iris's wagon and bring the replacement aspens home. As we reached the garage, I remembered Iris had used the wagon to transport pies to the bar mitzvah. But glancing at the sequoia, I realized a wagon would never hold three trees anyway. In that moment, I understood for the first time the phrase "Desperate times call for desperate measures." A decision was needed, so I made it.

"Come on, Joann, we're taking Mom's car. Since you're taller, you're driving," I said, with conviction. Stalling for time to reconsider my decision, I searched Iris's hiding places and scrounged $40. We felt nervous, so I suggested we try two shots of bourbon. It always worked for Mom.

Whiskey bolstered Joann's courage, and soon she sat behind the wheel. The nursery was five miles outside Sutter and normally a quick trip. Unfortunately, three minutes later, we stopped at a red light, and while we waited, officer Amos Putney pulled his squad car into the right turn lane, sitting parallel to me.

Deputy Putney was Sutter's assistant police chief. Power in the hands of idiots never bodes well. Saying Amos was an idiot gave him far too much credit. If his uncle wasn't the mayor, Amos wouldn't have a city job. He dispensed tickets for ridiculous reasons, including dirty windshields and improperly attached license plates. Drinking and driving while under the influence might get us strip-searched and jailed—which translated into being several years late for the dance.

Remaining in his car, Amos motioned for me to roll down my window. Looking at Joann, I asked, "What should we say if he asks for your driver's license?"

Continuing to look straight ahead, she replied, "We've been drinking, so tell him we left it at the liquor store."

Rolling down the window, a vision of Mom returning from China filled my mind. Not believing Joann's last comment, I smiled at Officer

Putney while whispering through my teeth, saying, "God, Joann! You're adding to our jail time? If Mom flies home to defend us, the death penalty is our best choice." Winking at Officer Putney, I asked, "Good morning, officer, what can we do for Sutter's brightest and most handsome policeman?"

Beginning to smile, Amos said, "You ladies know your rear license plate holder came loose, partially covering the number 8? Makes it look like a 3. Oregon law CLV–189.6, "Obstructing a License Plate," requires a $35 fine. I'm going to write you a ticket."

Thinking fast, I responded, "Officer, before you write us a ticket, could you tell me your availability to speak at the school safety committee? Joann and I are in charge this year, and we've thought about asking Sutter's celebrated crime solver to give the speech. We understand, of course, if your attention to duty doesn't allow time to share your expert knowledge. I shouldn't say this, but my mother, Judge Elizabeth Conner, sits on the Oregon Law Officer of the Year committee. On paper, you're one of three finalists, but unless some miscarriage of justice occurs, the award's all yours."

Digging the hole of deception deeper into the bullshit bog, I asked Amos if I could touch his strong hands. Joann grimaced as Officer Putney considered our invitation. He held out his hand, and I massaged his fingers as he inflated his chest, displaying a new-found pride.

A sense of fairness found its way into Officer Putney's heart. "Ladies, my original decision was too harsh. Oregon's Law Officer of the Year should fairly enforce laws. When you get home, fix the license plate holder and all's well. Call the station at least three weeks before you want me to speak and please put in a good word with your mother." As I rolled up the window, we heard, "Have a great day."

Joann pointed out, "Laurel, there is no school safety assembly, and the Oregon Law Officer of the Year seems questionable. That moron will wait until hell freezes over to receive a phone call and letter from Judge Conner. When nothing arrives, we'll be the focus of a manhunt."

"Look, Joann. There is a judge named Elizabeth Conner. She's a district court judge in Portland. Mom says there isn't a worse judge. If Amos doesn't win, what's he going to do—call Judge Conner and complain? As for the other part, I'll tell Amos I made a mistake. I'll say Principal Martin booked a different speaker without our knowledge and we'd like Amos to speak next year and proudly display his award."

"Fine, Laurel, but don't call me when Amos pulls up and hauls you away."

Satisfied we'd faced the worst challenge that two underage, slightly intoxicated teenagers could face, we continued our trip, leaving the worst behind us—or so it seemed.

Driving the gravel road to the nursery, we spotted a car driving toward us. The road ran through the forest, with pines lining both sides. As the distance between our cars quickly closed, it was clear that the large blue sedan was speeding. Wisely, Joann pulled over, offering plenty of room to pass, and we expected the road would shortly be ours. But a quarter mile ahead, five deer meandered onto the road, just in front of the approaching car. Caught off guard, the driver swerved—but momentum prevailed. Four of the deer perished, and then the car hit a massive tree head-on. The fifth deer continued across the road, unscathed.

Intuition took over. Forgotten were the penalties we would receive in several hours. Scared witless, we knew this person needed help. Joann hit the accelerator, and we covered the ground in record time. Avoiding the dead animals, Joann parked the car thirty feet from the wreck.

The blue sedan sat mangled around a tree, with flames shooting from under the hood. The fire was two feet from the driver, who sat slumped over the wheel. I ran over and tried opening the driver's door, but the twisted car frame prevented it from budging. Joann saw my problem and retrieved a tire iron, which we wedged between the door and the frame. Both of us tried to pry the door open, without success. The other three doors offered even less hope.

"Laurel, time's running out. Any great ideas?" Joann asked.

"The back windshield's broken. Help me knock it out." We took the tire iron, and in moments, the window was gone. "Come on, Joann!" I grabbed her hand. "Let's pull him out." I knew my best friend trusted me. Despite life-threatening risks, we didn't hesitate. We climbed onto the car's trunk and through the broken window into the backseat. Since I was smaller, I climbed up front to survey the damage and evaluate the situation. The heat made me sweat as the fire inched closer.

The man looked familiar, but I couldn't place him. There was a three-inch cut above his right eye, and blood poured from his nose. He started to stir, but there wasn't time to wait. "Joann, we need to tilt the seat and pull him out the rear window."

"My God, Laurel, have you looked at him? He's six feet tall and must be at least 220. Together, you and I don't weigh that much. I'm all for saving him, but that's pushing it."

I hollered back, "No, Joann, that's pulling it! We need to pull him, not lift him. If we can get him onto the trunk, we'll slide him to the ground. See if you can recline the driver's seat while I slow down the bleeding."

I pressed a glove against the cut, then tied it with a handkerchief from the glove compartment. Although my pressure bandage looked like an Indian headdress turned backward, it stemmed the bleeding. As I looked out the front window, the flames were rising higher and were within a foot of the windshield. Accidentally touching the steering wheel, my hand recoiled from the hot steering column. This guy was coming with me, or we'd die in the effort. I could not let a man succumb to the inferno to save my own life.

Joann managed to lower the backrest partway. I then pushed the man into a reclining position before crawling into the backseat. Dripping sweat, I looked at Joann and said, "The fire's spreading through the front windshield. You grab him under the right shoulder. I'll grab under the left. Pull like hell, because there's no time for a second chance. If we're unsuccessful, get out and leave me with him."

"Then we'd better make this work. I'm not leaving you here with Norman Dutton. I'm afraid you'll finish him off."

Come on! Was Joann kidding? I looked at the face of this man. Through the disheveled hair and caking blood, I recognized the guy who had threatened to expel me from school. His identity didn't matter. I'd never forgive myself if I left him to die. We grabbed his shoulders, and counting to three, Joann and I played tug-of-war with the grim reaper.

At first, he wouldn't budge. But by pushing our feet against the seat and pulling with all our might, Dr. Dutton soon rested on top of us in the backseat.

"Let's push him through the back window and get out of this oven," I ordered. The fire engulfed the front seat as we pushed Norman Dutton's body onto the car trunk. We crawled over him, took several deep breaths, and decided to move him away from the car.

I would like to say we carefully lowered Dr. Dutton onto the ground. However, the word *dropped* offers a better description. Every ounce of our physical and emotional energy was gone. We pulled the dentist toward Mom's car, resting as we went.

By now, the car was consumed in twenty-foot flames, and the close-by trees looked to be at risk. As we tried placing him in our car, a vehicle coming from the nursery pulled over to help. The man said he was Gary Sullivan, the owner of the nursery. We told him what had happened and said we were taking Dr. Dutton to the hospital. Mr. Sullivan wondered why we were driving to begin with—he obviously knew neither of us owned a driver's license. I explained to him why we needed to replace the neighbors' new trees.

"Ladies," he said, "you've done a remarkable job. It's clear you need to buy those trees and take the side roads home. This man needs a hospital, so I'll take him to town and bring back the fire department. That'll take twenty minutes. Get to the nursery and present my business card. Ask for the trees you need, and they'll load them. I suggest you scurry home because when the police and fire department arrive, they'll have lots of questions, if you get my drift. Help me load this man in the truck bed, then go! And remember, don't dillydally!"

We got Mr. Sullivan's drift. Placing Dr. Dutton next to fifty-pound bags of manure left me feeling satisfied and fulfilled. We tied him down so he wouldn't fall out, then got in the car and drove to the nursery.

Mr. Sullivan's business card brought us instant respect and three free Aspen trees. In fifteen minutes, the trees stuck out the trunk and we were driving past the still burning sedan. Thirty seconds later, a thunderous explosion rocked our car as the fire ignited the gas tank of the sedan. Black smoke billowed upward from the forest floor. As we reached town, fire and police vehicles raced past us toward the fire.

I was never so thankful to reach home. The fact that we weren't in jail, on fire, or recovering in the hospital was a minor miracle. I had no plans to tempt fate by saying, "Well, the day can only get better." I didn't want a volcano erupting under the house.

An hour later, three smaller trees stood in the Murdocks' aspen grove, and we had firewood for winter. "Laurel, the Murdocks will think something's odd. They left with seven trees towering over twenty feet. When they return, three of them will be shorter than fifteen feet."

"Well, Joann, the trees will be taller when they return. By spring, there shouldn't be much of a lag," I said optimistically.

We returned to my house to make soup and sandwiches. Despite Joann's reservations about Mark, it was exciting to have dates for our first formal dance.

CHAPTER 21

A Handsome Date Falls Out of His Chair

During the seventies, a formal dance was a rite of passage for teenage girls. At the time, the events of the seventies seemed radical, but they were tame compared with today. Girls seldom got their ears pierced or shaved their legs before ninth grade. Girls wore skirts at school, except for Fridays or days the meteorologist expected temperatures below twenty. Tattoo parlors admitted no one under eighteen. And makeup was regulated like nuclear weapons. Handling it required clearance from the highest authority: Mom.

Even though in Sutter, young adults could buy liquor "for their parents," makeup represented colored carnality, turning young women into wanton hussies. Teenage girls visiting the cosmetics department at F.W. Woolworth knew their parents would receive a call confirming they could buy the makeup. Mothers routinely supervised their daughters' facial applications, lest they start looking like Tammy Faye Bakker. But Joann and I already had pierced ears and were awaiting the premiere of shaving legs and wearing makeup.

The homecoming game would be starting soon, but more dance instruction before tonight's big event couldn't hurt. Ready to eat lunch, we sat down to watch *American Bandstand.* Successful dancing entailed knowing what new moves came from "the groove." *Bandstand* defined the groove. Considered the music bible of a generation, the show made artists stars and songs household hits.

Even my elderly grandparents in Wyoming watched it. I don't know why Gram and Pop enjoyed the show. In their courting days, they'd attended barn dances on Saturday nights. Whether it was the daring of the dance moves or the fact that it was reminiscent of younger years, *Bandstand* provided them with endless fascination. Pop would shake his head and say to Gram, "Mother, can you believe how they dance? They flip and flop like there's a bee up their ass. I'd love seeing an old-fashioned barnyard dance."

After Gram adjusted her hearing aid, she'd respond, "Now, Clark, if you remember, the reason we had barn dances is because the city outlawed dancing within the town limits. Our songs were considered 'the music of sin.' We never heard them broadcast over Cody's radio. Look how far these young people have come."

Sure enough, there we sat watching Al Green singing his two hits "Let's Stay Together" and "Tired of Being Alone." When the song ended, Dick Clark always asked, "What did you think about the music?" Although still quoted today, I never heard dancers say, "It has a good beat and you can dance to it." Teenagers weren't stupid. If the song didn't have a good beat and you couldn't dance to it, it wasn't on *Bandstand*. This was the reason Beethoven's Fifth never played on such a show.

The teens Dick Clark talked with knew every fact about the singers and their music. It was likely that writers scripted the questions to promote the music and performers. Had Dick asked anyone in my class, they wouldn't know who sang the song, let alone the song's title. I marveled at how well the young people danced, demonstrating such cool moves. If they weren't professional dancers with choreographed steps, I was missing something. All this aside, Joann and I watched them closely so we could re-create their steps.

When the show ended, it was one o'clock. The game started at one thirty. Denny would be here in four hours, and I needed time to get ready. If the game dragged on, I was leaving early. This afternoon, Sutter was playing Tigard, who hadn't won a game all year. Unlike the previous week, no trees fell on the field, and nothing unexpected occurred. The fans showed little enthusiasm. Perhaps after last week's game, they expected a more exciting performance. The crowd left early, as Sutter won 37 to 7.

When the game ended, my motivation to hurry home was at an all-time high. When I reached the house, Iris was still gone. She showed up twenty minutes later carrying three bags of groceries. Heading into the kitchen, she peered into the homemade beaver den and said, "I ran into Joann as I walked home from the store. She told me about all the troubles with Bobby and Jean."

I couldn't believe Joann had ratted us out. Clearly, she knew the consequences!

Iris went on, "I stressed to Joann that no one's ever sure with beavers. It's better to separate them before you're overrun and they chew down the entire forest."

I tried to find a fast path out of this mess, but for the first time today, nothing feasible came to mind. "Well, Iris, the intent was good, but without attention, trees quickly start to topple."

Iris gave me a strange look and then commented, "I suppose you're right, dear, but I was talking about finding out the sex of a beaver. Joann told me she rolled one of the critters over and still couldn't tell. Since beavers mate for life, before you can blink twice, there's a large extended family gnawing on your trees. Look at the Murdock home across the way. Can you imagine what damage five or six of these fellows could do to those new trees? In a few weeks, if they're still recovering, we'll separate Bobby and Jean. The last problem we need is a new batch of beavers!"

I offered to help Iris any way I could. She came over and hugged me.

"Laurel, this occasion is special, but it isn't a lifelong commitment. Tonight begins the first of many wonderful dates, but it's not a marriage proposal. Go and have fun learning the lessons only a man can teach. The words of wisdom I've passed on can't adequately replace a gentleman's unequaled touch upon the woman of his dreams. Get upstairs and bring Denny's dream to life."

I went upstairs and took a long, leisurely bath. After twenty minutes, I lazily emerged from the tub and dried off. Looking in the mirror, for the first time I sensed I had sex appeal. Instinctively, I knew: nature had crafted quality. At fourteen, age had also brought me a gift. Before time wilted my gifts, I hoped for the opportunity to make myself appealing to a man. Today, I'd give it my first try.

Sitting down in front of the mirror, I carefully applied my eyeliner, lipstick, and mascara. Then I called down to Iris, asking her to examine my beauty work. Within sixty seconds she had inspected me, making sure my makeup didn't make me resemble a clown. Then she fixed my hair.

"Dear, let's try the style you wanted," she said. "I think I can come close. You've got beautiful hair, but I'm not French like your new friend. Fashion has never been one of my strong points."

Within moments, my shoulder-length hair lay tightly rolled in a vertical scepter resting along the back of my head. The arrangement was as beautiful as Utannah's fashion demonstration in the dress shop had been. I finished getting dressed. The results turned out better than I expected. I hoped Denny would think the same.

I didn't hear the doorbell ring. Still upstairs primping, I turned and saw Denny. His eyes were scanning me from head to heels. Taking a deep breath, Denny proclaimed, "Laurel, you look incredible—a Renaissance masterpiece come to life. You are the hottest chick I've ever seen."

I was still shocked by the fact that Denny was standing outside my door, but his flattery was like music to my ears. "Thank you, Denny. I hoped you'd like it. I planned on giving you a quick fashion show when you came through the front door, but you'll have to see it here." I turned around, wiggling my butt several times. Swallowing hard, he released his inner heat by pulling the collar away from his neck.

Denny grabbed me by the arm. "Laurel, Iris is waiting. You have to see the downstairs. I've never been here, but I'm betting it doesn't normally look like it does now. Both of you probably worked the entire day."

We walked arm in arm out of Mom's room. Candles sat on the wall shelves along the stairs, lighting our path. Reaching the third-to-last step, a voice said, "Stop! Denny, please put your arm around Laurel's waist, and both of you smile." We did as the voice asked. Three consecutive flashes occurred before the voice continued, "OK, come on down, you two."

My eyes focused on the dining room table. Three blue candles illuminated two blue-and-yellow placemats, each candle radiating a romantic glow. Iris seated us at right angles to each other, our faces lit only by candlelight.

Denny said, "This is great. Something smells wonderful. Do you know what she's cooking?" Then he gave me an odd look, almost saying something but then deciding against it. "Here, Laurel, I got you a gift. I hope you like it."

He handed me the small package, which I carefully unwrapped. Inside sat a nine-inch shallow square blue box. I lifted the top, finding a gold braided necklace. It was a half-inch wide and sixteen inches long. I had never bought jewelry except for dime-store earrings. This was the prettiest costume jewelry I'd ever seen. I loved it and was overcome by Denny's generosity.

"Denny, this is beautiful. I love it. I'm certain you spent a great deal. It's truly special, just like you." He stood up, pulled down my scarf, and carefully placed the necklace around my neck.

Then Denny reached under the table and pulled out a dozen red roses. I didn't know what to say, and I started crying. "Denny, these roses are, are real, aren't they?" He nodded yes. I floundered, saying, "Let me get a vase. I'll be right back." I slid open the door to the kitchen, where Iris stood, surrounded by food and cookware

"Laurel, dear, what brings you into the kitchen? Go out and entertain Denny. The first course will be ready soon."

"Iris," I replied, "he just gave me roses. I didn't buy him anything. He laid his heart out and I'm about to run over it."

Iris responded, "Dear, you're feeding him dinner and going out with him. That's a great start. Denny's goal is close contact, as well as a kiss or two. Give him those, and by the end of the night, he'll consider his money well spent. Head back to the dining room and I'll bring the roses in a few minutes."

Iris soon brought us two shrimp cocktails. Denny's eyes lit up. "Wow, Mrs. Wimple, those look marvelous."

"Denny, I prefer you to call me Iris. I feel old when people call me Mrs. Wimple. Can you do that?"

"Oh yes, Mrs. Wimp—I mean Iris—I can."

As Denny and I finished the shrimp cocktail, Iris presented a salad with lettuce, bacon, and a tomato wedge. Denny stopped long enough to say, "Laurel, Iris cooks as good a meal as any professional chef. This food is outstanding."

Within minutes, Iris walked in holding the entrees. She carried garnished plates with filet mignon steaks, barbecued asparagus, and baked potatoes. Finally, she returned with the beautifully arranged roses, accented by baby's breath. She then went back to the kitchen.

Denny ravaged his steak, reminding me of a cheetah dining on water buffalo. Two-way conversation ended. I talked about my quarrels with the Duttons while Denny kept nodding his head. I didn't mind. I didn't expect him to solve my troubles, just listen. Once, surfacing for air, he said, "Laurel, can you please pass the hollandaise sauce?" But that was all.

Twenty minutes later, Iris slid open the kitchen door and asked, "How does everything taste, you two?" Noticing Denny's plate, she let out an audible gasp. "Oh, my dear boy, you still look famished. Give me your plate and I'll be right back." She quickly returned, presenting Denny with a second steak and potato. He smiled from ear to ear.

"Laurel, I can say without reservation that's the finest meal I've ever enjoyed! I believe I'll visit you and Iris quite a bit."

I knew Denny and Iris connected with each other. The perfect carnivore had found the perfect cook. From the kitchen, Iris said, "I heard that wonderful comment. Come in here and bring your glasses. I made a dessert I think you'll both enjoy."

In a few minutes, bowls of chocolate mousse topped with whipped cream and chocolate shavings graced our palates. Iris joined us. "I need to see if my mousse turned out OK."

Denny's eyes lit up as he polished off his dessert. "Iris, I've had chocolate mousse before, but none tasted this good."

Iris stood up, grabbing Denny a second dessert—this time a crème brûlée—and saying, "My dear boy, I'm touched you're enjoying my meal. My cooking defines simplicity itself. I cook everything from scratch, using the freshest ingredients available. I limit salt, instead adding various spices to enrich the flavor. Finally, I use alcohol in many of my dishes. I made your mousse using chocolate liqueur and cinnamon. There's no added sugar."

I knew Denny was absorbing every word. He was so absorbed in Iris's lectures on cooking, he lost track of time.

"Denny, it's quarter to eight. I think we should get ready to leave. It's a long walk, and I can't rush since I'm wearing heels."

"Gosh, Laurel, Iris was just giving a good talk about how cooking attracts wom . . . , I, um, mean admirers. I was hoping to learn a little bit more. Like she said, if I'm ever going to fix you a baloney sandwich, it's best I know what I'm doing."

I rolled my eyes and grabbed him by the arm, dragging him into the living room. We put on jackets as Iris came out to say good-bye.

Iris kissed us both on the cheek and said, "Denny, visit any time you wish. Even if Laurel isn't home, we can talk more about cooking. I don't plan to wait up, so call if you need something. You kids have a wonderful time. I'm eager to hear the details."

CHAPTER 22

Autumn's Don Lands the Dance of the Decade

Leaving the house a little after eight, Denny and I didn't arrive at the dance until nine fifteen. As I recall, we stopped to kiss on every block.

When we appeared, most of our class was already crowding the dance floor. Through bake sales and craft fairs, the PTA had raised enough money to hire a live band. Cliff Cleft and the Compositions stood onstage, ready to start their next tune.

As we took in the spectacle, I noticed Denny seemed hesitant to move forward. Then I remembered his fear of crowds. He hadn't said our code word, *Cher*, but I wondered if we should go back outside.

"Denny, are you OK?" I asked.

He responded, "Yeah, I'm fine. I've never taken a girl to a dance before. When I think about dancing, it doesn't make much sense. Why do people enjoy it? After all those dance lessons when I was younger, I still don't get it. Does it make sense to you?"

Thinking a second, I answered, "Well, dancing provides an excuse to hold your partner close, smelling her hair and hearing her breathe. It's a way to imagine how spending a life together might be. If a couple can't tolerate a few minutes of dancing, spending a lifetime together is asking for trouble."

Denny grabbed my hand, drawing me onto the dance floor, "God, Laurel, you're right. What was I thinking?" Cliff had started singing "Long and Winding Road," and Denny pulled me close, slipping one arm around my waist and placing the other on my back. "Follow my lead," he whispered.

"Boy, you've come a long way since earlier this week," he said. "Either you've been practicing or you move instinctively to the cadence of the music. I'm amazed."

Denny lowered his head, lightly kissing me. I lay my head on his shoulder, and he firmly held me as Cliff played "How Can You Mend a Broken Heart?" We moved across the dance floor effortlessly, tuning out the world. I sensed the two of us blending together, and for the first time, I felt unity with a man. Serenity like this was rare, and I didn't want it to stop. Maybe this accounted for the attraction between men and women: a person couldn't be whole without a mate. I looked up. Denny had closed his eyes. His breath brushed my ear, warm and soft. His strong hands, and the scent of cologne, kept me close. Heaven was holding me.

I saw Joann and Mark dancing a few feet away. They were dancing two feet apart. How odd for a slow dance.

Cliff stopped singing and announced an intermission. I told Denny to take Mark to the refreshment table. I motioned to Joann, and we lagged behind. "Hey, Joann, how's it going? From what I saw, Mark wasn't causing any trouble. Is he behaving?"

"Laurel, you won't believe it. You know, I had dinner at Mark's house and he started to get frisky, so I laid down the rules like you said. I didn't realize his older sister Mary heard every word I said." Surprised, I clapped a hand over my open mouth.

Joann continued, "Mary came over and asked to privately speak with Mark. They went into the study but didn't completely close the door, so I snuck over and listened. She told Mark if he kept kissing me, I'd eventually get pregnant. Mary reminded him he was too young to be a father. For most guys, her message would have hit home, but not Mark—he said he'd love to be a father!

"After slapping him, she reminded Mark that becoming a dad meant quitting school, getting a job, and learning to change diapers. That didn't faze him, either. Finally, she told him he'd never have time to play sports. Now he won't touch me. He's afraid holding will get me pregnant. It's feast or famine. I'm not sure what to do."

Confused and a bit worried, I probed, "God, Joann, it's not true that kissing leads to pregnancy, is it? Denny and I made out walking to the dance and never used protection. I don't know what protection anyone uses. I think sex causes pregnancy. Your brother said blow jobs cause pregnancy. I know Denny and I haven't done those. What to believe is confusing. Based on these rumors, it seems there are three ways to get pregnant. Kissing and blow jobs can't be enough. Somehow, sex plays an important part. I think Mark's sister was saying that kissing *leads* to blow jobs and eventually sex."

"Good God, Laurel that sounds right. It makes sense and explains how passion progresses to pregnancy. Once a guy gets oral sex, passion rages out of control, and soon you're in the backseat humping. Nine months later, a baby named Chevy drives into your world. Yup, that's the secret parents never discuss. Laurel, you're brilliant, but how can I convince Mark kissing is OK?" she pleaded.

"Hold on, Joann. Slow down. Are you 100 percent sure couples can't jump from kissing directly to Chevy? A Chevy doesn't show up without intermediate sex, right?"

"God yes! Quit second-guessing. I guarantee pregnancy doesn't happen without petting, blowing, and intercourse. Here's a way to remember it: FBI for Feel, Blow, Intercourse. You're safe as long as Denny's hands don't wander and his pants stay zipped. Look at his trousers every few minutes. If nothing's hangin' out, you're fine. Now what should I do with Mark?"

We caught up with the guys at the refreshment table. Everyone looked astonished to see Mitch and Tanice together. I whispered my love advice to Joann and decided to ask how Mitch and Tanice got together.

"Mitch, Tanice, it's great to see you both—especially Mitch," I said. "I thought you worked on the ranch today, so I'm surprised you're here."

Mitch was ready to respond, but Tanice interjected, "Here's the deal. Yesterday during lunch I was sitting by Mitch when Craig Russell walked up and said we'd have to break our date 'cause his leg was sore. What a shitty excuse! I'm sure he'll show up with Twyla Stone. She's always given Craig the hots, and her date, Darrell Gaven, developed appendicitis. Sitting there disgusted, Mitch said he was planning on castrating bulls today. He asked if I wanted to come and help.

"Well, between Craig and my brothers, men have really been pissing me off. I thought, *God, I'd sure like to cut off some balls.* So I accepted. Laurel, I have to say, today's a memorable day. Mitch treats a girl with respect. Besides ball bustin', we rode horses, had a picnic, and milked cows. I had such a good time, I asked Mitch if he'd take me to the dance. We scrambled and made it," she explained.

Mitch looked up, nodded, and continued sampling every selection on the refreshment table. Tanice and Mitch seemed a perfect fit. Defining the phrase "What you see is what you get," Mitch worked hard, cared for people, and said little. Tanice was the opposite: forthright, outgoing, and quick to express her opinions. Mitch would treat her like a queen—as long as the queen didn't mind having a horse and branding iron for her throne and scepter. They looked promising.

We talked a few more minutes before the band looked ready to start. Then I noticed Utannah arriving. She'd found a date, although I didn't immediately recognize him. Dressed in a dazzling gold-sequined dress with matching shoes, she had added a blue and gold scarf to complement the arrangement. Utannah's appearance approached perfection. Her gorgeous hair rested at shoulder length, strikingly offset by gold triangular earrings inlaid with lapis. Heads turned when she and her unknown date began to dance.

Denny escorted me to the dance floor, saying, "Man, Utannah looks great. Girls from France have a great sense of fashion." Reflecting on his statement, he recovered, adding, "Of course, I'm with the best-looking girl in Sutter. That guy she's with sure looks familiar, but I've never seen him in school. Do you know him?" Denny asked.

"No. I've never seen him. Let's dance that direction and maybe I'll get a better idea," I answered. The band played "She's a Lady," made famous by Las Vegas legend Tom Jones. We jived around the dance floor and eventually closed in on Utannah and her date. Denny was right—the guy looked familiar, but the dim lighting made it impossible to distinguish his features.

When the song ended, Utannah invited us over. I envied her style and demeanor.

"Utannah, that's the most beautiful outfit I've ever seen," I said. "You have a great sense of fashion. Your date must know he's with the most beautiful girl in the world."

She spoke up, "Well, Laurel, ask him yourself. I doubt that's true, since he's dated many beautiful women. Let me introduce you. Laurel, Denny, this is my date, Don. Donny Osmond," she said nonchalantly.

Momentarily speechless, Denny and I stood in suspended animation while the young man reached out to shake our hands. Looking closer, this guy had to be Donny Osmond. Millions of questions ran through my mind. Topping the list was why Donny Osmond was at our homecoming dance. Following that, I wondered if he was Utannah's boyfriend. After all, at that time Donny was a teenager.

Thankfully, Denny overcame the silence, saying, "Welcome to Sutter, Donny. We're glad you could join us. You have the privilege of escorting one of many beautiful girls attending our junior high." Utannah and I both blushed, trying to look demure. When he wanted to, Denny could express elegant thoughts in beautiful words.

Donny responded, "You're so right. When Utannah invited me, one look told me to accept. My managers are negotiating for me to perform in France. I met Utannah when I came to look at contract revisions and pick up visas through her father's home office. A young woman who musters the courage to ask me for a date doesn't come along often. I'm thrilled to be here. Last night, I performed in Portland, and I signed the contract this morning. Attending a dance is a great way to spend the little spare time I have. Usually, I can't do what regular teenagers do. Tonight, the crowd hasn't mobbed me. I'm hoping it stays that way."

Denny replied, "Well, it will happen. Look at Laurel—she's already starstruck. When the other girls figure out who you are, they'll know they've hit the lottery. If I were you, I'd dance where it's dark. We'll bring you refreshments, if you want them."

Donny asked, "What about the formal picture? I'd like to have a photo with Utannah. She's cool, and I won't get back anytime soon. Her picture will be great to have on a concert tour."

Awakening from my trance, I remarked, "Here's an idea, if you think it's acceptable." The four of us gathered around as I outlined my plan. With a few changes, Donny agreed to my simple scheme, and Utannah liked it even better. I asked Denny to find our chaperones, Mr. Olson and Ms. Fiorantino. Within a few minutes, we introduced them to Donny. He told the teachers about the problem that would arise once the class discovered he was in the crowd.

Utannah suggested precautions to prevent an unruly crowd. Between tunes, Ms. Fiorantino talked with the band while Mr. Olson confirmed that our celebrity wanted to go along with the plan. Then Mr. Olson ushered Donny backstage, as the band announced it was taking another short break.

Utannah, Denny, and I headed back to the refreshment table. Cindy Summers sat on the table's edge with her friend and fellow seductress, Lillyann Parker. Here with their dates, Ralph and Rodney, each girl chose this moment to display their advanced sexual skills. Using her tongue, Cindy tied a cherry stem into a knot, while Lillyann sandwiched herself between Ralph and Rodney. Low-cut blouses added to their sultry display, instantly hooking Rodney and Ralph.

Trying to keep mentally challenged boys from making another huge mistake, I said, "Hey, guys, good to see you. It's great you crawled out of hiding to attend the dance. I thought someone would report you for last week's fireworks display. Cindy and Lillyann are looking hot tonight—they make every guy jealous. If you two go to jail, there's less competition for these babes, so I'm impressed you're here. If it were me, I'd still be laying low. Well, I hope all of you have a wonderful time. Oh, look, here comes Mr. Olson with a sheet of paper. He probably just realized you're here. He's probably comparing your faces to the Wanted posters."

Rodney turned to Ralph and said, "You know, Laurel has a good point. There's no use pressing our luck. I don't want to repeat ninth grade. I think we should ditch this dance."

"You're right," Ralph agreed. "Cindy and Lillyann are fun, but they're not worth getting expelled." Turning to the teenage tarts, Ralph said, "Ladies, excuse us. Rodney and I need to find the back exit. We'll make it up in the future, we promise." Mr. Olson continued toward us as the boys quickly disappeared.

Cindy and Lillyann looked pissed. "Thanks a lot, Laurel," Cindy said. "We find a couple of decent guys who really care, and now you've chased 'em off. You're clueless how hard it is to find men we like." What a loaded statement. These two harlots loved anything with a penis. Thankfully, I kept quiet. Cindy went on, "I guess we'll have to search for men who appreciate us for our intellect."

Denny started to say, "Well, you'll be looking a long . . ." But I poked him, and he went on, "I mean you're going to look a lot—yeah, that's it—a lot for the right guys. Most men want a girl for their looks. They rarely consider a woman's intelligence." Both Lillyann and Cindy preened as Denny spoke, his words bringing wide smiles to their faces.

Mr. Olson hovered behind me and said, "All right, we're ready to introduce Mr. Osmond, so prepare to get the girls in line." The band wandered back onstage, picking up their guitars. Mr. Olson warned, "Here we go."

Cliff announced, "Ladies and Gentlemen, tonight we have a surprise guest you all know. He's with his date and wishes to spend uninterrupted time with her. However, he's offered to sing his two hit songs, sign autographs, and dance with three lucky girls. Write your name on a slip of paper and place it in the box on the refreshment table. We'll draw three names after he performs. Once he's danced with the winners, he requests privacy to enjoy the evening. In other words, leave him alone."

The crowd awaited to see if Cliff would produce a genuine celebrity. In the past, Cliff's surprise was his younger brother impersonating Elvis. Finally, Cliff got to the point. "Without further ado, Cliff Cleft and the Compositions welcome Donny Osmond, performing his new hit, 'Go Away Little Girl.'"

Donny took the stage, bellowing, "I'm excited to attend Sutter Junior High's homecoming dance. Thank you for having me. I dedicate this song to Utannah Donnay, who invited me to escort her. Thank you, Utannah. You're the best."

The crowd went wild and started screaming. Utannah shined at her compliment. In just three days attending junior high, she had produced the school year's highlight—or so it seemed that evening. Girls shoved their way to the drawing box. With Mr. Olson yelling, an orderly line started forming. Paper slips and pens appeared, with girls folding the slips and leaving lipstick imprints on each side. Donny quieted the students when he started singing.

Denny invited me closer. Within seconds, we had the darkest area of the dance floor. Dancing a slow two-step, my head on Denny's chest, I heard his heartbeat increase as Donny sang "Go Away Little Girl." For the rest of the song's duration, our lips never left each other. Oozing passion from every pore, young lust entangled our souls. I felt completely treasured.

As the song ended, I continued holding Denny tight. Emotionally spent, every fiber of my being lay woven in a fabric of exquisite sensations. Whatever intimacy was, I knew I had just shared it with Denny. Speechless, we walked toward the chairs to rest a moment. Digesting these emotions would take time.

Denny went for punch while I stayed seated. Joann and Mark materialized beside me. Joann exclaimed, "Laurel, how can you just sit? That's Donny Osmond up there. How did Utannah get him to accept her invitation? I want to know her secrets. As soon as they work out the chord structure, he's singing one more tune." Donny had the band on track and was ready to start. Joann surprised us, saying, "I'll dance with Denny; you take Mark!"

Looking rejected, Mark reluctantly escorted me onto the dance floor. Donny started singing his second big hit, "Puppy Love." Basking in the glow of my last dance, I felt no chemistry with Mark. But before the dance ended, we would share an intimate bond.

Holding me near, Mark shared, "Laurel, Joann and I aren't hitting it off tonight. Do you know what's going on? Something's changed since yesterday. Help me out, would ya?"

"Mark," I replied, "yesterday, Joann believed you'd cancel your date and bring Utannah. That's why she started swaying you with her seductive behavior. Obviously, her conduct succeeded because you returned her advances. But Joann didn't realize the passion she'd aroused. When she realized her error, she backed off—as it turns out, too far off. She overheard the discussion between you and your sister. Now she wants you to kiss her, but thinks you're afraid for fear of getting her pregnant. That's the story, in a nutshell."

"What I should do, Laurel? I can't tell you how much I love kissing her. But right now, I don't want any babies."

Clearly, Mark wasn't grasping the birds and the bees. I knew his sister had tried explaining the facts, but somehow they still eluded him. Moments ago, I wasn't sure myself. Thinking it might help to pass on my recent unconfirmed knowledge, I explained, "Look, Mark, here's the deal. I have it on good authority a woman can't get pregnant unless you feel her out, get a blow job, and end up having sex. All three are necessary or there's no chance of a baby," I pontificated. "In summary, kissing alone won't do it. So when you round up Joann, pucker up and go for it, cowboy."

Mark seemed as if a load had lifted from his shoulders. He looked me in the eye and said, "Laurel, you're the best. Now I get why Denny likes you. You're easy to talk to and know lots of stuff. Can I ask about something I've always pretended to know, but honestly don't."

Continuing our cheek-to-cheek discussion, I responded, "What's that?"

"Well," he continued, "what does it mean to 'feel a girl out'? I mean, you and I are holding each other and dancing. Is this feeling you out?" he whispered, seriously.

No brilliant words arrived. In fact, it took several seconds before I uttered a coherent reply. "Well, Mark, in a way, we're feeling each other out." I took Mark's hand from around my waist and pressed it on my right breast. "Now, squeeze," I commanded. Pointing at my breasts, I clarified, "When you grope these or other private parts of a girl's anatomy, that's 'feeling her out.'"

As he caressed my bosom, I noticed his gleam and a half-moon smile.

Then it dawned on me: I was relighting the fire Joann had worked so hard to quench. What an incredibly stupid move.

I was mentally searching for a way out of this blunder when Mark interrupted my concentration by saying, "Gee, Laurel, now it's becoming clear. One more question: can you show me a blow job? I don't understand it—or anything else involved with sex." Normally, this question deserved a slap, but since I sensed Mark was sincere, he kept his teeth.

He went on, "We go to church every Sunday. My parents never discuss sex, and the guys in school don't know what they're talking about. You seem to have the answers, and I'm not embarrassed talking to you. Joann will think I'm clueless if the time comes and I don't know the right moves. Last Monday, I asked Joann to the dance. When she accepted, I kissed a girl for the first time. I only knew what to do because I recalled the kissing scene from *Romeo and Juliet*. Otherwise, I'd have been lost."

He paused. "Damn, Laurel, I'm sorry about my cussing. Do you get what I'm tryin' to say? Learning relationship skills from a movie brings up more questions than answers. I'm too young to take the bus to Portland to see *Beyond the Valley of the Dolls.* I hear nothing's left to answer after seeing that."

Hmmm, maybe Denny and I needed to go on a field trip to Portland.

As we danced, I offered more wisdom. "Mark, to be honest, I'm no expert on love. The guys probably give better advice. Isn't there someone else you'd feel better discussing this with?"

He responded, "Laurel, we're here now. You hold the big advantage of being a girl. You know the secret answers about what makes a lady happy. Every man thinks women want a hunk handing out diamonds. Somehow, I imagine there's more to it. I'm in the dark. Tell me the truth, so I'm not the last guy who knows," he begged.

Relenting, I sighed. "OK, here's how someone explained a blow job to me." I softly whispered what I knew about oral sex as a prelude to intercourse. Then—from where, I'll never know—the key to a woman's happiness sprang from the tip of my tongue. Pleasing a woman isn't a mystery, I told him—a man just has to ask what makes her happy, then listen to the answer.

When I finished, Mark remained silent. His expression signaled that the last brick was laid and the foundation finished. Keeping me close, he murmured, "Thank you, Laurel."

"Puppy Love" faded into history, but I had just had my first explicit conversation about sex with a man. Intimate honesty didn't feel weird or funny. Until then, I couldn't remember a time when discussing body functions hadn't ended with giggling. Mark and I instantly became friends because we shared that special moment.

As the music stopped, he kissed me on the cheek and said with new-found energy, "I hope Joann's ready, because I plan to give her a hot time." Joann couldn't lose if Mark heeded my suggestion.

I gave him a wink, offering, "Give Joann all the heat she can take, but keep your pants zipped." He smiled and grabbed Joann, as she and Denny finished their dance. The crowd's applause was deafening as Donny took his final bow.

Cliff spoke into the microphone, "OK, troops, Ms. Fiorantino drew three names. We'll play three tunes and Donny will dance with each girl in the order drawn. Once the dances end, he'll sign autographs for fifteen minutes. OK, here we go. Let's see who wins the chance of a lifetime." Mr. Olson carried the winning names to the stage. Cliff gazed through his thick glasses and said, "Our first lucky lady is Lillyann Parker. Lillyann, come on over and meet Donny."

From the back of the crowd, Lillyann raced forward, rivaling Bob Hayes for the record in the hundred-yard dash. She reached Donny and smothered him with multiple kisses. I felt sorry for the famous young man. From his perspective, the price of fame must, at times, have seemed expensive—and Lillyann was one of those times. Their dance lasted three minutes. When they finished, Donny looked relieved.

Asking for a washcloth to remove the lipstick, he signaled the band to announce the second winner. Cliff called out Leslie Collier. Leslie was a quiet girl who never quite fit into the class. I suspected that, like Denny, Leslie suffered from fear of public places. But Ms. Fiorantino escorted her to meet Donny, and even though she completed the dance, she couldn't wait to get off the dance floor.

The final girl chosen to dance with Donny was Susan Small. She confidently walked up to Cliff and took the microphone. Without hesitation, she said, "I'm thrilled about this opportunity, but there's a girl here who's Donny's biggest fan. I'm passing my dance to Autumn Whitney. Come take my place, Autumn."

Susan whispered into Donny's ear as Autumn limped through the crowd to reach the stage. Autumn was a beautiful girl with short blond hair and freckles. Tonight she wore a white dress covered in red polka dots. Bound in pigtails, her hair shone like white silk. Male heads turned as she made her way through the audience. For the first time, boys noticed her for her beauty, not her handicap.

Autumn had cerebral palsy. The left half of her body had less strength than the right. In the seventies, special education classes weren't common, and Autumn attended the same classes required for every student. Our class did their best to shield Autumn from harassment, but she still endured endless teasing. Her IQ was normal, but her speech was difficult to understand.

Autumn loved Donny Osmond and his brothers. Multiple fan photos lined her locker, and the Osmond family's biography was the topic of her eighth-grade English term paper. For Autumn, attending this dance was a miracle. Her mother was a single parent, working three jobs to support five children. Her entire family lived in a trailer outside the city. Spare time to transport the kids was rare, and while Autumn's siblings rode bikes, Autumn could not.

As she approached Donny, her strength faded. Sensing her problem, Donny strode toward her, holding out his arms. Quiet came over the crowd; students wondered if they should laugh or cry, as they prepared to witness an awkward dance. There wasn't long to wait; the classic Bee Gees hit "Lonely Days" began its syncopated rhythmic percussion.

Alone on the dance floor—focused, as if savoring the last moments of life—Donny and Autumn opened their dance. Facing each other, they stomped their right feet in perfect cadence with the drums. The physical limitations Autumn suffered when walking disappeared as she started to dance. Without effort, they perfectly timed their footwork to present the image of a professionally choreographed performance. Flawless dynamic moves captured love's magic in the art of the dance.

Their electric performance was unequaled. When they finished four minutes of a syncopated tour de force, students, still stunned, remained quiet. Emotions Autumn could never express through words had surfaced in a way no one had anticipated. Even Donny looked surprised.

He invited Autumn to sit for a formal photo. The photographer took time creating the perfect pose. Donny sat in a chair with Autumn standing slightly to the side and behind him. Prior to snapping the photo, Autumn improvised. She completely moved to Donny's right, placing the side of her body toward the camera. Now in profile, she bent her waist in a precise right angle and touched the tip of her tongue to Donny's ear.

This impromptu tease produced a charismatic smile from both of them. The photo captured the innocent playfulness of two young people who could rarely be themselves. (Donny later signed a copy and sent it to Autumn.) Any remaining doubts I had about the existence of God tumbled away because Susan Small's selfless act of humility had given Autumn the opportunity to excel.

After the photo session, Donny took Autumn to the refreshments table. Utannah sat on one side of Donny and Autumn on the other. He autographed a wallet photo and wrote a special message on Autumn's dance program, thanking her for an outstanding dance and being his biggest fan. He added:

Autumn, you're more precious and priceless than the Hope Diamond. Love, Donny Osmond

Donny signed more autographs, then took Utannah onto the dance floor, where thankfully, the rest of the students left them alone for the remainder of the evening.

Everyone believed Donny never knew how much he had touched Autumn. But everyone was wrong. Within a month, attempting to copy her brothers and sisters, Autumn would try riding a bike. She was hit by a car and suffered massive internal injuries. She died en route to the hospital, clutching Donny's wallet photo to her chest. She was buried holding the photo over her heart.

Hearing of her death, Donny sent a second photo, which arrived in time for the funeral. This picture and Donny's message inscribed on Autumn's dance program sit in the trophy case at Sutter Junior High, paying homage to a special girl, from a special man.

Denny and I continued enjoying the dance until eleven thirty. The students started thinning out, so we walked over to French's Fry. Denny's stomach was again holding his brain hostage. Many kids attending the dance had already found seats. Since I hadn't talked to Joann after dancing with Mark, I hoped they'd join us to update critical gossip!

It was approaching midnight when Joann and Mark arrived with Jill Kennedy and her date. Sitting next to Joann, I quietly asked if she and Mark had found some common ground. Curiously, she probed, "I'd like to know just what you told him. Your information changed his game.

Mark started kissing me more and strangely enough, his hands were everywhere, as if he wanted to explore the topography of my body. Can you imagine?"

I wanted to say more, but Mark sat too close. Without specifics, I told Joann we'd worked together and defined confusing terms. Briefly, I mentioned that one phrase had entailed a small demonstration, which had allowed Mark to literally grasp its meaning. Joann wanted the details, but it wasn't happening here.

"Thanks for helping," Joann remarked and changed subjects. "Can you believe Utannah came with Donny Osmond? He's the catch of the century. And she looks fantastic; no wonder he said yes. And what about Susan giving up her dance for Autumn?"

Jill Kennedy heard us talking. She said, "I think it's the greatest gift I've seen anyone give, and Autumn rose to the challenge. Susan and Autumn just became two new best friends. Giving up the experience of a lifetime to provide a life-changing opportunity deserves recognition. I hope Susan gets a medal."

Jill's date, Tom Hardy, said, "Did anybody notice Elle Dutton wasn't at the dance tonight?" In our group, no one had noticed that Elle hadn't graced the crowd with her appearance. Tom continued, "Yeah, my dad was covering the emergency room today when they brought Elle's father in for treatment. Gary Sullivan, who owns the nursery, had Dr. Dutton strapped in the delivery truck and covered in manure to keep him warm. Anyhow, Elle's dad had second-degree burns, a concussion, and a three-inch scalp laceration. Dad patched him up, and I guess Dr. Dutton's stayin' in the hospital overnight.

"Dr. Dutton kept telling the hospital staff two teenage girls had pulled him out of a burning car. Said he would have died if they hadn't, 'cause the flames were coming through the window. The Duttons are offering $500 if the two girls step forward. Can you imagine how far five hundred bucks could go?"

Staring at Joann with a quizzical look, I knew she and I were thinking the same thing. How could we get that money without the Duttons knowing I was involved? Perhaps staying anonymous was best, considering the circumstances. This was one of those times when floating near the waterfall might take our raft over the edge. Unlike other troubles we'd survived, adding power to a gathering whirlpool might take me under, leaving Joann on the bank to watch helplessly.

We left French's Fry at 1:00 a.m. As the amazing night wound down, Denny walked me home. I complimented him. "Tonight was the best time of my life. You've made my whole week special. Thank you."

Denny beamed, squeezing my hand tight. He responded, "Laurel, thanks for being my date. I'm wondering if you'll go out with me in the future. We don't have to go steady—I'd just like to spend more time together. And to be honest, I enjoy Iris's cooking. Since she's currently living with you, it's better if you like me because I plan to visit several more times."

I poked him in the ribs. "Of course I'll go out with you again. I've always liked you, and you're fun to be around."

We reached my home and walked to the front door. I didn't want the night to end, and deep down, I didn't want Denny to leave. When we reached the front door, Denny held me close and we kissed as if it were our last time together. He stood there until I was safely inside the house. As he walked away he lifted his fist into the air with a thumbs-up. Clearly, he felt the night had been better than average.

I didn't relax for another hour. Thinking about the evening, my feelings for Denny brought back all the excitement I'd felt. I reflected on Iris telling me my first date had to be special. She'd gone out of her way to achieve that goal.

In the coming weeks, I'd remember this night as the island of tranquility in a sea of turmoil.

CHAPTER 23

It's a Nice Necklace if You Can Keep It

Sunday morning didn't see me stir until eleven thirty. The day was overcast—an omen for how the next twenty-four hours would look. I went downstairs but couldn't find Iris. Glancing into the beavers' box, I noticed they were gone.

Through the open door, I saw Iris watering the sequoia while repeatedly chasing Bobby and Jean away from the tree. She was fighting a losing battle until the beavers spotted Otis lying in the grass. Then they sauntered over to see if the dog had any parts worth chewing.

Watching their interspecies relationship made my stomach growl. With Iris doing yard work, making my own breakfast seemed best. I often cooked while Mom traveled. In fact, I'd prepared many meals—but saying I knew how to cook would be stretching truth to the breaking point. Today, I made what Joann called bumblebee eggs and zebra bacon. They earned these titles because when finished cooking, the eggs were black-and-yellow while the bacon was black-and-white. However, experience proved that any problems created by these breakfast variations were easily vanquished with ketchup or—even if highly suspect—Tabasco. Fortunately, for this morning's brunch, ketchup would do.

I was reflecting on the dance when Iris walked in. "Hello, dear," she said. "I'm glad you're up. I can hardly wait to hear about last night. Denny is such a love. You've found a handsome gentleman of the highest caliber. It makes me recall my teenage years. Before you describe the details, remind me, isn't your mother calling around five? I believe it's tomorrow in Peking, but it may still be today. Either way, it's afternoon here so tell me about last night." Iris's time frame had covered the world's time zones, so whenever Mom called, we'd be ready.

Still suffering from a testosterone hangover, I asked, "Gee, Iris, could you repeat the question? Did you want me telling Mom what the time is in Peking?"

"No, honey. There's no agenda at all. Just tell me about last night."

Omitting the breast groping and making out, I spent thirty minutes painting Iris a vivid picture. Her eyes lit up as I described how easy it was to follow Denny's dance steps. The story of Autumn and Donny brought tears to her eyes.

Taking off the necklace, I said, "This is the gift Denny gave me." I couldn't believe how splendid it looked in the daylight. "Look at this necklace, Iris. Have you ever seen costume jewelry so beautiful? It's the first piece of jewelry I've ever owned. I'm going to wear it every day." I handed it to Iris so she could get a closer look.

"Laurel," she asked, "have you carefully examined this necklace?" I admitted that I'd only done a cursory exam. "Let me show you something," Iris continued. "Inside the necklace, there's a trademark on the clasp."

Looking closely, I read "Tiffany & Co," with 18K behind the name. I told Iris what I'd found. She looked serious and softly said, "Honey, this isn't costume jewelry. It's made by Tiffany, one of the world's finest jewelers. This piece is almost pure gold, and while my knowledge of jewelry is superficial, I believe the piece is genuine. Where do you think Denny got this?" she questioned. "I hope he didn't take it from the family heirlooms. If that's true, you should consider giving it back.

"Well, he said he'd attended Opal Bernstein's estate sale. It's possible he bought it there." We both knew Mrs. Bernstein often wore expensive jewelry. When she died without heirs, it took two months to organize her estate and prepare it for auction. All the proceeds went to Opal's favorite charities.

"Denny did Opal's yard work for the last three summers," I said. "Maybe she gave it to him. I think it's rude to ask, since it's none of my business." Deep down, selfishness won over. I didn't want to return it. "What do you suggest I do?"

Iris looked at me lovingly. "Laurel, I know what this necklace means, especially after our discovery. Try to look ahead and see how this scenario might play out. Denny is a fine young man, but he is a young man. It might be a shock, but men often want physical favors in return for a gift. I stressed the same point when you accepted the roses. If Denny knows the value of this stunning necklace, he might expect more than a kiss. Do you understand what I'm saying, or should I just say it's possible he wants sex?"

I shook my head, recognizing her point. She continued, "So the question is: are you willing to pay that price?"

Man, for a relaxing Sunday, these questions rivaled detectives seeking a confession. Except for numerous times a day, my thoughts of Denny rarely involved sex. Since I didn't constantly dwell on it, why would he? Everyone knew girls matured faster than boys. Shouldn't Denny worry about me wanting sex? Yes, I had desires, but no plans of getting Lillyann's and Cindy's reputations. Why would Iris even ask? She wasn't judgmental or forcing me to answer, which made it harder to ignore the question.

"No, Iris, I'm not ready to pay that price," I said. "I like Denny a lot. It's possible I sort of love him; I don't honestly know." Curiosity challenged me to ask a question I thought I'd never ask. "Iris, how will I know when I'm in love and when it's right to have sex?"

Like the other big questions we'd faced, Iris didn't retreat from the answer. "I'm willing to answer your question, but always remember that your mother's opinions count far more than mine. While living under her roof, what she says goes. You can't say to your mother, 'Iris says this or that,' or we'll both be in trouble. Are we agreed?" I nodded my head, concurring.

"Let me remind you I've never married, so I have illusions about what love should be instead of how love truly is. I've had five men share my life; my experience with relationships comprises these five. What I tell you amounts to heresy in nearly every religion. However, church rarely substitutes for a life of experience. They say 'good judgment comes from experience, and experience comes from bad judgment.' Keeping that in mind, usually the first person you date rarely turns into the love of your life. Dating many men lets you understand what you want in a partner. You also discover if a particular man has those qualities. Just as important is exploring what your partner needs and whether you can provide it."

Iris reflected, "How will you know you're in love? Laurel that is a difficult question. First, know there's a difference between love and lust. Lust is a physical attraction sometimes leading to sex. In the beginning, it's usually lust, or physical attraction, that draws you toward a man. Only after spending time together do you begin to see his positive or negative characteristics.

"I believe the most important quality of true love is how a man treats you during your most difficult times. You're easy to love in sexy lingerie, revealing cleavage to your navel. But finding a man who will comfort and love you during your worst moments takes patience. Here's another tip: if you spend enough time together and know that life without him holds little meaning, he's usually the love of your life.

"Simply put, Laurel, a man who's your best friend celebrates with you in good times and supports you in bad times. That's far better than a man who only shows up to screw you senseless. Once in love, deciding about sexual intimacy becomes the next step. Only you will know the answer. Sex awards a unique, unforgettable sensation: both lovers feel bound together, as one. Sex with the right person provides the closest connection you'll ever share with another human. He's in your memory forever—and you, in his."

Wow. Iris had laid it out straight, holding back nothing.

Still, I needed more answers. "Iris, if you have sex, should you get married?" I asked. "Or should couples marry before they have sex?" I continued.

Iris pondered her response before saying, "The answer to your questions are 'no.'" I clearly looked confused because she quickly offered an explanation. "I know what you're thinking. We both grew up hearing sex before marriage is immoral and having sex means marriage must follow. The key word is *marriage*. Simply put, marriage is a contract, or a vow." She paused. "Do you know what a covenant is?"

"No, not really," I responded. "I've never heard the word."

Iris continued, "A *covenant* is a promise, which if broken, results in severe punishment. In biblical times, a covenant was a legal document between God and man. They slaughtered animals, cut them in half, and laid the halves in separated parallel rows. When men made promises to each other, or to God, they walked between rows of butchered livestock. If they violated their promises, they suffered the same fate: death and dismemberment.

"This is why you only enter a lifelong promise with someone you truly love. If you or your husband breaks the promise, the pain and difficulties are harsh. While it's proper to avoid premarital sex, couples overlook this opinion because they're in love but can't commit to a covenant. Obviously, they believe the punishment for premarital sex isn't equal to death and dismemberment. However, this doesn't grant you permission to be promiscuous. More importantly, don't enter marriage if you can't keep your vows. Picking the right man makes all the difference. I promise!" We both laughed.

I said, "While you've answered my questions, I still don't know what to do with the necklace. If I return it, Denny will think I'm rejecting him. Do you have any suggestions?"

"Tomorrow, if you give me the necklace, I'll take it to Neil Wilson's jewelry store. He'll estimate its value. I'll also find out if it was auctioned at Opal's estate sale. If Denny bought it inexpensively, we'll tell him what it's worth. If Denny lets you keep the necklace, I'll agree with one condition: if you sell the piece, Denny gets the first opportunity to buy it back for the original price. Do you agree that's fair?" Iris gave me a stern look, suggesting I should say yes.

"All right, Iris, your suggestion seems reasonable. Take the necklace, but please don't leave it overnight. Denny might show up, and I should be wearing it if he visits."

The afternoon went fast. I helped Iris prepare fried chicken, mashed potatoes with gravy, and glazed carrots. We ate early so we'd finish before Mom called. We didn't wait long—within ten minutes, the phone rang. I answered, and from an ocean away, Mom said, "Laurel, is that you, sweetheart?" Tears came to my eyes. With everything that had occurred during the week, I didn't realize how badly I missed her. I loved Iris, but I'd have given anything to hug Mom.

I responded, "Hi, Mom! Yes, it's me. How is your work in China? Great. Yes, Iris and I are doing fine. It's been a busy week."

Mom started peppering me with questions. Knowing Mom fretted over every detail, it was best not to increase her worries.

"Yes, we've checked on the beavers throughout the week," I said. "I can honestly say we've helped them survive and they seem like part of the family. Sure, if I remember, I'll take the Instamatic camera and take pictures. You have to know, Mom: it's a challenge to capture beavers in the wild." Which was true, unless the front yard substituted for the wild.

Mom wanted play-by-play descriptions of each day's ups and downs. Besides school, what else had kept me busy?

"Well, Mom, on Tuesday Iris, Joann, and I, as well as Nubs Fritzmeyer, decided to feed the homeless," I answered. "No, I've never done that before, but you know Iris, always helping people. We took sandwiches and ah, ah, juice, yeah, that's right—ah, apple juice—to the people who are less fortunate. Why apple juice, not milk?" I didn't know what to say. "How did we travel to the creek? You know, Mom, with Iris, it's safety first. She recruited the Baptist church's bus driver to give us a lift."

Mom changed the topic and started asking about the dance.

When her questions finished, I remarked, "Iris made us a wonderful dinner, then we walked to the dance."

I told her about Donny Osmond and the fun we'd had. From nowhere, Mom asked if I'd kissed Denny. "Just a peck on the cheek, Mom," I lied. Telling Mom about the countless times we'd made out, or about Mark groping my breast, didn't seem wise.

Next, she turned to school. "Yes, school's going well. Iris helped me present a demonstration on how cultures perceive God. It went fine, except for Elle Dutton causing a fuss." I described what had happened with Elle. I didn't mention the car accident, her father, or his desire to suspend me. Since no disciplinary action had occurred, it wasn't worth wasting time.

Mom said she had five minutes left. I knew Iris wanted to speak, and I needed an interrogation break, so I called Iris to the phone. Momentarily, I heard Iris say, "Marie, she's a lovely young woman, and it's my privilege to help. The young man who asked Laurel out is delightful. She's smitten with him, and I don't blame her. He gave her a beautiful necklace and a dozen roses. What young woman doesn't like that? No, don't worry about the Duttons. Leave it to me. If I need help, I'll call Bill Lansford. OK, let me see if Laurel will say good-bye."

I reappeared, trying to look as if I hadn't been eavesdropping. Iris said, "Laurel, your mother has to go. She wants to say good-bye." She handed me the phone.

Mom said, "Honey, just know how much I miss you. Not a moment passes that I don't wonder what you're doing." Thank God she had no idea. "I'll call again next week about the same time. If you have problems, run them past Iris. I love you."

"I love you too, Mom, and I can't wait to see you. Bye-bye."

It was hard letting her go because a week seemed a long time. During the past year, my mother's intelligence had declined rapidly. Other teenagers' reported the same problem. Joann told me her parents came up with the most irrational ideas, like us getting jobs and paying more attention to world events. They didn't understand the importance of listening endlessly to music and talking on the phone.

But even knowing how annoying Mom could be, her extended trip made me grasp life's emptiness without her. The only life I'd known was the life Mom and I shared, and I'd reached out and invited a guy into that world. While I felt uncertain, I couldn't go back to my prepuberty connection with Mom. I was enjoying surfing life's latest wave. While Mom sat onshore offering support, I was ready to challenge life's peaks and troughs. But was I prepared to leave the sheltered pool and swim in the ocean? After our phone call, I wasn't sure.

The rest of the evening stayed quiet. I hoped Denny would call, but as nightfall approached, I became less optimistic. I decided to call Joann for an update on Mark. She answered the phone, sounding happy to hear from me. I asked for more details about Mark. She said that Mark had stopped trying to "suck her tongue out" and had started groping her chest.

"Laurel, what did you say when you two danced?"

Describing our conversation in vague terms, I said we had discussed "communication between men and women."

Assuming the worst, Joann asked, "Laurel, you didn't offer him oral sex, did you? Talk about balls. That's really overstepping your bounds. If you felt he needed oral sex, I should have gotten dibs. After all, I was his date!"

"I didn't offer him oral sex," I said. "I let him feel my breast, so he'd understand the meaning of 'feeling a girl up.' Mark has a crush on you, Joann. He's trying to please you without causing more trouble. I tried helping him understand how girls think. That's all."

Joann sounded relieved. "Gee, Laurel, I was worried! I mean, a week ago you never had a date. If you're giving blow jobs, perhaps you've advanced too fast." Suddenly, Joann stopped talking, as if hit by a hammer.

Filling the void, I explained how Mark had coaxed me into sharing more details. I was describing how much he'd appreciated my frankness when the huffing from Joann warned me that she hadn't appreciated my lessons. That's when she blasted me.

"Thanks, Laurel; thanks a lot! Now Mark's stowing his tongue and squeezing boobs. That's wonderful. Why didn't you explain a blow job and tell him about FBI."

"Well, I did."

She paused. "You're kidding, right? You didn't really tell him, did you?" I said nothing as Joann went on. "Laurel, do you think of Mark as a new sports car?" I didn't think so, but I awaited to hear Joann's train of thought. "First he's speeding, and I have to pry his foot off the throttle.

Then you tell him I should grease his gearshift when he feels up the mechanic."

Continuing the theme, I retorted, "Well, Joann, you're the one who started his engine and revved the throttle. I'm not surprised that Mark's ready to set you in his passenger seat and take you for a test ride. I'm sure he expects you can properly handle his gearshift. He's a normal guy."

"Laurel, that's so insensitive. Thanks to you, he'll probably show up here with his dick hanging out. Imagine how embarrassed Mom will be if she opens the door. She's never seen the mailman deliver a dick before. If she doesn't faint, Mom will chase him off and ground me for a month. That's how it will play out because of you, Laurel."

Before responding, I decided to be brief. "You're right, Joann. Life as you've known it will vanish forever. Your parents will drive a stake in your bedroom floor and shackle you with a twenty-foot chain. I'm sorry for my behavior and I'll look for new friends since you'll be unavailable. Fortunately, Utannah's great and she enjoys a wonderful boyfriend. I wish you and Mark the best of luck."

Feeling peeved, I hung up. I knew I'd overreacted to Joann's overreaction. But at least for the next twelve hours, I wanted nothing to do with Joann's and Mark's love life.

The time was eight thirty. Iris was reading the *Sentinel* when I joined her in the living room. "Dear, you look upset," she said. "Is there a problem we should discuss? I'm available if you need an ear."

"Thanks, Iris. Joann's upset about information I told her boyfriend. The problem should mend itself. If the trouble doesn't improve, I'll ask for advice."

I said goodnight to Iris and went to bed wondering if the coming school week would be as exciting as the weekend. Little did I know . . .

CHAPTER 24

The Gauntlet Is Thrown Down to a Woman Not Yet a Knight

Monday started well. My first class was English. Mr. Schonbacher was ill, so we had a teacher who actually spoke and understood English. We thought of asking if Mr. Schonbacher was out with a serious illness. We could only hope. After English was PE, which today was uneventful. Then I headed to science class, which rotated with history.

Our teacher was Abernathy Tate. He taught chemistry, physics, and occasionally math. He always wore a dark suit, white shirt, and a black bow tie. His black-framed glasses accented his narrow nose and thin mustache. Without doubt, Mr. Tate was an intellectually gifted teacher. His knowledge of the physical sciences was staggering. Mr. Tate knew the periodic table by heart and seamlessly integrated physics and chemistry with everyday life. He transformed the complex into the comprehensible.

Mr. Tate was preparing to start when announcements came over the loudspeaker: "Laurel Montgomery, please report to Principal Martin's office. Brent Fuller, turn in your archery equipment."

Heads turned and looked at me. Students didn't go to the principal's office to get awards. Hopefully, he planned to inquire about the fireworks, but Elle Dutton's complaint made more sense. I asked Mr. Tate for permission to leave. He nodded permission, and I left through the rear classroom door. Two minutes later, I sat facing Mr. Martin's secretary, Agnes Reynolds.

I retraced the steps leading to my first visit with the principal. Honestly, there were only several words I regretted saying. I felt pleased with the message my project had tried to deliver. The phone rang and Mrs. Reynolds answered. "Yes, Mr. Martin. She'll be right in." Mrs. Reynolds said, "Laurel, Mr. Martin will see you. Come with me."

She opened the door, directing me to the biggest desk I'd ever seen. Previously, I'd avoided Principal Martin's office, but I'd heard about his dungeon of horrors. I carefully looked for his spiked paddle and stretching rack. My eyes were peeled for an ambush.

Mrs. Reynolds pointed to a large chair in front of the desk. "Sit down, Laurel," she said, then turned and quickly left. The door behind me closed with a click of the lock I can still hear today. I was now staring down the "Terror of Teens." I came close to crapping my pants until Mr. Martin said, "Laurel, you should know I'm not angry with you. Your grades make you one of Sutter Junior High's best students.

"I'm sure you're aware the Duttons have made accusations against you and Mr. Wright." I nodded my head. "Today, the school board met in emergency session and decided it was best to suspend you and Mr. Wright until an investigation is carried out."

Fear overwhelmed me. Suspending me made the board look good. This punishment went to the worst offenders, who rarely came back to school. I managed to ask, while starting to cry, "What's the reason? I didn't lie, cheat, or steal."

He responded, "Laurel, this isn't punishment; it's simply a time to review the facts. Plus, the board agreed to letting you continue classes at home until the investigation finishes. When that's done, most likely you'll return."

"Most likely?" I replied. "Is there a chance I can't come back? What about Mr. Wright? He only tried to teach us how religion influenced history. You're losing a great teacher if he's suspended!" I protested. "Not only that, the board's decision makes us guilty before we're even tried."

"That's not true," Mr. Martin replied. "You can do your studies, and Mr. Wright keeps his salary. But, for now, neither of you can attend school," he reiterated.

My courage started doing push-ups—and anger won out. My tears slowed and I confronted Mr. Martin. "If Mr. Wright and me are prevented from our duties, that's punishment. Unless I can call Iris Wimple, I won't leave school without being arrested." Feeling incarcerated, I deserved one private phone call.

Mr. Martin responded, "Mrs. Wimple is a lovely woman, but you should call your mother. Iris isn't your legal guardian, so she can't help you. However, the choice is yours. I'll step out, and you can use my phone."

Mr. Martin left, and I called home. On the fourth ring, Iris answered, "Hello, Montgomery home."

"Iris, it's me. Mr. Martin suspended me and Mr. Wright. The issue concerns the Duttons and their religious views. I'm confused because right now, it feels like I'm in prison. I could sure use help, if you know what I mean," I said urgently.

Iris replied in a calm voice. "Laurel, don't say anymore. Let me speak with Mr. Martin, and I'll be right over. Wait there, if you would, dear. I'm sure we'll resolve this without more carnage."

Opening the door, I motioned for Mr. Martin to speak with Iris. He took the phone.

"Hi, Iris, this is Chip Martin. I understand you're wanting to help Laurel, but you're not her guardian. Is Mrs. Montgomery there?" Mr. Martin paused. "Oh, I see. I didn't know she'd left town. Well, if there's a guardianship letter that should do." Again, a pause. "Yes, she can wait with Mrs. Reynolds until you arrive. This was the board's decision and I'm sorry it happened. All right, we'll see you soon."

Mr. Martin scowled at me, telegraphing the message *Now you've stirred up a hornet's nest.* Then he escorted me to a seat in the outer office. "Laurel, Iris wants you waiting here until she arrives. It shouldn't be long."

As I sat facing Mrs. Reynolds, I tried sorting out how doing an assignment could have ruined my life. No obvious answer came to mind. Within a few minutes, Iris walked through the door with Mom's law partner, Bill Landsford. Bill was the best litigator in Oregon. I didn't know him, but he held a fierce reputation as a courtroom competitor. How Iris had retained him on such short notice was anyone's guess, but if Mr. Landsford was involved, the school board's problems had just doubled.

Iris sat beside me, asking how I was, as Bill walked past a protesting Mrs. Reynolds and straight into Chip Martin's office.

"Hi, Chip," Bill said. "Here's a copy of the two-million-dollar lawsuit I'm filing against you, the board, and the Duttons. Subpoenas will be served by the end of today. I've petitioned Judge Faulkner to issue an injunction against Laurel Montgomery's suspension without a proper hearing."

Mr. Martin appeared dumbfounded. "Bill, why do this? The Dutton family filed a complaint against Laurel for verbal and emotional abuse. It's such a serious accusation that the board is practicing due diligence. I've told Laurel that until they reach a decision, she can continue her schoolwork at home. This offers a workable solution for everyone."

Bill Lansford looked Mr. Martin in the eye. "Chip, the district has expelled Laurel from her school based on only the Duttons' story. Telling me the board is practicing due diligence is an outright lie. The board assumes Elle Dutton's entire story is true but has nothing supporting her claim. That said, if the district suspends Miss Dutton, we'll accept suspending Miss Montgomery. However, if Elle Dutton attends school, so will Laurel Montgomery. If there's no response by noon, I'll file the lawsuit today."

Mr. Martin countered, "Bill, you're blowing the problem out of proportion. This is simply a case of tempers out of control. This trivial matter will surely sort itself out in several days. I would appreciate you giving the district some leeway."

"Mr. Martin," Bill said gravely, "obviously, you don't comprehend the gravity of this case. Separation of church and state versus the right of free speech is an issue the Supreme Court hasn't heard. If this matter weren't serious, the school's attorney, Emmitt Pilcher, wouldn't have called the board into emergency session.

"The second issue concerns which religions the Duttons find suitable to discuss in American schools. For their family, Christianity defines the one true faith; any religion taught to students should focus on Jesus Christ. This matter is much more than two equally smart students having a petty argument. Because these questions take years percolating through the courts, I want Laurel Montgomery back in class. Am I clear about the consequences of not reinstating her?"

"Yes, Bill. You're clear," Mr. Martin replied in a retreating tone. "I'll contact the board, as well as Emmitt Pilcher, and give you an answer by two at the latest."

"Good, Chip. I'll await your call. Have a wonderful day."

Mr. Landsford came over and introduced himself. "Laurel, I'm Bill Landsford; I work with your mother. Let's go outside and speak privately. It's been a rough day, but I'm optimistic it will improve."

We went outside to a stone bench in front of the school. Once seated, I noted Mr. Landsford was around forty, with graying hair and a trim physique. Directing his words at me, he clarified, "I'm sure you're wondering how I became involved in your case. Iris thought there might be trouble, so she phoned your mother and your mom called me."

Feeling unsure about my future, I asked, "Mr. Landsford, how much jail time will I get? I never pointed a gun at Elle, and I didn't punch her, like she deserved."

"Laurel, you're not going to jail. The reason you need a lawyer is because two powerful parties want to expel you. The first party is the school district; the second is the Duttons. They're both difficult to deal with. The good news is the school can't expel you for expressing your opinion. Your views may be unpopular, but the district doesn't employ you, and you're not representing the school. No valid reason exists to expel you.

"The board hasn't formally investigated your case. Essentially, they're trying to enforce a penalty without stating the infraction or providing evidence. Later today, a judge will issue an injunction against their decision until we know the facts. By tomorrow, you should find yourself attending school. We'll know later today. Do you have any questions?"

I thought a moment. "What will happen to Mr. Wright? He said nothing controversial, and his goal was teaching how different religions influenced history. It's true, the religious leaders who visited class taught the basics of their faiths, but no one was asked to join a specific religion. What did Mr. Wright do wrong?"

"Laurel, I'm impressed. You see the point. In my mind and yours, Mr. Wright did nothing wrong. But when you work for the school, the school provides guidelines for teachers. While I'm not completely sure, Mr. Wright may have violated those guidelines.

"In America, the Christian religion prevails. People aren't tolerant when folks talk about faiths that disagree with Christianity. For example, if you promote Christianity in the Middle East, you'll receive severe punishment. The Duttons are good examples of intolerance. They're fine if the school teaches students about Christianity—but discussing other religions constitutes blasphemy. That's why your skit brought controversy. It made students reconsider their understanding of God. You demonstrated how people's views about a divine power will differ depending on their culture and experiences.

"Parents who tell their children there's one true God don't like their kids thinking independently, which contrasts with the reason children attend school. The school district doesn't like students or teachers shaking up the status quo. That's why you're getting so much attention.

"Don't answer reporters' questions and don't discuss anything with friends. I know it's tempting, but friends are easy media targets. Seemingly private conversations find their way into print. Students from school might change or make up facts. It's likely the Duttons will exaggerate the story with negative publicity. And while bad publicity hurts, it hurts more if you use the press to retaliate. Refer reporters or TV news stations to me. I'll be in touch with you or Mrs. Wimple when something important occurs. I promise, Laurel, you'll prevail."

Mr. Landsford shook my hand, then headed for his car. I looked at Iris and uttered, "Well, what do we do now?"

"Dear, I've given the circumstances some thought. I've found in tough times, a banana split focuses your mind toward the solution. What do you say we head to the ice cream shop? I'll buy."

CHAPTER 25

If Heisenberg's Right, Maybe It Didn't Happen

Iris was right. After we ordered banana splits, I began to relax.

"Iris," I said, "what makes the Duttons so vindictive? I took responsibility for my actions and admitted to Elle I was wrong. I did as Mr. Wright asked, and look what happened. Adults often need one, but for me, needing a lawyer spells big trouble. Have I done anything that bad?"

Iris replied, "No, Laurel, you've done something worse. You motivated students to question established beliefs about their higher power. Presenting examples, you showed why people see God differently. Even worse, you asserted that gods of all religions are sacred—and, in fact, are the same god. Anytime you propose an argument against established beliefs, people defend the doctrine they've always accepted as true. They don't care who stirred their emotions. Whether it's you or the president, they'll pull out every weapon they have."

"What should I do?" I asked. "The Duttons won't change their minds. And look at Mr. Wright! He's a great teacher. Except for Elle, no one felt pressured to join a certain congregation. To be honest, today's the first time I've fully grasped the implications of my presentation. Where do we go from here?"

Iris looked me in the eye and said, "Laurel, I have a story. When I finish, you'll think I'm crazy, but it's worth trying. This story makes you think, *Can this idea really be true?* It involves science and focuses on what's real and what isn't. It will answer your question and support the existence of God. What do you say?"

God was the last subject I wanted to discuss. He was causing my troubles. However, Iris said this would provide answers, so I felt obliged to listen. "OK, Iris, I'm willing, but please get to point quickly. Right now, I'm not into deep thinking."

"Yes, dear, I'll make it as quick as possible." As Iris gathered steam, I settled for an eyes-open nap. "Early in this century, two scientists ruled physics. One was Albert Einstein and the other was Niels Bohr. Each man proposed a theory of atomic structure attempting to explain the composition of all matter.

"Two of Professor Bohr's colleagues were physicists who didn't get along: Werner Heisenberg and Erwin Schrödinger. Dr. Heisenberg proposed a mind-bending theory regarding atomic particles. He mathematically proved that, in the atomic world, the more accurately we pinpoint a particle's position, the less accurately we can calculate its momentum. Conversely, the same is true. Using big instruments to measure infinitely tiny pieces of matter always interferes with how those particles behave.

"Professor Schrödinger proved that atomic particles exist simultaneously in many different states. When we observe the particle, one of those potential states becomes real. Viewing the particle determines what it becomes. Both scientists showed that examining a particle changes its behavior. The idea is easily grasped if we observe young children. Kids behave differently when they know adults are watching. The presence of a grown-up affects their behavior.

"This theory's strangest part is a stunning conclusion: two identical particles produced together, or 'entangled,' can always communicate, regardless of their distance apart. Should the two particles separate, anything changing the first particle causes an instantaneous transmission to the second, telling that particle to copy its twin. There's no signal delay, even if the particles are separated by the entire universe. Professor Bohr helped combine these revolutionary ideas, and they form the basis for a branch of physics called quantum mechanics.

"As you might guess, Professor Einstein disagreed. He argued that just because you can't detect the force causing the second particle to change, it doesn't mean that force wasn't there. Einstein wondered how two particles an extreme distance apart could instantly communicate with each other. If matter behaved this way, it implied the existence of a signal that moved faster than the speed of light. Since nothing known, then or now, travels faster than light, how could this 'spooky action at a distance' change atomic particles located so far apart?

"Einstein felt quantum mechanics wasn't complete. He believed the second particle was changed by a local force, not yet discovered. For Bohr and Heisenberg, quantum mechanics solved many atomic problems. But despite their successes, no one ever discounted Einstein's comments. By 1962, both scientists had died without reaching a resolution.

"Seven years ago, a scientist named John Stewart Bell examined this controversy and described a way to determine an answer. He showed mathematically that Einstein was wrong, and eventually, a physics lab confirmed Bell's theorem, using precision instruments to measure time and distance.

"By now, you're thinking, there's no way the old windbag could link a scientific theory to a school suspension. To make the connection, let me ask, what mysterious force transports the message? No one's discovered the answer. What's your explanation, Laurel?"

"Well, Iris, you know some bizarre facts. Mr. Tate's never talked about Professor Hinsenbirch. Maybe he'll teach it in the second semester. But I can't use quantum mechanics to avoid getting expelled. Arguing that my demonstration didn't happen because nobody watched isn't true."

"Dear, it's Heisenberg, not Hinsenbirch," Iris said. "And I doubt you'll hear about quantum theory from Mr. Tate. It's usually taught in advanced college physics, so don't expect it next year either. You're correct, Laurel. You can't argue they didn't see the demonstration; they did! That's the point. Students saw a two-dimensional silhouette portraying God. From their own senses, they had to form an impression of God using their knowledge and background. Had I revealed myself, students might have associated my image with God. We don't want church leaders saying their junior flock thinks God looks like Iris Wimple."

Iris was right. Only I had known it was Iris behind the drape. Even Mr. Wright was unaware. I responded, "You're right, Iris. Telling Father Blevins that God's a woman who loves 'nerve tonic' wouldn't sit well in church."

"Laurel, you show no respect for your elderly nanny! Dear, if you'll stop derailing my train of thought, here's the point." At that moment I wasn't sure if Iris's train had all its cars. She continued. "Oh yes, now I remember! Because the kids never saw me, 'God' could exist for them in whichever form met their needs. Like particles in quantum mechanics, God remains formless until someone seeks Him out. Then He fills that person's specific spiritual void.

"So how can the Duttons know the real God wasn't behind the curtain? If we ask, they'd claim our explanation was impossible. Yet, they can't prove you're wrong. One of my favorite quotes comes from the rocket scientist Werner Von Braun. He built the Saturn V rocket that carried men to the moon. There's a picture of an astronaut's boot print pressed in the lunar dust, and below the picture are Von Braun's words: 'Always use the word *impossible* with the greatest of caution.' During my life, Laurel, some science fiction became truth.

"One observation about the Duttons: they don't often practice what's preached in church. A little spying might help the family to revoke their complaint. Right now, let's head home and wait for Mr. Landsford's call. Does any of this make sense to you, Laurel, or are you still upset?"

"No, Iris, talking about it helps. I wish I trusted physics. Something bothers me about how particles communicate. If the signal is immediate, it implies some undiscovered universal force connects all matter. Is that your take on it?" I asked.

"Yes, Laurel, I wholeheartedly agree. To this day, no scientist has defined that force. Do you suppose Dr. Bell discovered scientific proof that God exists? Surely, the powerful implications of Dr. Bell's discovery can't continue to be ignored. Perhaps science is reluctant to solve this problem, fearing the answer they might find."

We walked home and put Otis and the beavers outside. Iris commented that the beavers looked healthy enough to release into the wild. I hated to see Bobby and Jean go, but when I remembered the disaster at the Murdocks', I knew Iris was right. We agreed to return them in several days.

As we stood out front, a car drove up with *Sutter Sentinel* painted on the door. A man stepped out wearing a gray suit and a fedora. He carried a camera and notepad, as he introduced himself: "Hi, ladies, I'm Walt Staley of the *Sentinel*. There's a rumor you have been treating an injured baby beaver. I came to see if it might make a human interest story. Just looking at your yard, the rumor is true. Tell me how these beavers began living here."

I related the story about the wounded beaver and caring for both siblings. He interrupted, "Please tell me your name." I identified myself, while Iris walked toward the backyard. He continued, "Laurel, that's a wonderful story. I'll snap some photos for the paper." I posed with Jean and Bobby while he snapped away. "Do you plan on taking these guys to science class? My guess is most kids haven't seen a beaver up close and personal."

I answered, "Well, I haven't considered it. Right now it's hard to take them to school."

"Why's that, Laurel?" he inquired.

Ready to tell about my suspension, I noticed movement on the roof. Looking up, I saw Iris standing by the chimney adjusting the garden hose. In seconds, she sprayed the reporter, his camera, and his pride. Water dripped from fedora to feet as he ran toward his car. Iris then turned the hose on me. She yelled, "Mr. Landsford said don't talk to reporters. Did you think he was kidding? You deserve this hose as much as that reporter. Now come hold the ladder. It's hard for old ladies to scale ladders without body parts screaming for mercy."

Iris reached the ground, and we hurried inside. I ran upstairs and changed while Iris searched for Ben-Gay. When I got downstairs, she sat on the couch, smelling like a locker room and sipping a whiskey sour. "Laurel," she said, "today provided a lesson on deceit. You must know people are probing for information. These reporters make their living getting folks to reveal confidential information. Unless it's me or Mr. Landsford, refrain from discussing this issue with anyone, including Denny. Am I clear?"

"Gee, Iris, neither Joann nor Denny would say anything to cause me grief. Besides, I haven't done anything that deserves suspension. What could I tell my friends that they're not already aware of?" I said.

Iris took a breath and sighed. "It pains me to play devil's advocate, Laurel, but if that's what's required to keep you quiet, then I'll be blunt. Your class presentation was innocent, thought-provoking, and controversial. You fulfilled your assignment, providing a brilliant answer to an impossible question. Then this whirlwind developed into a tornado circling the issue of separation of church and state. Through the Duttons, you've forced the school district to deal with a live grenade.

"Their easiest solution is throwing the grenade away before it explodes, which simply means getting rid of you and Mr. Wright. That solves their problem and causes the fewest headaches. Everyone agrees teaching religion in public schools isn't appropriate, but studying religion's influence throughout history provides valuable insight.

"Where you broke new ground, Laurel, was finding the nerve to suggest the same God is the foundation of every religion. This philosophy you promoted is new religious thought, and history suggests society doesn't tolerate people reinterpreting the 'Word of God.' Burning at the stake, disembowelment, beheading, and genocide are all methods various cultures have used to erase new religious ideas. You should feel lucky. All you're dealing with is the possibility of permanent removal from school."

When Iris finished, crucifixion flashed through my mind. I had never considered myself a religious zealot. Suddenly, a thought occurred. "Iris, if my idea was so bad, why did you and Mr. Wright let me do it? I'm not crusading for a new religion. If you saw this coming, you should have said something."

"Laurel," Iris replied, "I can't speak for Mr. Wright, but the reason I didn't interfere is because I believed you were right. There lies the issue. New thoughts that people can't easily challenge causes mean-spirited reactions. Most people don't like change. The question you must ponder is whether you stand behind your convictions. Is what you proposed true, or was it a dog-and-pony show for a good grade? I'm guessing that deep in your heart, you know the answer. In the time I've been here, your maturity has amazed me. Your newfound insights won't abandon you now. If you believe your proposal, stand by your words."

Just then the doorbell rang. "You'd better answer it, Iris. If it's a reporter, I don't want to deal with him."

"Laurel, the way to face reporters is to close the door and lock it. This works every time. If they persist, call the police and report a Peeping Tom. I guarantee, a reporter doesn't want his own name in the weekly arrest report."

Iris opened the door, and there stood Bill Landsford. We invited him in, and he took a seat as Iris went to get iced tea. Mr. Landsford updated me on Mom's work in China, and he suggested her team was making rapid progress. With luck, she might get home sooner than planned. Since Bill had said he would call but had now shown up in person, I found it difficult to concentrate. Surely he was here with ominous news.

"I'm sorry to interrupt a quiet afternoon, but changes have happened since this morning. That's why I came in person. The good news is that the board agreed to let you return to school tomorrow morning. The bad news is that they hired an independent investigator to interview students who were in the classroom. We may do the same, but I'll avoid involving your friends unless absolutely necessary.

"By all accounts, you're well liked, and that's in your favor. There's also a rumor that someone contacted the American Civil Liberties Union. I'm hopeful we can resolve this before the ACLU makes the solution more complex. Right now, our threat of a lawsuit is making the school board reexamine expelling you. If the ACLU enters the dogfight, they'll sue the board to remove any topic about God. Expelling you and Mr. Wright solves the board's immediate problem, while writing guidelines restricting religious discussions satisfies the goals of the ACLU. Their efforts to oust you both shows the ACLU that the board's on track but needs time to consider changes."

I interrupted, "Mr. Landsford, like I said this morning, I'm more worried about what's happening to Mr. Wright. He brings history to life and make the past relevant to today. His punishment seems far worse than mine, and he's got a family to support. Everybody ignores his problem and focuses on mine. Can I call him and say how sorry I am?"

Bill Landsford mulled over his answer. Finally, he said, "Mr. Wright asked me to represent him. Before I agree, I have to make sure there's no conflict between your case and his. I know he'd love to hear from you, but any conversation between you two becomes discoverable and can end up in court. If you have an important message, write it down and I'll deliver it when I see him. Please don't contact him without talking to me. Also, the board's investigator will want to interview you. Tell him to call me, and don't say another word."

Iris had been quiet until this point. Now she asked in a concerned tone, "So where do we go from here, Bill? I don't want Laurel's life interfered with more than necessary. Teenage women have more important issues to deal with. Can you quickly resolve her predicament?"

"Iris," he replied, "the school board meets in ten days. I've asked the school's attorney to make Laurel's case the first issue on the agenda. He's agreed, if I keep from filing a lawsuit until after the board's decision. I've honored his request but stressed that any delay on the board's part means an immediate filing of the suit.

"When the board addresses the issue, they'll allow the public to comment. To address the board, people must ask for time on the agenda. If there's anyone either of you want to speak on Laurel's behalf, let me know by tomorrow. The schedule will fill quickly, and I sense passion on both sides. Nonetheless, Laurel deserves having her good character vouched for in public. Choose a person who knows you and will sincerely speak about your actions."

"Mr. Landsford," I responded, "can't I speak for myself? I know what

I did and why I did it. Iris has pointed out that I can't distance myself from what occurred. I stand behind my argument because I believe it's correct, and nobody's pointed out where it's flawed."

He responded, "Laurel, you are the best person to represent yourself. But I don't want you doing so. Your case stands a chance of going to court. Anytime you toot your own horn, folks think you're bragging. You'll have to address the board during the meeting, but if a respected person speaks about your integrity, it looks better. Anything you say can later be used against you. Unlike people who speak for you, we can't say you misspoke. It's best, although difficult, if you listen more than speak."

I turned to Iris and stated without hesitation, "If that's the case, Iris should speak on my behalf." Clearly, I'd caught Iris off guard. I continued, "Iris sat behind the sheet and portrayed God during the demonstration. She heard everything and she answered the students' questions. She's the best person to represent me!" I stated emphatically.

"Now, dear," Iris replied, "I'm not good at public speaking. Except for the garden club, I almost never talk to large groups. I'm flattered to be thought of, but I doubt I'm the proper person. Mr. Landsford has more experience speaking about important matters. He'd do a much better job. However, I'm happy to go and offer emotional support."

I glanced at Mr. Landsford with a *Please back me up!* gaze. I threw the ball into his court. "What do you think, Mr. Landsford? Who will it be, you or Iris?"

Without delay he replied, "There's no doubt Iris is the correct choice. An attorney presenting your case will alert the public that a lawsuit rests on the board's decision. Someone as well-known and loved as Iris, who can honestly describe your character, is precisely the right person—if, of course, she agrees. What do you say, Iris? Will you represent Laurel?"

Iris considered Bill's request and took a minute before speaking. "Laurel," she said, "I love you unconditionally. I've told you that. I agree with the message you so clearly defined. In my years exploring the world, I've seen nothing contradicting your conclusion. If I speak, the heartfelt truth is all I can offer. You're a good woman with much to give. My words might do more harm than good. But if you accept this possibility, I'll address the school board."

"Iris, I have faith in you. I know you'll be there if I'm expelled. I also know my true friends will stay around. The community knows and respects you for your kindness. Even if people don't agree, your words carry weight."

Mr. Landsford looked pleased. "Great! Iris will speak toward the end of the agenda. I want the last comments before voting to focus on Laurel's positive traits. Iris, what you say doesn't have to be long. In fact, shorter is better. However, the words you choose must be genuine and the overall message concise. I want the board knowing deep down that there's hell to pay if they vote to expel this sweet young woman from school. Can you do it, Iris?" he probed.

"I shall do my best, Bill. I will pray and leave it in God's hands. I hope the right words arrive when I need them," Iris responded.

"Then I'm heading to the office," Bill said. "If any problems arise at school, or if someone tries interviewing you, call me. I'll be in touch tomorrow."

Bill stood up, and Iris escorted him out.

CHAPTER 26

The Squire Picks Up the Gauntlet

The rest of my day was mercifully uneventful. I didn't hear from friends or even Denny. It was probably just as well. I couldn't explain my absence without going into specifics. After finishing dinner and homework, I went to bed, exhausted.

I arose to a breakfast of pancakes, maple syrup, and sausage patties. Iris complemented these with mixed fruit and orange juice. We engaged in small talk until I had to leave. Then she kissed me good-bye and I headed for school, trying to hold back my fear.

It was unusually quiet in my neighborhood. Normal sounds like car engines and barking dogs were uncharacteristically absent. The foliage had finished turning colors, and the sun radiated warmth. I tried to decide the best way to interact with friends, especially Joann. She was a masterful interrogator, and her subtle perseverance could coerce folks to surrender their secrets. She could read nonverbal expressions and was spot-on when deciphering the truth.

At school, I hurried to knitting class. I beat Joann, but only by three minutes. She came in wearing a navy blue skirt with a red blouse. Her hair was in a ponytail, and with makeup, she looked stunning. Looking at me with icy eyes, she asked. "And where were you yesterday? There are tons of crazy rumors flying around school. Mr. Wright was suspended for God knows what. Elle Dutton says it's because he preaches the devil's doctrine. She also said you were suspended, but obviously that's false. Here you sit."

Mrs. Gallagher appeared as Joann said, "What the hell's going on around here?" Mrs. Gallagher gave a slight cough. "Oh jeez, I'm sorry, Mrs. Gallagher. Excuse my language. I was telling Laurel I missed her yesterday. I need to watch my language better."

Mrs. Gallagher said, "I'll overlook it now, but next time, you visit the principal. This isn't the navy, and you will not speak like sailors. Do you understand, Joann?"

"I understand. And I want to avoid Mr. Martin's office. I hear he's busy suspending teachers and students." Mrs. Gallagher's eyes opened wide, but she said nothing more.

We were dismissed ten minutes before classes started. When Joann stopped to speak with Mrs. Gallagher, I saw the opportunity to bolt. Running away prevents false explanations, and Joann and I didn't share any classes except PE. That day, English and Mr. Schonbacher came first. If I could reach his room without Joann spotting me, I'd be fine.

The problem was Joann's locker. It sat next to Mr. Schonbacher's classroom. Ten feet past his door were the stairs to the second floor. I stood by the steps, peering around the corner. Joann came down the hall, tracking me. Grabbing a textbook from her locker, she glanced into Mr. Schonbacher's room, then headed toward the stairs. I darted up the stairs and ducked into Mr. Wilburn's room. I planned on giving Joann time to get to class, and then I'd run down to English.

Mr. Wilburn normally taught algebra II to sophomores. But for the first time, the school was offering it to freshmen with a high aptitude for math—which wasn't me. To be safe, I waited several minutes—a delay that turned out to be a major miscalculation. Just as I was about to leave, Mr. Wilburn closed the door and said, "Everybody take your seats. Put your books and notes on the floor. I'm going to hand out the tests, and you'll have fifty minutes to complete the exam. No one can leave until time's up. Simply turn in your test and take your seat until I dismiss class. You may read quietly while others finish. Does anyone have questions?"

As a test dropped on my desk, panic set in. I didn't think to raise my hand and say I was in the wrong class. My books still sat on the desk with the test on top. Instinctively, I grabbed everything and ran for the door. Nothing was going to stop me. I entered the hall and was quickly down the steps. In my hurry, I tripped on the janitor's cart. Notebook pages scattered everywhere. Embarrassed at falling, I still worried Joann would appear any second. I hoisted myself off the floor and squatted to collect my things. Joann walked right past me without looking down. Relief set in as I rose to my feet. But I'd dodged a bullet only to confront a grenade: I stood face to face with Elle Dutton!

Elle's face turned red as she gasped, "You! Why are you here? They said you were suspended! You shouldn't even be on school property, let alone stalking me. I'm reporting this to Mr. Martin, and you'll be arrested for trespassing!" She slammed her locker and walked off.

Utannah witnessed everything. She patted my hand, asking, "Laurel, are you suspended? I've only been here four days, but you should know Elle has you in her crosshairs and is looking for any reason to get you expelled. Perhaps your best strategy is to reach Mr. Martin's office before her. I'll keep her busy while you visit the principal's."

"Gee, Utannah, I'm sorry I can't discuss what's happened, but some-day you'll hear the story. Right now I have to keep quiet, but I think you're right. I need to reach Mr. Martin." I gave her a big hug.

"Laurel, it's not hard to sort out the facts. You know Joann's tracking you like wounded prey. From what I've heard, you should prepare for twenty questions when she corners you."

"Utannah," I said, "in ten days the board meets and the details will come out. Until then, if you see Joann, say that I'm happy to see her but I can't talk about my problems. Doing that would help. I'll make it up to you, I promise."

Utannah blew me a kiss and went to find Elle. I headed to Mr. Mar-tin's office. Thankfully, I was the only person waiting. Mrs. Reynolds looked up and asked, "What brings you here today, Laurel? Can I solve your problem? He's overscheduled his morning and already behind in his appointments."

"I just need five minutes. I have to tell him about an incident involv-ing Elle Dutton."

Mrs. Reynolds rolled her eyes as if to say, *Not again.* She lifted the phone and spoke quietly. Within thirty seconds the door opened and Chip Martin signaled me in. Today I wasn't afraid, and I noticed all the diplomas on his wall. Perhaps he did qualify as a principal. The State of Oregon had recognized him as Teacher of the Year in 1965.

I was pondering what kind of teacher he'd be when his booming voice intruded. "What trouble have you caused today, Laurel? Can you understand the grief you've created? Between the school board, your lawyer, and Dr. Dutton, I've been extinguishing fires since Friday. What disaster has occurred to increase my headaches?"

I explained the details, stressing that I didn't know where Elle's locker was when I tripped. I also said we hadn't spoken and I wasn't stalking her.

"Did anybody see this happen?" Mr. Martin asked. I told him Utan-nah had seen it all. Our principal seemed unaware of Utannah's enroll-ment. "Who the hell is Utannah Donnay? I've never heard of her. Are you sure you're not making this up, like that religious nonsense from last week? You have an active imagination. It's too bad your mother doesn't stay home. You deserve proper discipline for lying, and Mrs. Wimple is too kind to provide it."

As he talked, I started losing my temper. His opinions were biased, and I knew he didn't plan to help. I could forgive his comments about me, but Mom was another story. I couldn't let him talk trash about my mother.

"Mr. Martin, I see you were once Oregon's Teacher of the Year and you have many impressive diplomas. Owning all those credentials, I can't understand why you're as dumb as a snail. You don't know your new students, and you have no idea about my mother's character.

"Mom is an internationally known attorney specializing in business law. She earns four times your salary, has two secretaries, and deals with conflicts that make your problems insignificant. Best I can tell, your job is resolving students' problems, not complaining how kids make your job difficult. If you ever return to teaching, I'm definitely avoiding your class."

Mr. Martin fumed. I stood, gauging whether I could outrun him. He was overweight and smoked, but he looked formidable. He screamed, "Laurel, you're one smart-ass teenager! How dare you criticize me or my job! Those diplomas and the school board give me the authority to discipline students as I see fit. The fact that you disagree doesn't make that reality go away. Right now, I'm giving thought to suspending you. I should bend you over and spank your ass, but your lawyer would sue for child abuse. I've never had a student speak to me with such disrespect!"

The picture was clear: my principal planned to disregard my side of the argument. With the noose already around my neck, I saw no reason to hold back.

I interrupted, "Then it's high time a student talked to you with disrespect because respect is something you earn and you've fallen far short! You're biased, egotistical, and can't separate fact from fiction. Obviously, you have no interest in sorting out what occurred in history class. I'm ashamed having you as my principal."

I wasn't stopping. "Go ahead and suspend me. Just understand it will cause the immediate filing of a multimillion-dollar lawsuit. When Bill Landsford cross-examines you in court, today's conversation will sound like teddy-bear talk, and students' problems will seem easy compared to the ones he'll be handing you."

Looking me coldly in the eye, it was obvious he didn't care where his actions would lead. As he rushed around the desk, Mrs. Reynolds came in and stopped Mr. Martin. She whispered in his ear and he considered her words. Finally, he said, "Leave my office, and don't ever cross my path again. Doing so would be the worst mistake you could make. Leave now!"

I didn't waste time leaving. Mrs. Reynolds had a pad of pre-signed excused-absence slips on her desk. I needed one excuse for missing English. And since more beats one, I took the whole pad. Someday, I might covertly return them. Right now I didn't see that happening.

Fifteen minutes late, I walked hurriedly to math class and presented the excused absence to Mr. Olson. He smiled, suggesting I take my seat. Although I was tardy, I followed his lecture. Before class ended, I felt calm. Knowing I'd defended my beliefs bolstered my confidence. Any remorse for confronting Mr. Martin was gone.

Somehow, the idea that had rested in plain sight after presenting my beliefs sank in. Whether my premise about God represented inspired thought or dog dribble didn't matter. Opening our minds to new ideas and setting aside long held but incorrect presumptions was what counted. Until today, I had never valued how rare and extraordinary this opportunity was.

I was fortunate. Iris was living proof. Liked by everyone and recognized for her charity, she might state the ugly truth about a person's behavior, but she forgave if that person tried to improve. She led by example, showing me how respected and honorable people handled themselves. I knew that her way was the way I wanted to—no, needed to—live my life.

With my fears gone and math class ending, I walked into the hall with more self-assurance than I'd experienced in some time. This was fortunate, since Joann stood in front of Mr. Olson's door. Her posture made it clear she was looking for answers.

"All right, Laurel, cough it up," she ordered. "Mr. Wright's not here and you disappeared yesterday. Elle Dutton's saying the school's expelling you. I'm your best friend, so tell me what's up. If you can't trust me, who can you trust?"

"Joann," I countered, "Sunday, you said I'd screwed up your life by giving Mark advice. Now you expect me to tell you my troubles. Without explaining why, Elle's statements may soon be right. My lawyer says that's all I can tell friends, especially close ones. It's for your own good, just like talking to Mark. I tried hard to help Mark be the guy you wanted. Obviously, I made a mistake and upset you. I'm sorry. It won't happen again. When you can forgive me, we'll talk. Considering the pain I caused you, that may never happen. Right now, I'm overwhelmed with issues and need to move forward. Have a good day."

Her criticism about me talking to Mark had hurt. I wallowed in self-pity and wanted Joann to experience the same guilt I had felt.

It was noon, and time for lunch. I went to the cafeteria, hoping to eat in peace and quiet.

The first ten minutes were great. Then Mitch Hardisty and Susan Small sat next to me. They were close friends and I knew they wouldn't ask many questions. They said hello as Mitch opened his thermos and poured a beer. Susan said, "We heard you've had several bad days and wanted to perk you up. Is there any help we can offer?"

I smiled and replied, "Nothing specific, but the school's investigator will be tracking you down since you both witnessed Friday's events. I'm sorry you're involved in my problem."

Mitch devoured his first sandwich and mumbled, "They already told Suzie and me when to show up. I ain't tellin' 'em one damn thing. Ya did nothin' wrong."

"He's right," Susan agreed. "We interview right after lunch. We won't talk if you say not to. What works best for you, Laurel?"

Their sincerity humbled me. I softly said, "I appreciate your help, but please be completely honest. There's no need to cover for me. I did nothing wrong, so what you say should help me out. That's my request."

Mitch sipped his beer and said, "By God, Laurel, that's damn upstanding of ya. I'd like to hog-tie Elle Dutton and sew her lips shut. Elle should hope Tanice doesn't catch up with her! She's got some choice words to stuff in Elle's ears. I feel sorry for that little bitch. Before this here shit, nobody much liked her. Now she's dog meat. Oh—Susan and I sat here to get your blessin' for an idea we been a chewin' on."

Susan took over. "Mitch and I want your permission to form a protest group. We plan to protest in City Park, across from the school. We want to protect your good reputation. We've heard rumors that the Duttons are publicizing how much you harmed Elle. My parents run a paging service.

Yesterday, Dr. Dutton called asking us to page Jacquelyn Collier. Thankfully, she didn't answer his page."

Susan's information surprised me. Dr. Collier was a surgery professor living in Sutter but practicing in Portland at the University of Oregon Hospital. I knew she chaired the school board and that in 1971, she was one of very few women surgeons who had achieved a full professorship. She specialized in cancer surgery.

Dr. Collier kept a satellite office in Sutter, where she worked one day a week. Because of her schedule, people outside her practice rarely saw her. Her husband was an architect, and her oldest son was president of the junior class. Her youngest son had transferred to sixth grade after learning fifth grade wasn't a challenge. "You two can form a protest group, but I plan to defend my reputation when the board meets. I won't lower myself to the Duttons' tactics because it might make the situation worse."

Mitch had a quick comeback. "Laurel, the only way to win a battle with them folks is gettin' your hands dirty and beatin' the livin' shit out of 'em." He paused for a second of introspection, then continued, "In a respectacle way, of course. We're gatherin' your friends and showin' the public your good side. Fer me, that's always been your butt."

Mitch broke into a belly laugh as I started blushing.

Susan reprimanded Mitch by saying, "He's such an ass—like all men. You should slap him. Laurel, I don't know you like Mitch does, but your presentation helped me understand how people choose God. I don't feel confused anymore. Mitch and I think you're in a rough fight, and we can help. So, will you back our protest?"

"I can't stop you from protesting, but I have a request. Tell anyone who asked I had no part in this demonstration. I need to be independent of whatever happens. Will you spread that message among the students? My lawyer wants me quiet, so I can't attend. Agree to those conditions and you can start protesting."

Susan said, "I can agree with those, and Mitch will go along because I'm telling him to—right, Mitch?" I looked over, and Mitch reluctantly nodded his head. Susan continued, "I promise, Laurel, we won't use any names, but we plan to piss off some folks."

"Serves them sum' bitches right," Mitch piped up. "We was all doin' fine until that half-baked little twit threw pig shit in the fan. By God, if I could get 'er on the ranch for a couple days, we'd pry the corncob out of 'er ass." Mitch finished his second beer and said, "It's time to do that interview and head to history class. I wonder who's teachin' it."

As we left the cafeteria, I told Mitch, "You and Tanice make a great couple. And Susan, giving your dance with Donny Osmond to Autumn Whitney was the most unselfish act I've ever seen. You let her shine. I know she'll never forget it."

They went to do interviews while I sat in history class waiting to see who would assume Mr. Wright's role. It wasn't long before a short, balding man slowly eased the door shut and shuffled to the front of the class. Looking in his eighties, he weighed no more than 110 pounds. Short of breath, his shaking hands struggled to pick up the pointer. Utannah whispered in my ear, asking if I'd wager a quarter this guy wouldn't live another two hours. I took the bet. Considering he moved at a snail's pace, rigor mortis may have already set in. Even if this man survived, it was a fact I'd never hear his mumbling as I had a seat in the back row.

But without warning, his posture straightened and his eyes came alive. With a booming voice, he caught us off guard. "Good afternoon, students. My name is Frank Proust. I'm substituting for Mr. Wright, but I'm optimistic he'll return soon. It's important that you know I'm qualified to teach history, so let me state my credentials. I grew up in Nebraska, getting my undergraduate degree in history at the University of Nebraska. I then obtained my master's and PhD degrees in education at the University of Kansas.

"As some of you know, I taught history in this exact school from 1942 until 1956. Then I became superintendent of Sutter Schools from 1957 until 1964. I taught graduate history at the University of Oregon until I retired and moved back to Sutter. It shouldn't be a surprise that I taught many of your parents and coached some of your fathers in amateur boxing. Looking at me, you might think I've walked the earth since time began, and therefore, I should know all about history."

The class started chuckling.

"That's not entirely true, but I can say I've witnessed many events that have shaped the twentieth century. So today, we'll start discussing what occurred in the 1900s to make our civilization the most advanced it's been in human history. More innovations took place in the past seventy-one years than in all of recorded time. During my time here, our goal is understanding man's evolution from stones to skyscrapers. You've examined how religions influenced civilization. So let's look at other influences. I will tell and show you the discoveries that have improved our lives. Does anyone have questions?"

Cordell Pike raised his hand, "Are we going to talk about cars and football? Those things have to be two of the most important inventions of the century."

Mr. Proust replied, "We'll discuss the automobile industry. Perhaps, with some thought, I can work in football."

When we finished, the class loved Mr. Proust. He obviously enjoyed teaching history as much as Mr. Wright. Even Elle, who had started class with crossed arms and a huge pout, looked relaxed.

My last class was PE, where we played volleyball. Spiking the ball let me take out my frustrations. I felt better by the time I hit the shower and dressed.

It was cold as I left the gym and started walking home. I ran into Denny, who grabbed me tight and gave me a soft, delightful kiss. "Where have you been?" I asked. "I haven't heard from you in the last thirty-six hours. Aren't you ashamed, Denny Jensen?"

He looked at me with his gorgeous blue eyes and said, "Yes, I guess so. That's why I'm here to walk you home. Rumors about Mr. Martin, the school board, and Laurel Montgomery filled the halls today. Clearly, our principal and the board are out to get you. I'm here to offer support."

"Sure you are," I teased. "You're here because for two days, you've missed my lips. Don't try kidding me, buddy, I know what you're after. How did you plan to console me, young man?"

"Well, Laurel, perhaps I'll buy you a Coke and we'll sit on the park bench a few minutes. I'm sure putting our heads together will take your mind off these ugly issues. Doesn't that sound like great medicine for a wounded soul?"

Deep down, I couldn't wait to kiss Denny, but I hoped to do better. "Well, I don't know. I usually help Iris make baloney sandwiches and fill whiskey bottles on Tuesday afternoons." Denny gave me a quizzical stare. "If I sit with you, I'll be late getting home. Of course, if you wanted to come along and help, we could sit several minutes."

Denny grabbed my hand, and we sprinted to the park. I sat down while he bought me a Coke from the outdoor vending machines. When he returned, we cuddled together, and Denny gently kissed me. After a few moments, he whispered, "Laurel, chilly as it is, your lips are incredibly warm." His lips then turned to caressing my cheeks, inducing shivers with the warm breaths bathing my ear. Without doubt, Denny distracted me from my problems. For the next fifteen minutes I could think about nothing but him.

As we sat in the park, I noticed Iris coming toward us, pulling her wagon filled with groceries. Typically she shopped earlier in the day, but obviously she was running late. Denny and I hurried to help her. Denny said, "Iris, I heard you're making sandwiches and filling liquor bottles. I don't know why, but Laurel asked me to help. I said I'd do anything to be near both of you." I looked at Denny, shaking my head. What a brownnoser!

Iris seemed thrilled. "You're such a dear. If your parents approve, you can stay for dinner. We'll be happy to take you home after tonight's adventure."

Denny looked puzzled since he knew neither of us drove. I whispered, "I'll explain later, but you'll never forget the experience."

We unloaded the groceries as I read through *The Sutter Sentinel* Tuesday edition. I scanned for any stories about the events at school. On cursory examination I didn't see any related articles. One odd story caught my attention: "Bear Takes Car Ride on Main Street." I knew Iris would soon need help, but this story piqued my curiosity. I read on:

> On Monday, Florence Fritzmeyer and Iris Wimple found themselves driving a bear down Main Street. The two women had finished shopping at Mort's Market. They had bought multiple deli meats, as well as bread and condiments. Prior to visiting Mort's, they had purchased several bottles of bourbon, which sat in the trunk of the car.
>
> The baggers at Mort's routinely open Mrs. Fritzmeyer's trunk from inside the car. They loaded the vehicle as the women were inside, paying their bill. Since there were still several bags to carry out, the employees left the trunk cracked open. When the women reached their car, the trunk appeared closed so they put the remaining groceries in the backseat.
>
> The ladies prepared to finish their errands and didn't notice a bear open the trunk and jump inside. When they left the drive-through at First State Bank, the teller spotted the bear and alerted police.
>
> The women bought drinks at French's Fry drive-up, as

police dispatcher Ethel Twillager fielded multiple calls. Officers attempted to pull Mrs. Fritzmeyer over, but couldn't get her attention.

A roadblock was erected across Main Street, forcing Mrs. Fritzmeyer to stop. When told about the bear, she exited the car and assaulted the bear with her purse. While officers frantically explained the dangers of assaulting wildlife, Florence chased the bear from the trunk. She pointed out that since she was ninety-two, a bear attack was the least of her worries.

Examining the damage, officers reported that the groceries, including the liquor, were consumed by the bear. The bear got away but was later sighted in Mertyl Springfield's tree. The Wildlife Division arrived to capture the young male, but the bear fell out of the tree, clearly drunk. After watching the bear overnight, they released the animal this morning.

Both Mrs. Fritzmeyer and Mrs. Wimple are safe; their only casualty being "bear" pantries.

Iris had managed to avoid discussing this incident. I meandered into the kitchen, where Denny was enjoying a second piece of pie. "Say, Iris," I said, "usually you buy groceries on Monday; why did you wait until this afternoon?" I poked.

"Well, Laurel, occasionally time slips away and I don't accomplish all my errands. Yesterday, Nubs and I started on time, but events didn't go our way. Some days are like that, dear."

It was a perfect setup. "Well, Iris, the day goes better if you check the trunk for bears." Her eyes opened wide, but I didn't let up. "They're suggesting the bear was underage, and you're not supposed to give liquor to minors. You and Nubs should be ashamed!"

"Hindsight is always 20/20," Iris shot back. "Had we known a bear was hitchhiking in the trunk, we wouldn't have put the liquor there. Nubs and I are very conscientious about people interacting with wild animals. Yesterday was a rare event. I'm certain the bear needed the food more than we did."

"You're right, Iris. Besides berries and fish, a natural staple for bears is a baloney sandwich with stiff bourbon. You and Nubs were doing the wildlife a service."

As Iris gave me the evil eye, Denny looked confused for the second time today. He hadn't read the paper, and he had no explanation for the multiple liquor bottles sitting on the counter. I showed Denny the paper as Iris and I started a sandwich production line. Denny studied the newspaper while he bagged the sandwiches and placed them in a box. The liquor bottles didn't take long to fill—which wasn't the case for getting the distillery smell out of the kitchen.

When Iris finished opening the windows, she announced that dinner would consist of grilled baloney sandwiches. Denny seemed in gourmet heaven. "Iris," he said, "I love those sandwiches. My mom won't make them because she feels they're not a healthy dinner."

"Denny, your mother's right," Iris stressed. "I never prepare food without the right nutritional requirements, but tonight there isn't time. I feel bad not serving a healthy dinner, but I'll make it up to you. You've got thirty minutes until dinner, so don't go far. I'm not chasing you down when dinner is served."

I assumed Denny and I would go to the living room and "study" mouth-to-mouth resuscitation, but Denny said to Iris, "I want to read you an article I found in the paper."

Fear descended over me as I peered over Denny's shoulder. Small print at the top of page four announced: "School Board to Decide Fate of Student and Teacher Accused of Promoting Religion," by Walt Staley. Just the title implied Mr. Wright and I had preached religion and had been on the run until we were cornered and captured after a huge manhunt. Any Sutter residents who hadn't believed I was a heretic would soon line up to add a lash during my public flogging. I wanted to run and hide.

Denny sensed my attitude changing. "Laurel," he said, "let me read the rest of the story. Mr. Staley lists several points in your favor. There's nothing here that you don't already know."

I wanted Denny to stop, but Iris said, "Let's hear the rest. I'm sure Laurel wants to stop, but facing criticism is necessary to respond in a proper way. Ignoring self-weakness, right or wrong, usually returns to bite us on the butt."

Denny continued the story:

On Monday, the Sutter School Board suspended a junior high history teacher, as well as one of his students. The teacher is community volunteer Penfield Wright. Mr. Wright has taught history at Sutter Junior High for the last five years and has a résumé that includes local and national teaching awards. He has no previous record of disciplinary action. Because the student is a minor, the *Sentinel* is withholding a name until details are available. The school has not publicly provided reasons for the student's suspension.

Reportedly, the disciplinary actions occurred after Mr. Wright invited different religious leaders to teach students about the foundations of each specific faith. After the presentations, Mr. Wright assigned students a one-question test: explain, if they could, why diverse cultures see God in so many different ways.

One student presented her answer using different scenarios to depict the same God in different surroundings. Each skit tried to stimulate the student's five senses. Each student experienced different concepts about the Almighty, helping the young woman create an astounding reply to Mr. Wright's question. The teenager's argument implied that only one God exists and this Divine Entity presents itself in a manner familiar to each culture. Her presentation offered proof for a single god and described how a community achieves a closer bond with their higher power when He blends into their culture.

The broader implication of the student's presentation was that God adapts to meet the needs of progressing civilizations. Since many believe God never changes, this assignment and the young woman's answer have incited a growing controversy.

Most people living in Sutter are Christians. Initially, it was rumored that many Christian families complained to the school board, but investigation by the *Sentinel* confirmed only one formal complaint. This grievance came from Dr. Norman Dutton. We reached Dr. Dutton at home, where he is recovering from a fiery car accident. He said his daughter was forced to endure religious teachings contrary to the words of Jesus Christ. Concerned about his daughter's complaints and insults from the presenting student, Dr. Dutton believed he had no choice but to file a complaint.

He also expressed that parents, not schools, must teach children the correct beliefs of Jesus Christ. Dr. Dutton was confident that when the board meets, they will terminate both Mr. Wright and the student.

Our repeated attempts to obtain comments from both teacher

and pupil have gone unanswered. We contacted William Landsford, the attorney for both parties. Mr. Landsford stated that an independent investigation would issue a report to the school board. Depending on the board's decision, legal action is possible. Mr. Landsford did not say whether legal action would extend to the Dutton family, but "all choices remain on the table."

When Denny finished, we stared at each other. Finally Iris spoke up, saying, "Honestly, Laurel, the paper did you a service. The *Sentinel* could have slanted the article in favor of the board, but they kept an open-minded tone. Maybe I shouldn't have hosed down Walt Staley. Everything considered, we're lucky he didn't hang you out to dry." Iris laughed at her water humor. Denny and I shook our heads at a pathetic joke that was so bad it was funny.

I could tell Denny was entertaining a new thought. He said, "I didn't understand until now: the Dutton family has caused most of your problems, right?"

"It's true," I responded. "Elle was already intolerable when I aggravated it by insulting her. She called her dad, who came to school and filed the complaint. Mr. Wright had me apologize, but they didn't accept it. That's why I'm facing expulsion."

Just then, the phone rang. Iris answered, "Montgomery home." There was a slight pause and then, "Yes, Bill, she's here. Yes, looking at her now, Laurel seems an angel, but from what you've said, once she reaches campus, she turns into a devil child. Oh, I see. No, that's new to me, but she hasn't been home long. Today, Laurel's after-school project involved close observation of male courting behavior."

My face turned red, and Denny snickered. "Yes, that's why she's home late. Just a moment, I'll put her on the phone." Iris handed me the phone.

Mr. Landsford had heard about the incident in Mr. Martin's office. I described what happened that morning, without omitting any gruesome details. I told Bill what I'd said to Mr. Martin. I asked if a cordial way existed to defend Mom without using derogatory remarks. Deep down, I still seethed and firmly told Mr. Landsford I wasn't apologizing.

"Laurel," Mr. Landsford said, "I know you ran into Elle Dutton, and I heard what occurred between you and Chip Martin. I also know he didn't report your frank discussion to the board. He considered asking for an immediate suspension but wisely decided to contact the board's attorney, Emmitt Pilcher. Emmitt called me for our perspective, and I wanted your side of the story before returning his call.

"After today, we should assume Chip Martin isn't your fan. When we first met, I sensed his bias against you. Now we know his true character and his animosity toward you. Listen closely, Laurel. Between now and the board meeting, keep clear of Chip Martin. He's forming a mental list of reasons to hasten your departure. One more issue: did Mr. Martin touch you or threaten physical harm?"

Recollecting the duel at school, I replied, "Yes, he threatened to bend me over and spank me. He tried to catch me, but Mrs. Reynolds held him back. I didn't take any chances and left in a hurry."

Bill didn't hesitate. "Tomorrow, I'll petition the court for a restraining order. Are you available if I need you?" I wasn't sure about leaving school for court, so I gave the phone back to Iris. Bill updated her on recent events. With each detail, her face contorted, and she studied me with a probing stare.

"I see, uh-huh. Oh, heavens. Those words left Laurel's mouth? Well, yes, I understand your point. If she needs to attend court, I'll see she has a note with her. Thank you, Bill. What would we do without you? Yes, thanks for calling. Good-bye."

Iris hung up, looked me in the eye, and said, "You've had quite a day, Laurel. You didn't mention your verbal joust with Mr. Martin. Did you hope the postman would deliver a letter? And about Elle Dutton—don't you understand these people aren't your friends? Stop pulling her chain."

Denny interrupted my scolding, "Gee, I'd better leave. I'm interrupting an important family meeting, and my bicycle chain needs grease."

Iris grabbed his hand and said, "Sit down, young man. If you adore Laurel, she'll soon need your support. Our discussion won't take long. Now, Laurel, about you. Not disclosing your argument with Mr. Martin isn't acceptable. The moment anything serious occurs, you tell me! I'm responsible for you, and I have no intention of disappointing your mother. Another incident will not occur where I'm last to learn you're involved. Do I make myself clear?

"This isn't a game. Your actions are all potentially bad or good. And believe me, you're under the microscope! You started a growing controversy and I guarantee, it's one of many you'll handle before leaving this world. Quit fueling the fire, and start asking for help. Mr. Martin is your principal. Despite his inappropriate behavior, you're not prepared to confront him."

Experiencing humiliation in front of Denny, I started to cry. I hoped Denny would hug me. When he didn't respond, I sputtered, "What did you expect, Iris? He belittled me and insulted Mom. Should I have sat quietly and listened? He initiated the fight, and unlike most students, I hit back." Tears continued down my cheeks.

Denny pulled me close, and I cried on his shoulder. After a few minutes, I began to calm down. Resuscitating my self-respect, Iris spoke softly. "Laurel, you told Mr. Martin precisely what he needed to hear. In my mind, the important issue concerns Mr. Martin's having no respect for you or other students. Typically, he deals with disorderly students and rarely interacts with good students. He believes all student opinions deserve little credence.

"People earn respect from repeated good behavior. Mr. Martin doesn't know much about you, let alone your accomplishments. Ideally, he should find every student's hidden potential, but he doesn't have the skills. Until you've earned credentials and respect, you should seek help before defying an adult who holds tremendous power. I doubt Mr. Martin respects me either. But I guarantee you, Bill Landsford captures his full attention. Next time, don't argue. Excuse yourself and call me or Bill.

"Now, I've stated my concerns. You and Denny grab a Coke and relax in the living room while I make dinner. Later, we'll visit the homeless folks."

Denny and I sat on the couch. I still felt ashamed, but Denny rubbed my shoulders and kissed me on the cheek. He kept quiet and let me speak first. "I'm embarrassed. You probably think I'm trouble, after seeing this incident," I said. "At least Iris states her point and doesn't harp on it. I'm probably safe until tomorrow. Mom would still be ranting and raving."

"Look, Laurel," Denny said. "I realize that sorting through this mess must be difficult. I know you're a good person. You're popular *and* smart. I couldn't resist asking you out. You're the first girl who's made me feel that way. And honestly, if you agreed, I knew I was taking out a girl classier than me. A guy feels good knowing he's convinced the prettiest, brightest girl to go on a date. The boys think you're special, and they assume you have a boyfriend—or else, they'd be lining up to beg for a date. I never saw you with a guy, so I invited you."

"Denny, are you implying that my agreeing to your invitation was like bagging a trophy deer?" I jabbed. "Will my head hang on the wall next to your other women conquests?"

Denny looked embarrassed and searched for words to defend his honor. I had forgotten about his sharp mind. "Gosh, Laurel, my other conquests were playful practice compared to snaring you. I'm mounting your head right over my fireplace. That way I can celebrate Christmas by stringing lights from ear to ear." He grabbed my earlobes and eyed the distance between them. "I figure ten lights should work; maybe an ornament from your nose."

Denny's comeback dissolved my grief. I grabbed his arm and pulled him to the carpet. I climbed on his chest and started tickling him. He laughed so hard I wanted to continue, but when he mentioned possibly peeing his pants, I hopped off. No use taking chances. The beavers sat there watching until Denny called them over. When they got closer he ordered them to stop and sit; they did. Denny asked, "Didn't Iris say a few minutes ago she and Nubs were conscious about interacting with wild animals?"

I replied, "Well, obviously her idea of conscious interaction includes training beavers to sit and God knows what else. Before long they'll be trimming the hedge." As we returned to the couch, Iris called us for dinner. I advised Denny to avoid the animal domestication issue. It had been an emotional day, and I didn't want more heavy discussions.

Dinner passed uneventfully. Iris seemed delighted when Denny ate four fried baloney sandwiches, pasta salad, and peach pie. If Denny ever broke up with me, I figured Iris had an 80/20 chance of dating him.

CHAPTER 27

Advice about Women

After finishing dinner, we heard a horn honking. Iris said, "That's probably Nubs, parking by the house." She was right. The left side of Nubs's Cadillac had one rear wheel on the driveway. The rest of her land yacht sat diagonally on the lawn with its front a foot from the window. Iris wasn't kidding about Nubs getting *near* the house.

The wagon, sandwiches, and liquor were ready to go. Nubs unlocked the trunk, and Iris supervised us loading the supplies. Using a stick, I lifted the trunk cover and commanded, "Denny, stand to one side. These women occasionally transport dangerous bears. Caution prevents accidents."

Iris whispered something to Nubs as she got behind the wheel. Nubs lowered her window and asked Denny and me to come forward. We peered down upon a hunchbacked, dainty woman, who said in a sweet, melodic voice, "I hear you children are mocking our bear encounter. Let me be clear. If I hear one of your shitty remarks, you'll walk your asses off getting home. Now quit pissing around and finish the job! Do I make myself clear?" Nubs's expletives made Joann's language seem appropriate for Captain Kangaroo.

Denny and I packed the rations and sat in back. We cringed as we weaved along the highway, as if on a carnival ride without safety belts, and we held on as Divine Guidance decelerated the car and caused us to stop just in time at the trailhead. The relief we felt must have been like Columbus after ninety days at sea. We loaded the wagon, and our misfit relief party headed to the river.

When we arrived, the homeless group greeted us enthusiastically. I counted only seven people instead of the nine from last week. Ed helped us hand out sandwiches and liquor. He'd shaved and cut his hair. He wore a down coat and untorn clothing, which probably meant his previous week had gone well. I asked him where the two folks we'd met the previous week had gone.

"Well, miss—I done forgot yer name—Arnold's in jail 'cause he's a beggin' on corners, an' yesterday we found Warren dead. He ain't been well in the last few weeks. We figur' his liver 'splodid. Ain't uncommon with us folk. Lifetime a drinkin' tends ta pickle a guy's innards."

I told Ed my name and explained how I knew Iris and Nubs.

"So, ya lived in Sutter long, Laurel?" Ed wanted to know.

"Yes, my whole life. Mom's an attorney, and Dad left years ago. How about you? Were you born here?"

In a quiet and reassuring voice, Ed responded, "No, young lady. Born and raised in New York, I come west when I'as drafted. Years ago, I lived 'ere with ma family. Lost 'em 'cause of my drinkin'. Rumor is, they long since left these parts. Someday, maybe I'll see 'em again. It's my biggest regret. Can't linger on da past though. Since Friday, I got me a job with Milt Ordner. Milt had 'im a mix-up involvin' a 'spensive truckload o' furniture—evidently, done burned in a bonfire. He needed someone ta verify that da right furniture leaves the factory. It pays decent, so I bought me some thrift store clothes and traded my liquor fer better blankets."

"That's great, Ed! Hearing your story makes me forget my troubles. Plus, you make my problems look insignificant." Ed asked what was bothering me, so I told him about arguing with the principal.

"Laurel," he said, "one o' life's sad facts is ya can't make ever'one happy. Much as ya try, some folks just ain't gonna like ya. In my case, that's quite a few folks. While it ain't ma business, I'd tell ya to focus on da important values and da people who support ya. Joann, da lady I met last week, said you's both best friends. I'm surprised she ain't here this evenin'."

Ed's manner and ability to listen made it easy to be honest. "To be truthful, Ed, I didn't ask her. We had a falling-out, and I couldn't face her when the suspension happened. I'm afraid she won't want me as a friend anymore."

Ed replied, "Good friends know yer bad points and still want ya 'round. You can't run from yer fear. Face 'er and patch up yer petty differences 'fore it's too late to fix 'em. When yer facin' that school board, ya don't wanna be worryin' about losin' your best friend. Call 'er and set things straight. Tomorrow, school won't be near as bad as it was today. Wanna bet a candy bar?"

"OK, Ed. It's a bet—and I'll return next week to collect."

Iris interrupted by calling me to come and help bandage Jill's wounds. Earlier that day, Jill had startled a tomcat while scrounging for food in a dumpster. Iris always brought hydrogen peroxide, gauze, and antiseptic ointment with her.

I told Ed, "I'd love to continue, but I've already provoked Iris. I'd better go help." Ed patted my back, said good-bye, and walked over to help Denny find one of the addicts' ID.

Jill's scratches looked infected. While Nubs held up a blanket for privacy, Iris removed Jill's blouse. The wounds were red, and Jill's hand was swollen. Iris said, "Well, Jill, there's no fever. There's no facial scratches, and I don't feel swollen nodes under your arm. Typically, those findings indicate bacterium *Bartonella henselae,* or cat scratch disease. Cleaning these wounds with peroxide twice daily and applying antibiotic cream should cure it."

How Iris knew the organism responsible for cat scratch disease was anyone's guess. It was one of many bizarre facts crowding her memory. Momentarily shocked, I refocused when Iris said, "Laurel, take Jill's arm."

I held the arm as Iris treated the wound with half-strength peroxide and antibiotic ointment. Finished with bandaging, Iris instructed Jill to go to the hospital if she got a fever or the swelling increased. "Don't ignore this infection, Jill. Losing your hand isn't a problem you need. Next week, I'll bring some gloves to protect your hands."

Finished with Jill, we went to get Denny. He and Ed were talking intently, so we gave them time to spot us. Once we were seen, their conversation ended, and Denny said, "I'm not sure about our discussion. Two people should know each other well before discussing private topics. I'll consider your idea."

His comments made me wonder about the topic. Iris also looked curious. Denny stood up, grabbed the wagon, and we said good-bye.

Riding home, I encouraged Denny to tell me about their discussion. He seemed unsure what to say. Finally, he looked at me and spoke with reservation.

"I told Ed we were dating, and he asked how we got along. He wondered about our goals and how we'd achieve them. I said we liked each other but remained undecided about the future. Asking about our upbringing, Ed offered guidance about making you happy that he wanted me to consider. He asked my thoughts on his suggestion."

Denny was stirring my interest. I decided not to push too hard, too fast.

Denny said, "Now before you ask, I'm sensing your next question concerns what Ed said about making you happy." Denny had pegged me there. "I won't answer—because I find Ed's recommendation hard to believe. It's about developing a closer relationship, but I need another opinion."

"Another opinion," I repeated. "You plan on discussing a topic involving me with someone else, when you won't tell me? We've always trusted each other, but now I'm not sure. Tell me, Denny, who knows me better than me?" I said, emphatically.

Denny pondered a moment. "I understand, Laurel—I'll talk to someone who knows you well. I have to make sure Ed's words are true. I trust you—I really do. But your future counts, and I won't let a drunk's suggestion incorrectly guide us.

"I know nothing about girls. Guys at school think every girl's secret desire is to surrender to passion. They're certain that igniting a woman's desires is the key to helping her find happiness. In the men's locker room, teenage boys brag about their big crotch as the key to unlocking a girl's needs. Their knowledge comes from rumors and bad information, passed down from older brothers. Many guys claim they've driven ladies to ecstasy. I don't believe them. Maybe it's similar with girls. So before we talk, I'm finding out if Ed's advice will really make you happy."

Right now, Denny's bullshit *wasn't* making me happy. But I had to settle for his flimsy explanation.

Miraculously, Nubs found Denny's home without scaring any of Sutter's citizens. Denny and I walked to his front door. I'd never kissed him with Iris present, and that wasn't changing tonight. I surprised Denny by holding his cheeks and sensually kissing him. Then I smiled, winked, and said goodnight.

When I reached the car, Iris commented, "Well, you and Denny are getting along famously. If he ever collapses, you'll be able to provide satisfactory mouth-to-mouth resuscitation. And I thought he came just to enjoy my cooking. Boy, was I ever wrong."

Iris let the zingers fly, but when she finished, I was ready. "Make fun of my kissing, Iris, but we kiss in the open. Someone I know publicly claims she never domesticates wildlife but has secretly taught beavers to follow dog commands. Talk about hypocritical behavior. What example does it set when the woman raising me preaches one thing and practices another?"

Nubs piped up, "Iris, shall I pull over here and kick her out? Walking home in the cold never hurt anyone. Why do you put up with such nonsense?"

Nubs watched Iris considering her proposal. "No, Nubs, keep driving. Toss her out here and she'd return to Denny's house. You saw their behavior. When we reach home, she'll suffer the consequences."

Iris was kidding, but why tempt fate? Keeping quiet seemed like the best plan.

Nubs dropped us off and I finished my homework. It was now the time I regularly talked with Joann. Ed had recommended forgiveness, but I wasn't ready to call and mend fences. Iris served a dessert with bananas sautéed in brown sugar, rum, and vanilla extract. The bananas were topped with vanilla ice cream and hot fudge.

While Denny's affections distracted me from school problems, Iris's desserts came in a close second. We each held a small bowl, with a larger bowl for Otis. Otis loved ice cream, so he got dessert too. Iris placed the dog bowl on a towel, and I expected Otis to show up soon.

I was enjoying a spiritual hot fudge experience when I noticed Bobby and Jean downing the dog's dessert. Otis wasn't anywhere around. How odd—he rarely missed out.

"Iris, do you see those beavers eating ice cream? Do you think we should take it away? Otis is missing out."

"Don't worry, dear. Otis is enjoying dessert in the kitchen. I made Bobby and Jean their own treat. After all, these beavers are growing mammals. They nurse at birth, so dairy products can't be bad. I left off the hot fudge and nuts because they're not good for them."

I was incredulous. "You think alcohol-laden bananas provide good nutrition? They're herbivores, Iris." Remembering the incident across the street, I stated with certainty, "And really, Iris, you think nuts are bad for them? They chew down trees faster than chainsaws! I hardly doubt cashews will constipate them. That reminds me, they haven't chewed any wood products for at least three days. Their teeth won't stay sharp eating ice cream. You've tamed these two. Soon a game warden will knock at the door with a warrant for harboring wild animals."

Iris interrupted, "Laurel, quit blowing our refuge out of proportion. I've spoken with Warden Morley and explained how we found the beavers and what we're doing. He's so pleased that tomorrow he's coming to present us a Friends of Wildlife award. He's arriving at four, so hurry home."

I couldn't believe it. We were receiving a Friends of Wildlife award for turning wildlife into friends? I shook my head, finished dessert, and decided I needed sleep. This day, like many lately, had produced many unusual events. Drifting off, I wondered what Denny wouldn't tell me. I decided it must involve sex. What else would men discuss that involved pleasing a woman?

I planned to bring it up when we were alone. I wondered how he'd respond.

CHAPTER 28

A Betrayal of Trust

E verything went well the next morning—until I reached a spot a hundred yards from school, where I heard a roaring noise. As I got closer, I could see hundreds of students in the city park across from the school chanting, "IF LAUREL GOES, WE GO!"

Many signs urged Mr. Martin to bring back Mr. Wright, while other banners encouraged people to boycott Dr. Dutton's dental practice. A Portland Channel 8 TV reporter was interviewing Susan Small; Mitch stood behind her. From her hand gestures, I sensed she had no reservations about stating her cause on live television.

I realized that if I were discovered, I'd be the lead story on the evening news. I instinctively moved backward, considering how to enter the school unnoticed. The only alternative to the main entrance that I knew about was an old service tunnel that ran between the gym and the junior high. It was a utility corridor, restricted to maintenance men and rarely used, which I had learned about when Joann's brother showed us the entrance. He said he used the hiding spot to make out with girls. Definitely good to know!

I retraced my steps, following an alley to the gym, then entered through the rear janitor's door, opening it quietly to avoid a squeak—the PE offices were thirty feet away. Careful to shut the door quietly, I walked along a short, dark corridor leading to a staircase. I had reached the lower landing and just stopped to get my bearings, when suddenly a hooded person appeared before me. Scared witless, I believed I'd found the lair of a deranged killer. I turned, ready to run, when the killer removed the hood. It was Joann. I sat down, totally speechless.

Joann squatted, looked me in the eye, and said, "Now do I have your attention?" I nodded affirmatively. My adrenal glands were doing push-ups, making my heart pump like a locomotive. Joann said, "It's just an inkling, but I'm guessing some trivial event occurred between Sunday and today. You're probably wondering how I concluded that. I'll admit you're better at linking clues, so see if my reasoning is sound. First, you're suspended; then, you're not suspended. Then I try talking to you and you walk away. Today, everyone knows you had a pissing match with Chip Martin. And, unknown to me, Mr. Wright's a devil worshiper. Finally, most of our class are protesting on your behalf. So what are you not telling me? Fortunately, I know how your clever brain thinks. I figured you'd enter the school using the tunnel. Start spilling the beans," she demanded.

Gathering my wits, I replied, "Look, you were upset after I talked with Mark. You were mad, and apologizing was all I could do. I didn't plan on making your life miserable. I did it because Mark had no experience with girls and he wanted to impress you. My goal was making your friendship one to remember. I look out for you, even if I don't get it right."

Joann started sobbing, and I followed suit. We pulled each other close, and Joann rested her head on my shoulder. She asked, "What miracle can save you from this mess?"

I had no idea what to say. She continued, "Just know that whatever happens, I'll be beside you. We always figure it out."

Suddenly we realized we were late for knitting, so we headed to Mrs. Gallagher's room. She wasn't there, and while we waited, I noticed the absence of normal early morning chaos. Ten minutes prior to our first class, Mrs. Gallagher walked in. Surprised to see us, she said, "My heavens, how did you get in? School is locked to keep out reporters; they'll open the doors five minutes before class. Laurel, are you aware this protest is supporting you?"

"Yes, Mrs. Gallagher, I know what's happening and I'm trying to avoid it. I came here to stay out of sight because I'm not starring in that media circus. Would you excuse us from knitting while this is sorted out? Six days should work. Besides, if the board expels me, you'll only have Joann."

"Laurel," she said, "you're this school's most gifted student. Nothing you've done warrants a permanent suspension. Mr. Wright is somehow involved, and he's well respected by the faculty. The teachers support him and have decided to see he regains his job. The joy of teaching is seeing students experience new ideas for the first time. Our job is to stimulate your minds. When students express unique ideas, it's appalling the board wants to ban them. We shouldn't punish students for doing exactly what the teacher assigned.

"Laurel, I know this mess is hard for you, but I guarantee you will survive and be better than before. This school has dodged this issue for years. They must confront the topic, not sweep it aside. Meanwhile, I'll excuse you from knitting, and you may use my room as a refuge. That's a secret between the three of us. If you want to talk, come see me. Anything said will stay confidential."

I thanked Mrs. Gallagher. Home economics wasn't for me, but she'd definitely gained my respect. She and Joann were taking a risk to support me, and Mrs. Gallagher risked the most: she could face Mr. Martin's wrath for aiding the enemy. We got up and headed off to our first class.

The morning went well. Susan and Mitch were in science class, but didn't speak. When I looked their way, they flashed a thumbs-up. How had these two organized a protest? Susan was a beautiful and popular girl, and Mitch was a tough guy who didn't care about his reputation. Both were good friends, but I never dreamed they possessed the skills to coordinate a demonstration.

While Susan had used her popularity to convince students to protest, Tanice and Mitch had used less subtle tactics. Later, when events died down, I learned Tanice had hidden in the boys' locker room before a ninth-grade football game ended and covertly taken pictures of players exiting the shower. She threatened to post the photos in the women's locker room—using the caption "Which Football Player Has the Smallest Dick?" This motivated the football team to protest, holding a banner exclaiming, "We Line Up with Laurel."

Mitch had taken a more social approach. Any student joining the protest received a ticket to *The Biggest Party Ever*. Planning the event at his parents' ranch, Mitch promised food, go-carts, horseback rides, a dance, and prizes. He guaranteed two beers to any student with a parent's permission slip, although how he planned to authenticate the slips wasn't mentioned. In the seventies, few freshmen were interested in local politics. But a free party, minus the parents, was an event every kid wanted to attend. After the party was announced, people took notice and the crowd tripled.

Meanwhile, Denny was gathering intelligence. It would take a year for me to discover he'd had a part in the scheme. And many years before I learned how he had discovered important information relevant to my situation. Denny's job was covert surveillance: watching the Duttons, Mr. Martin, and the school board was his responsibility. In ninth grade, we didn't know laws existed governing surveillance of others. But Susan and Mitch agreed that if Denny were caught, ignorance of the law sounded like a good excuse. Neither of them recognized Denny's intelligence, but they knew he wanted to help. Denny wisely recruited kids from the photography club—students who didn't mind waiting for the perfect photo.

The only problem Denny and his agents had was having to miss school to watch their targets. Utannah solved this difficulty. She remembered the pad of excused-absence slips I'd acquired, and after science class, she asked to borrow them—explaining that I shouldn't ask why. That was fine with me. She had picked out my dance wardrobe, and the result was astonishing. I asked her to hide the pad at home though—last year, administrators had searched every locker after finding a joint, and I didn't want them coming across anything damning in mine.

Before lunch, Mr. Wilburn spoke over the intercom. "Your attention, please. Will the student who ran out of math class yesterday please return the test he or she took. Mr. Martin will accept it with no questions asked." I had forgotten about grabbing the test. I wasn't sure how to proceed, but returning it to Mr. Martin didn't seem wise since my future education already hung by a thread. Later, I heard someone had for the first time received 100 percent on the exam, and Mr. Wilburn convinced Mr. Martin that the stolen test had some role in that score. Three students showed up for the reward claiming they had found the exam, then misplaced it.

Mr. Martin punished them for lying. They had to stay after class for thirty days and empty every trash can in school. So someone else was being disciplined for my actions, but why they took the bait always puzzled me.

I was eating lunch peacefully in the home ec room when I heard a commotion from Mr. Martin's office next door. Although I didn't yet know who they were, the American Civil Liberties Union had sent representatives to see Mr. Martin and members of the board! When they arrived at twelve thirty, everyone retired to the conference room, which shared a non-insulated wall with home economics. The two rooms also shared common ductwork, which amplified the voices next door.

The idea to record the discussion hit me out of the blue. A voice suggested this discussion might impact me, and recording it might prove useful in the coming weeks. The only difficulty was locating a tape recorder—the audiovisual department closed over the lunch hour. Not that it mattered, since the AV instructor always verified what school business you needed a tape recorder for. I doubted that taping administrators and the ACLU qualified as school business.

I headed to the drama department. Mr. Garvin, the teacher, kept five recorders so students could practice their lines. I hadn't taken drama, but I knew Mr. Garvin because he had coached me on the eighth-grade track team. He wanted me to return in the spring, but until now, I'd procrastinated giving him an answer.

Finding the door unlocked, I entered with the plan of borrowing a recorder and leaving a note. To my surprise, Mr. Garvin was there, reading. "Laurel. What brings you here during lunch? I hear you've caused quite a stir. Is the rumor true?"

Feeling rushed, I replied, "Mr. Garvin, because of that stir I need to borrow a tape recorder. If you don't ask questions, I'll return it today and promise to join the track team. But I desperately need it, right now."

"OK, Laurel, I trust you. Just promise me I won't be fired or sitting in jail."

I said if I were caught, I'd confess to "borrowing" the machine without his knowledge. I left with a recorder, new batteries, and two fresh tapes. There was also a plug-in microphone with a long cord.

I hurried back to home economics and, using a table knife, unscrewed the duct cover. I inserted the microphone into the duct and replaced the cover. To conceal the recorder, I hid it in a yarn basket. Unless someone looked carefully, I felt the setup would stay undiscovered.

I could listen for twenty minutes before I had to leave for classes. I pressed record, hoping the batteries and tape would last the entire meeting. I also hoped the chaos from home economics wouldn't blur the conversation next door. I got my notepad and listened to the discussion. Apparently only superficial chatter had occurred while I was gone—and I soon knew why.

Mr. Martin opened the conversation. "Ladies and gentlemen," he said, "this is the school's attorney, Emmitt Pilcher. Our three school board members are Allison Bond, Webster Simpson, and Andrew Capellan. Now that Emmitt's arrived, please tell us your concerns."

An unfamiliar voice said, "Ladies and gentlemen, my name is Mel Corcoran. I'm an assistant attorney with ACLU. This is my associate, Robin Bruce. We're here because of reports that a history teacher invited religious leaders to lecture students about the world's six major religions. I'm sure you're aware that the First Amendment states that 'Congress shall make no law respecting an establishment of religion, or prohibiting the free exercise thereof.'

"Your school isn't part of the federal government, but the Fourteenth Amendment extended the Bill of Rights to state and local governments. The Supreme Court has used these amendments time and again to prevent mixing of religion and government. We belief this school violated the separation of church and state. We find nothing in the school's charter that bans religion on school property—and it needs to be there.

"This meeting is to help you voluntarily correct these discrepancies so the ACLU doesn't file suit. You all know that court is expensive and ultimately increases costs to the taxpayers. If we can agree on revisions without involving the court, both sides can move on."

Silence prevailed as school officials considered the ACLU's demands. Emmitt Pilcher interrupted the quiet. "What kind of revisions would the ACLU consider satisfactory to avoid a lawsuit? Your organization is premature in approaching our school district. The events you describe just occurred last week, and disciplinary proceedings are set for next week's board meeting. Currently, a private investigator is gathering the facts. He'll deliver his report to the board and other relevant parties two days before the meeting.

"Town leaders founded the school's charter in 1922. It shouldn't surprise anyone that during the Prohibition years, the community focused on religion. Banning God from school constituted blasphemy. Check other school charters throughout the country and you'll find the same attitudes influenced many school districts. Why did the ACLU choose Sutter to advance their goals?"

Ms. Bruce replied, "For years, religion from Sunday has crept into school Monday through Friday. In the United States, Christianity has been the usual culprit, but now other faiths have gained ground. An example is the Pledge of Allegiance, in which children recite the words, 'one nation under God.' Though 'God' is not specifically Christian, the phrase might offend atheists or agnostics.

"Sutter went beyond the Pledge of Allegiance by allowing religious leaders to preach the positive aspects of their religions. Sources state that these leaders never discussed the turmoil their faiths created throughout history. Unfortunately no atheists were invited to present an argument against God's existence. This implies that students must follow a particular faith or face eternal damnation.

"We chose Sutter because here, other issues, like school segregation and low-income education, aren't concerns to distract from our main topic. The ACLU considers Oregon a liberal state, and therefore it's easier to bring about change here. If we visited the Bible Belt, many students faced with this dilemma would switch to private schools, forcing public schools to close. This mass exodus would harm agnostic or atheist students more because they'd have no choice but to attend a religion-affiliated school."

She continued, "Our demands are straightforward. We want the charter amended to ban references to God and religion. Strict penalties should occur for violating the charter. Forcing students to endure religious teachings is reason to expel the student and fire the teacher. If your district complies, we want Sutter Schools to lead by example on how to keep religion in parochial schools, where it belongs."

Board member Simpson interjected, "No matter what we decide, it seems we can't avoid the spotlight. If people in Sutter wanted publicity, they'd live in Portland. Can't we make these changes without unwanted news coverage?"

Mel Corcoran answered, "The ACLU believes Sutter has a critical role in making the Supreme Court define the boundaries between school and religion. You can pursue a legal battle or accept our suggestions and revise the charter. Your progressive thinking will offer other districts a path to adopt similar policies. Without doubt, some school system will reject our suggestions, and legal challenges will result. We're asking your district to cooperate and set the precedent."

Ms. Bond remarked, "Your ultimatum is a form of extortion. The board could make the changes and petition the court to prevent the ACLU from publicly mentioning Sutter schools."

Mr. Corcoran shot back, "Ms. Bond, you may see this conversation as a threat, extortion, or perhaps a warning. In truth, we're discussing actions my organization will take depending on your board's decision. It's true, the district could ask for an injunction, but this would mean going to court, which both sides wish to avoid. There's also a good chance the injunction won't be granted.

"Regardless of the result, a public record exists, which quickly becomes available to the press. The board has freedom to decide whatever it feels is correct. Our purpose is personally communicating the steps necessary to improve the learning experience and describe how the ACLU plays a role."

Andrew Capellan, the third board member to comment, said. "I can't speak for Webster or Allison, but for me, the answer is simple: we expel the student, fire the teacher, change the charter, and set a precedent. Twenty years from now, the district's trailblazer reputation will remain an important chapter in Sutter's history. The board should embrace the ACLU's suggestions and move on. What do you think, Chip?"

Until now, Mr. Martin had been quiet. "I think Penfield Wright is an excellent teacher. I'd hate to lose him. Our best option is offering him a nonteaching position with reduced pay. If he accepts, that's fine, but it's likely he'll reject the offer and resign.

"The student is Laurel Montgomery. You won't meet a more cunning teenage bitch. Surely, she's behind the bullshit across the street. Her grades are outstanding, but her disruption of school events and her treatment of the Dutton girl provide good reasons to expel. To ensure the board has solid grounds to dismiss, I'll provide written evidence describing her behavior.

"We need three school board members to agree with my recommendation. The board knows that Miss Montgomery's attorney has threatened a lawsuit against the district if she's expelled without due process. This is why the district hired an independent investigator. We've made him aware of what evidence is required to support her expulsion."

Principal Martin's comments stabbed me like a knife. How could my class presentation have caused such a typhoon of wrath, drowning my life in despair? I remembered discussing the existence of God with Iris. Right now I needed God. Listening to the conspiracy against me unfold, I felt no power greater than myself. But despite feeling spiritually bankrupt, I decided to pray.

I asked God to lead me out of this calamity. Help was all I prayed for, simple and direct. If God listened to my first request, I didn't want to sound greedy. Then the bell rang, signaling five minutes before classes started. The door to the conference room opened and someone said, "Thank you, Mrs. Reynolds," and the door closed.

Chip Martin started speaking again. "My secretary just handed me a note saying the girl's attorney now represents Penfield Wright. He wants a callback this afternoon. Before responding, I'd like some idea of what

Allison and Webster think about this proposition. Andrew's made his position clear."

I was running out of time and needed to leave. Students were starting to wander into Mrs. Gallagher's room, and being caught in another wrong class wasn't part of my plan. I left the tape recorder running as I hurried out, still stunned by Mr. Martin's plot. In six days, the entire town would witness the scheme unfold in a way no one saw coming.

CHAPTER 29

Mr. Wright Knows What's Right

When school finished, I hurried to Mrs. Gallagher's room. She was in the hallway telling students good-bye. Truthfully saying I'd left something behind, I went and found the tape recorder. The batteries were dead, but the recording had used the entire cassette. Optimistic it had captured the complete meeting, I sprinted out the door.

Returning the recorder to Mr. Garvin, I asked to keep the tape until a copy could be made. Mr. Garvin consented, wished me luck, and reminded me to show up for track.

I left school via the tunnel. I suspected Mr. Landsford would want this information, so I decided to pay him a visit. A block from school, I noticed the media circus had tripled since morning. It looked like high school students had joined the crowd. I remembered to avoid publicity.

At Mr. Landsford's office, I waited while Kay Formby, his secretary, told him why I'd come. We soon sat facing each other.

"Laurel, Kay says you have new information. Tell me what's up." I explained what I had heard and how I had seized the moment. Bill had Kay bring a tape recorder, and we listened to the entire discussion. What I'd previously heard was bad, but the remaining discussion was even more astounding. After I'd left for class, Mr. Martin had asked Webster Simpson and Allison Bond about their thoughts on the ACLU's requests. For the first time, I heard their chilling response.

"Chip, no matter what's done, I see no way around court," said Webster Simpson. "The girl will sue if she's expelled. Is there any other evidence highlighting her bad behavior that might justify your solution? That would provide ammunition against a lawsuit and reinforce our decision."

Mr. Martin replied, "Do you all remember last month's cheating scandal?" No one spoke, but the board must have remembered the event, and Chip Martin continued. "Since you all sat on the disciplinary committee, I didn't think you'd forget it. That's why I invited each of you to today's meeting. The cheating students and Laurel Montgomery are connected."

This was news to me! I didn't belong to the ring of eighth-graders the school had punished for cheating in math. Mr. Heatosky, the math teacher, used variations of the same tests from one semester to another. If students acquired previously completed tests, chances were they would score well. The students involved had a poor academic history, so when they all scored eighty-five or above, Mr. Heatosky caught them. I knew I had nothing to do with the scandal, so I didn't worry.

Mr. Martin went on, "Five of last year's recovered tests belonged to Laurel Montgomery. We're unsure how the eighth-graders got the tests, but we suspect Miss Montgomery sold them. This provides another reason the board should expel her. It's also possible she took one of Mr. Wilburn's algebra tests. An investigation is underway. However, even if the students stole her tests, it was Miss Montgomery's responsibility to protect her previous course work."

Allison Bond asked, "What about the other tests? Which student owned those? We can't discipline one student if we don't discipline the other."

"Allison, those tests belonged to a student who's moved from Sutter. He only attended one semester."

Ms. Bond continued, "Chip, you realize nothing was done to discipline Miss Montgomery when we punished the others. Now, a month later, you claim she provided the tests that encouraged the cheating? This is very irregular. How do you explain the delay?"

"Allison, checking the facts takes time. Confirming those tests belonged to Laurel Montgomery took Clyde Heatosky and me two days of comparing grades between the eighth-graders' current exams and Laurel Montgomery's 1970 exams. They matched. The test grades on the stolen exams matched Ms. Montgomery's scores in the teacher's grade book 100 percent. We've thoroughly confirmed our facts, and this explains the delay. Reaching early conclusions is as harmful as the problem we're facing."

"That's all fine and good, Chip," stated Ms. Bond. "But is there a paper trail showing the progress of this investigation? If not, it's speculation, and I guarantee I won't support unsubstantiated claims. If there's any loophole in your conclusion, the entire district will pay handsomely. When Devlin Myers returns from the Mayo Clinic, he'll double-check every fact. He wouldn't hesitate firing you for any indiscretion. So, do you still accuse Laurel Montgomery of leaking the exams?"

"Board members," Mr. Martin pleaded, "each of us know Devlin's developed a bad case of stomach cancer. He's undergoing surgery in three days, and odds of completely removing the tumor are low. Even if surgery is a success, he'll be gone six more weeks. I have my notes on the investigation and can write a chain of evidence report. I'll have Emmitt review it before submitting it to the board. Emmitt, what are your thoughts?"

Mr. Pilcher continued the reasoning. "Considering the paths this problem might take, your suggestion offers the least risk to the district. It's critical that your accusations about selling old tests, or negligently caring for them, can withstand Bill Landsford's inspection. We may still go to court, but with solid facts, both sides could reach an inexpensive settlement."

I wanted to say something in response, but Mr. Landsford told me to wait until the tape finished. I hadn't seen those math tests since last year. I kept them on the floor of my locker, but since I never locked the locker, anyone could have taken them. Before summer break I had cleaned my locker and assumed the tests were there with the rest of the junk.

Andrew Capellan asked, "Are we all three agreed? Can we form a majority to offer Penfield Wright a non-teaching job and expel the girl?" I heard whispering but couldn't decipher the words. After thirty seconds, Allison Bond announced to the ACLU, "The three of us will support your requests and Mr. Martin's plan. If new details arise, we may reconsider. The final concern is how Tibor and Jacqueline view this case. A unanimous vote would be great, but knowing them, the vote will probably be split. Are there other issues we need to address?"

Mr. Corcoran said, "I'll follow up with a letter reviewing our discussion. In response, we'd like a return letter agreeing to our goals and a time line showing their implementation. A paragraph should be included asking the ACLU to approve the charter's final wording. Unless there are more questions, I think we're finished. Thank you for listening to our concerns. Please have an enjoyable day."

Chairs scraped the floor as people stood and exited. Emmitt Pilcher said, "Chip, I'm telling you now: if this plan fails, you'll become the scapegoat. The board members will quickly sacrifice you to protect their own hides. You should strongly consider hiring a private attorney until this finishes. I'm the school's counsel and, therefore, cannot individually represent you. Should the unthinkable happen, a personal attorney can limit damage and negotiate contract buyouts. My suggestion deserves serious thought. Also, remember that this meeting never occurred."

"Don't worry, Emmitt, I'll take your advice, and I assure you that no records exist of this discussion."

We could hear footsteps as they walked away, then silence.

Mr. Landsford remained quiet, considering what to do. The phone rang and he answered. I heard Kay Formby say he had a client. Mr. Landsford said, "Fine, Kay, I'll be out."

He turned to me and said, "Laurel, wait here. I have a surprise for you."

Wonderful, I needed more surprises! So many bombs had dropped during the last week, I was looking for foxholes. Whatever Mr. Landsford planned, I hoped it didn't add stress.

He walked back in with Penfield Wright. Mr. Wright was dressed in a sweatshirt, Levis, and work boots. If I hadn't known he taught school, I'd have taken him for a logger. It mattered little. I jumped out of the chair and gave him a hug.

He kissed me on the head, asking, "Laurel, I've worried myself sick about the trouble I got you into. The words 'I'm sorry' fall far short of returning your life to normal. I would never ask students to do an assignment if I knew it would cause so much emotional pain. I hope someday you can forgive me."

Without knowing it, Mr. Wright had given me another tutorial. Knowing he would probably lose his job and the opportunity to support his family, he was taking responsibility for my problems. It wasn't his fault, and I didn't blame him for anything.

Bill Landsford said, "Just a moment. You both should know that attorney-client privilege protects your discussions only if I'm present. This means opposing attorneys can't ask you questions about conversations with your attorney. Until this is finished, don't speak with each other unless I'm included. Is that clear?" We agreed.

Mr. Landsford continued. "Penfield, I'm sorry we ran into your appointment time, but Laurel brought me a recording that concerns you both. This tape is illegal; Laurel recorded it without informing the involved parties. Still, we can't ignore the content. You'll hear three-fifths of the board agreeing to dismiss both of you without examining the evidence. We'll listen again, and then I'd like your thoughts."

The tape rolled again, and Mr. Wright's anger increased as it progressed. As it ended, his chiseled face froze in disbelief. Then his expression turned to resolve, and he stated, "That's all horseshit. I can't believe the board has lowered itself to do the ACLU's bidding. Chip Martin disappoints me. The man who recruited me now conspires to fire me."

Mr. Wright focused on Bill Landsford. "The assignment's goal was showing how religion influences history. Accomplishing that goal only happens if students understand the major religions. I implored the speakers to focus on principles of their faith, not preaching. That's precisely what they did. Perhaps asking students to examine peoples' different perceptions of God went too far? There was no plan to start a heated debate."

I spoke up. "Mr. Landsford, Mr. Wright is telling the truth. Except for Elle Dutton, I don't know any students who claim they heard a sermon. It's the first time someone clearly explained to me the differences between the religions. Most adults don't even understand how each faith is different."

Mr. Wright asked, "I assume your friend, Joann, was behind the curtain. Am I correct?"

I recalled Iris's talk about Dr. Heisenberg. I saw no reason to reveal her identity. Promoting the uncertainty of "God's" identity was the point of the presentation. What advantage was there to revealing someone's identity so an investigator could ask questions?

I responded, "I won't identify the person, but it was a trusted friend. This person didn't know what students would ask. The questions and answers weren't written before class."

Mr. Wright replied, "Well, Laurel, the answers were insightful and understandable. I think you have a friend worth keeping."

We sat several seconds while Mr. Landsford contemplated our words. Finally, he spoke. "Both of you have confirmed information I received through different sources. Neither of you can reveal this tape exists. Laurel, that includes Iris. I know she's your caregiver and insists you tell her the truth, but anything you tell her won't stay secret. Opposing counsel will have her describe your conversations in detail.

"Some legal research is necessary to have any hope of using the tape. Even finding a loophole, I may decide it's too risky to use. Does either of you have anything to add?"

Mr. Wright was surprised to learn Iris was looking after me. Having met each other through Catholic charities, they still occasionally got together for coffee. He told me to say hello. I told Mr. Wright he was my favorite teacher and we'd survive this ordeal together. We shared a final hug, and I started home.

Joann intersected me several blocks from the house. Swimming practice had ended and she was headed home. She wondered why I was late, so I told her I visited my attorney. "God, Laurel, seeing a lawyer makes you sound like a criminal. Do you feel like Charles Manson?"

"Almost," I replied. "I haven't stabbed anybody or tattooed a swastika on my forehead, but after today, I'm sharpening my knife. If you see the headline, 'Three Board Members Stabbed to Death,' keep quiet—promise? My attorney speaks with the media and keeps me muzzled. That's hard with you and Denny—there's a lot to say. I trust you both, but I don't want either of you in court. If you don't know anything, you can't be called to testify."

Joann replied, "Your friends are helping in many ways. Many witnessed the events in history class, so the details spread fast. Every student tells the same story. The question they ask is, 'Who represented God?' Would it stretch our friendship if you shared that information with me?"

"Someday, I'll tell you," I reflected. "The presentation's goal was letting everybody sense God without me painting a portrait. People believing in God paint their own picture of a Supreme Being. Unless a church puts a face with a name, God doesn't have a photo. Jesus was from the Middle East. Did he really look like a white Anglo-Saxon hippie? I doubt it. Besides, why force the person behind the sheets into court. Everybody wants God's identity. I don't understand why."

Joann responded, "It's strange, Laurel. I'm not sure I can explain it. You know Gilbert Turner has the hots for Kathy Vendrowski? They're both in your history class. Gilbert told Kathy how calm and relaxed he was after you read 'God's' answers. Kathy admitted she had the same feeling. I don't know the questions, but neither of them expected that the person portraying God would provide such meaningful answers. They first suspected you planted the questions, but Gilbert found who wrote them. Each kid confirmed that he or she had written the questions in class. Gilbert and Kathy want the person's identity because they have more questions."

"Joann, Iris made the candy and pie provided during the presentation. You've had her desserts. There's liquor in everything. It's her cognac-infused truffles that made Gilbert and Kathy calm. I'm glad they verified the questions weren't planted. Knowing what happened behind the sheets, I doubt the person portraying God provided their rapture. You can trust me on that one."

A block from my house, we stopped. A huge commotion was engulfing the neighborhood. TV trucks were lined up along the curb, and reporters were everywhere. I doubted they'd come to report on the growth of the sequoia. Police signaled for traffic to keep moving as neighbors watched, trying to unravel the reason for chaos.

I said to Joann, "Looks like I'll have to run the gauntlet. I'll run for the house. Maybe Iris will see me and unlock the door. What do you think?"

Without hesitation, Joann said, "Stay here—let me handle it!" She walked down the block, and reporters immediately encircled her. She talked several minutes before the media mysteriously packed up their gear and left. When the caravan had disappeared, she came and found me. "It's OK, Laurel; they've left."

Not believing my best friend had intimidated gung-ho reporters, I slowly emerged from behind the Johnsons' doghouse. Whatever her con job, it had worked like a charm. We joined each other and walked to the house. I asked, "What fairy tale caused the reporters to leave? Once a tiger smells a scent, it continues hunting until it catches its prey."

Proud of her achievement, Joann smiled. "You're right; they don't stop unless they're hunting the wrong prey. Hoping I was you, they instantly mobbed me. I admitted we'd met, so they wanted every detail. Saying I wasn't qualified to answer their questions, I suggested they ask you. I said you were in seclusion and hesitantly slipped them the address, telling them that the heart of the town's trouble resided there."

"Damn, Joann, whose address did they get?" I asked. "Only a sick mind guides tigers to unsuspecting bait." I smiled and said, "Perhaps that's why it's a brilliant idea. But use caution so you don't find yourself with my troubles," I warned.

"I'm not worried," Joann replied. "I gave them Chip Martin's home address. Dad occasionally needs a fourth person for golf, so he has Mr. Martin's unlisted number. I supplied reporters with that as well. It should keep both groups occupied for a while."

I gave Joann a hug. My best friend had saved me from a miserable press meeting. Earlier that day, I had worried our friendship was on the rocks. Thankfully, I was wrong.

CHAPTER 30

Life's Greatest Accomplishments Require the Greatest Risks

When Joann and I walked through the door at five o'clock, Iris was in the kitchen cooking. Joann sat down while I went to get Cokes. I asked Iris if she had enough dinner to add Joann. She nodded yes and said we needed to talk.

This didn't bode well. To my knowledge, "needing to talk" meant I had done something wrong. As with the math tests, I knew I could be blamed for trouble I hadn't caused. I asked, "Iris, if Joann stays, can she listen to our discussion? If it's trouble again, I need the support."

"Don't worry, Laurel. Ignoring the media's intrusion on my lawn work, I'm not upset. In fact, the *Sentinel* took my picture today when the game warden presented the Friends of Wildlife award. I'm sorry you missed it. I fed the reporters banana cream pie, hoping they'd write my story. Convincing them you weren't home was thankless. They believed I was lying. By the way, why did they leave?"

I explained Joann's scheme and she started smiling. Iris responded, "There's the reason to involve Joann in our discussion. Head into the living room and get her mother's permission to stay for dinner. I'll call out when it's time to eat."

When I reached the living room, Joann was glued to the TV. Without turning, she said, "Bring your butt here and watch this, will ya?"

A Portland evening news commentator said, "We're in Sutter, outside the Montgomery home. Reports suggest that Laurel Montgomery, the young woman responsible for the religious controversy surrounding this town, may be inside. Minutes ago, the junior high principal, Robert 'Chip' Martin, pulled into the driveway. There's speculation he's negotiating a compromise between both parties. Let's see if we can get Mr. Martin to comment."

The reporter soon poked the microphone in Mr. Martin's face. "Mr. Martin, will the Montgomerys settle this dispute? Is that your reason for coming, or are both parties still far apart?"

Chip responded with a lie. "Well, the district is open to any suggestion that brings the parties closer together. The board won't make a decision until the investigator concludes his report. We'll present the independent findings to the Montgomerys and their attorney. Both sides can then evaluate whether a settlement seems reasonable. Neither side wants this going to court."

The reporter continued, "So, knowing the opposition inside, can you say what concessions you're asking for?"

Chip Martin grinned and said, "Sure, if you're interested. First, I'll ask for a scotch and water. Then I'll review today's mail. After that, I'm looking forward to dinner and conversation. Look, I'm happy to answer questions, but not here. Call my secretary and schedule a news conference. We like to keep the neighborhood quiet. Thanks." With that Mr. Montgomery walked into his home.

The reporter stammered and then said, "Based on breaking news, we just learned Robert Martin is having a sit-down dinner with the Montgomery family. He hopes the home's intimate surroundings are conducive to both parties settling their dispute. We'll keep you updated as more information comes in."

Joann said to me, "We've found the world's dumbest reporter. For experts, they're clueless about how stupid they sound. What's worse, Mr. Martin had no clue the reporters were deceived. It's hard to know who's the dumbest. Someday, the reporters will grow a brain and track you down. After school, you can avoid them by taking the lake trail entrance a few blocks away. Walk to your neighbors' gate, enter their backyard, and hop the chain-link fence to reach your kitchen door." I never knew why our backyard fence didn't have a gate to the lake trail. Joann's suggestion sounded reasonable, though cumbersome.

Iris interrupted by calling us to dinner. As we seated ourselves at the kitchen island, Iris served glazed carrots, chicken Kiev, pasta salad, and O'Brien potatoes. Once she sat down, I decided it was the right time to discuss serious matters.

"Ok, Iris, Joann's here. Tell us what the problem is."

"My, Laurel, you're certainly impatient! Typically, dinner starts by focusing on how everyone's day went. After everyone checks in, we move to specific topics. I haven't even greeted Joann. How are you doing, my dear?"

Joann's face was stuffed with potatoes, so she nodded while her cheeks bulged. "Iris, you know, I'm fine. I avoided picking up lice in PE and didn't make a daily visit to the principal, so I'm thinkin' today was good." What a stupid response! I couldn't believe what she'd said.

Iris had cooled down from yesterday. Now Joanne made it look like I'd been to the principal's office today. Then she dug the hole deeper. "Hey, if you want to discuss Laurel's behavior issues around Denny or her school problems, I can leave."

Iris's eyes shot open. Behavior issues with Denny? Problems at school? Sure, I had problems, but they couldn't get worse. And unless Denny wanted to discuss sex, I didn't have "behavior issues."

Joann continued, "Let me finish this great meal. You know, swimming zaps my energy, and I still have homework."

"Joann, Laurel and I can address the things you've mentioned later, but right now, I want to discuss the necklace Denny gave Laurel last Saturday." I could hardly wait.

I'd forgotten about our Sunday conversation. Obviously, Iris had more information about my new jewelry. Joann jumped in, "Yeah, that necklace is stunning. I didn't know it was a gift from Denny. With all the distractions that night, I didn't think to comment. Jewelry that nice probably set him back fifteen bucks. What's your worry, Iris?"

Iris responded, "I showed the necklace to the jeweler, Neil Wilson. His reputation's good, and I felt he'd give us an honest appraisal. He confirmed Tiffany & Co. made the necklace. It's from the 1930s or early 1940s. Such jewelry is rare in Oregon because Tiffany's business was back East. Only a few pieces found their way west. He appraised the necklace at $2,500."

Stunned, I stopped chewing, lowered my fork, and gave Iris a look of *What the f— did you just say?* Joann was also in disbelief, but until she pounded her chest, neither of us noticed her choking. Even then, it took more disbelief before I slapped her between the shoulders. Despite her color returning, I remembered her stupid answer to Iris, so I added a few more smacks. Breathing better, Joann gave me the evil eye.

I asked Iris, "Did you say $2,500?" As Iris nodded affirmatively, I began to see the possibilities in newfound wealth. Holding back my excitement, I commented, "I'm sure Denny didn't know its value. I probably should return it."

Joann had the astonished look one gives a person examining the inside of a gas tank with a match. "Are you kidding?" she exclaimed. "Why would you return it? He wanted you to have it—if you return it, he'll think you've rejected him. Remember, you already rejected him last week—and look how well that worked. Keep it, and let peace prevail."

Thankfully, Iris intervened. "Joann, let me ask you a question. Assume you dated Denny and discovered the value of his gift. If you told Denny the truth and offered to return it, what would your honesty tell him? More importantly, if he knew the gift's value and insisted you keep it, what would that say about Denny? When you care for someone, short-term pain often leads to long, loving bonds."

Not surrendering easily, Joann responded, "I grasp your point, Iris, but if he realizes the value and takes back the necklace, he might dump Laurel. Then she's stuck with sadness. There's no consolation prize." Tact wasn't one of Joann's strong points.

Iris replied, "Joann, you've overlooked some important points. Life's great accomplishments require great risk—love is at the top. Also, a man who wants the necklace rather than a woman's love isn't a man worth having. Wouldn't you agree?"

"Yes, Iris, the man isn't worth keeping, but the necklace is. Let him learn from his mistakes," Joann persisted. "Rather than take a risk, Laurel should keep quiet. Does Laurel have any choice or must she honor your decision?"

"The decision is up to Laurel," Iris said. "This is about integrity. It's an everyday pursuit, trying to gain and follow high moral standards. Since I can't reverse most decisions, I must live with them. This is true for every living creature. Knowing right from wrong is essential because, remember, people are already judging you by your decisions. Many folks remember you as the senior who set the books on fire or the kid always caught speeding. It won't matter if you win the Nobel Prize, their memories will be about today's behavior.

"When Sutter's citizens associate a name with the school controversy, it won't be Chip Martin's. If Laurel Montgomery is that name, people should recall a young woman who defended her words and told the truth. Integrity isn't negotiable. That's why you talk with Denny. That said, I've droned on too long. Help me with the dishes, and then do whatever you wish."

We washed the dishes, and then Iris said she was tired and planned a hot bath, followed by reading in bed. She said goodnight, leaving Joann and me alone.

I asked Joann, "What should I do about the necklace? Iris indicated how she feels. I hate to disappoint her."

Joann propped her head in her hands, and said, "Iris sure makes you feel guilty, doesn't she?" I nodded affirmatively. Joann continued, "I was sure of my opinion until she discussed your lasting reputation. I doubt the necklace will affect your future, but I see her point. I've changed my mind and agree with what she told you. You'd better tell Denny."

"God, Joann, nothing like waffling on your firm opinion," I commented. "And yes, Iris can make anyone feel guilty. I'll get the necklace and we'll head over to Denny's. No use putting it off. Considering today's events, tomorrow won't be much better."

Joann stalled, trying to find an excuse to avoid visiting Denny, so I prodded her along. "If Denny wants the money and not me, I'll need support. You're coming, so forget trying to slither away!" We headed out the door, Joann looking disgusted.

We soon reached Main Street and strolled through downtown. Except for bars, most businesses closed at five. Passing Josephson's Laundromat, we spotted Rodney Talley and Ralph Schumacher fiddling with the washers and dryers. Now, the schemes occupying their time branched in many directions, but laundry made no sense. I noticed Joann shaking her head in disgust. Both of us gave these guys latitude in their exploits, but we suspected they weren't waiting for a washer.

We marched in and yelled, "You're busted!" Their well-practiced fight-or-flight response made them bolt for the door. Running past us, they made it outside before stopping and marching back in. Rodney said, "Ralph and I about shit our pants. Shouldn't you two be studying or something?"

Joann said with resolve, "You two aren't doing laundry. If you don't tell us what you're doing, we're turning you in. And we haven't forgotten the football fireworks either. So cough it up."

At that time, sophisticated tamper-proof washers and dryers didn't exist. The Coke machine wasn't any different. The refrigerator-sized metal box had a six-inch-wide glass door. The door started near the top and ran three-quarters of the way down the machine. Angled thirty degrees upward, ten different brands of soda pop rested in round slots, all in bottles, not cans. Putting a dime in the slot released the rollers, and the parched sufferer could open the door, grab the bottle neck, and be holding an ice-cold soda. A bottle opener on the machine popped the cap off the bottle.

Washers and dryers were less complex than vending machines—a fact that hadn't escaped Rodney and Ralph. "Come on," invited Ralph, "we'll get you a pop." Thinking back, Ralph never said he'd "buy" us a pop. He went to the Coke machine, opened the door, and asked, "What would you like?" I preferred Coke and Joann chose root beer. Rodney produced straws and a bottle opener. Leaving the angled bottles in the slots, he popped the caps off the sodas and inserted a straw in each bottle. He suggested, "You can't poke your heads in there together, so one of you should go first. We'll finish our business and be back."

As Joann started sucking on her root beer, I watched the boys. Rodney and Ralph visited every laundry machine, inserted a wire in the change dispenser, and tapped the dispenser with a mallet. Removing the wire produced coins everywhere. We finished our sodas as they completed their "business." Remembering our integrity, we put two dimes in the Coke machine.

Ralph and Rodney came over holding their jackpot. Joann and I were accessories to robbery, but compared to the football pyrotechnics, tonight's corruption seemed tame. The boys had sheepish grins as I pointed out, "You guys robbed the laundromat. Aren't you ashamed? What's worse is you did it in front of witnesses. Are you planning to kill us so we don't squeal? The hole where the tree stood isn't filled. That's where you should bury us!" Joann agreed.

Ralph said, "Look, Laurel, tomorrow there's a test in ol' man Olson's math class. We've gotta study. Tonight we can murder ya, but not bury ya. We pride ourselves on thoroughness: we finish the project in the planned allotted time, or we don't start. Next week, we'd be happy to kill *and* bury ya. We'd be studying now, but they empty the change on Thursday mornings. You know, a year ago, Andrew Capellan bought the laundromat from Ernie Josephson. Rumor has it Mr. Capellan's not your supporter. Susan Small needed money to buy ads that support you in *The Sutter Sentinel*. We told Susan we could find the money—that's why we're here. We're not stupid, you know."

Joann replied, "Right, Ralph. *Stupid* doesn't describe you two. *Imbeciles* is more appropriate, though Laurel and I agree that if we see supportive ads in the paper, there's nothing to worry about. If those ads don't run, you're both dead. Understand?"

Rodney brought up a rare valid thought. "Laurel, there's a lot on your plate. The last hitch you want is your name associated with a robbery. If we're reported, the police will want your source. You'll have to say you were involved. Nearly every student is on your side. Most have volunteered to support you. Ralph and I have talent for raising money. When all's said and done, if we haven't supported you, turn us in. The deal's square with us. Do you and Joann agree?"

I had to trust these two con artists. The trouble they'd caused over previous years had yet to cause serious harm. I liked these guys, and deep down they each had potential. Rodney and Ralph had time to change, but Iris was right. Every person made a choice between good and bad. Only limited time remained to change people's first impressions. When that time elapsed, the ranch we lived on would place its brand. Today, the branding iron glowed in the fire. A fair answer to Rodney's proposal eluded me.

Thankfully, Joann responded. "Yeah, I know what's happening, and we have a deal. It's only a matter of time before Capellan figures out he's missing money. This adventure should be limited, if you get my drift."

We shook hands and left the laundromat. I thanked Joann for helping and looking after me. Growing up was my goal, but the pace of maturity occasionally caught me napping.

We walked to Denny's house in silence. The stillness was odd, but it felt right. We saw our childhood trickling away as the glacier of innocence melted into the river of reality. I was happy not to have to raft the river alone. The calm stream of two weeks ago lay miles behind, and whether peace existed beyond the rapids, no one knew.

CHAPTER 31

A Wealth of Laboratory Information

We reached Denny's home and rang the doorbell. Mrs. Jensen answered and invited us in. "I'll bet you ladies are looking for Denny." We nodded in unison.

"He's downstairs working on God knows what. I hear bangs daily, but frankly, I'm afraid to ask. Someday a mushroom cloud will originate downstairs and destroy the neighborhood. Thankfully, we've updated our home insurance. Take this plate of cookies downstairs, but watch your step. This afternoon he dragged home more stuff. The stairwell's cluttered from top to bottom."

Mrs. Jensen wasn't kidding. Heading downstairs with chocolate cookies, we had to climb over cameras, dark clothes, and walkie-talkies. When we reached the landing, we found ourselves staring at an experiment we'd never understand. The huge laboratory staggered Joann, and even I noticed the lab had expanded since last time.

Considering the passionate distraction of my first visit, I recalled few details about the project. "My God," Joann said, "I had no idea Denny's lab was so large. I know he's smart, but this lab beats what we have in school."

A voice hollered, "Mom, is that you?" Denny's location wasn't obvious, but following the sound, we found him under a table connecting electronic circuits. Colored wires ran in every direction. I assumed he had a diagram to keep track of the connections. Later, I learned the diagram existed, but not on paper.

Covered in dirt, Denny hopped up and dusted his pants. God, was he gorgeous. I wanted a kiss but practiced restraint.

He said, "Did you two come for homework help? Or did one of you miss me and couldn't stand it?" His words tipped my scale. I ran over and gave him a hug and kiss. Always a man with a sharp wit, Denny said, "I'm glad one of you missed me; wanna try for two?"

Joann loved a challenge. She walked over, pecked Denny on the lips, and commented, "This lab amazes me. Whatever you do here wasn't learned in junior high. What's the purpose of this equipment? Maybe you've rigged this scheme to impress women?" Joann kidded. "No—let me guess—you have an altruistic invention that will make the world a better place."

"Well, yes, that's true," Denny replied. Then he explained solar panels and their potential for future energy. When he finished, Joann looked sorry she'd asked. Denny shined a bright light on his solar panels, and a radio started playing. If Joann had any doubts, she'd now experienced Denny's intellectual gifts. Denny faced her eye to eye and said, "See, I'm not just another pretty face." Boy, he had that right.

We sat down and ate cookies, and I told Denny we needed to talk. He offered his attention as I unfastened the clasp on the necklace. Looking confused, he asked if the necklace had caused a neck sprain. Wondering why this brilliant teen would deduce that a necklace had caused a neck sprain, I replied, "No, my neck isn't sprained—it's the necklace," I said.

Still not firing on all cylinders, he replied, "Oh, well, that's different. You're at the right place. I can fix it if I can see what's wrong." He took the necklace and carefully examined it under a microscope. Joann and I watched with amazement as Denny remarked, "Gee, Laurel, it needs cleaning, but nothing's broken. What's the problem?"

"Denny, the necklace works fine. The problem is its value. I'm worried this is a family treasure and you don't know its worth."

Denny considered his answer. Finally, he said, "It's strange, but the necklace came from Opal Bernstein." Without any prompting, he explained. "During the last three summers, I mowed Opal's lawn. I did errands and watched her home whenever she traveled. We became friends, and she paid me well. Last summer, she was diagnosed with terminal cancer. Opal asked if I needed any tools from her late husband's workshop. I was visiting the shop, searching through tools, when her bulldog, Petunia, joined me. Petunia was sniffing some old apple baskets, and before I knew it, he scared up a rattlesnake. I didn't witness it, but the snake bit the dog."

I didn't know where this story was going, but I hoped it would get there soon. Denny continued, "Petunia started seizing, so I carried him to the house and told Opal to get the car. Then the dog stopped breathing. I'd read this 1966 article about mouth-to-mouth resuscitation, so I gave it a try. While Opal got the car, I gave the dog mouth-to-mouth. During the ten-minute drive, I resuscitated that dog. Do you know how much bull-dogs slobber? Anyhow, when Petunia stabilized, the vet credited me with saving his life. We returned to Opal's home so I could grab my bike. But before I rode away, she explained what Petunia had meant to her, especially after her husband died. Since she had no relatives, she gave me this box, because she said I was her extended family."

Denny reached into the hardware cabinet and removed a blue enamel box. Inlaid with gold, the box was the size of a kid's square lunchbox. Denny produced a key and unlocked the lid. Twenty to thirty pieces of exquisite jewelry rested in silk-lined compartments, including diamond earrings, a Rolex watch, two ruby bracelets, and a large emerald ring. One gold necklace had a diamond chain and a pendant with a half-inch circular diamond surrounded with sapphires. It was the largest diamond I'd ever seen. Quality names trademarked every piece: Cartier, Tiffany, and Harry Winston were just a few of the names on the custom creations stored in the jewelry box.

We sorted through each piece. "Denny, this jewelry is incredible!" Joann exclaimed. "Do your parents know about this? My God, I can't imagine the value of this stuff. Why isn't it locked in a safe?"

Until then, I had never been interested in jewels. The only jewelry I'd seen were pieces worn by everyday people. This jewelry was spectacular in every detail. These quality designs decorated the models in women's magazines but rarely a junior high school student. These beautiful gems captivated me. I wondered if their size correlated with the depth of love a man had for a woman.

Emerging from fantasy, I commented, "Denny, didn't they sell Mrs. Bernstein's best jewelry at auction? I remember the *Sentinel* reporting that her jewelry fetched fifty thousand dollars—and you're saying these weren't included? Were these her favorites? For most women, they're gifts of a lifetime," I said.

Denny replied, "Yes, she told me this jewelry box contained her favorites. Her father was a New York City banker. Some of this jewelry were gifts he gave to her mother. She considered them heirlooms. Opal's late husband, Dwight, purchased the rest. I attended the auction to bid on her safe. I almost won, until I realized my parents would wonder why I needed a safe. Besides, how would I lower a seven-hundred-pound safe into the basement. Eventually, I figured nobody would suspect a teenage kid had anything valuable, so the jewelry's on the shelf."

Joann and I believed Denny's story, but we still hadn't addressed what had brought us here. My mind said I was justified keeping the necklace. After all, Denny's other pieces held more value than mine. Keeping the necklace wouldn't be stealing his future college funds. However, I remained haunted by Iris's words. Knowing the value of my necklace, would he let me keep it?

"Denny," I said, "this necklace appraised for $2,500. That's too expensive for a girl on your first date. It's more than most engagement rings." Holding the necklace out, I stammered, "I can't accept this because we haven't created the devotion this necklace represents. Does that make sense?" I wanted to know.

Denny answered without hesitating. As he spoke, Joann's presence faded, and the two of us seemed alone. He spoke in a sincere tone. "Laurel, I'm a nerd. I don't fit into our class. People think I'll never amount to much. No girl cared about me, until you." He paused, letting his words sink in.

"Few girls would risk embarrassment hanging out with me. When a popular girl I adored agreed to a date, it blew me away. For the first time, I fit in. For once, I wasn't outside, looking in. Tell me the value of a lady who thinks you're worth a chance."

I never knew Denny suffered from low self-esteem. He'd always seemed to fit; yet, looking back, the popular students had shunned him from their club.

Denny continued, "Laurel, I know the value of the necklace. Tonight should prove it. I didn't expect a lifelong commitment. I gave it to you because you're the first person, besides my parents, who accepted me as I am. When I think about our first kiss, I still get a shiver. You keep the necklace. It's insignificant compared to the gift you've given me. If we break up tomorrow, there's hope someone might like me and I won't live life alone. Thanks for saying yes."

Tears ran down my cheeks as he softly kissed me. I had gotten my answer, and it wasn't the response I'd expected.

As I held him, sobs came from behind us. I released Denny and saw Joann leaning over the solar panels, bawling away. I've since learned that if two women are present, one rarely cries alone. That night was no exception. Adding to the drama, men don't know how to react when women cry. The obvious answer is: *let them cry.* But somehow, this response escapes men of all ages. Denny searched for water, Kleenex, and cookies—anything to halt the saltwater flow threatening the future of solar energy.

Soon Joann and I relaxed, but Denny sweated profusely and looked emotionally drained. We all sat, eating cookies, knowing we'd expressed some heartfelt emotions. Knowing Joann was hearing every word, Denny still had expressed his soul. We'd all formed a bond of trust, and Joann and I would keep it. Finally, Denny handed me the necklace and we said goodnight. Emotionally exhausted, Joann and I walked home.

Joann broke the silence. "Laurel, I'm either jealous or sad. Denny isn't a typical guy coasting through ninth grade. He's the smartest person I know. However you caught his attention, he's decided to let you—and now me—into his reclusive life. I'd like to help Denny feel normal, but clearly he's not and never will be. But God, girl, he's everything you could want in a guy. He's smart, handsome, rich—and doesn't brag. His wants to improve the world, and from my view, he's got hot lips. I think you're the key piece completing his puzzle."

I considered Joann's observation and said, "Here's what's strange. I know what people say, and I'm aware Denny does nothing to change their impressions. Except for a few, he doesn't care what others think. I'm stuck on him, and he really cares. To me, he isn't different, or if he is, perhaps I'm different too. I don't know.

"Here's another mystery. Yesterday, we took Denny when we went to help the homeless. Do you remember Ed? Last week you talked with him. Anyhow, Denny and Ed had a deep conversation. All I know is their discussion involved communicating with women. I asked Denny to tell me what it was about, but he said he needed to think and verify facts. All I could imagine was advice about sex. I mean, isn't that what guys usually discuss?"

Joann cut to the chase. "Laurel, when I said you were the piece completing his puzzle, I didn't mean that kind of piece." I had no idea what Joann meant. I assumed couples in a relationship eventually discussed sex. I expressed this and asked Joann to explain.

"God, Laurel, lately you've come along so well that I forgot your complete lack of knowledge about sexual slang." She took time to explain *piece* in its sexual connotation.

Pondering this new lingo, I knew I'd remember it if used in a sentence. "So Joann, would Ed tell Denny to ask me for a piece? And if does ask, should I agree? If I say yes, how many pieces are appropriate?" I pressed.

"Laurel, what are you planning?" shouted Joann. "Are you transforming from Cinderella to slut in a matter of hours? We're almost fifteen, but I'd never put out—I mean, give Denny sex—until I was older. There's no rush. Look how I turned Mark on. Trust me, right now, you don't need the hassle."

I interrupted, "I turn fifteen in two weeks. That's not a long reach to maturity. But, I agree with you. I asked Iris about the right time for sex, and I'm not ready. Turning fifteen won't change my feelings."

Joann stared and said, "You discussed sex with Iris? I doubt Iris has ever had sex, let alone knows anything about it. I can't talk with Mom, and Dad says, 'Ask your mother.' Let's face it, Laurel—Iris isn't your normal adult."

I agreed. "She's different. But you know Iris is easygoing and usually says something intelligent. Compared with Mom, Iris doesn't even blush at intimate questions. She said the personal issues we don't discuss often mean the most. The last two weeks, we've talked about guys, religion, sex, love, and the Heisenberg Uncertainty Principle. She was fluent in every subject.

"I love Mom, but I feel better with Iris when it involves the mess at school. Iris hasn't guaranteed it, but she radiates the feeling that everything will be all right. It's odd, Joann. My vision of 'all right' is never close to how 'all right' eventually turns out. That probably doesn't make sense. But if I have a goal that's worthwhile and a solid plan to achieve it, the results are usually better than I expected. Is that true for you?" I asked.

Joann said, "My goal right now is graduating from high school. Thanks to your extra credit plan, I'm getting five minutes closer to my diploma. And tell me: what is the Heisenberg Uncertainty Principle? I missed that in science."

During the rest of our walk, I explained quantum mechanics and how objects aren't real unless you observe them. I detected doubt when Joann pointed at my neck and commented, "Laurel, if Heisenberg's correct, that necklace doesn't exist until we look at it. We could have closed our eyes and avoided tonight's interrogation party!"

We stopped at Joann's home, where she hugged me and said, "The Heisenberg Uncertainty Principle, huh? There's no question: you're

Denny's missing piece." She patted me on the back and said, "See you tomorrow. Thanks for removing the boredom from my life."

I arrived home late and stayed up doing homework, finishing at midnight. Changing into my pajamas, I couldn't bring myself to remove the necklace. Mrs. Bernstein had provided me a gift I'd treasure all my life. Drifting to sleep, I wondered: if I were Denny's missing piece, what did the whole puzzle reveal?

CHAPTER 32

An Interview about Math and God

I awoke to Iris knocking and reminding me I was late. I saw the time, and indeed, I was forty minutes behind schedule. I attempted to save time by trying on two outfits rather than six. Reducing my hair brush-strokes from a hundred to fifty trimmed more minutes. I hurried downstairs and sat down for breakfast. Iris never disappointed. The smoked Gouda, crab, and cherry tomato omelet caressed my taste buds.

The phone rang, and I heard Iris say, "Good morning, Bill. Yes, we're fine." Iris paused and kept nodding. Finally, "No, if we need to show up, then we'll be there. Can I ask him questions? What do you mean, no? That seems unfair. Well, that doesn't leave much time. It gives me twenty minutes to change and put on my face. Bill, I know you're married. Your wife wouldn't tolerate such a stunt. Since I never look better no matter what, I'm letting you off the hook. We'll see you soon, dear." She hung up.

This wasn't good. I was certain that "we" referred to Iris and me. I was also sure "Bill" wasn't Buffalo Bill—it had to be Mr. Landsford. Whatever "we" were doing, it meant missing school.

Confirming my suspicions, Iris said, "Laurel, Bill Landsford has summoned us. The school's investigator arrives at nine to interview you. Mr. Landsford told the investigator he was sitting in and recording the session. Apparently, the investigator isn't happy, but his happiness isn't a priority. On a nicer note, Bill convinced the school to excuse you all day."

Most kids would happily sit through unpleasant questions to skip school the whole day. But knowing three board members had already decided their votes, I felt the interview would be a waste of time. Obviously, Mr. Landsford disagreed. He knew everything and still wanted me there. Despite my misgivings, I planned to cooperate.

Since I wasn't rushing to school, I turned on the television. After the last week, it was getting hard to surprise me, but as I flipped the channel knob, both Portland networks were reporting the pandemonium at City Park. Cameras panned today's massive crowd, which easily dwarfed yesterday's protest. Looking at two groups taking sides—with police standing by—I couldn't believe people gave my words such powerful influence in their lives.

Reporters said students from Oral Roberts University had come to Sutter last night, while the NAACP had arrived this morning. The university students promoted a solid Christian school education as a fundamental condition to enter college. Members of the NAACP supported Penfield Wright. The news agencies estimated eight hundred people were trying to outshout their opponents in the drenching rain.

One reporter noted, "No one's interviewed Laurel Montgomery, the young woman at the center of this controversy. Reports confirm she attended school yesterday but left for an undisclosed location. We'll continue our attempts to find Miss Montgomery and bring you an exclusive interview."

I switched the TV off. One fact was certain: the predators roving the town had increased dramatically. Some had an appetite for school administrators, but all awaited the chance to devour me.

While Iris dressed, I called Joann. I wanted to tell her I wasn't going to school. The phone answered on the second ring.

"Hello," she said. I swallowed wrong, and started coughing. I couldn't get a word out. "Laurel, are you croaking?" she wanted to know. "Why are you calling now? I'm leaving for school and time's too short to gab. Whatever your worries, we'll talk later. See you at school. Meet me in the tunnel."

Joann hung up. I hadn't said a word.

I let it go. If I upset Joann, we'd address it later. Iris appeared, wearing black leotards and an orange skirt. I hadn't previously seen any cellulite below the knees, but her leotards left no doubt. Completing her outfit was a white blouse showcasing an embroidered pony over the pocket. I assumed she wore the green baseball cap because she was previewing a Halloween costume. And although that wasn't true, thinking of Iris as a pumpkin was more palatable than admitting she was a fashion schizophrenic.

"All right, dear, I'm ready. Did you talk with Joann?"

"Well, Joann talked, but saying I talked with her would be stretching it." I told Iris about the news story and why we should leave through the back door.

At the window, looking toward the street, Iris said, "You've got a point. They've seen through Joann's ruse. I can't climb the fence in this outfit, so here's the plan: I'll distract the reporters while you escape. When I'm finished, we'll meet at Bill's office. They'll follow me, so make sure you've vanished before I'm close. There'll be hell to pay if you aren't!"

I headed out back, climbed the fence, and reached the trail in seconds. I got to the sidewalk using a shortcut I'd discovered playing hide-and-seek as a child. One block away, a whirlpool of reporters engulfed Iris, hoping for new gossip. I was trying to figure out a way to hear her response without edging closer when someone tapped my shoulder. Convinced a reporter had cornered me, I turned, ready to run. To my surprise, there stood Utannah. I hugged her and asked why she had come.

"Hey, Laurel, I'm glad I found you! I came to warn you that the school's a war zone. Protesters and reporters are everywhere. It's a challenge just reaching the building."

"Don't worry, Utannah. I'm not headed to school." I explained what I was doing and why. "But thanks for warning me. I'll keep that in mind for tomorrow. You know the students are talking about Donny Osmond; my God, how did you land him for a date? He's the real story, not my troubles," I exclaimed. "Do you think he'll ask you out again?" I asked.

Utannah laughed. "I like Donny a lot. He's fun but reserved compared to other boys I've known. I tried to kiss him, and he held back. I've never been with a guy who didn't want to kiss me. Usually, the girls play hard to get, not the other way around. Can you think why a young man wouldn't want to kiss?"

"Utannah, even in everyday clothes, you look spectacular. He's Mormon, you know. Kissing on first dates probably isn't allowed. It's likely the French are more outgoing than the Mormons. Try your charms on another guy. I'll probably be suspended by next Friday, but I'll help you find a guy."

Utannah looked puzzled. "Don't be so sure they'll vote for a suspension. The board hasn't heard that investigator's report. He interviewed everyone from history class. The next day he returned and asked questions about stolen math tests. I wasn't sure how math tests related to history, so I wanted an explanation. He wouldn't answer, so I left. I think he's framing you," Utannah said.

I confirmed, "I know he's *not* on my side, so today won't be easy. I have to reach my lawyer's office before the reporters trailing my nanny catch sight of me. We'd better get moving."

Utannah tagged along until we reached Mr. Landsford's office. She wished me luck and took an alternate route to school. I scanned the sidewalk; seeing that no one cared to brave the morning chill, I slipped in the front entrance without drawing attention.

No one was present, but within five minutes, Iris trudged through the door. She looked disheveled. Fearing a long conversation, and knowing silence was golden, I decided not to ask Iris about her experience on the way here. When Kay Formby arrived, she served soft drinks and coffee. She said Bill was meeting with the private investigator, working out the format for my interview. She implied it wouldn't take long. Iris put herself back together and expressed her legal thoughts.

"Laurel, I'm no lawyer, but supposedly, it's better to answer yes or no unless you're testifying in court. Apparently, offering details provides more evidence against you."

I agreed. "Yes, that's true. But clearly explaining my viewpoint to the board may keep me out of court. Except for Bill, nobody's asked for my assessment. If I don't explain my answers, this guy will say I didn't cooperate—and that's what the board wants. Iris, they're looking for reasons to expel me. Until I address the board, this is my only chance to defend myself," I said with conviction.

Iris squeezed my hand, saying, "Laurel, for me, the last two weeks have been special. You allowed me into a young lady's most memorable moments—a role usually reserved for mothers. Your mom has entrusted me with you, and we won't disappoint her." Focusing on me with steely eyes and speaking with grit, Iris said confidently, "I'm the person presenting your perspective to the board. It's a serious responsibility, and though I haven't personally handled critical controversies in some time, be totally assured: we will not lose.

"Remember, I was there, so my account won't differ from yours. People fear that your perspective might be right. This board will see and hear the truth. If education means helping students understand the world, the board can't censor religious beliefs that Christianity disagrees with. People experience horrible days. The purpose of faith, any faith, is helping us through bad times when nothing else works.

"Throughout history, billions have found comfort in a higher power. Whether in church, school, or Macy's department store, people can discover a faith that provides serenity. A school that doesn't encourage students to cultivate a proven repair for wounded souls is beyond understanding. If someone tries faith and it leaves them wanting, they can stop and try a different one—or become an atheist. They lose only time, which seems a small price if they find serenity. That's what you tried to explain. People shouldn't be appalled—they should applaud! My answer to this argument forms the core of my being. I intend to make five board members feel the same way."

I asked, "Have you decided how you'll persuade them? Unless you have a direct line to God, wonderful baked goods and looking after their gardens probably isn't enough. Those are your talents. Can you use them to convince the board you're as wise about religion as you are about cooking and gardening?"

"Laurel, that's a wonderful insight! I never thought of that. Your suggestion makes sense, and I may do something along those lines." Iris was considering my suggestion when Bill Landsford appeared and took us to the conference room. We were seated at a massive walnut table surrounded by twenty chairs. Original art decorated three walls, and a gold-framed mirror hung on the fourth. Beneath the mirror rested a serving hutch with numerous refreshments. A microphone hung over the center of the table. I found the setup intimidating and decided to move near the door.

Mr. Landsford used a serious tone. "Thank you for coming on short notice. After we've talked, the investigator will begin. His name is Harrison Shepard. He consults for the FBI and the CIA. His job is interviewing applicants who will handle secret information. I assure you, he knows if you're lying. We'll swear you in so a court may admit today's interview as evidence. If you're uncertain about an answer or don't know, tell Mr. Shepard. If you want advice before you answer, ask for time to consult your attorney. Do not lie! If you decide a previous answer is wrong, tell me. If necessary, we'll say you misspoke and ask to clarify your comments. Do you have questions, Laurel?"

One question came up. "I know Mr. Wright's here. His car is parked outside. Can he sit and listen? I'd like to know he agrees with my answers. It's important to avoid saying the wrong words and getting him fired."

"Laurel," Bill said, "that's why Mr. Wright can't attend. There can't be the appearance that you two agreed on the answers prior to your interviews. It looks better when you give the same and haven't spoken to each other."

Unbeknownst to me, Mr. Wright would see and hear everything taking place—he sat behind a two-way mirror just above the serving hutch.

Mr. Landsford hadn't lied. Penfield Wright and I never discussed our answers, and if we did, our attorney was always present. If our stories agreed, events must have unfolded as we testified. Mr. Landsford had engineered a legal plan that would leave no trace of Mr. Wright's presence.

Bill went and got Harrison Shepard. He was a small, balding man nearing sixty who personified the ninety-eight-pound weakling I'd seen in Charles Atlas ads. His suit was worn, and he didn't appear organized. I started to relax. He arranged his notepad and introduced himself in a soft dainty voice. He thanked me for missing school so he could finish his investigation. Letting me know his only purpose was finding the truth, he repeated many points Mr. Landsford had already explained. And then we began.

His first question came in a booming resonance, catching me off guard. "Miss Montgomery, where are your eighth-grade math tests, and can you produce them?" Truthfully, I was almost certain who took them, but I wasn't completely sure.

"No, I don't remember," I responded.

He continued, "Did you destroy them, give them away, or misplace them? Surely, a young lady with your intelligence has some idea how eighth-graders got those tests. Think carefully: how did they get those tests?"

I replied thoughtfully so I wouldn't contradict myself. "Mr. Shepard," I replied, "do you know where your eighth-grade math tests are? Probably you don't, and neither do I! And I won't waste time locating them." Mr. Landsford, smiled, apparently pleased with my retort. Summoning newfound courage, I continued, "Unless you connect last year's math tests with history class, I won't address them again."

Mr. Shepard appeared taken back but was not easily deterred. He continued his inquiry. "Miss Montgomery, I understand your frustration over these questions. You may not know your math tests played a major role in a recent cheating scandal. It's important to know if you supplied your tests to the students. The cheating issue, along with what occurred in history class, are concerns I need to explore. It helps you to thoroughly answer my questions. You may choose not to answer; however, doing so could raise suspicion that you're withholding critical facts. That impression will not favor your future."

I turned to ask Bill a question. Iris was asleep on the couch. I only hoped my faithful guardian wouldn't start snoring.

Mr. Landsford said, "Miss Montgomery would like to go on record with a statement that should conclude your math test questions. I agree with her. There are no connections between those tests and the religious issues discussed in class. Also, for the record, evidence exists that the only purpose of these irrelevant questions is pursuing a witch hunt started by Mr. Martin and three board members. Simply stated, there aren't enough grounds to expel Laurel, so they're making them up! It's very likely proof exists to support our claim. If I need to subpoena board members, I won't hesitate. Laurel, please make your statement."

I had no negotiating experience, but I knew Bill Landsford had just sent a powerful message to the board. The tape would be difficult to use, but implying to the board we had knowledge of their scheme was a psychological shot across their bow. I felt a slight glimmer of hope.

Doing my part, I stated, "The honest answer is, I don't know where those math tests went. I didn't sell or give them to anyone. I put old assignments in my locker, to study for finals. During the school year, my locker becomes cluttered. Since I don't lock the door, it's possible someone stole the tests. When the school year ends, I throw out old assignments, so it's possible those tests were retrieved from the trash."

Mr. Shepard absorbed everything and said, "Very well, Miss Montgomery. If that's your final word concerning the tests, we'll move on."

We spent two more hours discussing what the religious leaders had told the students, and their handout comparing faiths. I confirmed how their short talks had enlightened me and that I believed their goal wasn't to recruit new members. I explained that Mr. Wright had wanted us to understand how religion shapes history and felt the best approach was having leaders of many faiths help students see how religions impact the world with their differences and similarities.

Finally, Mr. Shepard wanted to discuss Mr. Wright's assignment. Iris slowly stirred, and Mr. Landsford's ears perked up. I asked for a short break. I needed assurance I was doing well. My answers wouldn't land an intelligence job, but my only aim was finishing high school.

During the break, Iris apologized for napping. "I don't understand the appeal," she said to Bill. "Sitting for hours, tolerating endless questions and not saying a word; how do you find this job enjoyable? Personally, I've never slept better," she commented.

Bill countered, "Iris, do you remember first grade, when the teacher said listening was better than talking? *Silent* and *listen* have the same six letters: if I'm not silent, I'm not listening. Remember, once someone's testifying against us, I ask the questions. Laurel is testifying on her behalf. I'll only ask questions to clarify her previous answers. Should we go to court, I don't want to reveal questions now that opposing counsel hasn't thought of. Laurel's mother is a master interrogator. She's the best lawyer I've ever seen when it involves cross-examining a witness. That's why she's in China and I'm here. Because the US wants to create a solid trade agreement, they asked Marie to be the lead negotiator."

My mother, the lead negotiator? Surely, he was kidding! This woman couldn't discuss sex, dating, or female physiology without Jack Daniels. If Marie Montgomery was America's best at bargaining, achieving terms with China seemed grim. Remembering my arguments with Mom, I hoped World War III didn't break out.

Bill focused my attention. "Laurel, you're doing fine. I'm guessing his next inquiry will explore your answer to the history assignment. He'll probably ask what Mr. Wright expected when he issued the assignment. He'll attempt to use your impressions as a source of questions for Mr. Wright. Make it clear you can't speculate about Mr. Wright's expectations, and suggest it's better if he asks your teacher. It will greatly shorten your interview."

Kay handed me a soda, and we resumed the interview. "Miss Montgomery," Mr. Shepard said, "who was the person behind the drapes during your presentation? No one seems to know, so I'm curious."

I replied truthfully. "Mr. Shepard, it's my guess God was behind the curtain." Bill cringed as I continued. "Nobody actually saw a human being, and the answers reflected the wisdom of a higher intelligence. Because God appears differently to every person, my illustration showed how difficult it is to associate a common face with God. I won't say any more. The person helping me out wouldn't want you pestering them."

"You do understand, Miss Montgomery, that the person behind the curtain could corroborate your story? Do you still assert that God Almighty was behind the curtain? If so, you're wasting a valuable opportunity." I nodded, signaling I didn't plan to change my story.

He continued, "This leads to my next question. How did you conceive your answer to Mr. Wright's assignment?" I looked at Bill, who encouraged me to answer.

Before doing so, I clarified my previous answer, "Mr. Shepard, I'm sure God or God's representative was behind the sheets." Watching Iris knit, I proclaimed, "I'm also certain that if asked, 'God' would defend me now. Frankly, I don't need to prove God was in history class; it's the school's responsibility to prove he wasn't. Mr. Wright's assignment sparked an idea. As each religious leader spoke, I saw no reason why a limitless God couldn't fulfill all their beliefs. I'm not religious, and my family rarely attends church. From various discussions, I'm convinced now more than ever that some entity participated in creating the natural and manmade wonders we know today. I'm also sure my perception of God is similar to others'. Assuming that's true, if I described my perception to someone holding a similar view, our pictures of a Supreme Being would still be different.

"My presentation asserted that humans will never completely agree on their conceptions of God, but God agrees with each person's conception of Him. This is the reason I believe one God can, and does, encompass all people. When people see past their religious differences, peace becomes real—for example, in Turkey, Muslims, Christians, and Jews coexist. On the other hand, when faiths magnify their differences, wars result and civilizations suffer severe setbacks. That's the lesson I think Mr. Wright was trying to teach—but ask him yourself. I'll state without hesitation: no preaching occurred with any speaker. They only described the principles behind their faiths."

I decided I was done and said so. Mr. Shepard had more questions, but I'd had enough. I looked at Bill and said, "I have nothing more that's relevant. I'm finished."

Mr. Landsford knew I wasn't changing my mind. "Harrison, Laurel is correct. There's little more she can add. Your last few questions drifted into topics involving freedom of speech. If further relevant questions arise, call me and I'll send the answers in a signed affidavit. If there's nothing else, let's break for lunch and you can interview Penfield this afternoon."

Shepard reluctantly agreed and ended the interview. After Shepard left, Bill summoned Mr. Wright to prepare for the afternoon interview, indicating he'd call later to share his thoughts. Iris and I decided to head home.

Iris asked, "Well, dear, how are you doing? Are you worn out, or is there energy left for a nice lunch? If so, let's try for a table at The Roasted Pear. Don Caster owns the restaurant, and Nubs says he's the best chef in town. I'd like to try it, and since you're vacationing today, we should splurge."

I was emotionally exhausted—but I had never eaten at a gourmet restaurant. I thought it was a perfect way to salvage the day. "I'd love to eat there. Mr. Caster must be an outstanding cook. You should see the lunches Mr. Olson brings to school. They look and smell great. You're probably hungry after such a long nap," I grinned.

"Laurel, you assumed I was asleep, but I heard every word. At my age, you rest when you can."

As we prepared to leave through the rear entrance, I had one more volley of words for Iris, "Well, if you heard anything, it was between snoring and your lips puttering like a hot rod. What an incredible gift. You should know that I have only $1.50 for lunch. That works at Woolworth's, but I doubt it covers The Roasted Pear. Can I pay you back?"

"Nonsense, my dear. I received a new BankAmericard, and I'm eager to see how it works. Lunch is the perfect opportunity. Apparently, you swipe the card, and later, a bill arrives. There's no reason not to use it. Of course, credit cards are a fad—cash will always be king. When your mother returns, ask her about getting a card for you. If you're caught without money, a card like this might prevent trouble."

Surveying the hundred-yard alley, Iris and I headed toward the restaurant. Iris remarked, "Since we're farther from Bill's office, I doubt anyone will recognize us. There shouldn't be any reporters, so I think taking Main Street is fine." I looked at the orange pumpkin beside me and wondered how no one would spot us. We stood out like red dye in a gallon of milk.

I countered, "For peace of mind, let's continue down the alley. I'm not taking any chance of having to answer more questions." Iris agreed, and we continued our unusual journey through Sutter's alleys.

Interesting discoveries await in places rarely seen. Recycling was rare before the late 1970s, and any item considered garbage went in the trash. Paint, oil, and toxic chemicals made up the garbage collections of the businesses lining the alley.

At the end of the block, we ran into Ed. It was odd seeing our homeless friend away from the stream. He'd driven Milt Ordner's truck to Oakley's gas station and was waiting for service. Within seconds, Mr. Oakley washed the windows, filled the tank, and checked the oil. Ed checked the straps securing the furniture. He looked well-nourished and groomed.

He came to greet us. "Of all the folks walkin' down the alley, you're the last two I 'spected to see," he stated. "And, Laurel, shouldn't ya be attendin' school?" he asked.

I almost responded when Iris interrupted, "Ed, I see you're doing well. You're correct. Laurel normally attends school during the week, but because of recent issues, we're using today to examine our options."

Ed knew the issues. "Yup, I read 'bout the sitiation you's facin'. Laurel, can't help ya none, but ya outta know, ya got my support. I wouldn't be standin' here without the charity you, your friends, Iris, and Nubs been a-givin' us. Mr. Ordner hired me, give me a cot in the coffee room, and just yesterday, he done give me a raise. I've saved ma money ta bring food and clothes to ma homeless friends. Gettin' me a roof over ma head and regalar meals makes me feel I'm leadin' the good life. Least I can do is share ma good luck. I can offer ya a lift, wherever you're headin'." Before Iris could object, I told Ed we'd love a ride.

Ed drove us to The Roasted Pear. After prying Iris from the truck, Ed said, "Iris, I got information that may help."

"Ed," Iris replied, "we need any help we can get. If you know something, it's safe with us."

Ed continued, "Occasionally, I gossip with Milt's secretary. The other day, we was yakkin' when Milt phoned his attorney. Apparently, the school's plannin' to enlarge the high school and remodel the power plant. Mr. Ordner decided ta provide the $1.5 million coverin' the whole project, provided the board don't toss out Laurel or that history teacher. Milt's a good Catholic, and he feels God and a tenth-grade education was all he needed ta succeed. He don't want that experience taken outta school. Accordin' to Mr. Ordner, 'If the board goes hog-wild with 'liminatin' religion,' he's gonna give the money ta the City of Sutter."

Ed's revelation added more complexity to the already confusing situation. Iris asked, "Ed, is the school aware of Mr. Ordner's proposal, or is everything still confidential?"

"I ain't sure," Ed responded. "Milt said somethin' about discussin' it with Dr. Collier. The doc's on the board and took care of his late wife. I do know this information ain't for publicizin', and if Mr. Ordner finds out I told ya, he'll fire ma ass. Whatever ya do—don't say nothin' ta no one! Can ya promise me that?"

I realized I was the sole guardian of all the relevant details—and it left me feeling exhilarated. Clearly, Bill needed Ed's information, but until Bill received it, only I knew every fact. Knowledge is power, and I didn't know its addictive grasp until I experienced it firsthand. Mr. Wright often quoted Lord Acton's phrase "Absolute power corrupts absolutely." History had proven the truth of these words time and again. If Ed's revelations didn't help produce a well-thought-out defense, three board members would prove Lord Acton right.

Iris and I reached the restaurant and selected a lovely window table. There were fresh linens, a rose, and enough forks and knives for three people. We both enjoyed a lunch of strawberry arugula salad with bacon vinaigrette, beef tenderloin sandwich, and caramel apples with vanilla ice cream covered in chocolate sauce. Iris also allowed me one glass of 1969 Margaux, from the French Bordeaux region.

It was two o'clock when we left the restaurant. School was in session, and the news vans were downtown so reporters could eat. We took the residential route home because Iris had talked to the media that morning, so it was likely they'd remember her. We discussed how to get Ed's information to Bill Landsford. We couldn't call because our phone might be tapped. Clearly, a way had to be found.

Iris wondered if I'd spoken to Denny about the necklace, since she'd been asleep when I returned. I considered telling her the details, but I decided not to reveal Denny's superb jewelry collection.

"Yes, after you retired, Joann and I went to Denny's. I needed a witness to verify what I'm about to tell you." Iris groaned as I continued. "Denny knew the piece was valuable, but he still wanted me to keep it. Opal Bernstein gave it to him for saving her dog. Since Denny didn't buy the necklace and it's worth a lot, we came to an agreement. If I sell it, we'll split the money."

My answer didn't satisfy Iris so she persisted. "Are Denny's parents aware of the necklace?'

"No, they aren't. It was a gift, and Mrs. Bernstein died shortly after she gave it to Denny. He decided not to tell them and didn't give me a reason. It's not a family heirloom, so we should respect his decision. I offered to give it back and he declined."

Iris hesitated, analyzing my argument for keeping the necklace. Finally she said, "I'll be honest, Laurel. I'm not 100 percent comfortable with this gift. I worry Denny wants more than you can give. I don't know him well and can only judge based on the short time we've spent together. During those limited hours, I'm convinced the boy is wise beyond his years. Denny's so intelligent, he not only sees the needs of the future but he has ideas to achieve them. I'm guessing his genius is a blessing and a curse. He knows he doesn't fit in."

She went on, "I'm sure my conclusions are correct. My sixth sense rarely lets me down. If my summary's correct, you're the first young woman he's allowed into his world. What's more, you're the only girl he'll ever confide in and value."

As she continued, I believed Iris must be a psychic. She was agreeing with everything Joann had said.

Iris went further. "Denny may become famous, but he'll be different from Hollywood stars. A new girlfriend every week isn't his style. He isolates due to low self-esteem and the fact that few people think at his level. It's an assumption, but he's probably stunned you agreed to a date. So, Laurel, it won't matter what women he meets—only you will hold his heart. Even if you break up, thinking of you will inspire Denny to accomplish great things. He'll want to prove he's worthy of your time and affection. As I think about his motives out loud, I agree, you should keep the necklace. Another woman won't possess the piece because Denny believes only you are worthy of wearing it."

I asked Iris, "Do I have to be so important in Denny's life? We discussed how connections fade with time. I can't see my future in two weeks, let alone next year. How do you understand Denny's thoughts? Essentially, he confirmed everything you described—except me being the motivation for his work."

Iris responded, "Dear, leave next year alone and deal with today. Are you harmed knowing thoughts of you enrich his day? How can that possibly cause trouble? Laurel, you're a gift to many, but the greatest gift to only one. When a man believes you're his gift of a lifetime, he's worth a second look." Iris winked.

She continued, "Experience is the answer to your question about knowing Denny's thoughts. Over the years you meet many people. How people act, dress, or use facial expressions to highlight their words are things associated with their character. With time, you begin to link actions with thoughts. Sometimes I'm wrong, but not often.

"Think about it, Laurel: with every person, you form a first impression. If someone holds a switchblade, you know to retreat. It's rarely that obvious, but your health may depend on it. Be wary and only give your trust and respect to people you truly know. And always remember: never *give* away your trust or respect. These are dividends people must earn.

To know if they're worthy of these assets, look for responsibility, selfless-ness, fairness, and tolerance. Consider your friends now. It's likely you prize them because of those traits."

I thought about Joann. "I guess you're right. I've never thought about my friends that way, but they do have those qualities. But it still isn't clear how you can define Denny and what motivates him. To me he seems complex, but somehow you're able to simplify him."

Iris commented, "During my life, I've met people like Denny. They're usually selfless, responsible, and fair. If anything, tolerance will be his obstacle. Most people won't be worthy of his time because they can't think at his level. Adventure, for Denny, involves unraveling science. The reward for new discoveries are thoughts of pleasing you, or—if you're together—you! Money and fame aren't important. Whether you accept it or not, you're the pivotal lady shaping his life. Do everything reasonable to remain his close friend. He'll never let you down."

"Iris, do you know why men give women so much influence? It doesn't make sense. In the last year, I've noticed the boys never stop chas-ing the girls. Except for Cindy Summers and her crowd, the girls play a more subtle game. However, underneath their coy surface, they're just as competitive. What suddenly makes girls and guys so desirable? Do you have any idea?"

"Oh, honey, that's a loaded question," Iris answered. "Do you want the simple answer or the complex biological answer? Either works, if you don't mind the time it takes to get to the point."

My day had involved difficult thinking—more than any kid not attending school should experience. "Simple works best, Iris. After this morning, I'm not into details."

Iris grinned and said, "I'm sure, dear. The simple answer is: girls have a vagina and boys, a penis. Complicating those anatomic facts, sex hor-mone production begins around twelve in girls and fourteen in young men. Those hormones stir the elixir of desire, and men and women seek out what the other possesses."

She stopped to let her remarks settle in. I understood somewhat. Last year, guys held no appeal. Then, four months ago, I decided dating a boy was OK—if I was his first date! I wanted an unused 1971 production model of a new guy. Now I was parked with the brightest model and a yearning to use his features.

Vaginas were different. I'd owned one my whole life, and the last three years, it had caused nothing but trouble. I'd recently learned vaginas had many slang terms—all of them strange. How did *tail* or *pussy* begin to describe a vagina? I had no idea.

Joann had enlightened me about men chasing "tail," but she too was clueless as to why men used these terms. These were lessons for women that were never taught in school. Specifically, guys used all these terms to describe the same female body part. Upon growing older, my horizons expanded, along with the definitions. It took two more years before I understood that for men, each of these terms automatically included breasts. Still, everything considered, I never expected Iris Wimple to speak the word *vagina*. Who knew she even had a clue? Once more, I'd misjudged her.

"How's that for getting to the point?" Iris asked. She continued summarizing her thoughts. "Laurel, you hold the immense power of the vagina. I can't begin to stress how the six-inch vacuum between your legs can exert control over almost any man. This is another great argument for a higher power arising from the void. Any woman with half a brain and a little makeup can control continents using judicious sex.

"Mr. Wright focused on what alters history, but he probably avoided how sex changed the world—perhaps more than religion. Why, in 1936, the lair between a woman's legs convinced King Edward VIII to resign the British throne. Even Marilyn Monroe entranced President Kennedy by pleasing his sexual palate. Throughout history, empires rose and fell because cunning women with evil intent used their weapons of man destruction. Vaginas force men to abandon common sense. That's the point, in a nutshell."

Iris waited for a response. Astounded by her frankness, words escaped me. I never expected the mating ritual to be described in such blunt terms. Mother never said *vagina,* and I doubted Grandma knew what a vagina was. I couldn't picture my grandparents having sex. All they did was work, watch *Lawrence Welk,* and play canasta. Iris made it sound like people over thirty still had sex—and might even enjoy it. Obviously, Iris had experience playing this game.

Finally, I had an intelligent thought. "Iris, your answer was simple, but seems out of focus. Aren't men captivated by the woman wrapped around the vagina, rather than the body part itself?" I asked. "After all, a vagina is just empty space. How could men like sex without the right woman surrounding the void?"

"Your logic is perfect, dear," Iris replied. "However, young men abandon logic for instinct. Their primitive drive seeks satisfaction, without any rational thought toward the woman. Men live by the motto 'Sex without love is an empty experience, but as empty experiences go, it's the best.' Drinking makes this instinct worse. Alcohol transforms the ugliest woman into Miss America.

"When men finish sowing their oats and emerge from their alcoholic or hormonal stupor, they develop the concept of finding a loving woman. Most men succeed, but some never do. A fellow Denny's age who hasn't yet embraced his own physiology—let alone the philosophy we just shared—is an advantage. You can share memorable times without Denny trying to remove your pants. That won't last long because shortly, he'll want more. Enjoy his innocence, Laurel. Quickly, the purity ends, and you'll experience having to set the hurdles a man must jump before you surrender yourself."

Two blocks from the house, the media was still present. I took the shortcut to the lake trail. Walking past our fence, I noticed an object embedded in a wooden fencepost. The device was a camera, and it was attached to a cable hidden by shrubs along the fence. We were being watched! I climbed the fence and entered through the back door.

Iris was peeling carrots. She asked, "What took you so long?" I explained what I'd found. Iris commented, "It's incredible, the steps reporters take to pursue a story. Damaging our fence goes too far. Keep looking; other cameras may exist. How do you think we should tackle this?" she asked.

Denny seemed a good bet. As I prepared to call him, the phone rang. I let Iris answer and after three seconds, she shouted, "Laurel, it's for you."

Holding the handset, I heard Joann say, "What's your reason for skipping school today—sick, depressed, or just pissed off?" I described my day and said I'd gladly have traded places. I told her about our surveillance problem and enlisting Denny's help.

"My God, woman!" she exclaimed. "They might have bugged your phones. Tell Iris not to cook. Leave it to me. I'll round up Denny, and we'll be there in an hour." She instantly hung up. It was four o'clock.

Paranoia set in, and Iris joined me in the living room. When we sat down, she suggested calling Bill Landsford to pass on Ed's information. "We probably shouldn't use our phones," I warned. "Joann says a camera in the fence might indicate they tapped our phone too."

"Joann may be right. Since I'm not cooking, let me walk to Bill's office and give him the information." Iris changed into her red-and-orange sweat suit, put on her tennis shoes, and headed out the door. The media tried cornering her, but she jogged on past.

In the silence I recalled the words of the three board members. I knew their investigator intended to fulfill their agenda; I feared my answers to Mr. Shepard's questions had made my case worse. So many variables made it impossible to guess the result. I wondered what kind of God would place me in this predicament. Did He hold some divine purpose? What trouble had I caused to deserve this punishment? Was this a test, or did it represent the first of many difficulties life would throw my way?

Maybe the purpose was teaching me to weather tough times and grow from the experience. I could either abandon believing in God or embrace Him and seek Divine help. When the idea of one God adapting to everyone's needs first came to me, it offered a decent answer to my assignment—nothing more. But over the last two weeks, I had become convinced I was right. After all, if my spiritual idea was so crazy, why had it incited a huge protest?

Unlike Darwin's theory of evolution, my proposal had no scientific backing. Nothing about spirituality had objective proof. People now protested as they had in the 1850s, but unlike Darwin, science wouldn't exonerate me. The only true proof that serenity could be found through one's belief in a higher power lay enfolded in the heart. Whenever I tried doing what was truthful, just, and loving for everyone involved, a reassuring voice resonated praise from the core of my soul. My fears decreased, and my worries declined.

Maybe my proposal could work for others, maybe not. But whether people grasped the message didn't matter; what mattered was that the idea worked for me. However peace occurred, God had adapted to meet my needs. I realized that the solution to my problems came from within. Outside fixes only brought temporary happiness. After that, they failed miserably.

Someday, I'd understand how to easily tap this source, but today, I didn't know how to begin. Years passed before I regularly decoded the secret to achieving tranquility. They were devotion, self-examination, and setting right my wrongs—every day, for the rest of my life.

CHAPTER 33

Hatching a Plot
over Chinese Sweet-and-Sour

As I pondered my revelation, the doorbell rang. Thinking it was a reporter, I almost ignored it—but I decided to look through the blinds. Utannah stood there, alone, so I opened the door and invited her in.

"Hey, Laurel, I wanted to hear about your interview and invite you to a party."

We sat in the dining room and I described my day. As we talked, the beavers came over and sat at Utannah's feet. Momentarily surprised, she said, "Are these beavers? I'll bet they're common pets. I love animals, but before they distract me, let me tell you why I came.

"I'm having a slumber party tomorrow night. It's short notice, but I wondered if you'd come. I'm also inviting Joann, Tanice, and Susan. So far, everyone's said yes. Six seemed like too many, so Elle isn't invited. I know that disappoints you," she said, flashing a grin. "We'll listen to records, play games, and talk. But instead of American food, my mother is serving French cuisine. What do you say?"

"I'd love to come, Utannah. Mom's working in China, and a family friend is looking after me. When she returns, I'll ask, but you should count me in. If you stay for dinner, Joann's bringing food. I've discovered someone's secretly watching the house, and supposedly, Joann's solving that problem as well. Please stay. We could use more ideas."

Utannah called her mother and returned. "Mother says I can have dinner, but Dad's picking me up by seven. I said I could walk home, but my parents behave like we're still in Paris. I hope we solve your problem before Father arrives."

In ten days, the beavers had become used to human contact, and they loved Utannah holding them. But the beavers reminded me that surveillance wasn't my only problem. Convincing Mom to get Otis hadn't been

RITA JONES ⸺ 253

easy. Surprising her with two beavers after a long stint in China would be much harder. Iris would have to step up and help me out.

I could offer them to Utannah, since she believed beavers were a common household pet. But if she accepted, it wouldn't be long before her parents realized I'd made my problem their problem. I liked Utannah. She exuded sophistication but never belittled others. I hoped she'd teach me her style. People on the West Coast had abandoned formality years ago, and setting aside etiquette allowed people to justify their lower standards. The French projected sophistication that seemingly lifted them above daily calamity. Since calamity had recently ruled my life, rising above it sounded good. This was the noble goal I aspired to.

We held the beavers until someone pounded on the door. Looking out the window, we saw Joann and Denny. Joann was using erratic hand gestures to emphasize her point, while Denny looked as if he couldn't wait to escape. I opened the door and they hurried inside.

Denny held three bags of Wong's Chinese food and breathed a sigh of relief to be free from Joann's yapping. Together, they portrayed proud hunters who'd bagged their limit of sweet-and-sour chicken. I kissed Denny while Utannah greeted Joann. We put the food in the oven to keep it warm while we sat in the living room and waited for Iris. I asked Joann about her idea for the surveillance camera.

"Oh, I didn't have any ideas except rounding up Denny. He'll look at it and suggest a solution. I didn't know Utannah was coming. I hope there's enough food." She pointed at Denny. "One bag is just for him."

Since Iris wasn't back yet, Denny went to see the camera. Joann and Utannah went along, while I set the table. I was placing the napkins when Iris got home, exhausted. "My heavens, those reporters are relentless. They're searching but can't figure out how you've evaded them. They keep following me, hoping I'm headed to your hideout. I've reaffirmed that I'm only housesitting, but they don't care. Apparently, teenagers arrived, so the press thinks you're home. It's going to get harder to leave the house. Has Joann arrived?" she asked.

"Yes, and she brought company. The three of them are outside examining the surveillance setup. Denny's the only one who understands anything. But I think he's disappointed because he feels Chinese food is inferior to your cooking."

Iris beamed as I went on.

"My other friend, Utannah, dropped by—she invited me to a slumber party tomorrow night. I told her I needed your permission. She also invited Joann, Susan, and Tanice. May I go?" I pleaded.

"Dear, do you trust this young woman and her parents?" Iris asked.

"Honestly, I've never met her parents. Her father works for the French consulate, and I don't know about her mom. But yes, I trust them. Utannah's lived in Sutter two weeks. She's trying to blend in and make friends. I like her and don't want her feeling rejected. Also, her mother is preparing French food for dinner. After lunch at The Roasted Pear, I'm eager for more. By the way, what did Bill say about our news?"

"Let's finish the slumber party first. You can certainly attend. Leave Utannah's phone number and I'll call her mother. Unless our conversation raises a red flag, consider yourself included. As for Bill, we only spoke briefly. He'd finished Penny Wright's interview and was hopping mad. I'm not sure why. He found Ed's information helpful but said he'd examine it with other recently discovered facts. Do you know what facts he's talking about?"

I shook my head, hoping my nose wasn't growing longer.

"Bill said he'd call back and that he valued our help. Now, I'm starving—what's for dinner and when are we eating?"

I said Chinese was the entrée and asked her to call the others. When they entered, I introduced Utannah to Iris, and we enjoyed a meal of sweet-and-sour chicken over rice, with crab wontons.

Utannah asked, "Denny, what should we do about the camera—take it? Since surveillance without a warrant is illegal, they won't report the camera missing. That choice seems simple," she said.

Denny stopped serving his second helping, leaving others time to quickly grab some chicken and rice. While we scrambled for our fair share, I noticed a gleam in Denny's eyes, followed by an evil grin. Continuing to chew, he said, "You're right, Utannah. We could disable it without trouble, but I have a better alternative. The camera is an opportunity for misdirection. The right scheme could catch the school board off guard. Whoever placed the camera works in the media or for the school board. The people behind it should believe a good story, and eventually their film will find its way back to the board.

"Utannah, here's your role. Would you visit Sister Sarah Agnes and get an enrollment application for Catholic School. Say you've recently moved to Sutter. She'll ask when your parents will schedule an interview. Say you're not sure, but don't give her your last name or phone number.

"Iris, can you arrange the patio table so the camera captures someone sitting there? The camera has a telescopic lens and sits fourteen feet from the table. The other detail is ensuring the patio trash sits at the end of the table, since the garbage is the key to the plan."

Denny asked Joann, "Can you look like Laurel? There aren't many public pictures of you two, so it would be hard for the media to notice the differences—a close likeness would work fine. What do you think?"

Denny caught Joann off guard. She thought makeup was her strong point—but I disagreed—she looked better without it. Her peach complexion highlighted beautiful cheek bones, and most days she only wore lipstick. Extra touches hid, rather than spotlighted, Joann's splendor. Right now, she probably wondered how to downgrade her image attempting to resemble me. Joann replied, "I don't know. I've never disguised myself.

Utannah jumped in. "I can make you look like Laurel if you let me apply the makeup." Joann consented and breathed a sigh of relief.

Denny had given everyone a task except me. Whatever he was planning, I wanted a part in my own defense. Forcefully, I said, "Denny, what am I doing?"

Denny assigned me a scriptwriting project, then wove our parts together so we all saw the big picture. The plan was wicked and laced with deceit—we loved it. We decided to carry out the plan Saturday afternoon. Utannah, Joann, and I would need time to sleep after a slumber party.

We finished our plan just as the doorbell rang. It was Utannah's father. Utannah introduced him to everyone. He was handsome and impeccably dressed, reminding me of Rock Hudson. I was smitten, and Iris clearly felt the same way, maneuvering herself close to him. They discussed the upcoming slumber party, and Iris got Utannah's phone number. Mr. Donnay offered to take Joann home, so we all said good-bye.

Iris gave Denny some pie, and of course, one piece led to three. Vanilla ice cream complemented his dessert and launched him into gastronomic heaven. When he finished, Denny kissed me and said goodnight.

Once again, our home was quiet. I asked Iris, "Do you like Denny's idea?"

"Dear, I said from the beginning we'd have to lower our standards to win this fight. Nothing illegal is occurring. Perhaps the best feature is that no one will doubt the information. People believe their sight, and everyone knows the camera never lies. Besides, no one imagines junior high students contriving such a story. It's a marvelous plan."

"Iris, you've sure made my day better. Your support made all the difference, and lunch was incredible. Thank you for being more than my guardian. You're like a mom and grandmother rolled into one. I sort of hope Mom stays away a bit longer. It's been good for me having you here."

I kissed Iris and planned to start Denny's assignment. I also needed a bedroll for tomorrow's slumber party. Mom stored the sleeping bag in the upstairs hall closet with everything else we never used.

I dreaded opening the closet door. It was stuffed with junk, and a falling booby trap awaited the uninitiated. Each piece of junk had its proper place, and moving one piece automatically moved others. Mom had threatened to declutter the closet, but one look reminded me why she always procrastinated. Organizing our closet wasn't a task for the timid.

As I rummaged around, the sleeping bag materialized on the top shelf, behind some photo boxes. Instead of getting a proper stepstool to reach it, I decided to use the bucket on the lower shelf to stand on; in the past, it had easily supported my weight. This time, however, as I moved the boxes and grabbed the sleeping bag strap, the bucket collapsed. Down came the bag, the boxes, and me.

I knew the bucket had crumpled because of poor design—I certainly hadn't gained weight. Getting to my feet, I discovered I was fine; unfortunately, hundreds of old photos lay scattered along the hall. Putting the pictures in order would take hours.

The photo boxes divided the snapshots using year markers. I collected the prints and used the stamped development date to reorganize them. I had never seen these photos before, and I was captivated. I came across pictures of Mom taken when she attended law school. One photo showed her posing in traditional cap and gown, holding a degree. Others showed me as a baby, including the day I arrived home. Then, searching through photos labeled "1957," I found one of a man holding me. I'd never seen a picture of my father. Could this be him? Only Mom knew for sure.

Continuing my unplanned project, I came across a single photo showing the man in close-up. His face look familiar, but I couldn't place it. I kept several photos out to discuss with Mom after she returned. After an hour, I'd reorganized the prints. I took one final look at the close-up from 1957. Recognition came instantly this time, and again, life's roller coaster started to dive. A second later, I yelled, "Iris, come up here. I need you now."

It's a misconception to believe elderly people are slow and feeble. Bounding three steps per leap, Iris Wimple, wearing red pajamas with cold cream masking her face, conquered the staircase like Hillary summiting Everest. However, unlike Sir Edmund, she didn't have oxygen. As she stood puffing, recovering from shortness of breath, I popped the photo in front of her face. "Iris, is this Ed? You know, the guy working for Milt Ordner?"

She nodded her head yes. Then her color returned and she spoke. "Yes, Laurel, that's Ed, although at a much younger age. Where did you find it?"

I told her how it had unexpectedly appeared. "Why would a picture of Ed be in Mom's box of old photos?" Showing her the other pictures I'd kept out, I asked, "Do you think Ed is my dad?"

Iris took my hand and said, "Let's sit down and discuss it." We entered my bedroom and sat on the bed. Iris wrinkled her face, and with the cold cream, she resembled an elderly clown. However, she had a serious look. Holding my hands, she said sincerely, "I've lived here since 1954, but I didn't meet your mother until 1964. And I've never met your father," she admitted. "But, Laurel, I believe Ed's your dad."

"But why? Maybe he was just a family friend—until alcohol ruined his life. Perhaps he's related some other way. If he's my dad, I want to know. Let's call Mom. It's morning in China," I reasoned.

Iris quickly responded. "I believe Ed's your father because Tuesday night he confided in Denny that he was your father. Ed knew your birthday and your mother's birthday, as well as her middle name. When Denny said Ed had wanted advice about women, it involved him meeting you and telling you the truth. He asked Denny how you'd react. That's why Denny remained quiet while riding home. He didn't want to tell you unless he knew Ed was telling the truth.

"The next day, Denny called me, wondering what to do. We decided Ed must be your father, but the truth should be confirmed by your mother. The pain resulting from wrong conclusions would exceed the pain of the truth. Laurel, I believe that photo wouldn't be in your hand if your mother had no reason to keep it. I'm guessing that soon she planned on using that picture to tell you the story."

Everything fell together. My dad's complete name was Marcus

Edward Montgomery. I knew he had grown up in New York and enlisted in the navy. When we talked, Ed had admitted as much. Questions clouded my mind. Mom never said much about Dad, but the little she had said wasn't good. I had imagined my father resembled the devil. He'd run off and never paid child support. Mom had absorbed his debts, which took years paying off. To my knowledge, Dad never checked on us. I was convinced the man was an ass.

Yet, from my short time with Ed, I truly liked him. He had admitted his faults, hid nothing, and made steady progress using AA. If Ed was my father, how did the extremes of good and evil live within the same man? The bigger question was: could Ed remain sober?

"Iris, what should I do? I have so many questions, but I don't know where to begin."

"Well, wherever you begin, don't call your mother. I'm sure your mom knew that someday you'd inquire about your father. Imagine her guilt if she discovers you're facing a second life-changing event when she can't help. It's bad enough you're facing this added complication, so let's avoid increasing your mother's remorse.

"What about inviting Ed over to dinner early next week? I'm happy to speak with him and see if he's ready to meet and willing to answer questions. Knowing something about the AA program, the ninth step of their twelve-step program requires Ed to make amends to you. If he hasn't reached step nine, it's only a matter of time. Like all twelve steps, it's critical for achieving and keeping long-term sobriety. But remember, Laurel, Ed's not your priority. He's waited thirteen years, so a little longer won't hurt. You must stay focused on what won't wait. I think calling Denny and letting him know you've discovered the truth would help. He's tried hard to keep the secret."

The thought of phoning Denny brightened my mood. "That's a good idea, Iris. I worried that Denny had consulted Ed about asking me for sex. It's a relief knowing I'm not facing that."

Iris shook her head. "Honey, you have no idea what men discuss. They probably touched on that topic as well. My thought is, don't bring up sex during your phone call. Never set fire to a young male's sexual arsenal, which stores a vast supply of powder kegs. It's difficult for women to outrun the blast. Thank him for the comfort he's provided and remind Denny he's always welcome. Say you look forward to seeing him tomorrow. You can never stroke men too much."

I thanked Iris for her advice. By now, the cold cream on her face was dry. It looked like the Arctic ice floe had broken apart, revealing a flesh-colored ocean. I knew the cold cream wouldn't help, but if Iris was happy, so be it.

I reached the phone and dialed Denny. We talked almost half an hour. Denny was thankful he didn't have to tell me about Ed. I did my best to extract every detail about their conversation, but Denny reiterated the discussion in under a minute. It was my first lesson on how men minimize issues. In the years since, I've learned guys can spend days together and rarely discuss anything significant.

Women, on the contrary, place significance on every trivial conversation and can instantly recall every detail. Feeling I had pried the most out of him, I dropped a reminder about tomorrow's slumber party and that I wouldn't be available. Denny said he had plans, so it was fine with him. He didn't offer any details.

We said goodnight, knowing that in thirty-six hours, we'd see each other and his grand plan would unfold.

CHAPTER 34

Reporters for Breakfast

Thankfully, it was Friday. This week hadn't gone well, and the coming week promised to get worse. In seven days, the board would issue its decision and the drama would decrease—unless, of course, we went to court.

I devoured breakfast and was ready for school. Iris took Otis out back and stood in front of the surveillance camera while I climbed the fence and got on the trail. Three blocks from school, I noticed many cars parked on side streets. Getting closer, I understood why: the park overflowed with protesters. By my estimate, eight distinct groups were now protesting something.

The students would soon be in class, and I wondered how others found time to demonstrate. Great jobs rarely let employees take unplanned leave just to protest. And for folks not having any income, wouldn't finding work be more productive than protesting? There were more demonstrators occupying City Park than there were people living in Sutter.

Standing there, amazed, I entertained the idea of disguising myself and selling sandwiches—I could make a fortune! But as I considered the ethics of profiting from a protest I'd initiated, someone tapped my shoulder. Turning around, I stood face-to-face with a woman reporter. She introduced herself as Tamara Teague from Channel 12 News. I hadn't heard of this station, but I rarely watched the news. Ms. Teague said she was on her first assignment and looking for a personal story from someone who knew Laurel Montgomery. She wondered if I knew anything.

I knew Bill wouldn't be happy, but Tamara seemed desperate. I liked her and decided to do the interview. Before starting, she asked for my name, but I declined, preferring to remain anonymous. I tucked my hair and covered it with my stocking cap. She pointed toward the camera, signaling we were live.

"This is Tamara Teague with Channel 12. We're here with a student we'll call Jane, to protect her privacy. Jane goes to Sutter Junior High and attends many classes with Laurel Montgomery, the young woman at the center of this controversy. Jane, how well do you know Miss Montgomery?" The microphone swung in my direction.

"We're good friends," I answered. "We grew up together, and we can almost read each other's minds."

Ms. Teague retracted the microphone, "Have you seen Miss Montgomery since this dispute started? And if you've talked, what are her thoughts?"

"I've talked with Laurel since this began, and I think she's doing well. She's well supported and seems willing to face what's ahead. It's hard facing a principal who wants you expelled. This school would benefit if they replaced Mr. Martin. He can't communicate with students, and he's determined to banish Laurel."

"Do you know why Mr. Martin feels this way?" Ms. Teague inquired. "Is it because Miss Montgomery forced the school to face this issue, or is there another agenda?"

Responding carefully, I answered. "Laurel has kept quiet, but students overheard Mr. Martin accuse Laurel of creating trouble and increasing his problems. He shouted at her and came close to physical violence. Students know Mr. Martin was named Teacher of the Year in 1965. But we wonder why he's not still teaching if he's such a great teacher. It's quite possible they promoted Mr. Martin to protect innocent students from his uncontrollable temper."

Tamara probed further. "Jane, that's an angle we haven't heard before. Why do you suppose that is?" she asked, clearly not listening to my previous answer.

"It's simple, Miss Teague. People focus on Laurel, not the circumstances. I was present when Laurel presented her project, and I assure you, no preaching occurred. She answered Mr. Wright's assignment so well, students started rethinking their views about God. Some parents, primarily the Duttons, complained to administration. Faced with a difficult problem and no idea how to handle it, Mr. Martin responded in anger."

"That's very insightful, Jane. Just a few more questions. Obviously, Mr. Wright is your teacher. How would you describe him?"

Here was my chance to promote Mr. Wright. "I can't say enough about what an excellent teacher Mr. Wright is. History comes alive because he highlights historic events that shaped today's world. He takes time to emphasize the lessons learned from man's greatest achievements and failures. That's why he wanted us to know about the six major religions. How people worshiped God reshaped history. He's my best teacher."

"One more question, Jane. Do you know where Laurel Montgomery stays? Reporters have watched her home without any sightings. There's only an elderly woman who insists she's looking after the home while the owner is gone. Isn't it hard to hide in a small town like Sutter?" Tamara asked.

"Well, Ms. Teague, I'm not sure. If she wants to meet, she calls and tells me where to go." Lying with feigned sincerity, I proclaimed, "I know she's living elsewhere."

"A final opinion, Jane: how will this turn out?" I was already on a limb by giving this interview. The question was an opportunity to pound the nail of fear into three board members.

"Honestly, it doesn't look good for Laurel. As I said, several students overheard Mr. Martin and three board members talking to the ACLU. During that meeting, they decided to demote Mr. Wright and expel Laurel. The ACLU threatened a lawsuit if they don't rewrite the school charter to forbid religious discussions."

Tamara Teague faced the camera and said, "Thank you, Jane, for revealing new facts. Live from Sutter Junior High, Channel 12's Tamara Teague. Back to you, Lou."

Ms. Teague grasped my hand and held on to me, but I wasn't sure why. Her hazel-colored eyes glowed with excitement. She asked, "Jane, can you verify the conversation between the board and the ACLU? Are there minutes, or by any chance, a recording? Can you even prove the meeting occurred? Miss Montgomery's future likely depends on it."

Acknowledging the tape wasn't possible. Bill didn't know how—or if—he could use it. The recording provided decisive proof but had been recorded without the speakers' knowledge. I could face jail time. While I wanted neither, jail seemed better than expulsion. I told Ms. Teague, "Give me your business card and I'll check around. I'm not optimistic, but if something surfaces, I'll call." She seemed thrilled about the opportunity of breaking a story. I left for the gym, hoping the interview concluded today's surprises.

The morning went well. I saw Denny and Tanice, who agreed to lunch in Mrs. Gallagher's room. Denny was eager to see what Iris had packed for my lunch. Tanice only wanted peace and quiet. I asked if she and Mitch were still dating.

"I gotta tell ya, Laurel, Mitch is the best. Besides being older and mature, he's smart and knows ranching is his goal. He also has a romantic side. On Tuesday, he gave me an oil painting of his favorite horse, Piglet. I was surprised Mitch had artistic talent. Ya know, Denny, you outta try applying yourself. There are schools for guys like you. A little work, you'd be the best grocery clerk in Sutter."

I considered speaking but decided Denny could defend himself. Taking a moment to find the right words, he said, "Tanice, let me clarify your words. Mitch, the guy who's smart and knows his future goals, named his favorite horse Piglet?"

Tanice nodded, clearly not getting the irony. Denny continued, "You know, that inspires me to improve. You're right, Mitch has an intellect few could equal. If I spent more time with him, maybe I'd pick up his special talents. I'll find him and ask for help," Denny said seriously.

Tanice looked surprised. "When I finish lunch, I'll ask him. I don't think he'd mind. You're one of the few who realizes Mitch has much to offer. God knows, if the other guys in this school had Mitch's skills, our class would get respect."

Denny persisted, "One more question, Tanice. Does Mitch get his best ideas chewing tobacco, drinking beer, or both? I probably should start doing his routine. I'll get different results if I don't follow his path," he explained.

Tanice stood up wearing a puzzled look. She said, "That's a good question, but I'm not sure. I'll tell Mitch to find you. Denny, I'm glad you're taking initiative. I'm happy to help anytime." She waved goodbye and left.

I shook my head at Denny. "You're terrible, you know that? You should've shown her your lab. It worked for Joann."

"Laurel, she's smitten with Mitch. Tanice thinks he's more mature because he's sixteen. Only a few know he repeated fourth and fifth grade—and barely became a freshman. Intellect probably doesn't matter in their relationship. If I tried to show Tanice that Mitch still lacked intellectual growth, what good would it do? Let's face it, Mitch is a good guy and knows more about ranching than I do. Love or infatuation or whatever lets Tanice see him in the best light. I won't hurt her feelings or start bashing Mitch. Tanice cares and she supports you. Despite her misguided thoughts of Mitch, she's always reliable. You don't need me ruining a good friendship."

We were alone, so I asked Denny, "Do you think Ed's my dad?"

"Well, if he isn't your dad, someone told him all about you. Plus, pictures of Ed wouldn't be in that photo box. Someone in your family's past photographed Ed holding you. He could be a distant relative, but Ed claims he's your dad, and I don't doubt him. What are you planning from here?" Denny wondered.

I responded, "Iris will talk to him and invite him for dinner. I've got questions Ed needs to answer. Mostly he needs to explain why he abandoned us. Right now, I'm not up to facing him. However, if we don't meet soon, I'm afraid Mom won't allow us to meet later. Ed's not drinking, so there's a chance he'll answer honestly. Getting close to Ed carries risks because alcoholics often return to drinking."

Denny said, "You don't have to meet him now. Your mom's gone another month. The other crap ends next week, so wait and see if he drinks. If he's still sober after the board meets, sit down and talk to him. With your situation, today's the only day you can improve. Tomorrow comes soon enough."

"Denny, do you believe in God? And if you do, tell me why."

Denny turned and said, "Man that came out of the blue. I'll answer, but tell me why you asked."

I explained. "Mr. Wright's assignment made me think about the existence of God. Iris said not to answer questions about God unless I thought he was real. She emphasized that I couldn't understand why people saw God differently if I'd concluded God wasn't there to be seen. We studied the arguments used by philosophers to prove God exists. You're incredibly bright. I wondered what you thought."

Denny replied. "No one's ever asked my opinion concerning God. Our family doesn't attend church, but Mom always checks 'Christian' when she fills out the census. So, yeah, I believe in God, but not like most Americans. Studying science and discovering nature's laws supports being an atheist, and there's no doubt science has unlocked the doors hiding nature's unpredictability. In the past, when people didn't understand why nature harmed them, they believed they had displeased God. With time, science took away those fears.

"I think God exists because of the elegant principles governing the physical world. As science breaks atoms down to sub-atomic particles, the questions become more intriguing. This probably doesn't make sense, but when physicists study small particles, the behavior of the particle depends on how it's examined. It's called the Uncertainty Principle. Uncertainty makes the atomic world hard to predict. Even so, the structure of all matter follows a form of mathematics called quantum mechanics, which allows scientists to accurately describe an atom's behavior. The rules governing the universe can't be random chance. Quantum mechanics shows even randomness has order. While the problem of linking atomic structure to planetary physics remains unsolved, the way science has linked seemingly unrelated discoveries suggests a supreme design. Does that make any sense?"

I surprised Denny. "Actually, I do understand. Iris told me about the Uncertainty Principle. Until then, I'd never heard of it; now it comes up twice. What's the probability of that?" I kidded.

Denny scratched his head, clearly amazed Iris knew anything about quantum mechanics. "Jeez, Iris is the most interesting person I've ever met. Having never gone to college, she knows a lot. I've been around bright people, but I'd love spending time with Iris. Wherever she gained her knowledge, it's impressive. I've never met anyone her age who's even heard of quantum mechanics. The high school physics teacher probably can't describe how it works. You're lucky Iris is around so you can ask her questions. If you don't, I promise you're losing out."

Denny was right, but in ten years of asking Iris endless questions, I still didn't understand her. From previous visits, I had learned to listen to and follow her advice. I didn't care how Iris had collected her wisdom. Although several days later, she would divulge her secret and pass some unique wisdom on to me.

We left the classroom heading in different directions. Walking past the administrative offices, I saw a public notice listing the agenda and rules of order for the "Special School Board Meeting." Three topics were on the agenda.

First, the board planned to discuss ways of financing the high school remodeling project. Then they were presenting an award to Brett Moore, honoring his football achievements. Brett remained in Portland but continued to improve. Thursday, he was coming home to start rehabilitation. Hope had faded for significant recovery, but some remained optimistic. Permanent damage was the diagnosis, and he wasn't expected to walk or play football again. Confined to a wheelchair, without cognitive or physical abilities, Brett required lifelong supportive care. A young man's tragedy afflicted his family and the entire town.

Finally, the meeting would turn to the disciplinary actions against Mr. Wright and me. After the investigator presented his findings, the public would comment, and then Mr. Wright and I would have thirty minutes for rebuttal. The board planned to decide our fate and finish before midnight. Originally scheduled for a regular classroom, the meeting was being moved to the high school auditorium-theater so more people could attend.

In six days, Mrs. Reynolds would remove this notice. I hoped I'd be present to see it.

Friday afternoon remained quiet. The previous day, when Utannah invited us to a sleepover, she asked us to bring sleeping bags and anything else we needed. For me, this amounted to a backpack. But later, when I found Joann, she had an oversized suitcase with her. "God, Joann, are you planning to stay? It's only one night. Why the large bag?" I asked.

She looked at me, offended. "Look, Laurel, other than dinner and games, do you know what Utannah has planned? I don't. So I brought my swimsuit, winter clothes, and twenty-four record albums. I prepare for any activity. Can you imagine being without the right clothes if we hit a late movie? Talk about disasters."

I considered her comment, then said, "If you recall, the last time we did something unplanned, you were naked; why change now? Plus, at a movie, nobody sees your outfit, so it doesn't matter. All I know is that we're meeting at French's Fry and waiting for Mr. Donnay to pick us up. I haven't heard about a movie. Utannah's family is probably experienced at hosting parties. Being a diplomat, I'm guessing her father's well versed in social gatherings."

Joann had a weak excuse. "You've forgotten: I had to pack makeup and an outfit for tomorrow's movie production. I'm leaving the slumber party and staying with you. I have to dye my hair, rehearse my lines, and star in Denny's matinee. When I think about it, you're responsible for my huge suitcase."

While I considered Joann's explanation, Tanice walked up carrying a small purse. Since Tanice never carried purses, curiosity overcame me. Adding to the mystery, she didn't have a sleeping bag. I commented, "Tanice, it's great you're carrying a purse, but it's not your style. Do you need anything else for the sleepover?"

Making me look like an idiot, she said, "Hell, yes, and it's all in my purse." Opening the purse, she extracted deodorant, panties, five dollars, and a folded plastic bag. "See, everything's right here."

Joann looked incredulous. "Wait a minute," she said. "Something's missing. Where's your sleeping bag and warm clothes? No woman stays overnight with less than twenty essential items. I'd say you're missing about sixteen."

Tanice explained. "God, Joann, why so much crap? I've got clean underwear, pit juice, and my inflatable pillow." She pulled a white cloth from her purse. "I also brought money and a pillowcase. I'll borrow a blanket and sleep on the floor. Am I missing anything?" she asked.

While Joann recited a list of fashion essentials, I looked outside to see if we could leave school without using the tunnel. Clearly, Friday was a day off for protesters. The park was deserted, and reporters were absent. Still, I wasn't taking chances.

I interrupted Joann's sermon on choosing the right shoes. "Let's leave. No one's watching the school. We'll take the fast route. It beats dragging a suitcase through the tunnel." Suitcases with wheels wouldn't exist for several years, so short distances worked best.

We carried Joann's luggage five blocks to French's Fry. After a quarter mile, we knew the bag topped fifty pounds. I sat down, resting my back and threatening Joann, "Whatever's in here better brighten everybody's night," I warned.

Susan and Utannah soon joined us. After we ordered a Coke and fries, Utannah announced this was our last American food until tomorrow. She described tonight's plans. Dinner and games filled the agenda until ten o'clock. Then, to Joann's satisfaction, a clandestine event awaited. Knowing my name would headline the newspaper if caught outside after curfew, it took courage not to appear hesitant and spoil everyone's fun. Utannah said the only weapon we'd need was sixteen pennies—so how could that cause trouble?

I wouldn't know until the rumors started on Monday that the adventure would boost morale and, in a unique way, exacted revenge—on someone truly deserving it. During my college years, the technique would relieve the feeling that I needed to strangle somebody.

To this day, I thank God for the French.

CHAPTER 35

Let's Chew on a Great Dinner
and Hit the Town

Around five o'clock, a large station wagon pulled up outside French's Fry. Utannah's father clearly anticipated Joann would bring her entire wardrobe. He drove a blue Vista Cruiser, which could hold six passengers and their luggage. The Oldsmobile was eighteen feet long and seven feet wide, and sported a huge engine. The blue beauty boasted nine miles to the gallon.

We piled in, trying to sit comfortably. Every inch of space behind the driver was filled. Joann's stuff took up most of the space, and the four of us made do with what remained. Since seat belts weren't standard, none of us were restrained.

In minutes, Utannah's father was on the way. Mrs. Donnay needed several food items for dinner, so we stopped at the grocery store. Mr. Donnay ran in to grab a few groceries. Fortunately, he wouldn't be gone long: Utannah was threatening to show us the new driving skills she'd learned in vacant parking lots.

She told us it had started after accompanying her mother to the store. While Mrs. Donnay shopped, Utannah slipped behind the wheel and practiced driving. She suggested we try this only if our mothers were planning to spend at least thirty minutes shopping. Utannah hoped to attempt highway driving the next time her mother hosted a formal party.

Tanice, looking to advance the cause, said, "Hell, Utannah, there's no need to wait. If you come to Mitch's ranch, you can drive their truck. There's all highways and roads. You can even drive a tractor if ya feel the urge. Mitch had me drive the pickup last weekend. I was horrified when I hit a tree, but it didn't matter since the truck had a cattle guard across the front. Sure enough, there wasn't a damned scratch. He said hittin' trees was fine but runnin' into livestock would cause holy hell. I still tore off a barn door and clipped the chicken coop, but I avoided anything with four legs.

"When we finished, Mitch said I deserved a shot of Jack Daniels. The whiskey hit the spot, but when I tried the chewing tobacco, I thought I would puke. When your dad holds an embassy party, avoid that crap. Let those heads of state do the chewin', and make sure they're carryin' a spittoon," Tanice advised. Utannah assured Tanice that after dinner there were no plans for chewing tobacco.

Susan piped up, "Oh, Tanice, it's not that bad. When Mitch and I started our protests to support Laurel, I loved the tobacco smell. Mitch offered me a pinch. I enjoyed it so much, I paid Mitch to buy me an entire roll. I brought some along, in case you haven't tried it."

The thought of chewing made Joann gag, but Utannah and I joined Susan. Tanice politely declined. Susan used her thumb and forefinger to pull three dips from a round can. Making sure the tobacco was moist, Susan helped us place the dip between our lower lip and gum. At first, I wasn't sure I would enjoy this new experience, but Susan said to let the juices build before passing judgment. After we'd savored the taste for five minutes, she advised we spit it out and try another dip.

The three of us were preparing to indulge again when the car door opened. Mr. Donnay had returned with the groceries. While not uncomfortable, I felt I needed to spit pretty soon. Utannah's father said he had one more errand and then we'd hurry home. The three of us chewed the same wad for fifteen minutes before pulling into the pharmacy.

To our dismay, he used the drive-through. By this time, the tobacco had lost its taste and the texture was like string. The car ahead of us had to argue over insurance coverage for another twelve minutes, and as we got to the window, the three of us were desperate to spit.

As we left the pharmacy, Utannah whispered for me and Susan to join her in the back of the car. After we had crawled through the obstacle course, she rolled down the rear window and we spit our guts out. Susan and I then proceeded to vomit. I felt sorry for the couple riding on the Harley, but there was little we could do. We waved and rolled up the window. I don't know about Utannah, but I never chewed tobacco again.

Utannah's home was in a gated community near the center of town. The gate attendant greeted us and waved Mr. Donnay through. I'd never been inside this complex and couldn't believe the magnificence of the homes. The splendor of Utannah's house was beyond that of any ordinary home. The house rested on one acre, and a semicircular driveway led to the front entrance. Trimmed shrubs lined the driveway while mature trees provided an elegant touch. The architecture showcased a two-story colonial design with a brick exterior and emerald window frames. Fireplace chimneys ran up two sides of the home. A three-car garage abutted the driveway. Milt Ordner and Opal Bernstein had gorgeous mansions, but this home seemed the prettiest Sutter had to offer. I couldn't wait to see the inside.

Mrs. Donnay greeted us at the door. Without a doubt, Utannah's mother could have been a model. She had dark silky hair and blue Asian eyes. Her light-yellow dress stopped two inches above the knee; a wrapped orange silk scarf cascaded around her neck and over each shoulder. I could see where Utannah had learned fashion and style.

The entryway inside the home opened to both stories. The foyer showcased a crystal chandelier, and below the chandelier sat a pedestal supporting a huge bouquet of fresh flowers. On each side of the pedestal, curved staircases with turquoise-inlaid oak rails welcomed guests into the home. The staircases connected to a bridge that linked the master bedroom on one side of the house to the rest of the second floor.

We walked into the formal living room. The ceiling was eighteen feet high, with another chandelier directly over the center. The living room's focal point was the circular wall forming the back of the house. This wall held ten eight-by-two-foot rectangular windows. Five windows sat at ground level, with five more directly overhead. Attached to the living room was a wainscoted walnut study. On the opposite side was a superb kitchen. I assumed Utannah's room was upstairs.

The home carried an air of formality, which seemed appropriate considering the diplomat and his family who lived here. I knew Joann was lapping it up, like me. Tanice, in contrast, looked as if she didn't fit into this environment. Everything looked expensive—and probably was. But the aroma from the kitchen took our minds off breaking expensive French heirlooms. Having dined at The Roasted Pear, I knew how good food tasted. When a concerto of flavors blended in a melody for the palette, the French never played second violin.

Mrs. Donnay asked us to call her Cateline. Utannah later told us her mother's name was old French and meant *purity*. I saw nothing about Mrs. Donnay that contradicted the appropriateness of her name. Cateline spoke English with a French accent. "Ladies, may I have your attention for a few moments?" she asked.

We stopped talking and listened. "Dinner will not be ready for at least an hour. We have bruschetta appetizers, and various kinds of soda pop. If you prefer, I have also made peach iced tea. I suggest you get your appetizers and drinks, unpack, and dress for dinner. If you need anything, let me know. I will call when dinner's ready."

We hurried for the kitchen and loaded our plates. Utannah brought the entire appetizer tray as we headed upstairs. Arriving at her bedroom, we guessed that it was six hundred square feet—plenty of room to unroll five sleeping bags. Tanice asked for a blanket and was instantly at home. We played records, talked about boys, and enjoyed the bruschetta.

In a corner of Utannah's room, I noticed something rolled up and covered with towels. When I asked her about it, she winked and said, "It's for later."

Excitement built as we donned our finery for the event we were about to experience. It felt wonderful to be dressing for ourselves—not the guys. Eventually, Mrs. Donnay poked her head in and told us dinner was ready. Like migrating wildebeests, we stormed down the stairs as if there wouldn't be enough seats. We were beating cheeks to the dining room when Joann put out her arm signaling us to slow down. As the rest of us reached the foyer, we understood why.

The dining room table was set formally, with an embroidered tablecloth and fine lace napkins. A dozen short-stemmed red roses graced the center of the table, while crystal candleholders brightened each end. Each place setting held French china and sterling silver utensils. Also present was an elegant name card marking where each of us should sit. I thought The Roasted Pear was formal, but I sensed French diplomats had higher standards than the town's best restaurant. I'd soon experience how true that was!

All of us tried to look dignified as we approached the table. We had never felt so grown-up. Mr. Donnay sat down last. Cateline had done the cooking, but she had hired a woman to serve dinner and clean the kitchen. She explained that on formal occasions, it was important for a diplomat's spouse to be present and engage in conversation. With Vivaldi's *The Four Seasons* playing softly overhead, I couldn't imagine how any event could be more official.

For thirty seconds after sitting down, the dining room was silent. However, with five teenage girls present, thirty seconds of silence strains the physical laws of nature. Each of us had two wine glasses, and when the server began filling them—one with a red wine, one with a white—we all started talking at the same time. I wondered how this would go over in a formal household, but to my surprise, Utannah's parents simply smiled and appeared pleased that their daughter had made new friends.

Mrs. Donnay interrupted, "Girls, may I have your attention. Tonight we've provided excellent wine selections. We understand this dinner may be your first opportunity to sample French vintages. Utannah grew up on wine because the French drink wine the way Americans drink milk. We serve these wines because this meal honors classic French cooking. The chef selects the wine to complement the food. If you prefer not to sample the wine, feel free to ask for a different drink. We would never enforce our customs on any of you. Should you choose to drink wine, these two glasses will be your limit."

Mrs. Donnay had immediately made herself a superstar. Utannah's parents had trusted us to act as adults. If we wished to keep their trust, we needed to behave like adults and not abuse the privilege. Swirling the wine as he spoke, Mr. Donnay gave us a lecture about how to judge the aroma and how to sip the wine. He described the many types of wines, as well as some of the best wine-and-food pairings.

When his talk ended, the assistant served the first course. The initial dish was a truffle salad with arugula, white wine, parsley, and a dash of walnut oil. I'd never heard of truffle—or that these fungi top the list of the world's finest delicacies. Utannah told us we were eating black truffles harvested from the caves of France. Trained hogs helped find the precious delicacy, which sold for $500 a pound. We made sure no truffle went uneaten.

The salad was delicious, and I enjoyed tasting wonderful French food for the second time this week. When we finished, the assistant removed the salad bowls and served the *soupe à l'oignon.*

I had eaten French onion soup once in the school cafeteria and held it responsible for two days of gastric grief. I had intended never to try it again. But little voices told me I'd miss out if I didn't sample this dish. To this day, I've never tasted a more delicious bowl of soup. Many times since that evening, I've tried to find a recipe to compare with Mrs. Donnay's soup, but re-creating this masterpiece still escapes me. The toasted baguettes, freshly made beef stock, and French Gruyère cheese simmered together pleased the palate in a symphonic taste-bud orchestra.

The soup alone made an entire meal, but I suspected this dinner promised much more. As the soup bowls vanished, Mr. Donnay suggested we cleanse our palates with sips of chilled white wine. *Domaine de la Bongran* was on the wine label; it was a French chardonnay. Utannah's father explained that most wines were aged in oak casks, but this vintage aged in a metal cask, making it more remarkable.

Mr. Donnay went on to describe how the French view meals differently from Americans. The French didn't consider dinner a sprint but rather a stroll down the culinary path. They designed the meal to encourage family conversation, using incredible food to entice people to stay at the table. When Iris cooked, our dinners were fast and planned around watching television by 7:00 p.m. Utannah's home used the dining room to stimulate appetites and run daily issues by the family.

No one noticed sixty minutes flying by before we had even seen the entrée. This was a slumber party like no other. All the girls, for the first time, fully absorbed the feeling and splendor of maturity. The records, games, and pizzas of previous sleepovers didn't compare to tonight.

Mrs. Donnay brought me back to the present by proposing a toast. We knew what a toast was but had never experienced one. It was the start of a new tradition as we raised our wineglasses and listened to Mrs. Donnay, who said:

> Listen my ladies, choose wise.
> Good friends are often disguised.
> The people you meet
> are often quite sweet,
> but may tempt you with little white lies.

> Look for a friend who proves humble;
> In running a life, who won't stumble.
> They'll treat you as art,
> with joy in their heart
> and pick you up when you tumble.

> Tonight, new friends we will find.
> Who lighten our load in a bind.
> These friends who are best
> May they lessen life's test
> and always bring peace to your mind.

Touching our glasses together, we cheered. Now I understood how Mrs. Donnay contributed to her husband's career. She was smart and quickly put guests at ease. It was no wonder Mr. Donnay had risen quickly in the diplomatic ranks. It had surprised no one when he later became the French ambassador to China. His wife was unquestionably his partner.

I hoped someday I would marry a man with whom I would play a similar role. I imagined how difficult marriage would be if couples didn't share their goals. A ship can't sail two ways at once.

Our entrées arrived as we finished the toast. I wasn't sure what it was, but Cateline, sensing confusion, said, "Ladies, this is *Hachis Parmentier*. It is a typical French dish, with a US theme of meat and potatoes. I take tenderloin steak, onions, garlic, and thyme, and I mince them. I do the same with carrots and leeks. They're covered with homemade mashed potatoes. I'm not sure it beats the burgers at French's Fry, but try it. Should you be starving later, my husband will make a burger run."

Susan quietly enjoyed her dinner and said in a soft, sweet tone, "My limited experience with whine involves my younger brother Paul, who complains all the time. Until tonight, the only French cuisine I've ever tasted is French toast from a package. If you'd like to adopt me, I'm willing to help around your home. With your cooking skills, I'm sure you're underpaid."

Mrs. Donnay replied, "I'm guessing the only reason you're joking about adoption is that you enjoy our French customs. Utannah wishes we could be more like Americans since our way of life seems stuck-up." Thinking Utannah was crazy, every of us gave her an incredulous look.

Cateline went on. "She talks about Tanice castrating bulls and riding horses, while she says Joann knows more about rock music than Dick Clark. As far as Mr. Donnay paying me, don't get me started. He's owed me for years, and that's not likely to change. We're not adopting you ladies, but you're always welcome to visit. We're returning to France next summer, and if permitted, please join us. Then Utannah can show you what French life truly entails. Despite a different setting, the French have the same problems found here."

Tanice was sorting through what she'd just heard. "Whoa, whoa, whoa! Did you just say we could come to France? If we visited Paris, where would we eat and sleep? I mean, I don't need much: some money, two days' clothing, a blanket, and a canteen should cover it. I could wash my clothes in the stream running through Paris and sleep near the Awful Tower. I'm sure nobody would mind."

"Tanice," Utannah said, "you'd stay at our home and we would be happy to feed you. You can't do laundry in the Seine river—that's the Ganges in India. In Paris that gets you arrested. The Eiffel Tower is a great landmark to visit, but crimes against tourists are frequent. People who sleep there often get mugged. But come to Paris and I'll show you why people love the City of Lights. I'm sure you've all read about French history—and so much starts in Paris. Please give it some thought."

We finished our entrées, which put hamburgers to shame. I started feeling full and hoped there weren't many courses left. I excused myself to visit the bathroom, and when I returned, an individual lemon soufflé decorated each plate. Cateline explained that lemon custard was inside the soufflé while lemon chiffon ice cream sat atop it, making it soufflé à la mode. The tartness of the soufflé's shell contrasted with the sweetness of the custard in an exquisitely blended culinary creation.

I wondered if home French cooking was my grown-up reward for having spent five days in the adult world. I enjoyed not feeling like a kid, and I think my best friends felt the same way. The dinner marked a milestone on another front: our horizons had expanded from Oregon to France. Until that evening, our world had been strikingly small. The Donnays were giving us a glimpse of a much bigger world.

It didn't seem that long, but dinner lasted three hours. We stood up from the table at eight-fifty and cleared the table despite Cateline's objections. Mr. Donnay excused himself to make overseas phone calls. When we finished, Utannah's mother thanked us and reminded us to arise by ten for an informal brunch. Mrs. Donnay said she and her husband would sleep soundly in the guest room, rather than the master suite next to us. She planned on retiring soon and asked us not to make a mess.

We meandered upstairs with the energy of lions that had recently finished eating two weeks' worth of gazelle. Feeling tired, the promise of sleep beat out six more hours talking and playing records. I started putting on my pajamas when Utannah said, "Don't get ready for bed. We'll be heading out in two hours. I have a great idea."

Immediately, we speculated about our destination, but Utannah wouldn't budge. She suggested we play Hearts or listen to records, but we were to avoid falling asleep. We tried following Utannah's directive but fell asleep before the first album ended. I was vaguely aware of Mr.

Donnay's opening the door to check on us. It was midnight and highly unusual for five girls to be quiet.

After he closed the door, I heard a snicker. Drifting back to sleep, I awoke thirty minutes later to a flashlight blinding my eyes. "Wake up," Utannah whispered. "You can sleep more when we return. I've prepared an adventure that's way overdue. Help me wake everyone so we can move out."

We tapped each girl's head, and soon everybody was awake, but dazed. As Utannah handed us sweaters, Joann remarked, "I'm glad I brought my outdoor gear. I'll put on my makeup and we can do whatever's planned."

Tanice and Susan both looked Joann square in the eye. Tanice said, "Why do you need makeup? It's twelve thirty in the morning. Nobody gives a flyin' fuck. I don't know what we're doin', but the only folks taking pictures will be the police. If you're plannin' on lookin' just right for your mug shot, then do it damn quick."

Tanice continued, "It's my guess Utannah wants us tucked in by morning." Utannah nodded, agreeing. "So don't be dickin' around."

Tanice impatiently tapped her watch as Joann applied makeup in the record time of one minute, fifteen seconds. Utannah turned on a flashlight and opened her bedroom window. Uncovering the mysterious lump, she ordered, "I need someone to unroll this heavy ladder and get it out the window. We can't turn on the lights because the neighbors might get curious."

Tanice went over to take a look and without hesitation unrolled a sixteen-foot rope ladder with hooks that draped over the windowsill. She volunteered to climb down first, and in moments, stood at the base, stabilizing the ladder. In the movies, it's easy to climb down rope ladders. But doing it for the first time made me appreciate rescue guys dragging victims down burning buildings or cliffs. I had trouble keeping a purse over my shoulder. Joann's purse was so bulky it should have been dropped by parachute.

Once we were on solid ground, we assembled between two pine trees, where Utannah described the plan. It was a simple, well planned, deliciously nasty idea. This excitement went beyond records and games. Utannah reached under one of the trees and pulled out a bag containing supplies. We were wide awake and eager to begin a commando mission for the ages.

We had to be cautious. On weekends, midnight was the curfew for kids under eighteen. It was already one o'clock, and we knew it wasn't just cops we needed to avoid. Upsetting nocturnal older citizens could make them summon a squad car. I'd learned from experience that older people spend their time tracking other peoples' habits and homes. This vigilance can be good or bad. Tonight, it would be bad.

Utannah had brought black shoe polish to darken our faces, but staying out of sight would guarantee escaping trouble. We avoided the front entrance of Utannah's gated community because the attendant tracked folks coming and going. Three homes down, we entered a backyard where Utannah was pretty sure there was no dog. The house bordered a nine-foot fence surrounding the community.

Approaching the side of the home, Utannah directed us to climb the trellis and step onto the wide fence. She pointed out that the master bedroom was inside a nearby window, so silence was mandatory. It took fifteen minutes before every girl stood on the fence. Certain a nine-foot jump would cause broken bones, descent down the other side posed our next problem. But Utannah had prepared by surveying our route and working out the solution: we walked along the fence for fifty feet, stepped into an adjacent tree and climbed down. Dimly lit streets and dark alleys offered a quick but noisy journey to within half a block from Principal Martin's house.

Susan and Joann had talked constantly about boys the entire journey. Joann related my perceived indiscretion of telling Mark about a blow job. I felt vindicated by what I'd done when Susan said, "Gee, Joann, I'm just as bad. I've never heard of a blow job." Joann didn't hesitate to explain in graphic detail what Susan needed to form a vivid picture.

Arriving behind Chip Martin's home, Utannah raised her hand, signaling quiet, just as Susan blurted out, "No way, Joann! No woman would ever put a dick in her mouth! You're full of crap!"

Before Susan uttered another word, a hand appeared and stifled the sound. Tanice gave Joann the *As soon as I silence Susan, I'm killing you* look, while Utannah scurried us behind some nearby shrubs. In seconds, a window lit up in the home behind the Martins'. A head popped out, and a flashlight swept the alley and yards.

Knowing the shrubs didn't provide enough cover, Tanice didn't say a word, but the message was clear: if you make a sound, we're all dead. Five minutes seemed like thirty, but finally, the flashlight turned off and the window closed. Everyone breathed a sigh of relief before Tanice said to Joann, "What the hell were you thinkin', tellin' Susan about hand jobs while we were sneakin' around back here? You coulda done that during English class! We almost got caught, and eventually we'd face the jerk principal livin' next door. That'd be fuckin' great! We're tryin' to keep Laurel in school, not join her at home. Joann, you're a dick wad!"

Joann countered, "We didn't discuss hand jobs, and I had no plans to do so."

Susan interrupted, "Hey, Joann, Tanice, what's a hand job? It sounds better than a blow job, especially for the girl. Can you explain it?"

Utannah came to the rescue, saying, "Look, we'll discuss any specific job when we're back at the house. If we're doing this, we need to start now. Focus and stay quiet! Everybody understand?" We confirmed with a nod.

Rather than go back in the alley, we climbed the fence into Mr. Martin's backyard. Joann, Tanice, and Susan examined the house perimeter to locate the phone line running into the home. Meanwhile, Utannah and I inspected the door locks. Once they had located the phone line, Tanice removed the cover plate and loosened the phone cord wires from the screws holding them in place. She buried the ends of the cord under a shrub, completely disconnecting phone service.

We surrounded the back door so everyone could learn the art of "pennying in." Utannah kept one penny and handed me five more. Two inches above the lock, we put two stacked pennies between the door and the doorjamb. Below the lock, we employed the same technique. Now came the hard part. Could we insert a third penny into each of the penny stacks? Our goal was squeezing the deadbolt so tight against the strike plate that the doorknob wouldn't turn.

While Joann pushed hard against the door, Utannah slipped a third penny into the upper stack. I softly hammered the penny in place with the help of a rubber mallet Utannah had brought along. We performed the same feat with the bottom stack of pennies. Our confidence grew when we tried turning the doorknob and the bolt wouldn't budge. We smiled, knowing the Martins wouldn't be leaving this house—at least not through the doors.

Tanice boosted Susan on top of her shoulders so she could unscrew the backdoor lightbulb. Then we followed the same routine with the front porch light and door.

We put on black caps and sunglasses and gathered around the tall tree in the Martins' front yard. Then Utannah repeatedly rang the doorbell, attempting to wake everyone. She waited a moment and repeated the process. As the lights went on upstairs, we lobbed toilet paper rolls over the tree. A face appeared in the window and quickly disappeared.

Within thirty seconds, lights illuminated the entire first floor. Someone glared at us through a closed window but soon discovered they couldn't see much with the inside lights on. The first-floor lights went off, and a flashlight pointed through the window. We saw the flashlight turn and head toward the front door. Two minutes of yanking on the door produced a scream of "Goddamned son of a bitch!"

The flashlight beam turned and headed for the back door. Tanice broke away from us and went around back to make sure Mr. Martin didn't escape. We still had goals to accomplish, but we were ready to scram, if necessary. I stood to the side of the tree, where I could view the second-story bedroom. A woman stared out the dark window, looking from side to side. The other upstairs windows showed no movement.

Moments later, the flashlight revisited the front door, then stopped and turned right. Indirect light profiled Mr. Martin dialing the phone. After several tries, he realized the phone was dead. Looking up, our principal saw Tanice standing at the window, taunting him as she shook her index finger from side to side. Finally, she joined us as we heard Mr. Martin yelling, "I'm going to castrate you little fuckers." I was relieved knowing he thought we were boys.

"What took you so long?" I asked Tanice. "I was getting worried."

"When he turned on the first-floor lights, I thought he might signal a neighbor by turning the lights on and off," she explained. "I searched for the main electrical shutoff switch. The box sat near the rear door, and it wasn't locked, so I killed the power." God, I was proud of Tanice. She was a special friend with knowledge ideal for this adventure.

Unrolling our ninth roll of toilet paper, we noticed a front window rising slowly. Two hands pushed upward with obvious difficulty; numerous coats of paint had sealed the window seams. Sensing we needed to leave, we searched for Utannah's bag, where we'd put all our items back so no evidence would be left behind. Utannah had printed her name on the bag, so we didn't dare leave it behind.

We hunted everywhere, but as the window reached halfway open, we knew it was only seconds before one angry occupant would interrupt our revelry. Mortal danger trumped retrieving evidence, so as the window opened, the bag search abruptly ended.

Suddenly, I spotted a masked figure rushing to the open window and slamming it closed. Unfortunately, Mr. Martin's fingers prevented it from completely closing. Our principal possessed a gift for reciting vulgar phrases. Every cussword I'd ever heard flowed in poetic profanity.

The person who closed the window then flipped Utannah her bag and dashed toward the front door. He shook a gallon container with both hands, and then took off the lid. Smoke began billowing out, making it difficult to see the masked man dislodging the pennies from the door-jamb. In the meantime, smoke started coming from the backyard too.

We should have left at that moment, but this stranger intrigued us. Out of the smoke, the figure appeared and kissed each of us. I was the last in line; he grabbed my head, giving me a sensual kiss, and said, "Run." I couldn't see his face, but he kissed great and his cologne seemed familiar.

Looking up, I saw that Mr. Martin had opened the window and was slowly crawling out. When he reached the ground, he turned to help his wife. The masked figure gave me a pat on the ass, encouraging me to leave. Without hesitation, I ran through the backyard and headed toward the alley, where the girls were waiting. I heard expletives not far behind, and from our spot in the alley, we saw bright flashes in front of the house.

The masked man ran down the sidewalk, with Mr. Martin running and yelling, "Rodney, you little bastard. When I catch you, you're dead." Lights came on throughout the neighborhood, and sirens sounded in the distance. A fire truck had arrived out front of the Martins' house, and we heard another one heading toward the alley. The police arrived thirty seconds later.

Wearing street clothes, we didn't fit in with the neighborhood kids who'd gathered in their nightclothes to watch the commotion. There was no place to run, and the shrubs that previously sheltered us sat three feet from where the second fire truck was headed. Tanice hollered for us to follow her. She was in the backyard next to Mr. Martin's home. Parallel to the house sat a huge boat, which had been carefully backed in. Tanice lifted the tarp covering the boat's lower level. We crawled up the boat ladder and lowered the tarp as the second fire truck turned down the alley.

Once inside, we walked down two steps into a small living area.

There we found a galley, a bathroom, and multiple beds. Looking out the portal, we saw hoses being pulled along the ground, ladders coming out, and firefighters headed into the smoke—everyone was looking for the fire's location. Everyone except one person: Susan had spotted Mrs. Martin crawling along the ground between the fence and the shrubs. She reached the toolshed and quickly disappeared inside. In the smoke, the firemen hadn't noticed.

Utannah asked, "What do you suppose that was about? She should have put on eyeliner and lipstick, but her appearance wasn't worth hiding over. With a nice hat she could have avoided the toolshed."

Joann's breathing finally slowed down. "Does anyone have a clue what just happened? Jeez, Tanice, slamming the window down saved our butts, but I didn't understand what you were shaking at the front door. And thanks for the kiss—you're good. I've got to practice my technique."

Tanice replied, "Hey, I didn't pull the window down. It was some guy—sounded like Rodney, from what Mr. Martin was yellin'. And I sure as hell didn't kiss you. I'm not into girls, but if Mitch doesn't work out, maybe I'll switch. Ask me in a few weeks."

The firemen had smothered the smoke by putting a swimming pool's supply of water on the two plastic containers. One of them pronounced, "Those jugs should head to the lab for analysis. It smells like jet fuel to me. Maybe they're poorly made bombs."

Fire chief McShane walked over, picked up the jug, and sniffed it. "Really, boys," he said, "how many bombers take da time to put da paper from da toilet all over da tree before dey blow up da principal's home?" He took a swig from his flask. "What was in dis jug was a mixture of 30 percent glycerin and 70 percent distilled water. Ya shake it together, uncork it, and yuv got instant smooke. Wish I'd known it when I was a kid. Dis is just kids pullin' a fast one on deir principal. Dey did a right good job, too. Dere's a woman hidin' in da backyard toolshed. I suspect she ain't da lady of da house, and da kids got wind of it. Hell of a way to go public. Gotta give 'em big balls for creativity. Tony, go check and see if she's all right," the chief ordered. "Den we'll be on our way. I'll talk to da police and finish her up."

The fireman knocked on the shed and the door cracked open. He exchanged a few words with the woman, then said, "Chief, all's good. She's fine." The firemen started cleaning up, as Mr. Martin pointed his finger at the police sergeant.

"Look, officer, I want those boys arrested and prosecuted to the fullest extent of the law. I know who these hellions are, and all five deserve juvenile detention. I want to be repaid for my phone, doors, and lights. They caused extensive damage, and on top of the repairs, it'll cost plenty to get the toilet paper out of my tree."

The police officer took Mr. Martin's forefinger and pushed it aside. "Mr. Martin, let me put things in perspective for you. Screw in the lightbulbs, reconnect the uncut phone line, and let the wind blow the paper out of your tree. Frankly, I don't find any problem with your doors. There's no sign of illegal entry or malfunction. Maybe the reason you couldn't open the doors is because your hands were more interested in the woman hiding in the shed. If we investigate, I'll need her name and address, and there will be a write-up in the newspaper. It's guessing on my part, but unless Mrs. Martin enjoys living in the toolshed, that woman isn't your wife. If I were you, I'd be happy nothing tragic happened and let it go. It's totally up to you, of course."

While Mr. Martin sorted out his future, the chief's revelation had all of us whispering simultaneously. "My God," Tanice said. "Of all nights, we picked the night Chip's bangin' his mistress. Can you fuckin' believe it? Worse, he's going to find out who did this and silence them. You watch, next week we'll be in little pieces being fed to the bears. That's what happens in the movies."

Susan weighed in, "I think the guy who kissed us knew Martin and his mistress were together and wanted pictures—I'm pretty sure a camera caused those flashes in the smoke. Why would someone need pictures?" she asked.

"Shit," said Tanice, in despair. "We've wandered into a blackmail scheme. Besides Martin, the guy takin' the pictures might threaten us too! We should lie low for a while."

Joann suggested, "All we need to do is find the photographer and make a deal. We'll promise to keep silent, and everything will be fine. We'll ask for copies of the photos so when Mr. Martin threatens us, we're protected. We ought to hang around and identify the woman hiding in the shed. That information will be priceless."

Utannah looked at her watch. "It's four thirty," she said. "The *Sentinel* said the sun rises at six thirty. Father always checks on me before seven. If we're not in bed, you know what will happen."

As we looked out the porthole, it appeared Mr. Martin had decided not to file charges. The firemen left, with the police right behind. If Mr. Martin would just rescue the woman in the shed, we could head home. We couldn't leave without knowing the woman's identity.

Ten minutes later, all was quiet—and a woman cautiously left the toolshed. Her bathrobe had come undone, revealing the slinkiest black teddy I'd ever seen. It was see-through and sparsely covered anything private. It surely cost $20, and considering how slinky it was, she might as well be naked. I didn't understand what convinced a woman to wear such shoddy clothing. My thoughts abruptly ended as I realized the woman sharing Chip's bed was Amelia Dutton—Elle Dutton's mother! Life suddenly became interesting.

Our principal and Mrs. Dutton retreated into the house. We were about to get out of the boat when the entire watercraft shuddered, knocking us onto our butts. Metal banged on metal as Utannah placed a finger to her lips and a voice said, "There, Willy. Hook up the safety chain and brake lights and we're sailin'."

A screen door slammed, and a woman said, "Here, Elmer, you and Willy have fun. If you have more engine trouble, the lake's only sixty miles; I'll come get you. Don't drink too much beer, now."

"Thanks, Maxine. We'll be back by two and we'll have salmon for dinner," the voice said. Two truck doors slammed, and the boat began to move.

Tanice lifted the cover and looked out. "Great!" she exclaimed. "You guys won't believe this, but we're goin' fishin'." Considering the equipment scattered about, I believed her. "If we don't get off this boat soon, we'll be sixty miles up Shit Creek, followed by fishing in Shit Lake," Tanice proclaimed. "Joann, you got any bright ideas?"

Joann had been brushing the tangles from her hair. Surprisingly calm, she asked, "Tanice, where are we?"

"Hell, Joann. If I knew, I wouldn't 'a asked ya!" Tanice said, signaling for Joann to come look. Poking her head out, Joann spent several minutes observing our surroundings. I imagined Utannah's steadily receding home with each passing second.

Finally, Joann said, "OK, we're at the intersection of Summersby and Third Street. I think he's headed to the I-5 interchange. Presuming I'm right, we'll intersect Woodberry Lane, which is close to Utannah's house. When he slows down for the four-way stop, we'll hop out. It's the only way I see us in bed by six thirty."

Susan had a serious look. "We need a backup plan. I've asked myself what problem would make these guys stop so early in their trip. I have an idea."

Susan told us exactly what to do. Having only a few minutes before we reached the intersection, we untied the boat cover we'd been hiding under, leaving only the front edge of it tied down. Along the back edge, we attached five lead sinkers from the tackle box.

Utannah had discovered two six-packs of beer in the refrigerator, and soon I held a Pabst Blue Ribbon in each hand like everyone else. Tanice looked at her beer and then at Utannah. "Don't you think we should get off the boat before we celebrate? I've got to admit, I've had ice-cold beer in the summer—there's nothing better. But I've never had a beer before eight in the morning. However, I am a little thirsty." Tanice found the can opener, put two holes in the top, and took a long swig.

Utannah said, "I didn't give you the beer to drink. When we get to the intersection, start tossing the beer cans in front of the truck. I've heard American fishermen love their beer, and the liquor stores won't open for hours. These guys will surely rescue their beer. Between a threatened beer supply and the boat cover thrown over the cab blocking their view, they'll have to stop—we should have almost ninety seconds to find cover."

Tanice finished her Pabst, nodding her head, "Hell of an idea, Utannah; let's kick ass."

Out the side of the boat, we saw we were approaching the intersection. We started throwing cans in front of the truck, which the truck's headlights lit up as they bounced off the pavement. A muffled voice said, "Well, I'll be a donkey dick, Elmer. Them's beer cans flyin' around. They gotta be comin' from the boat!"

We each grabbed a sinker attached to the boat cover and lobbed them over the truck cab with all we could muster. The truck slowly rolled to a stop, so there was little wind resistance preventing the cover from furling over the cab. Elmer slammed on the brakes, and the deceleration almost bounced us from the boat. We had stopped.

While the fishermen sat blaming each other for not having secured the cover, we scrambled from the boat, running for the large bushes off to the side of the truck. The fisherman took their time gathering their beer and retying the boat cover and were soon on the road again. They never saw us, and we emerged from the bushes sighing with relief.

We needed to set record time running to Utannah's. The town's curfew had lifted at 6:00 a.m., but we had twenty minutes to get home. We made it to the tree and climbed on top of the fence. But as we were walking carefully to the trellis, the back door of the neighbor's home opened and out came a big German Shepherd. This posed a serious problem.

"Do you know if this dog is vicious?" Susan asked Utannah.

Utannah said, "Yes, his name is Taz; it's short for Tasmanian devil. He's a trained guard dog. He's blind, deaf, and from what I've seen, pretty arthritic. He's about fourteen years old. Does that help?"

Susan said, "We'll have to take our chances. Time is short, and if the owners are like my parents, they've gone back to bed for a while. Does anyone have food?"

We searched our pockets and found two pieces of jerky and a box of Milk Duds—not a feast, but worth trying. We passed the Milk Duds to Susan, who was first to descend the trellis. Taz peed on every bush and eventually rested on the doormat. Susan tossed a Milk Dud onto the porch in front of the dog. His sense of smell still worked, and he tracked the candy and polished it off.

Susan descended the trellis while we threw more Milk Duds on the far side of the yard. The other girls made the descent, snuck through the back gate, and waited on the trail. I was the last girl down, and as I touched the ground Susan said, "Damn, I've run out of Milk Duds. Where's the jerky?"

Joann responded, "I threw it away, of course. God only knows how old it was, and I didn't want to poison someone's dog." I loved Joann, but there were moments I wanted to strangle her. Right now, I envisioned a hangman's knot.

I decided to run for the gate. Tanice held it wide open, and I sprinted like a jaguar. And then, a miracle: the arthritic, blind German Shepherd bolted like lightning and caught me three feet from the gate.

Anticipating a grisly death, I prepared for the ravenous grip around my neck. A gaping mouth with long, sharp teeth aimed straight for my head. I felt the searing pain—wait. It wasn't pain: it was slime. Taz was licking my face. The thought had occurred how dog bites might prevent me from facing the school board. But this dog was saving me from one misery to face another—guard dog, my ass.

Slowly, I got up, as Taz continued licking my face. We patted him on the back and hurried to Utannah's home as the sun rose over the horizon.

The ladder hung where we'd left it, and we scurried up to the bedroom. It was a quarter to seven.

Utannah was fortunate to have a bathroom attached to her bedroom. Five girls crowded in to remove the shoe polish we'd applied to our faces. It was harder than we had imagined, but multiple applications of soap, nail polish remover, and cold cream removed most of it. Joann suggested we looked like a family of raccoons.

Hearing movement downstairs, we crawled into our sleeping bags just before the floor creaked outside the bedroom. We heard a soft knock. No one moved. The door squeaked as Mr. Donnay opened it and glanced inside. Cateline was right behind him.

He said, "The ladies look like they've had a good time. I'm sure they've only slept a few hours. They'll hear the news soon enough." The door closed and footsteps receded down the hall.

I wanted to know what the news was, but my curiosity would wait. Settling in, I realized how special this night had been. Five girls had forged a lifelong bond through the common danger we had shared. As sleep overtook me, I felt content, knowing my friends would support me in days to come.

I awoke to sounds of a shower in Utannah's bathroom. Looking around, I saw that Tanice was missing. It made sense: being the only girl among a band of brothers meant rising early to reserve bathroom time. It wasn't any easier competing with five girls. We knew if Joann claimed the bathroom, we'd have to wait until she finished. I decided to be next in line. I got out of my sleeping bag, realizing I was sore from head to toe. Perhaps the medicine cabinet would have some aspirin.

Someone knocked on the door. Cateline carried a pot of French espresso to wake us up. Except for Utannah, we'd never heard of espresso. I took the pot, thanked Cateline, and assured her we'd be down soon.

Tanice emerged from the bathroom, and I pointed to the espresso. "There is a God," she remarked, pouring herself a cup. The cups were smaller than coffee mugs, and Tanice remarked, "I hope people don't buy espresso by the cup. You'd go broke before you got a decent helping." She looked at it, swallowed the entire cup, and started coughing. Once her gagging stopped, I found the aspirin and started my shower.

It was the nicest shower I could remember. Along with the aspirin, the hot water soothed my pains. I washed my hair, then concentrated on scrubbing my face. Once finished, I felt human again. As I opened the door, Joann dodged past Susan and Utannah, claiming the bathroom.

Tanice slowly sipped another cup of espresso. "You know, Utannah, this stuff isn't half bad if you sip it. I'd like to know the recipe. This is my fourth cup, and I'm feeling a buzz."

Utannah told Tanice, "They make espresso with finely ground coffee and water that's almost boiling. It's more concentrated than American coffee and has two times the caffeine. You should stop, unless you enjoy sitting on the toilet all day." Tanice considered the suggestion as Utannah said to Susan, "You and I will go to Mother and Father's bathroom. They have his-and-hers showers. Joann will take a while."

"Tanice," I asked, "Who was that guy taking photos last night? He had to know Martin and Amelia Dutton were together; otherwise, why take pictures? Their affair must be new because in Sutter, secrets don't last long. The rumor mill runs rampant. Do you suppose there's another reasonable explanation? Maybe Mrs. Dutton is his sister or some other relative," I suggested.

"Let me think a moment. You're probably right. Put yourself in Mr. Martin's place. Your wife and kids are gone. You're feeling lonely, so you invite Mrs. Dutton, your 'close' relative, over to visit and provide loving 'friendship.' Her family has probably left town this weekend, so the arrangement works well. You sit around a cozy fire, with sister in her see-through teddy and you in your skimpy shorts, playing checkers and sipping fine wine. It gets late; the heat doesn't work, so she shares your bed, providing body warmth. It makes perfect sense to me."

"That's precisely what I mean, Tanice. I can think of many reasons they might spend time together. We should give them the benefit of the doubt," I suggested.

Tanice leaned forward, two inches from my face. "Laurel, are you fuckin' crazy? Relatives never visit other relatives wearing a see-through teddy. Most wives don't wear teddies after a few years. Women use lingerie for seduction. If you want to get Denny's attention, wear a teddy. He'll set a record undressing, and you'll soon be naked as well. The reason a teddy lasts a long time is because women don't keep them on. Never wear one unless you're planning a night of hot, steamy sex. My Aunt Pearl says they drive men wild. No, Laurel, Amelia Dutton isn't Mr. Martin's cousin or sister; if she is, it's a weird family."

CHAPTER 36

It Ain't Liz and Dick,
but It Will Do

We finished a lovely breakfast of smoked salmon Benedict, French pastries, and fruit. I wondered what news Mr. Donnay had been talking about but decided not to bring it up. I would find out soon enough. We finished breakfast and thanked the Donnays profusely for their hospitality.

Joann's mom showed up at ten and offered to take the four of us home. Utannah reminded me she'd be over that afternoon to help with Denny's diversion plan. During the short ride home, I fell asleep. I was thankful Joann decided to go home for a few hours. The thought of unloading all her belongings made me nauseated.

As I arrived home, I noticed the sequoia. It looked a foot taller than just a few days ago. I didn't know what Iris was feeding it, but obviously it was working. I dragged myself in the house, where Bobby, Jean, and Otis greeted me. The unlikely trio were becoming fast friends. Otis had never liked water, but over the last week he had started joining the beavers whenever they scurried into the wading pool Iris had set up in the front yard.

I knew Saturday was the day Iris typically ran errands. She went to the market, paid bills, and visited with people she met during the course of her errands. I decided to watch TV and doze on the couch. The television was tuned in to Channel 12—and there sat Tamara Teague next to the news anchor. He asked Tamara if she had any updates on yesterday's report, and the tape began rolling, showing my back to the camera. Thank God, I was unrecognizable.

The entire interview played, and the camera returned to Ms. Teague. "Since we first aired this piece yesterday," she said, "several major developments have occurred. We've heard from Allison Bond and Webster

Simpson, who have firmly denied such a meeting ever took place. We have tried to contact Andrew Capellan, without success. Tibor Kirshbaum did not answer our phone calls because it's the Jewish Sabbath, and Dr. Collier was in surgery. We have left messages for both of them.

"Also, we have received several anonymous calls stating that the voice of the young lady interviewed was consistent with Laurel Montgomery's. Channel 12 has been unable to find a current picture of Ms. Montgomery, so we can't confirm or deny these statements."

"Thank you, Tamara."

My interview had made the news and stirred the school board's pot. I felt good about doing the interview. Keeping my emotions bottled up never worked for me. But if Bill Landsford had seen it, I feared a lecture would be coming my way. I expected a phone call from my attorney any moment.

I pulled up the blanket and continued napping, the TV providing perfect white noise. My belly was full, and I felt cozy and warm. Otis and the beavers rested near the fireplace, and with the house pin-drop quiet, I quickly fell asleep. It lasted almost two hours. Then deep in my subconscious, I heard a phone ring. Finally, I was awake enough to realize it was the phone intruding on my dreams. I answered, "Montgomery home."

"Who's speaking, Laurel or Iris?" I cleared my throat and responded, "This is Laurel; who's calling?"

There was a one-second lag before I heard, "Hi, dear. It's Mom calling. How are you doing?" I couldn't believe it. I hadn't talked to Mother by myself in two weeks. I immediately snapped out of my groggy state.

"Mom, it's great to hear from you! But why are you calling a day early? Iris is out doing errands, and I'm home recovering from a slumber party. If you want to talk to Iris, I'm not sure when she'll be back."

"No, honey, it's OK. The reason I called today is that we rescheduled a big meeting from Thursday to tomorrow. Tomorrow, we're meeting with Chinese Premier Zhou Enlai. Premier Zhou is second in command to Chairman Mao Zedong. If he accepts the proposals we've developed in cooperation with the Chinese government, it will speed up my time frame for returning home."

"Gee, Mom, that's great. So you think you'll get to come home early?"

"It's possible, Laurel, but I won't know until tomorrow. We'll be scrambling to deal with changes after tomorrow's meeting, so I'll have to wait and see. Tell me what your week was like."

I related to Mom my experience overhearing the school board and my interview with the investigator. I told her about Utannah's slumber party—leaving out several minor details. Mentioning Ed came to mind, but since Mom was away and preparing for an important meeting, my revelation could wait until her return. Finally, we discussed the camera found in the fence and what we were planning to do in the next several hours. Mom asked, "Does Iris know what you're planning today?"

"Yes, Mom—she helped organize it. Without her suggestions it wouldn't be as effective. Iris is wonderful to me. She can't replace you, but she's loving and has a subtle way of helping me see her point. She's going to speak on my behalf at Thursday night's school board meeting."

Mom sounded concerned. "Laurel, do think Iris is the best choice? Bill Landsford speaks to juries every week. You should give serious thought to having him speak for you. Maybe I should call him."

"Don't, Mom. Bill agreed to my choice. He's talked with the school's attorney, and I'm sure the board knows what's at stake. Bill feels we should try to keep our presentation simple and sincere. Mom, you don't need to worry. Iris has a special way of making her point when she wants to. If it's OK with you, I'm going to stay with Iris."

"Honey, I'm torn between a duty to the United States and my love for you. If I were home, I'd still have Bill represent you. I love you very much, and I miss you even more. How are my plants?"

"Funny you ask, Mom. Remember the giant sequoia? Iris transplanted the tree in the front yard, and it's growing rapidly. I knew these trees grew tall, but this one was five feet tall when she planted it, and I swear it's grown three feet."

I decided a little deception wouldn't hurt since our house rodents were quickly becoming domesticated. "The only problem we're having is the sequoia attracting the two baby beavers living by the lake. Iris was ready to chase them away until she discovered one had a neck wound. We took them in and are trying to nurse them back to health."

"Laurel, honey, do your best to avoid letting the local wildlife use our house as a rest home. You probably didn't consider it, but we have neighbors who take great pride in their yards, especially the Murdocks. I'm sure you and Iris will do what's right. Honey, I have to go. Know I love you and I'll be praying for you. I'll call Wednesday or Thursday if possible. Tell Iris hello and I'm sorry I missed her. Bye-bye, dear."

"Bye, Mom. I love you." Tears filled my eyes. Now I truly knew what a major life issue was—and she was half a world away. The sobbing started and I wallowed in self-pity.

I knew this poisonous emotion needed the right antidote—and Iris was the answer. She'd know the right words to mend a hurting soul. I hoped she'd get home before the others arrived. In the meantime, the comfort of a hot bath would be a good alternative.

My friends would be here in forty minutes, so I ran upstairs. The bath was an old claw-foot tub where I could relax. I poured in bubble bath and got in, letting the hot water continue to run as I lay back and closed my eyes. My worries drifted away, and I started feeling sleepy again.

I had just fallen asleep when I heard the doorbell. It rang again, and I tried to wake up. God, I must have overslept! I tried standing, but my legs were deadweight. My thighs felt as if a heavy anchor held them down. I reached through the bubbles and discovered the problem: a beaver was resting lengthwise on both of my legs. How he, she, or it had crawled into the tub remained a mystery I'd figure out later. Lifting my amphibious pet, I crawled out from underneath and let him sink back to the bottom. I pulled the plug and yelled, "Come on in, I'm just getting dressed. I'll be right down."

Immediately realizing I might have invited the press into my living room, I peeked down the stairs to see who was there. Opening the door, Joann and Utannah strutted into the living room. Joann said, "Can we come up? We need a makeup mirror and a place to spread our stuff."

I waved my arm, and soon Joann and Utannah were in the bathroom getting ready to make Joann look like me. I asked them to listen for the doorbell while I dressed. I finished dressing and was heading downstairs to wait for Denny when I heard Utannah screech, "Joann, did you see it? A creature slithered from the tub and waddled out past the door. It resembled a large snake—maybe an anaconda."

"Utannah, get down from the bathroom counter," Joann replied. "The animal isn't an anaconda. Oregon isn't the natural habitat for snakes that size—South America seems more likely, but frankly, I'm not certain. I'm guessing you glimpsed one of the beavers coming from the tub. Come finish my hair and makeup so I'm ready for my movie preview. Denny's supposed to arrive any minute."

"You're telling me Laurel's family lets the beavers bathe in the house?" Utannah asked.

"Utannah, I've known Laurel a long time. When Iris Wimple comes over, nothing happens the way you expect it to. I can't describe it, but Iris is just different. She's a lovely woman, but doesn't seem to fit. I promise, when Mrs. Montgomery returns, it will seem like nothing strange ever happened."

"Laurel's a wonderful friend," Utannah said, "but in Paris, pets aren't treated in such luxurious ways. We typically visit the zoo instead of creating one in our living room."

Joann replied, "Join the crowd, Utannah. Our daily behaviors are strange, but they make more sense over time. As for Iris, her behavior won't fall into the 'making sense' category at any time."

I sauntered downstairs to finish creating file folders and letters to be used as props. I'd worked on them during Friday's English class. I hoped Utannah had done her part and picked up the application forms from Sister Sarah Agnes.

The doorbell rang, and there stood Denny, holding a bag. I let him in, and he looked to see if we were alone. Seeing no one, Denny dropped his bag and pulled me closer, kissing my neck and working his way to my mouth.

He was a great kisser. I loved every variation of his lips on mine, but there was one lust-evoking kiss that turned me into erotic putty. I hoped it was coming. He gently closed his eyes, parting his lips slightly as he put them a quarter inch from my mouth. I felt the heat from his breath as he leisurely pulled me closer, using his powerful hands on my lower waist. Our lips barely touched for several lingering seconds, making me long for a full deep kiss. Moving at a snail's pace, he pressed his lips against mine until our lips sealed. He whispered, "Laurel, I love you, and I missed you very much."

Between this melting kiss and telling me he loved me, Denny had hooked me. I couldn't get away—nor did I want to. Looking up at him, I didn't hesitate to say, "I love you too, Denny. You're more special than I ever imagined and more than I ever hoped for. Deep down, I know you're my soul mate."

Neither of us could articulate exactly what it was that we gave each other, but it lifted me out of my self-pity and forced me to face my problems. We both sat for a moment. I didn't know what was running through Denny's mind, but I tried to consider where we were going.

Fortunately, my introspection had to wait, as Utannah guided Joann down the stairs with a paper bag over her head. Reaching the living room, Utannah removed the bag, and we stared at Joann from behind. Joann turned around slowly, and I swore I was looking at myself in the mirror. Her cheeks appeared lifted; Utannah had applied makeup and eye shadow perfectly.

"My God, Utannah, that's incredible," Denny said. "I need a picture." Incredibly, he pulled a camera out of his bag and asked if we would pose together. He took distance and close-up shots that focused on our faces, eyes, and hair. Thirty-some snapshots later, Denny replaced the camera in the bag and went through our props.

Joann had the file folders, letters, and glasses. She was ready. Still amazed, I examined Joann more closely. She wore a sweater with a letter J embroidered on each arm. This didn't make any sense, so I asked Utannah what the purpose was.

Utannah explained, "Our director said he didn't want Joann to look exactly like you. So I made obvious changes that anybody who knows you would easily spot. Unlike you, Joann is wearing glasses. You don't wear glasses, so I'm guessing most close friends will notice. Putting the J, for Joann, on the sweater was another noticeable change.

"The small mole to the right of your upper lip is a beautiful birthmark, which I didn't put on Joann. Whoever placed the camera won't notice these differences because they see exactly what they're looking for. The media never lets details hold up a good story."

I knew these friends were incredibly clever and trying to help any way they could. We walked to the back door with Joann. Denny said, "Joann, do you feel ready to go?"

Joann signaled she was. "All right, Utannah, Laurel and I will stand in the neighbor's yard to your right. It keeps us out of the camera's view. Remember, there are no second takes. Joann's acting must be perfect with our first take. If you can't remember what to do, scratch your nose and I'll raise a tablet with instructions. Don't rush. Remember, you're supposedly considering your future. OK, give us ten minutes to get in place and then slowly come out the back door."

Utannah, Denny, and I scrambled out the front door. I went next door to tell the neighbors we were using their backyard to film a movie for school. Wishing us luck, Mrs. Tidbury seemed excited we were shooting a movie. After assuring her we didn't need extras, we took our places.

The back door opened. Joann came out carrying a bottle of Coke and looked up, enjoying the sun. She took a seat at the end of the picnic table, facing the camera. The trash can was right next to her. She pulled out the files, laying them flat on the table. Slowly, a grimace came over her face, giving her a pained expression. She sat quietly in deep thought for the next several minutes. Then hesitantly, she lowered her head and raised the first file in front of the camera.

Written on the file in big black letters was "Letter of Intent to Change Schools." Joann pulled out a piece of stationary and set it on the table. She then removed a second sheet of paper and started copying from the first sheet. After writing for ten minutes, she shook her head from side to side, wadded up her letter, and threw it in the trash. Twice more, she went through the same ritual. On the third attempt, she stopped, seemingly satisfied with the result. She put this letter in the file and set it aside.

Next, she held up the second file. I had labeled the file "Application to St. Mary's School." She removed the multipage admission form and began filling it out. Then, looking resigned that St. Mary's was her future, she placed the application in the file.

Unknown to us, Joann had concealed a freshly cut onion in her sweater pocket. Cloaking the onion in her hand, she held both hands to her face, accenting her glum look. The tears came slowly at first, but as she kept the onion near, a torrent began running down her cheeks.

Suddenly, to everyone's surprise, Iris came out the back door, visibly concerned. Her entrance wasn't in the script; disaster loomed over our production. Iris sat down next to Joann and gave her a hug. Unaware that an onion rested in Joann's hand, Iris started to cry. I hoped the camera wouldn't pick up the smile on Iris's face once she realized Joann was holding an onion.

In a few minutes, Joann picked up the files and her Coke. Iris patted her on the upper back, and they went inside. Denny hopped over the neighbors' back fence to the lake trail, making sure the camera was still running. He gave a thumbs-up, and soon we joined Iris and Joann in the dining room.

Looking flustered, Iris apologized, "I'm sorry I'm late. I walked down to Mort's to buy groceries. I hadn't planned on being gone too long, but I ran into Nubs at the store. She asked me if I wanted a ride to the Save Laurel rally going on in the city park. I told her it would be fine as long as I was back here by two thirty. But when we arrived, we couldn't find any parking!

"Well, wouldn't you know, Horace Perkey's home is right across the street from the park. He was sitting in his rocking chair enjoying the commotion, so Nubs drove up onto his patio, almost hitting the poor man. We asked if we could park there so we could join the protest. Horace said parking would be OK as long as we agreed to help him into his wheelchair and take him along.

"Crossing the street was a challenge, but once we reached the crowd, we joined right in. Horace even got a 'Save Laurel' bumper sticker on the back of his wheelchair. Well, time went by faster than expected, and suddenly it was a half hour before I was supposed to be home. We started leaving the park and caught the attention of the reporters. I guess we must have been the oldest protesters at the rally because they lined up to interview us.

"Starting with Horace, they asked why he had decided to attend the rally. It was obvious they didn't know the man, or they never would have asked. Horace didn't even hesitate.

"'You know, at age eighty-five, it's not often a widower gets asked by two babes if they can take him somewhere,' he said. 'I told 'em anywhere they wanted to go, I was in. Now I'll grant ya, I've lost a hell of a lotta brain cells over the years. But why is the goddamned school board afraid of a fourteen-year-old girl and a decorated marine? He's an excellent teacher, and she's an honor student. Instead of interviewin' me, you ought to be askin' those stupid bastards what the hell their thinkin' is.

"'You know, I fought in World War I so the people in this nation could keep the freedoms they enjoy. Last I knew, one of those liberties was freedom of speech. Doesn't that liberty extend to the classroom? I went to college from 1904 to 1910 and got my master's in chemical engineering. I heard lots of crap from professors that was just plain wrong. Was my life ruined? Hell, no! Did I want 'em fired? Hell, no! The reason we go to school is to learn other views and ideas. If you want to censor thought, go live with the damned communists! See how well that works for ya.

"'Boys, the critical question here is, when do we teach our kids the techniques of critical thinking? Throughout their lives they'll hear and see a great many ideas. They can't get rid of people who dream up these ideas, but they can sure as hell ignore them. School provides a place where kids can learn who they should trust. I'll grant ya, parents should be on the top of the list, but they can only help you with what they know.

"'School is where kids expand their horizons. The school board is protecting students from knowledge that makes our world understandable. It's a damned shame.

"'That's enough outta me. Let's go home, ladies, and have that threesome we've been talkin' about.'

"So," Iris said, "when I finished, it was almost three, and that's why I'm late."

I was the first to speak. "Don't worry, Iris. I think it's great you hung around to have a threesome with Horace. He probably feels like a new man, having you two ladies sandwich him with love. You know, the other night, Denny, Joann, and I had a threesome in his lab. It was incredibly emotional—but fulfilling. I think next time, we'll do it at French's Fry. It's fun joining other students when Denny quits participating. He's only good for about fifteen minutes, but Joann and I can go on forever."

I noticed Utannah whispering in Joann's ear. I heard her say, "Did you, Laurel, and Denny really have a ménage à trois?" Joann shook her head in disbelief as Iris blushed and Denny shrank behind his *Scientific American.* I wondered what I'd said wrong.

Iris interrupted my train of thought. "Nubs and I knew Horace talked like a sailor, but what could we do? Elderly people say exactly what they think. They don't care how people react because they're not trying to impress anyone. Horace fits this description, and I knew it before he spoke. We should have marched him right by those reporters. If they put him on the news, they'll have to censor every third word. I was standing right behind him looking like I approved of everything he said. I don't want to be on television!"

In her quiet French accent, Utannah stated, "Mrs. Wimple, when I watch TV, I never remember who's standing in the background. My father's in charge of preparation work necessary to negotiate agreements between France and other nations. When heads of state meet to sign an accord, father stands in the back. No one remembers him, nor do they care. He explained to me that everyday people have so many of their own problems, they rarely remember others'.

"Father stressed that if I tracked other people's faults, I'd be ignoring my own. In time, I'd be the town gossip. The other point is: I don't know how old you are, but in the short time I've known you, you've embraced our idea to help Laurel, and you seem liberal and open with your thoughts. You offer suggestions but never impose your will on others. These aren't traits I normally associate with elderly people."

"Oh, Laurel, where do you find such lovely friends?" Iris asked me. Addressing Utannah, Iris went on, "Utannah, there are some issues I'm passionate about. I try doing what's right as best I can, but even that changes over time. From time to time, this country has made and enforced laws that were obviously wrong. I can't go back in time and change them or help the people those laws harmed. But I can do my part to make sure the right decisions are made in the future.

"The reason I try to keep an open mind is that I know that I might be wrong. At times in my life, I have been wrong—and then I had to swallow my pride and apologize. Admitting to another person I was wrong is the highest hurdle I've ever jumped. Countless times, I've had to change my perspective and admit my errors. It's easier admitting I'm imperfect by staying out of the spotlight. I'm guessing your father would agree. What would you think about removing Joann's makeup and letting me take all of you to French's Fry?" Iris said. "My treat."

We had a memorable time at the diner. Iris fit in with our young group. Kids liked her because she was a trusted friend. Iris didn't judge, and she kept our thoughts confidential. Around her, none of us needed to change our regular behavior.

That day, friendship and love ruled the moment, and expressing our feelings came naturally. I didn't foresee the rolling black clouds rising to a crescendo in the dark days ahead. In less than a week, Iris Wimple would suddenly be gone, and I'd never see her again. When she left, my days of childhood innocence would depart with her.

CHAPTER 37

Question Authority

Saturday evening and Sunday were calm. I told Iris that Mother had called and would try to call again before Thursday. I described how fun the slumber party was and how formally the Donnays lived.

Iris commented, "It's important to see how foreign families live their daily lives. It makes you examine your own life and change the parts you dislike. The United States has no monopoly on the world's riches. Should you visit France, I hope you tour Monte Carlo. The wealth and splendor of the principality are magnificent. However, as I've said, having thousands of material goods won't make you happy. Many wealthy people have problems on a much grander scale.

"Speaking of problems, Bill Landsford called after seeing last night's ten o'clock news. He wondered if I'd seen a certain story, which of course I hadn't. I stood in the bedroom half naked, rolling my curlers and applying cold cream, while he described your classmate, Jane, who had shared confidential information with a reporter. The news disguised the young woman's identity. Bill wondered if you knew her."

I saw no reason to lie. "Iris, I'm Jane. I was walking around the protest when a reporter came over and asked if I knew anything. Assuring me she wouldn't show my face, I described the facts. Frankly, Iris, I'm tired of this secrecy and the games surrounding it. The reporter seemed to need a break, and I thought telling her some details would help us both. I'm sure Mr. Landsford doesn't approve, but I don't care."

"Well, dear, the story was on this morning's news. It's caused a stir, and it's staying in check only because it's the weekend. Bill was very pleased because he thinks the story has scared the school board. With respect to your mother, lawyers handling a case that may go to court like controlling as many factors as possible. It frustrates attorneys when clients endanger their own case. I'm not a fan of telling the public a tape exists when it doesn't, but planting an impression that the board is conspiring against you only helps."

I wanted to tell Iris about the recording, but I held back, remembering Mr. Landsford's words: if Iris didn't know the tape existed, she could honestly say so in court.

Iris continued, "We'll see if yesterday's soap opera surfaces in the next twenty-four hours; if so, it should stoke the fire." As we sat together, Iris took my hands and looked me in the eye. "Honey, the next few days will be some of the most difficult days you've ever faced. I wish I could live this experience for you, but I can't. I've thought about the pearls I might offer to help you face this difficult time, and the only solution I have is prayer.

"We've talked extensively about the existence of God, but I can't make you believe in the Almighty; it's something you have to desire because you feel it's right. Even this desire isn't a feeling I can transfer to you. People turn to God when they're in pain and out of options. People often pray because they can't understand how unexpected events came to be. Wars offer a good example. We pray for our loved ones who must fight, but we have no good explanation of why we're fighting. If you're in fear, prayer may help. I can't say which religion is correct, but trying to love and serve others is a common theme for every faith. People forget this theme when they argue over which religion is right."

I reflected on previous topics we had discussed. "Iris, you believe in God, don't you?"

"Yes, dear, I do. For me, God is a reassuring feeling I have—not something I own. No matter what happens each day, I feel protected and loved. I used to fear death—and constant fear is a horrible feeling. God took away my fear and now I enjoy life. I'm at the end of my days, but I'm convinced death is a short stop for my body and spirit. You and I are composed of molecules that probably belonged to another person. It's exciting to think one day I might be a fraction of someone else.

"When I'm gone, my spirit will live on, for a few years, in the people whose lives I've impacted. If people I've spent time with incorporate some of my good deeds into their behavior, it's the supreme compliment. In the several times this occurred during my life, it was the greatest honor another person could bestow. No other gift has given me more satisfaction."

"Iris, will praying help, even if I'm still sorting out God?" I asked. "I'm sure I believe, but I can't fit it together. Just when something seems clear, more questions arise. The religious leaders who visited class stressed that

God demands devout faith. To me, that suggested I shouldn't ask questions but rather accept an established religious view. I'm having a hard time doing that because my questions won't stop coming."

"Laurel, always ask God your questions. Principles concerning God that can't be questioned are usually false. A God you can believe in will answer all your questions. The answers may not come when you wish or be to your satisfaction, but they will come. A God who is real welcomes your challenge. Mr. Wright would be first to point out what happened when the Germans didn't question Hitler. Don't fall into the trap of blind obedience. Apathy is the absolute worst character trait: it allows bad to triumph over good. If you pray to God sincerely, he'll hear your prayers—especially if He's asked to lessen your problems so you can help others."

"Iris, you can't be even near dying. You're full of energy, and I've really enjoyed having you here. I'm lucky to have you by myself. Mom isn't like you—I don't know why. She's often worried, on edge, and sometimes crabby. You're never that way. You tell me what you expect without all the emotion. It'll be hard when she returns. It's a relief knowing you'll support me during the coming week. I'd be more stressed if I had to deal with Mom. You give me that comfortable feeling God gives you."

"Laurel, I hope I live up to your compliment. Bill can still speak for you; I won't be offended if you change your mind. Litigation has given him speaking finesse that's far better than mine. Thursday, we'll have one chance to impress the board. I want a presentation so powerful, the school board will have no choice but to keep you and Penfield."

"I don't know, Iris," I said, recalling the secret meeting. "Intuition tells me they're getting rid of us both. I know if I'm expelled, Mr. Landsford will sue, but when the case ends, I'll be ready to enter college. Honestly, I don't relish the thought of high school at St. Mary's. Sister Sarah Agnes would never tolerate my questions about God."

"Laurel, like me, there you are, living in fear. Live in this moment and worry about today. We'll cross the Sister's bridge if we have to explore that trail. The future rarely unfolds the way we believe it will. But right now, it's time for ice cream—and I've got a new topping to try."

Iris went to the kitchen while I tuned into Sunday night TV. I wasn't focused on the news but on the days ahead. Iris returned in several minutes carrying a tray. There were two bowls with three scoops of vanilla ice cream and two large glasses containing a dark green liquid. She gave us each a serving and sat down.

"Dear, pour about a quarter of your crème de menthe over the ice cream. The rest you should sip slowly."

I hadn't heard of crème de menthe. Picking up the glass, I poured several spoonsful over my ice cream and sampled a small sip. I noticed a peppermint taste with a kick. The more syrup I sipped, the finer it tasted. I had ordered many flavors of ice cream at French's Fry, but I'd never seen this syrup on their menu. I finished off my glass and felt less anxious about the coming week. "Iris, this is excellent. I've never had anything like it. I don't suppose I could have more?"

"I don't suppose another glass would do harm, but when we finish, it's time for bed. Between nursing the sequoia, herding beavers, and cooking, I'm tired. I don't expect the next several days to be better. Please hand me your glass."

Finishing my second glass of this wonderful elixir, I was ready for bed. Still sleep deprived from the slumber party, I slept the best I could recall in weeks.

When I awoke at seven o'clock, nine hours of uninterrupted rest had left me with plenty of energy. I couldn't imagine what Iris had said last night to remove my worries, but for this week, whenever she spoke I'd have to pay careful attention. I'd showered and dressed when Iris knocked on my door. When I opened the door, she stood holding the newspaper and smiling.

"Laurel, you're in the *Sentinel.* Let me show you." We sat on my bed reading the front page. "Student in School Religion Controversy Decides to Leave" was the headline. Underneath the caption were two photos. The first showed Joann sitting at the picnic table holding a file labeled "Letter of Intent to Change Schools." The second picture showed the letter recovered from the patio trash. The letter had been uncrumpled and described my intent to leave school. I had to smile. We had achieved the success we'd hoped for. The text read:

In a copyrighted story, *The American Enquirer* has gained exclusive proof that Laurel Montgomery, the Sutter teen involved in the junior high's religious controversy, has written a letter to the Sutter School Board. The letter details her plans to change schools within the next two weeks. Through sources, the *Enquirer* obtained a photo of Ms. Montgomery writing the letter and drafting the final copy.

The Sutter Sentinel has sought to gain an interview with Ms. Montgomery, but at this time, Ms. Montgomery's location remains unknown. Sources report she attends school and at other times remains in seclusion. Ms. Montgomery's reasons for leaving school are unknown, but the decision relieves the school board of a difficult burden. Still remaining is a future decision about history teacher Penfield Wright.

The final decision will be made Thursday night at a special session of the school board. The school expects many people, so the meeting has moved to the Sutter High Theater. Starting time is six o'clock, and the meeting will likely go late into the evening.

The public may address the board provided they call ahead to get on the agenda. Attorneys representing all parties suggest people having similar opinions band together to write a group opinion.

The board's attorney, Emmitt Pilcher, wants the public to be aware that because of the volatility of the issues involved, security will be tight. Protests or inappropriate behavior will lead to removal from the theater and possible arrest.

"My God, Iris, they took the bait—hook, line, and sinker." I felt elated. "I hope Bill understands our goal since we didn't get his approval. If he calls, will you explain our thinking? He'll probably take it better coming from you."

Iris gave me the evil eye, as though I had asked her to turn stone into clay. "Yes, honey. You know I enjoy bantering with lawyers. You kids dream up a scheme and leave me holding the bag. You'll be lucky if he doesn't come to school and beat you to a pulp."

Breakfast consisted of baked eggs, sausage, and fresh raspberries. Iris had placed a pansy on each plate to accent our meal. "Why the pansies, Iris?" I asked.

"Please, let me explain," Iris said. "Although small, the pansy blooms year round, showing a majestic face while surviving nature's gauntlet. A pansy has a pleasing fragrance, plus it's rich in vitamins A and C. Like you, this flower is tough outside and gentle within. A pansy reminds me of you: resolute, beautiful, and tough."

Words wouldn't come. Iris believed in me more than I believed in myself. I knew my many faults. So did Iris. How could she know my many flaws and see any virtue?

"Iris, you're too kind. I can't see any trace of those qualities within me." I started crying, and Iris rounded the table to embrace me.

"No one sees good or bad within themselves," she said. "This is why we need friends. When we're at our lowest, they support us until we can support ourselves. Laurel, I wouldn't praise you if my heart didn't believe it was true. This isn't a hollow try to inflate your ego. I want you to discover and use your inner strength, which this week will demand.

"You and I haven't touched on spiritual awakening, which is the key to a happy life. Whether you believe in God or whether you don't has little to do with spirituality. Realizing that magnificent godlike gifts come from within you, and developing those gifts to solve your hardest problems, is what makes your life whole. Believers, atheists, and agnostics will debate God's existence until the end of time. All of them are missing the point: it's impossible to argue about the existence of God without already possessing the godlike powers to do so. This is why African tree frogs don't debate the issue on *Wild Kingdom*. Where humans gained these powers is irrelevant.

"Religion is different from spirituality, but for many, it works just as well. Multiple faiths comfort billions of people around the world. Often, they use a god outside themselves as the source of their spiritual foundation. Some faiths use science and nature as their foundation. Few folks realize that their god can provide the necessary inspiration to use their incredible gifts in the most effective way. So providing comfort isn't God's only purpose. He can provide the courage to persist in the face of failure, and persistence leads to innovation, which drives mankind forward. Unless a religious leader stresses these truths to his congregation, people will rarely see or tap their potential.

"Laurel, tap into the spiritual power you have, and the next four days, while difficult, will swing in your favor. Lose faith in what you know is right and the school board will prevail. Laurel, you must promise me you won't repeat what I'm about to say."

I crossed my fingers.

"Good friends tell me events will happen Thursday night that aren't on the agenda. If half this information is true, significant changes will follow. If it's all true, people will know you're the only person able to unravel multiple events. Intelligent men will want your insight. Today, the school is setting the stage so you can shine. Do not waste this opportunity."

Iris kissed me good-bye, and as I walked away she yelled, "I'll call Bill and tell him not to believe everything he reads."

I couldn't decipher what Iris meant by me unraveling events. I worried about stage fright, but I knew I could stand in front of the board and state my case. I'd memorized my lines and rehearsed them in front of the mirror. We'd sent a draft to Bill Landsford for his revision and approval. Nothing I could remember writing would entice intelligent men to want my insight. Iris's words made her sound like she was talking about the Three Kings looking for Baby Jesus.

Still, I knew better than to doubt her. The woman displayed an uncanny knack of being correct. I decided to start searching for my power within.

CHAPTER 38

A Woman to Respect and Adore

By now I had perfected my route, and I reached school without difficulty. I wasn't expecting multiple questions about remarks in *The Sutter Sentinel,* but students wondered if I were leaving. What could I say? I told friends and teachers I wouldn't comment until after the board's meeting.

Unfortunately, I kept seeing Mr. Martin. We didn't speak, but his big smile and good-bye waves indicated he'd read the paper. I wanted to confront him about Mrs. Dutton, but even knowing I *could* remove that smile offered sound satisfaction.

During lunch hour, I walked to the high school, where protests were absent and students didn't recognize me. I hoped previewing the stage would make me familiar with the setup for Thursday night. I wandered the halls knowing that today might be my only experience at Sutter High. I followed posted signs to the auditorium, and then, looking in both directions, I snuck in.

Initially, I thought I'd entered the lobby, but after adjusting to the dim light, I found myself onstage. Eventually, the dark void revealed hundreds of seats. The stage crew had added folding chairs to provide extra seating. The podium stood stage right and angled toward the audience. On stage left was a long table with a green tablecloth. Six leather chairs sat behind the table, with a microphone in front of each seat. Nameplates identified each board member and attorney Emmitt Pilcher. Like the podium, the table angled forty-five degrees toward the audience. The American flag stood on the right side of the podium and stage left showcased the Oregon state flag. A sixty-by-thirty-foot picture screen provided background for the entire setup. This screen attached to the floor with its bottom hooks looped through O-rings recessed in the hardwood.

Normally, schools are noisy, but in the theater, I could have heard a mouse turd drop. Walking the stage caused the floor to creak and sent echoes every direction. I needed to remember that if I whispered to Bill, our conversation might be overheard. Standing behind the podium, I imagined speaking to the board. I recited my presentation, knowing this was my only chance to practice. Then I repeated my speech, adding emphasis to key phrases.

I continued until I heard the stage door open and close. High heels echoed behind the stage, and within seconds, an incredibly tall, striking woman emerged, carrying a black bag. Her shoulder-length brown hair was sculpted to accent her face. A one-piece forest-green dress, complemented by matching heels, made a powerful, commanding impression. I hoped she hadn't heard my speech, but I didn't know.

"How do you do? I'm Jacquelyn Collier, chairperson of the school board."

I introduced myself. "Laurel, it's a pleasure to meet you before Thursday. Do you have a few moments?" she asked. I nodded affirmatively, and she motioned me to sit at the table.

"I came to inspect the arrangements for Thursday night's meeting. I can't imagine the difficulties you've endured in the last two weeks. Can you talk without Mr. Landsford present? It's often helpful talking face-to-face. It's how we doctors work. Two people working together accomplish more in a week than a committee does in a year."

"Well, Miss—I mean Dr.—Collier—I'm supposed to avoid talking to anyone. There's a lot I can say, but I guess it must wait until Thursday."

Dr. Collier noticed my cut from last Friday's covert field trip. "This arm wound is deep," she said. "It looks infected. May I look at it?" I truthfully said I'd cut my arm on a branch. Trying to not muddy the waters, I didn't say the branch was on Mr. Martin's tree.

She opened her bag, which doubled as her purse. Out came antibiotic ointment, and she dressed my wound. "There, we're finished. Clean the cut twice a day with soap and water. Apply this antibiotic cream and wrap it with gauze. Can you see me next Tuesday, Laurel?"

I said I'd call for an appointment. "Good," she said. "Now we have a doctor–patient relationship. Do you understand the agreement?" I told her I didn't.

She continued, "It means anything we discuss is private. My professional oath binds me to that promise. Whatever you tell me is confidential. Today's conversation won't factor into my board decision unless you give me written permission. Is my explanation clear?"

"Yes, it's clear. You sound like you've said this before," I commented.

"Laurel, when I do surgery, its important patients clearly understand what I'm about to do to their body. Medical words are complex, and people often won't ask questions. But surgery has risks, and it's essential patients know the reasons they're taking those risks. I want our conversation to be just as open. Perhaps together we can reduce everyone's troubles."

I talked with Dr. Collier for forty minutes. I discussed the recording and Mr. Martin's affair. Dr. Collier had the rare capacity to listen without interrupting. Her steady eye contact told me she understood and took my concerns seriously. She often shook her head in disbelief. When I finished, she asked me to clarify several points, then looked at her watch.

"Laurel, it's almost time for afternoon patients, and I know you're late for class. Let me give you a lift and express my thoughts."

I looked around the stage. Here's where I would face life's first fork. Recalling recent advice, I prayed God would support me on whichever path was chosen.

Reaching her car, I felt incredible respect for Dr. Collier. I had no understanding of the path she had followed to become a surgeon in a male-dominated profession. But her intellect and compassion were undeniable. Once seated, Dr. Collier said, "Laurel, thank you for the truth. Clandestine meetings and affairs are relevant surprises the board must face. I will seek advice before acting on this information, but you have my full support. I will do everything to keep you in junior high."

She scribbled a number on her business card and handed it to me. "Here's my home phone. Call anytime. Also, it's best if we don't discuss this meeting with anyone. Mr. Pilcher is as protective as Bill Landsford. And don't forget: schedule an appointment for your arm."

I thanked her for the ride, realizing I was twenty minutes late—but I hadn't given all those excused-absence slips away.

When classes ended, I met Joann and Tanice at French's Fry. As Tanice sat down, she said, "Damn, Laurel, why didn't ya say you were quittin' school? I've been bustin' my butt for ya. Then you pull this idiotic stunt out of your ass. Tell me, is it the week before your period, or are you fuckin' crazy? Three days ago we discovered a gold mine of information, and now it's worthless. I'm doin' other things since you're backin' out."

Before Tanice continued bashing my character, I interrupted, "Tanice, if you shut up, I'll describe what's going on." She stopped mid-gasp. "We faked the story, Tanice. Look closely at the picture in the newspaper. It's Joann. Utannah made her look like me." Joann had the article and handed it to Tanice. "If you look closely, there's no mole on her face. It's not me."

"Damn," Tanice said. "After Friday's bonding experience, why didn't you include me? I'm trustworthy, you know."

"Tanice, this was Denny's idea. He arranged it Saturday on a moment's notice," I fibbed. "You weren't intentionally excluded, I promise. You're one of my best friends, and I appreciate your help. I trust you and Mitch. You've both risked supporting me and I can't thank you enough. Please don't take this personally."

"Oh, hell, Laurel, Saturday I went to the ranch. Honestly, makeup, fashion, and all that crap aren't my strong points. You both know that. I'll never be smart like you two. When school's over, I won't miss it. Hard work beats hard thinking. Tell me what to do and I'll do it. Maybe that's why we made a good team Friday night."

Joann and I couldn't argue. Even now, if I want a practical answer to a question, I call Tanice. She never sugarcoats words or acts pretentious. Her perspective is usually correct after I remove the cusswords. But right now, Dr. Collier was my mentor: she was straightforward, and her intellectual responses made profanity unnecessary.

We left the diner by four. Joann and I walked home, noticing the media had returned. The newspaper article had rekindled the fire. Iris stood in the front yard with a man I didn't recognize. Reporters were asking questions, and it appeared she was answering them.

We said good-bye, and I took the lake trail, eventually winding up in our backyard. Between Otis, Bobby, Jean, and a family of rabbits resting in the grass, I wondered if Iris was gunning for another Friends of Wildlife award.

CHAPTER 39

Father's Day

Entering the kitchen, I heard voices near the front door. When I went to the living room, Iris was sitting on the sofa—with Ed. Anger and fright immediately gripped me—and that was just for Iris. Why was she surprising me this way? Sure, we had discussed inviting Ed for dinner, but why now? What was the purpose?

Ed stood up, offering to shake hands. I paused, deciding how to respond. Finally, I shook his hand and greeted him. I took the chair facing Ed.

Iris spoke first. "Laurel, I see your shock. I'm sorry for surprising you with Ed's visit. We ran into each other, and asking him over felt right. He's dining with us, and I thought you might have questions. I'll bring you some chips and dip, as well as sodas. Then I'll make dinner while you two talk." She soon returned with the snacks and was quickly gone again.

I sat quietly, facing the devil. I hadn't prepared questions, and none were coming to mind. Ed broke the silence. "Laurel, Iris told me all about you. I want you ta know how proud I am of you and your accomplishments. I'm sorry this nonsense with the school board come up. Anything I can do ta help you—maybe answerin' your questions?"

I wanted to despise Ed, but his kindness made it impossible. To pass judgment when I remembered nothing seemed unfair. Mother had rarely discussed him. The deep lines woven across his face spoke volumes about the hardships and fights he'd survived. But today, he sat before me well-groomed, nicely dressed, and willing to face his daughter's rigorous interrogation.

For a decade, I'd banked numerous questions to ask my father if the chance ever arose. Swallowing hard, I asked, "Ed, were you married to my mother, and am I your daughter?"

There, I'd said it! Suddenly, an incredible load lifted off my back. I'd heard that the word *catharsis* meant "releasing a strong emotion," but I never recalled experiencing one until now.

Ed didn't hesitate. "Yes, Laurel, I did marry your mother, and I am your father."

I didn't expect what Ed said next. "Before we get specific, I want ya to know how seein' you makes me feel. I'm a drunk. I'm no damn good, and my life has been a failure 'cept for one gift to the world: you. Marrying Marie and havin' a young woman like you for a daughter is the reason God put me on this earth. You're the only good I ever done. In my wildest dreams, I never 'magined a daughter so damn smart and beautiful.

"Today, you added purpose to ma life. The difficult moments hauntin' ma past have ended because of the grace you've granted me, however brief the moment. The shame I been a-feelin' from abandonin' you has decreased knowin' how far ya come. Today, ya done took a big ole' weight offa ma shoulders."

Ed and I were swamped by emotions. We stood and hugged each other and he held me protectively, kissing my head and patting my back. Lack of a father had left an unrecognized hole in my soul. Now, I held my missing piece, and I didn't want to let go. I sensed Ed felt the same way. Finally, we sat down together and Ed said, "Laurel, let me tell you what happened. It'll probably cover the questions you got, but I'll answer any others you want."

He started filling in the past. "Your mother and I met in 1955. Your mom was attendin' her third year of law school in San Diego, and I was an aircraft mechanic stationed at the naval base. Your mom's trainin' brought her on base to view a military court-martial. Laws for folks in the armed services come from the Uniform Code of Military Justice, which is different from civilian law. My senior enlisted rank made me eligible to sit on the jury.

"Your mother was in the audience. I'd never laid eyes on such a gorgeous woman. I went to the commissary for lunch, and she was sittin' alone enjoying a sandwich. I asked if I could join her. To my surprise, she said sittin' with a member of the armed services would be an honor.

"The trial was scheduled to last three more days. Each day, I met your mom for lunch, and we'd walked around the base. After two days I was smitten. I wanted your mom for my wife.

"The day before deliberations, I noticed your mother conferring with the defense attorney. The meeting was unusual because civilian lawyers needed special permission to argue in military courts. The case involved national security, and somehow President Eisenhower intervened, stopping the trial. The jury read and confirmed the letter—and the judge dismissed the case. Whoever had involved the president saved the life of a young naval officer.

"After court, I caught up with your mother, and she told me about her second-year law internship. Ranking highest in her class, she had been offered a wide choice of summer internships. She chose the White House."

I couldn't believe it! Mom had never mentioned it!

Ed continued. "President Eisenhower wanted formal controls for the use of nuclear energy. The FBI had vetted your mother, and she had received top-secret clearance, which allowed her to prepare a draft of the Atomic Energy Act of 1954. Using her clearance to research the prosecution's charges, she discovered that high-level secrets would have to be revealed to prove the man's innocence. She had called the president, and he had intervened. Thanks to your mom, the truth won and secrets stayed secret.

"I had no doubts about marrying your mother. Four weeks later, we had a small wedding and a weekend honeymoon. We both worked hard, and I finished my navy service while your mother finished law school. She worked for the Department of Defense, and I worked as a private aircraft mechanic.

"Drinkin' is popular among enlisted men. I took my first drink after basic training, and soon I was outdrinkin' everybody. I was honorably discharged, but your mom knew my drinkin' was a problem. We made a good living, and I drank to celebrate. I also drank when I was mad, sad, glad, afraid, and alone. I couldn't face any emotions without drinkin'.

"In 1956, your mother got pregnant. Knowin' I was goin' to be a father, I stopped without a problem. Havin' my first child was excitin'. When your mom miscarried halfway through, it threw me over the edge. I started boozin' again, and it quickly got worse.

"Over the next year, I lost my job, my friends, and our savings. Went to jail four times. When your mother said she was pregnant with you, I tried to stop. But unlike the first time, I shook, sweat, and had horrible anxiety attacks. Only alcohol cured my symptoms.

"A month after you's born, Marie told me if I didn't quit, she'd leave. Three months later, I come home from the bar to find my belongin's in the front yard and new locks on the doors. The divorce summons found me at the YMCA three weeks later. Who coulda blamed her? I loved liquor more 'an I loved her.

"I was homeless for five years. One day, while I's drunk, I robbed me a bank. I ran, carrying three bags a money, but I passed out three blocks from the bank. They arrested me without a struggle. Thirty-four days later, the court found me guilty and give me sixteen years in the Oregon State prison. It was there that I found Alcoholics Anonymous.

"I attended meetin's so I could get outta ma cell. But over the months, the program begun makin' more sense. Prisoners who showed up enjoyed their work and learned better skills. We stayed outta trouble and tried helpin' others. They released me last year for good behavior, waivin' ten years off my sentence. I come back to Sutter to start over. I ain't drank in a while, but I wasn't ready to face you or your mom. I needed a job and shelter before I could make those amends."

I sat still, continuously eating chips and dip. Ed had covered many years and I wasn't sure where to begin. Alcohol had ruled his life and caused so much harm.

"Ed, why didn't you just stop drinking and not start again?" I asked. This seemed the obvious solution to his problem. "If I get stung by a bee, I'm going to avoid bees," I explained.

I ate more chips as Ed continued, "I can't argue with your logic, 'cause it's hard to understand if ya ain't never had it." I grabbed a few more chips, as Ed changed his train of thought and said, "Ya know, dear, them chips ain't good for your heart. Ya oughtta limit yourself so ya don't croak 'fore your time."

"Yeah, Ed, you're right," I agreed. He continued explaining how, whenever he had obsessed about drinking, he'd felt compelled to hit the liquor store. He said that once the compulsion started, nothing could stop him.

"I'm still not sure why you didn't quit after a few drinks," I reiterated.

Ed sat silent several seconds. I continued to finish off the chips. "Laurel, why are you still eatin' the chips?" Ed wanted to know. "You agreed they're bad for you."

"Jeez, Ed, have you ever tried eating just a few chips?" I volleyed back. "It's impossible. I only plan to eat four or five, but I never stop until I've finished the bag. Once I eat that first chip, I can't put the bag down. Surely, you've experienced the same craving," I remarked. Suddenly, my words sank in. Ed's point belted my brain like a bat crushing a home-run ball.

Ed looked at me and said softly, "Yes, Laurel, if anyone understands craving and the inability to stop at just one, I do. Alcoholics Anonymous says, 'One is too many and a thousand never enough.' Alcohol behaves like potato chips: once I consume the first drink, I can't stop."

Truly understanding how liquor had owned Ed was powerful. Potato chips weren't liquor, but I grasped how a substance could enslave a man. It required incredible skills for a slave to free himself and avoid being recaptured. "Ed, you're wrong," I said. "You've produced two, not one, gifts to the world. On your own, you got and stayed sober," I pointed out.

"Laurel, your insight is excellent, but in one way you're wrong: I didn't get sober alone. I only stopped my drinking when I asked a sober alcoholic for help. He told me I had ta find a personal power greater 'an myself and pray for that power to keep me sober. You've probably ain't never heard it described, but what I had was a spiritual awakenin'.

"I'd always believed in God, and I tried different religions. Never did get sober. Alcoholics Anonymous suggested the power I needed lived within me. They told me they had a way to find and tap this resource. I had to admit I was a drunk, confess my faults to another man, make good for the damage I done, and share my 'perience with other drunks. It worked. My awakenin' came when I found myself carryin' out tasks I coulda never done with my strength alone."

"Ed, have you been talking to Iris?" He shook his head. "This morning she gave me the same message. She said I'd have to locate my inner strength to face the school board. Do you think you could help?" I asked. "There isn't time to confess my many sins. What should I do?"

"Listen, Laurel, you ain't an alcoholic, and I know ya haven't been alive long enough to cause much trouble. First, I need to convince ya that the power you seek is within you. Let me ask a few questions. Ya ever held a newborn baby?" he asked.

"Yes. When Mrs. Mayer had her daughter, Mom and I took dinner, and I held the baby for several hours," I answered.

"Holdin' that baby, did ya see any signs leadin' ya to think she'd grow up to lie, cheat, or steal?" I admitted I hadn't seen those traits. "Did the baby make you want to love and nurture it?" he asked. I said yes. "Did ya see signs the newborn was hateful or lived in fear?"

"No, Ed, I didn't see one fault. The baby seemed perfect to me," I explained.

"Laurel, do ya think God is perfect? If ya answer yes, ya hafta admit ya were holdin' a little part of God. People in this world teach the child good and bad, but deep down lies God's purity, present before birth. That purity gets hidden as the child grows, and eventually it becomes so buried, no one sees a trace of the purity within.

"Rediscoverin' that goodness demands siftin' through a lifetime of garbage to find the pearls of perfection. What I've told ya is true for everybody, but only those living in hell seem willing to undergo the painful soul-searching necessary to discover their inner power."

Ed must have been right. I'd heard the same argument from the religious leaders, Iris, and now him. I couldn't find fault in their logic. Three independent sources had recited the same message. Each source was reliable and gained no profit from spreading their message. The thought of God existing in me was radical, but it felt right. This postulate was a discovery I would have never made without help. I knew with certainty that this principle was "God's Honest Truth."

By now, Ed and I were both emotionally exhausted. I had found my inner strength, and Ed had found a daughter. We had both found a moment of serenity in the chaos of life. I didn't know where our relationship would go, but time was on our side. I felt anxious about telling Mother my discussion, but I'd ask Iris to help.

Like Houdini, Iris appeared out of nowhere and invited us to eat. Tonight, she served rotisserie chicken, mashed potatoes, and mixed vegetables, with chocolate cake for dessert. Since Ed had gotten a job, his meals had improved, but it was obvious he hadn't feasted like this in years. When Iris stood up to refill the sugar bowl, I whispered in Ed's ear, "Ask her for more of her famous chip dip, and you'll make a friend for life."

Iris was ready to sit when Ed remarked, "Iris, your cooking is superb. May I refill my plate?" In a flash, Iris grabbed his dish and returned with a reloaded plate. As Ed finished his third helping, I imagined serving him and Denny together would compel Iris to stock the pantry ahead of time.

We finished dessert, and I told Ed I had to start my homework. He understood and gave me a kiss. We promised to see each other soon and make up for lost time. When Ed left, I flopped on the couch.

"Iris, I'm exhausted, and I've done nothing strenuous. I've never felt like this before," I said, puzzled.

"Well, sweetheart, emotional exhaustion is ten times worse than physical exhaustion. Formally meeting your father for the first time falls into the first category. I had no plans to invite Ed over, until I saw him delivering furniture close to Mort's.

"He offered to drive me to the house, and I told him about your date with destiny. Not knowing Ed had a clue, I told him how we'd discussed tapping into your inner strength. He seemed interested when I told him I had problems explaining the idea in a way you understand. He offered to help, and with reservations, I accepted his offer.

"Now, you might disagree, but looking back, the meeting went well because you two had no chance to imagine the various scenarios. The anxiety before an important event is usually worse than the event itself. Someday, in retrospect, you'll look back and agree I was right. Until then, I apologize and accept responsibility for your tired soul."

My routine at this time of night was finishing my homework and calling Joann. Over the last two weeks, I'd added Denny to the lineup. It took an hour to discuss everything twice and say nothing relevant. Tonight was no different.

It was ten o'clock when I finished my telephone rounds. I went to bed knowing the final countdown launching my future was underway. Ed and Iris had taught me I couldn't alter the course of the rocket—only the attitude of the pilot.

CHAPTER 40

A Revelation of Mind and Self

Tuesday and Wednesday came and went in a blur. Iris and I visited the homeless people, and with help from Denny, Joann, and Nubs, we took plenty of food and whiskey. Serving less fortunate people focused my attention on the everyday blessings I received. Folks living outdoors reminded me how much I took shelter and indoor plumbing for granted. If I was expelled, those luxuries weren't going away. Perhaps my higher power was starting to emerge.

Thursday morning, a tangerine-orange sun dawned, radiating heat I normally felt in Denny's arms. Sleeping soundly, I basked in the warmth of an erotic dream. Now in our early twenties, Denny slept beside me as we cuddled naked, in a pearl-white room. A saltwater scent of the ocean drifted in through open balcony doors. As I slept, Denny awakened and placed his hand on my cheek. Turning my head, he French-kissed me as his hands explored the peaks and valleys of my female anatomy.

Our passions ascended and soon, we were making love. Worries about knowing what to do quickly faded as instincts took over, and lust momentarily replaced love. Denny knew how to please my sensual spots and in moments, vibrations racked my body as I shook in an endless climax.

Oh my God—this part wasn't a dream! Waking up, my face was flushed and my thighs were warm. The pleasure of my first orgasm was overwhelming. Heat waves pulsed outward from my erogenous core, increasing the intense pleasurable sensation. The hedonistic tingling faded leaving my body rigid and my senses on overload.

I felt rejuvenated and horny at the same time. I wanted Denny now—right now! In my mind, he appeared. Applying increasing pressure to stimulate my desire, I imagined both of us making love again. I could feel Denny pulling my hips close and before long, we both achieved simultaneous satisfaction.

After lying in total bliss for a short time, my libido started to fade.

Embarrassment replaced the incredible satisfaction I'd experienced. This wasn't how proper women behaved. Being certain normal women never masturbated, I knew I must be a slut—another pea in the same pod as Cindy Summers. What would Mother and Iris think if they knew I had masturbated?

If Mom found out, she'd confine me for years—hands in shackles, preventing me from diddling myself. Experiencing a first orgasm could happen anytime—why today? Many years would pass before I learned that women who started their day with a climax usually had a better day.

The clock showed six thirty. Home economics had paid off: I appreciated rising early and knowing how to work a washing machine. I stripped my bed and put the linens in the washing machine. I made my bed with fresh sheets and decided I'd surprise Iris with breakfast.Unfortunately, my cooking skills were not advanced. When Iris wandered down, I had finished burning the bacon and eggs. Because there was little I could do to harm fresh fruit, it saved breakfast.

Iris cleaned her plate, complimenting me, "Laurel, thank you for surprising me with a breakfast I won't soon forget. How come you're up early?"

Not wanting to lie, I responded, "I was thinking how Denny would react if I'm expelled. I tried to concentrate on different issues, but thoughts about Denny 'kept me coming' back to my part in this mess. It's possible he'll leave me if I'm expelled. I guess there's no choice but to deal with it."

"Honey, remember our discussion. If Denny cares for you, he'll stand by you. Right now, I'm hearing fear in your voice. Today is not the day for a pity party. Move past Denny and focus on the present. We have a busy day, beginning with you going to class. After lunch, I'll meet you at Bill Landsford's office. He plans on reviewing final instructions. Your mother will definitely call during our meeting."

Her voice rose as she continued, "Before her call, collect your thoughts. Crying and whining will make Marie feel guilty. With all due respect, your mother's work affects far more than the board's decision about you. I know those words are tough, but they're 100 percent true. Your goal is to assure your mother that her absence isn't a problem. She must feel confident that everything is fine."

Defending myself, I said, "I'm committed about what I'm telling Mother and the board. The only person not committed to what she's saying is you! I haven't heard a peep about your plans," I scolded. "Honestly, I doubt you've committed any thought to tonight." I regretted the words the moment they flew off my lips.

Iris projected a radiance I'd never seen. Softly, she took my hands and held them. She spoke in a calming voice: "Laurel, I'm sure you know I've been around a long time. During my years, I've lived my life doing good in a bad world. There isn't much I haven't seen or done. Without doubt, few have experienced more.

"I've often witnessed poor judgment lead a person into hell. Only people who unconditionally forgive themselves and those who've harmed them ascend from the cauldron to the peak of serenity. Forgiveness never changes anyone's past, but it always changes everyone's future.

"Tonight, I plan to use my experiences to make the board understand their folly. I hope for a positive result, but if I fail, please forgive me. Whatever happens, know God loves you, and let that guide you in seeing the good in me and the board. Finally, humble yourself and accept the board's decision. If you succeed in forgiving, perhaps you'll realize my words are the golden key—not the lock."

"Iris, I'm sorry about how I spoke to you. I hope you'll forgive me. I know you'll come up with a unique presentation. I shouldn't ever have doubted you. Over the past several weeks, you've shown qualities I should strive to emulate. And then there's God. You helped me get a perspective without emphasizing one religion over another. The theories we discussed gave me enough information to form my own idea of a higher power. Most of all, you and Ed showed me this power lives within us all. I have more self-confidence and self-respect than ever. Those are the gifts you've given me, and I love you with all my heart."

We embraced each other, and I kissed Iris on both cheeks. She dabbed the tears in her eyes and remained quiet while she tried to compose herself. "Honey, I accept your apology. Your stress is incredible, and you've dealt with it better than I expected. It's almost finished. Just stay focused. We won't return home until after the meeting. See to it you have your notes for this evening. I'll bring dinner, and we'll ride to the theater with Bill. Now, off to school while I figure out what I'll say and do."

Dozens of reporters were roosting in the front yard. Hoping it was the last time, I took the back route to school. Suddenly, Tamara Teague came out of nowhere and ambushed me.

"Laurel!" she said. I instantly looked in her direction. "Laurel Montgomery—that's who you are—am I correct?" she asked. I considered running, but my instinct said to stay and talk.

"Yes, I'm Laurel," I admitted. I saw joy in Tamara's eyes, as she realized she was the first reporter I'd granted an interview. She asked if I would answer a few questions, and I agreed on one condition: the interview could only air after the meeting began. She accepted my terms. After I put it in writing, she signed and we began.

When we finished, I walked away as Ms. Teague signed off. I was happy to speak my mind. Thinking back on what I'd said, I decided to make changes to my presentation that evening.

When classes ended, Joann caught up with me and explained, "Laurel, we have a plan to baffle the reporters waiting to interview you. Susan saw a show discussing how the Secret Service transports the president. She studied their methods and added an idea of her own. You must convince Bill to stop. It's critical. I promise."

Recent events made me wonder what they had planned. I gave Joann a long hug and kissed her on the cheek. I had spent time with her as far back as I could remember. My emotions remained stable until we parted, and then the tears flowed as I imagined us not graduating together.

I walked for twenty minutes before reaching Bill's office. Checking in with his secretary, Kay, I soon sat in his empty office while he took a call. Iris wasn't anywhere around. Five minutes passed when Kay said, "Laurel, Bill would like you in the conference room."

Mr. Landsford was on the phone when I entered. He turned and handed me the phone, saying, "Laurel, this call's for you." Only Iris knew I had an appointment with Mr. Landsford; I thought the media had tracked me down.

Holding the receiver to my ear, I said, "Hello." Static echoed in the phone as Mom's voice tried to break through. "Laurel, is that you talking, or is it Bill?"

"Hey, Mom, it's me, Laurel. Can you hear me?"

"Laurel, honey? I don't know if this call uses an undersea cable or a satellite, but our connection is horrible. How are you coping, dear?"

"Well, Mom, I'm in Bill's office preparing for tonight's meeting. Iris hasn't arrived, but she'll arrive soon. Today, I've had support from my friends, teachers, and even Dr. Collier. The future feels a little more optimistic."

Recalling that Iris had told me not to upset Mom, I knew my next question was pressing my luck, but this morning, my luck was good; I decided to press for more. "Hey, Mom, have you seen Dad since he left home?"

The silence seemed like an eternity.

"Laurel, why are you asking? You have more urgent matters, unless . . . my God, Laurel, have you found your father? Tell me the truth, young lady! If he's bothering you, I'm coming home and filing a restraining order! The man is not worth the powder to blow him to hell! The answer to your question is no, I haven't seen Ed—nor do I plan to see Ed! He ruined the best years of our lives! Tell me why you're asking."

I sensed from Mom's tone that she still harbored hostile feelings toward Dad. Wisely, I decided that trying to change her mind was futile. Iris had reminded me actions speak louder than words. If Mom ever agreed to meet Ed, he'd have to demonstrate how much he'd changed. Choosing my words carefully, I said, "Well, Mom, I was searching the hallway closet and came across some old photos. Three photos showed you and a handsome man standing side by side. One image showed the same man holding me as a baby. I assumed it was Dad.

"On Tuesday nights, Iris and Nubs feed the homeless down by the river. I've been tagging along. I met a man named Ed, who lived in a cardboard box. He's older now, but he's the same man in your photos."

With my next few words, solid ground began to tremble. "I'd spoken with Ed twice before I discovered the connection. Based on our conversations, I'm sure Ed's my father. You've said I can't run from my problems. It's a matter of time before I see him again, and honestly, I want to confront him—preferably on my schedule and not his. What do you think, Mom?"

"Honey, I didn't imagine this would pop up during my absence. Ed's not going anywhere. Your focus must be today's board meeting. You can speak with Ed and tell him your suspicions. You need to know the truth, and since you're fourteen, I can't protect you forever. If the discussion can wait until I return, that's my preference. What does Iris think?" she asked.

"Iris thought I shouldn't disturb you with this matter until you got home, but she agrees with your suggestion. She's known Ed a while and says he's sober and progressing in his recovery. He landed a job with Milt Ordner and found a place to live."

"Laurel, life unfolds in unexpected ways. God has a reason for you meeting your dad. We'll never know His intent, but time adds perspective. I have a few minutes left, so here's my advice. Don't elaborate; say only what Bill tells you to say. If they ask a question, answer it if you can, but don't guess. If you're unsure, say, 'I don't know.' Look the board straight in the eye when you speak. Doing so projects honesty and confidence. Panels find it difficult to vote against people displaying these qualities. Whenever the meeting adjourns, I want a phone call! Do you understand, Laurel? No waiting until tomorrow."

"Mom, I understand. You know it will be expensive, but I'll call. I love you, Mom."

"I love you too, darling. Stay alert and good luck. Bye-bye." She hung up.

I was ready to fight!

CHAPTER 41

Preparing for Battle

After assuring Mr. Landsford that the article in the paper was false, we reviewed his copy of the investigator's findings as well as my presentation. During this time, Iris remained absent. Most likely, she was finalizing her argument. Iris was a visual person and liked to have props available when she was teaching.

It wasn't a surprise that Harrison Shepard's report determined that Mr. Wright and I had colluded to preach religion. His summary stated that I had caused Elle Dutton "severe mental anguish." My actions, it seemed, were "equivalent to beating her with an emotional bat."

While his accusations were untrue, his only evidence supporting my involvement in the cheating scandal was Chip Martin's chain-of-evidence letter. Mr. Landsford considered other statements about the cheating scandal to be hearsay. When we were close to finishing, Mr. Landsford said, "Laurel, you're one of the best-prepared clients I've ever had. I'm familiar with the suggestions your mother passed on to you, and I agree. The only advice she left out is this: if you choose not to answer a question, you're given that right. The drawback of not answering the board's inquiries is they will assume you're hiding critical facts. Whatever you decide, don't refuse to answer more than three questions. If you do, they will vote to expel you."

"Mr. Landsford," I responded, "I ran into Dr. Collier several days ago and told her what happened. She believed me and promised to vote in my favor. I need two more votes to stay in school. Right now, I can't think of any question I wouldn't answer."

Mr. Landsford hesitated a moment. "Look, Laurel, normally, I'm not this straightforward, but with you, I'll state my gut feeling. Dr. Collier is an outstanding doctor and a wonderful person, but her first responsibility is meeting the educational needs of the students. Doing what's best for the school supersedes doing what's best for you. I spoke with her yesterday. She'll vote in your favor, provided we present a case justifying her decision. In other words, if you and Iris display outstanding character and integrity, you'll succeed. Screw it up and I guarantee Dr. Collier will not fall on her sword to save your ass. Dr. Collier spoke with Tibor Kirshbaum. His son told him the entire story and he is on your side.

"I think Ms. Bond is our target. She clearly states that her vote depends on decisive evidence that you took part in the cheating ring. The only evidence Shepard lists in his report is Chip Martin's letter. Martin wants you expelled, and he is not a disinterested party. The weakness in Shepard's investigation is not having an independent source confirm the allegations in Mr. Martin's letter."

"Look, Mr. Landsford, I've been holding back," I said. "Chip Martin is having an affair with Elle Dutton's mother, Amelia." I explained how we had gained this information. "That's why he's out to expel me. Also, we used the concealed fence camera to convince the board they could stop preparing their case against me. The girl in the *Sentinel* is my best friend, Joann."

Bill pulled out some photos. "I received these in the mail yesterday. They arrived without a letter of explanation. I'm not familiar with Mrs. Martin or Mrs. Dutton, so I had no idea who these represented. Do you have any idea who took these pictures?" he asked.

"No, I don't have a clue," I replied. "I got the impression he wasn't an adult."

Thinking back, I realized it had to be Denny. I'd noticed his scar the first time I kissed him. Why was he spying on Mr. Martin? What else hadn't he told me? Bill pondered what I'd said. "Laurel, the reliability of this evidence is critical."

He lifted the phone and said, "Kay, come in for a second?" Within thirty seconds, Kay Formby was by Mr. Landsford's side. "Kay, Dr. Dutton's your dentist, isn't he?"

"Yes, Bill. He's been our family dentist for many years."

Bill showed Kay the photos, asking, "Do you know Mrs. Dutton, and if so, is that her in the picture?"

"Yes, I know Mrs. Dutton, and that's her. I must confess I've never seen her in a negligee before—especially outdoors. Our investigators just get better all the time, don't they?" she kidded. Bill thanked Kay, and she returned to her desk.

"Laurel, are there other secrets you've kept hidden?"

I admitted I'd done both TV interviews with Tamera Teague and that the second interview would air tonight. I saw Bill wince. "Laurel, you'd better hope Ms. Teague doesn't broadcast the story at five thirty. Couldn't you have waited one more day?" Bill said in a frustrated tone.

Reaching into my pocket, I produced the contract. "Here. This is her signed contract guaranteeing she won't tell the story until the ten o'clock news."

Bill seemed impressed. "This isn't bad, Laurel. Did you learn this language from your mother?" he asked. I admitted Mom had unintentionally taught me several legal points. I knew about torts, mergers and acquisitions, and even criminal law.

Just then, Kay escorted Iris into the conference room along with the wagon, which was loaded with clothes and food.

"I'm sorry I'm late again. I walked to the theater to examine the stage and prepare my presentation. Seeing the setup, I realized I needed a specific piece of furniture. I decided to call Ed. I borrowed the school secretary's phone and called Milt Ordner. Mr. Ordner granted my wish, and Ed delivered exactly what I needed.

"I had the stage crew prepare the sets and lighting for my presentation. After dropping by Blitzer's Lounge to bend the mayor's ear and share a drink, I hurried over. I've even brought a late lunch."

Recalling Iris's episode with her "nerve medicine," I shuddered to think what verbal arrows she was aiming at the heart of the board. I needed to search through the wagon and be sure her nerve medicine hadn't hitched a ride. The tonic magically appeared at the most inconvenient times.

"Let me get the food, Iris," I said. "You sit down, talk with Mr. Landsford, and rest."

I searched the wagon, finding a makeup kit, a three-course meal, and a copy of the Marine Corps manual. I couldn't imagine why she needed the manual until I saw written on the inside cover "Property of SMMC Wright." It looked as if Mr. Wright had lent his personal manual to Iris, but the reason wasn't clear. Thankfully, I discovered no tonic.

I wanted to ask Iris what she had planned, but Mr. Landsford beat me to it. He said, "Iris, give me an idea what your presentation involves. I understand you want to keep it secret, but I don't like surprises. I need to be sure your speech won't harm Laurel's chances of staying in school."

Iris responded to Mr. Landsford without any signs she'd been drinking. "Bill, do you have faith in God?" she asked. Bill answered her question by nodding affirmatively.

Iris continued, "Try having the same faith in me that you have in God. The idea behind my plan is a Houdini variation I dreamed up myself. It's divinely inspired and beautifully crafted. You must have faith that God will carry me through."

"I don't have much choice," Bill said, blowing out a big breath.

Iris had prepared chicken salad sandwiches, pasta salad, and chocolate cake. She'd made a three-day supply of meals. I prayed we wouldn't need them. Bill said his sandwich was the best he'd ever eaten.

Iris smiled, saying, "I prepare each meal like it's my last masterpiece. Someday soon, that will surely be the case. By the way, Bill, the source motivating my cooking also inspired my presentation. Perhaps that gives you some comfort."

Mr. Landsford said, "It's five-thirty. Here's my parting wisdom. The events unfolding tonight are important, but the board isn't the highest authority. If their decision goes against Laurel, we will take the case to court. Emmitt Pilcher is an excellent attorney. If he sees the evidence we have involving Chip Martin and members of the school board, Emmitt will avoid a trial at all costs. Chances are good we could settle the case. Let's hope we don't have to resort to the legal system, but understand: we have a backup plan. Any questions?"

I piped up, "Yes. Can we drop by French's Fry and pick up my friends? They want to escort me to the meeting. I told them you'd probably say no, but they swear they have a plan to help me avoid the press."

Bill responded, "How come everybody has a plan I don't know anything about? This case has more secret operations underway than the United States government. Let's pick up the ladies and see what surprises await."

The weeks, days, and hours had ticked down. My future, while monumental to me, wasn't the important question on trial. What hinged on tonight's decision were the foundations of diverse thought and the right to express them. Could my earthly soul defend the magnificence of our God-centered Constitution? It seemed a lofty challenge for a fourteen-year-old woman and an elderly nanny.

I prayed God would see us through.

CHAPTER 42

A Divine Response to a Devil of a Deed

We went downstairs and packed Bill's Chevy Suburban. Bill's vehicle could have doubled as a small bus; fuel efficiency and smaller cars were years away. We loaded Iris's Radio Flyer wagon and seated her in the shotgun position. I jumped in back, and we headed to French's Fry.

Dozens of kids sat outside. I scanned the crowd—my girlfriends never sat indoors—but nobody resembled my bosom buddies. Then suddenly, the back door of the car opened and four girls crawled into two backseats. Bill and Iris did a double take, and I just stared. Except for their wardrobes, all four ladies looked exactly like me!

Bill exclaimed, "Well, I'll be damned!"

It took time figuring out everyone's identity—all four looked precisely like me. Utannah had applied the makeup brilliantly, matching every detail right down to the birthmark above my lip.

Joann punched my shoulder, "Well, what do you think?" she asked. "Utannah started working on us after school."

Bill said, "It's incredible. Your scheme will baffle the press, especially if you all answer the same question differently. They won't know who to believe. I'd still caution you to keep moving. This isn't the time to give a long interview. Let's get into the auditorium and find our places."

Iris added, "How lovely, girls. What a scrupulously wonderful ploy. Those reporters have pestered me endlessly and brought bad karma to my sequoia. You're wonderful for supporting Laurel, even if the devil has occupied your brains."

Susan spoke up, "Laurel, you're getting out fourth. Most of the media should surround the first three girls, which will clear a path to get you inside. And this goes for everyone: if you can't move, don't tell reporters your name but offer to answer their questions. Speak briefly and move when you can."

Tanice seemed to agree. "Tanice," I asked, "you're not carrying pepper spray, are you? Cameras are everywhere. If you plan on maiming reporters, stay out of the limelight."

Tanice shot back, "No pepper spray, but I have brass knuckles and a knife in my purse. Here's the best part, Laurel: if I have to wallop someone, they'll think you did it!"

Boy, she had a point. No doubt her purse contained every item she described, as well as other unmentioned surprises. I didn't have any bodyguards, but I felt well protected.

It was a five-minute drive from French's Fry to the auditorium-theater. As we drove past city park, droves of people were protesting, many holding "Expel Laurel" signs. The crowd outside the theater stood packed behind restraining barriers, while reporters moved about freely. People lined up to receive free tickets for one of six hundred seats. Police and state troopers stood at each entrance and roamed throughout the crowd. Reporters awaited my arrival with their cameras and lights. I felt like a movie star about to attend the Academy Awards.

Mr. Landsford pulled to the curb. Before leaving his office, he had called the police department, described his Suburban, and told them we were on our way. After we stopped, two officers opened the front doors, and Iris and Bill hopped out, leaving the car running. A police officer jumped in, ready to valet the vehicle. Bill came around to the passenger side and opened the back door.

"Jeez, Iris, look at the people. There must be five or six thousand," I noted.

Iris curbed my amazement by saying, "Well, dear, anytime there's rumor of a public hanging, people show up in droves."

As Joann exited the car, the press surrounded her yelling, "Miss Montgomery, Miss Montgomery." Law officers tried to run interference to no avail. Joann started speaking, and the crowd noise dwindled. Moments later, Tanice emerged from the Suburban. Occupied with Joann, reporters took a minute to realize Tanice must be the "real" Laurel trying to avoid the media. They quickly engulfed her.

In under two minutes, the rest of us exited the Suburban and produced mass confusion for reporters and law officers. As I answered questions, one obnoxious reporter started harassing Tanice. When she opened her purse, I got ready to tackle her. I felt relief when she pulled out lipstick and walked away. That reporter didn't know he'd just dodged losing his teeth.

Entering the lobby, we heard, "Folks, we've handed out the last ticket. The fire marshal won't allow more people into the auditorium. Loudspeakers and restrooms are outdoors for folks who wish to stay. Thank you for your patience."

While police cleared the lobby, we walked down the aisle to seating specifically reserved for the Wrights and me. Most of the fifty seats were for Mr. Wright's large family; my small group consisted of seven. Reaching the first row, we found ourselves seated just below the podium. I turned and faced the audience. Behind us sat the Van Skoks, the Jensens, and Nubs Fritzmeyer. Ed and Milt Ordner sat by my teachers on the opposite side of the Jensens.

Students I'd grown up with stood and applauded as I arrived. No television cameras were allowed because there wasn't enough space. Reporters had special closed-in seating and could only take still photos until the meeting started. After that, no photos would be allowed.

On the opposite side of the center aisle sat the Duttons, ACLU representatives, and Mr. Martin. Norman Dutton had his arm in a sling and wore a cap to cover his head wound. Amelia Dutton sat next to Mr. Martin. Joann whispered, "Look at that tent pole in his pants. Do you think he can avoid boning her until after the meeting?"

I responded, "God, Joann, what a dirty mind. You're as bad as Mark. You should consider putting the strength of your libido to good use. I've said before, we don't know for sure, so quit giving them grief; they might just be close friends."

Joann lowered her head, commenting, "Yeah, right!"

When I turned around, Denny had joined us and started kissing Susan Small. Since we were all facing the stage, Denny had assumed Susan was me. Susan looked surprised, but with Denny's talents, she wasn't objecting. Denny looked confused but was clearly enjoying a different set of lips.

I saw no reason to promote competition. I whispered, "Denny, I'm over here." Standing straight, he saw all five girls and kissed each of us. When he got to me, I slipped him the tongue to signal he'd hit the jackpot. He produced an evil grin and sat down, taking my hand.

At six o'clock, the school board trustees walked on stage, with Emmitt Pilcher accompanying them. The last person to appear surprised the audience. It was Superintendent Devlin Myers. He received a well-deserved standing ovation. Dr. Myers had gone to the Mayo Clinic when diagnosed with stomach cancer. Recent reports stated he was near death, so no one had expected his attendance. Tonight he looked healthy, though somber. Glancing at Chip Martin, I noticed he was sweating and twiddling his thumbs, most likely because he and Dr. Myers didn't see eye to eye.

As the lights dimmed, the school board seated themselves, and Rabbi Edelstein led the audience in the Pledge of Allegiance, followed by a blessing. Each board meeting opened with a prayer presented by different religious affiliations. It didn't matter that the crux of this meeting was the separation of church and state; no one had thought to change the format.

After finishing, Rabbi Edelstein descended the stairs and Jacquelyn Collier spoke. "Ladies and gentlemen, on behalf of my colleagues and school attorney Emmitt Pilcher, we welcome you to this special meeting of the board. We're especially delighted to have Superintendent Myers seated with us after his long illness. We look forward to his comments and insight. Tonight, we'll begin discussions on funding the high school remodeling project. The second agenda item is an award presentation to Mr. Brett Moore for leading three winning football teams. Finally, the board will address disciplinary action against student Laurel Montgomery and history teacher Penfield Wright."

Dr. Collier continued, "Our first discussion deals with choices for financing improvements to the high school. The most feasible choices are seeking private donations or asking voters to approve a tax bond. Board member Simpson has studied the issue and will provide an update. Mr. Simpson?"

Webster Simpson pulled his microphone closer. "Ladies and gentlemen, Sutter High was built in 1946. It's served us well but is overdue for improvement. The boiler is failing, and there is no air conditioning. We use more audiovisual equipment now than in the past, requiring three times the electrical outlets in current classrooms. The plumbing is outdated, and more restrooms are necessary. Based on recommendations for bringing the school up to code, the cost will exceed two million dollars. Raising the mill levy five points allows retiring the bond in eight years, assuming most taxes come from corporations.

"We have several offers from private citizens. The advantage is a significant tax write-off for the donor and no tax increase for the voters. However, conditions exist that may pose barriers to accepting private donations. Addressing this further, we have two community leaders to present proposals for the board. First is attorney Hattie Daniels."

Hattie Daniels was an estate attorney specializing in charitable trusts. She walked to the stage, and after giving binders to each board member, assumed the podium.

"Members of the audience and trustees, thank you for the time to explain this funding proposal. I represent an estate with significant funds for charitable causes. This person placed a tremendous value on education. Unfortunately, the estate didn't keep up with taxes, so I've reserved significant funds to clear the estate. Until the IRS is satisfied, the estate can only offer $400,000 a year over the next five years, with no guarantee on the fourth or fifth years. The last two years depend on the estate paying its final taxes. I understand this isn't the ideal choice, but it's the best I can offer today. I'll gladly address any questions from board members."

Mr. Capellan asked, "If I understand correctly, the estate guarantees $1,200,000. Can the district receive the guaranteed amount as a lump sum rather than paid out over three years?"

Ms. Daniels responded, "No, it isn't possible. The client invested in blue-chip stocks, which produce significant dividends. The estate stipulates the initial amounts, with the balance contingent on how the school uses the funds. Four hundred thousand dollars is the yearly limit. I've outlined excerpts from the will and details of the proposal in your binders. May I answer any more questions?"

No one responded, so Mr. Simpson said, "Thank you, Hattie. The board will read the proposal and respond within four weeks. We appreciate the donor's generosity."

Webster Simpson continued, "Our next presenter is Milt Ordner, who will present a second alternative for private funding."

Milt took the stage and was showered with applause. Despite his tough exterior, he'd funded numerous city projects and created many jobs. Milt stood behind the podium. Unlike Ms. Daniels, he had no prepared statement. He spoke from his heart.

"Board trustees and citizens, I've had the great privilege of living in Sutter most of my life. With my late wife, I built a business from a small store into a large corporation. My motivation to persevere in difficult times was faith.

"When we had little else, God filled the gap. Tonight, this board decides whether to exclude God from Sutter's schools. We can't challenge the fact that freedom of religion was a defining force in the establishment of the United States. In addition, arguments between religions have caused millions of deaths throughout history. My question to each trustee is: how can students learn these truths if they're not taught in school? Parents can't always know history, just as they may not know math. That's why our children attend school.

"Discussing God's influence on civilizations explains what faith has accomplished—it doesn't promote it. If students don't understand these motives, the world won't improve. You may disagree with what happened in Mr. Wright's class, but knowing Penfield, I'm certain there was no intent to change your teenagers' beliefs. If this board dismisses the allegations against Ms. Montgomery and Penfield Wright, I will give three million dollars to the school."

Supporting his promise, Mr. Ordner withdrew a check from his wallet, approached the board, and handed it to Webster Simpson. A close-up of Milt's generosity was strategically projected on the screen hanging behind the board members. Like almost everyone, I'd never seen a check for three million dollars.

Milt returned to the podium and said, for all to hear, "If the trustees make the wrong decision tonight, I will instantly tear up that check." Without taking questions, he then left the stage, leaving a confused school board with a very slippery treasure.

Andrew Capellan adjusted his microphone, "Mr. Ordner, you may try to intimidate the trustees, but we have a duty to the school district. While your offer is generous, money cannot buy the board's vote. I'm sure my colleagues agree."

Allison Bond added her opinion. "Mr. Ordner, thank you for your generosity. I appreciate your passion for God and your wish to help Ms. Montgomery and Mr. Wright. I also know how much the high school needs the money, but I agree with Mr. Capellan: the disciplinary decision rests upon facts, not money."

Dr. Collier concluded, "Milt, your offer is extremely generous. I hope you'll let us keep your check until after the vote. If the decision doesn't meet your expectations, I will personally return your donation."

Milt stood from his seat, saying, "Dr. Collier, that's fine, but Iris Wimple asked to borrow the check for her presentation, so I agreed. Please lend it to Iris, if necessary."

Mr. Ordner had spilled the beans. I looked over to ask Iris what was going down, but she'd disappeared. Mr. Landsford said he thought Iris had run to the ladies' room. I hoped that was true, but somehow I knew the bathroom was the last place she'd be.

Dr. Collier conferred with the high school secretary, Mavis Turner. After several exchanges, Dr. Collier stated, "Ladies and gentlemen, our award to Brett Moore must wait. He's coming from Portland, so when he arrives, we'll interrupt the discussion. Since we've changed the agenda, the board will hear statements on the disciplinary actions against Laurel Montgomery and Penfield Wright. Emmitt Pilcher will read the accusations, as well as the summary of an independent investigation. The board will read the filed complaints and listen to members of the audience. Emmitt?"

Mr. Pilcher strutted to the podium. He thanked Jacquelyn Collier and started by reading the complaints filed by the Duttons, the ACLU, and the International Atheists Coalition. He then turned his attention to the investigator's summary.

"The statements I'm about to read are from an independent investigation conducted by Harrison Shepard and Associates, based in Portland. The complete investigation is available in the superintendent's office."

As Mr. Landsford had expected, Mr. Pilcher placed emphasis on excerpts from Chip Martin's letter and Elle Dutton's emotional turmoil. I glanced at Elle and saw that both she and her mother were sobbing. Dr. Dutton looked as if he'd flog me if given the opportunity. When the allegations were finished, I could tell the audience was swaying toward Elle's defense. Compared to me, Rasputin looked like a saint.

Mr. Pilcher then invited audience members to express their opinions. The initial ten speakers supported our dismissal. Their first spokesperson was a man from Britain I'd never seen before. He introduced himself as Ronald Dalwin. His title was Director of the International Atheist Coalition. I was thankful he had only five minutes.

"Members of the board, I've traveled far to expound on the truth. It's abundantly clear there's nothing scientifically proven to support the existence of God. People can believe what they wish, but we all know Santa Claus isn't real." Several of my classmates looked at their parents in disbelief.

"In addition, teaching such delusions offends every child who doesn't believe in God. It places pressure on these children to accept a philosophy that they and their parents find intolerable. Churches and parents—not the schools—share responsibility for teaching children religion. I wholeheartedly support removing both individuals from the Sutter school system."

Feeling demoralized, I wiped away tears, but they continued to flow. As the speeches continued, people knowing nothing about me referred to me as "the rodent infesting our schools." I now understood the idea of bullying: even when I was down, people kept piling on.

Mr. Landsford noticed me sinking and said, "Hang in there, Laurel. Our turn is coming, and I need you ready to fight." I wanted to go home and crawl under a blanket. This verbal abuse was total crap, and Sister Sarah Agnes was looking better every minute.

The final presenter was Amelia Dutton. Dr. Dutton and Elle remained seated as Mrs. Dutton addressed the board. "Trustees and citizens of Sutter, speaking for my family, I'd like to thank the independent investigator, as well as Principal Chip Martin for his support. Mr. Martin, would you stand, please?"

Martin rose as the adult audience clapped and the student contingent booed. Mrs. Dutton continued, "My family has belonged to the Presbyterian Church for many generations. Several weeks ago, our daughter Elle was forced to endure teachings contrary to our beliefs and repeated insults by Laurel Montgomery. The emotional pain caused to our daughter hasn't subsided. We aren't prudes. We're aware that students say insults and commit harmful acts, but the demonstration in Mr. Wright's class reached a new low. My family and faith demand this board carry out justice. The trustees must fire Mr. Wright and expel Laurel Montgomery. Anything less adds salt to our wounds. Thank you."

Relieved I'd survived the harsh criticism, I awaited the next ten speakers. People I'd never met came to my defense. Three of their arguments were based on the fact that because I wasn't employed by the school, the board had no grounds to restrict my free speech. Four other presenters praised Mr. Wright and me for making students think critically about how different conceptions of God impacted the world. Two speakers emphasized that the school board had no difficulties with Christianity being routinely talked about in history and literature classes. Since this was true, why should the district restrict discussions concerning non-Christian religions or any other spiritual ideas? After all, they noted, no one had to accept any of these alternative concepts if they disagreed with the philosophy.

The last speaker was Twilley Blomberg, who was president of the

Sutter Women's Book Study Club. She offered to have her members read passages from the scriptures of all six religions as students rotated through study hall. Right now, Twilley's suggestion was about the only thing I could think of that would make my school experience worse. Thankfully, the board felt the same way. As the trustees tried to appease Twilley and avoid a student revolt, the deep hole I was stuck in started to fill, and a ladder to the surface appeared. When Twilley Blomberg was kindly escorted from the stage, I was ready.

By luck of the draw, Mr. Wright presented first. Like Iris, he'd disappeared during the atheist presentation. Yes, something was afoot.

Dr. Collier said, "Our next speaker is Penfield Wright." Dr. Collier looked around and, not seeing my history teacher, announced, "Mr. Wright, if you're present and wish to address the board, now is your opportunity."

Two spotlights came on, illuminating the top entrance of the center aisle. Everyone turned and watched as a lone marine stood at attention. He wore his Blue Dress uniform, composed of a dark blue jacket and spotless white trousers. His cover and belt were the color of snow. A brightly polished brass handle sword, set in a chrome scabbard, hung at his side.

Walking upright and proud, he took slow, precise steps as he approached the stage. The Navy Medal of Honor hung around his neck. Above the cuff of each navy blue sleeve were seven hash marks, representing his many years of service. The insignias near the top of the sleeves showed three inverted chevrons with four rockers. Prominent between the chevrons and the rockers sat the Marine Corps emblem. Only one person had the privilege of wearing this insignia: the Sergeant Major of the Marine Corps. This rank belonged to the highest ranking enlisted man in the Corps.

The audience rose in tribute, forcing the board to follow suit. We knew of Mr. Wright's service to his country, but his distinction as a Medal of Honor recipient and his military position astonished the entire crowd. Every person continued standing until Mr. Wright reached the podium. Standing straight, he saluted the American flag, then walked to the podium, where he removed his cover and directed the audience to sit.

America's highest military decoration went to soldiers exhibiting valor above and beyond the call of duty. For many, the cost of receiving this distinguished medal was sacrificing their lives to save others. I remembered my discussion with Iris about unconditional love.

Unconditional love of freedom embodied itself in the marine standing on stage—-and everyone knew it.

His entrance was a master stroke of political theater. Whatever his alleged offenses, if the board fired Mr. Wright, they would commit political suicide. Few men received the Medal of Honor, and only one held the rank of Sergeant Major of the Marine Corps.

"My name is Penfield X. Wright," he began. "I am accused of asking religious leaders to lecture in my class."

Staring down at the board members, he continued. "Without hesitation, I admit to asking such devout men to teach my students—and proudly so. The reason we sit here tonight, peacefully discussing our differences, is because of God's influence on our forefathers. Faith has guided the progress of man since the dawn of recorded history. If schools do not teach this critical point, we shelter kids from the truth. I believe it's better to teach the dangers of scorpions rather than find out firsthand. If having learned men explain the foundations of their beliefs defines preaching religion, you have no choice but to terminate me. On the other hand, if teaching young adults to understand what motivates their fellow man provides a path to befriending him, then perhaps you should reconsider.

"One further comment: in a few moments, you will hear from a bright, outgoing young woman. If anyone is to blame for her appearance here tonight, it is I alone. Laurel Montgomery completed her assignment with an original and thought-provoking answer. She carried out my directive, as did every student in world history class. Summarizing her project, she insulted Elle Dutton, and as a result, followed up with a sincere apology. Since the Duttons have confirmed their belief in Christianity, they know that forgiveness, not retribution, is the cornerstone of the teachings of Jesus Christ. Please remember this when you decide the fate of Miss Montgomery. Do you have any questions?"

Andrew Capellan confronted Mr. Wright. "You're a retired veteran, and yet you have the gall to dress in the uniform of an active soldier. Having served myself, I know that is a violation of the military dress code. I rose to the rank of corporal, and I know your dress is inappropriate. I applaud your support of Miss Montgomery, but you ignore all the facts. Mr. Martin has provided a solid foundation implicating Laurel Montgomery in a cheating scandal. Emmitt Pilcher summarized Mr. Martin's letter of proof when he read the conclusions. Unless you support dishonesty, you should be careful where you tread."

Penfield Wright took a breath and quickly launched a verbal counter-attack. Embracing his medal with white gloved hands, his teaching voice took over. "Sir, I wear my uniform because this medal grants me the privilege of doing so. I do not wear this decoration often or tell many people it exists. The medal is not about me, but about three men. In 1967, a helicopter was shot down three miles inside enemy territory. On board were an assistant secretary of state and a two-star general. If these people had been captured, it would have had bad consequences for the United States: the president ordered that they be found and rescued at all costs.

"I was in command of the twenty-five-member team sent in to rescue them. We found the wreckage, but everyone had died when the helicopter crashed. We recovered the remains of the secretary and the general, as well as the crew. As we left the site, we were ambushed and forced to fight our way out. Fourteen men were killed and the rest of us wounded. The three of us who could move dragged the remaining eight men to safety. When we went back for the helicopter victims, my two buddies were killed, and I lost part of my leg."

Mr. Wright lifted his trouser pant leg, revealing his prosthesis.

"All the rescued men survived and are alive today. In that experience, I learned to judge character and integrity in my fellow man. You are correct; I am unaware of the facts surrounding Laurel Montgomery's participation in cheating. But let me state, for the record, I've lived my life following the Marine Corps motto, *Semper Fidelis*. This Latin term means 'Always Faithful,' and it represents the responsibility we owe to our country and fellow soldiers.

"From everything I know, based on experience, Miss Montgomery has the integrity and honor this district should strive to instill in every student. Terminate me if you wish, but do not expel this bright young woman for thinking in new ways. Mr. Capellan, we teach students to think. Will this board expel every student who comes up with an innovative thought? If the answer is yes, you'll have my resignation by morning."

Andrew Capellan sank into his seat, totally deflated. He didn't ask another question for the balance of the meeting. The other trustees understood Penfield Wright had won this battle. It was time to cut their losses and retreat. Mr. Wright once again turned, saluted the flag, and walked offstage to a standing ovation.

I noticed Bill Landsford snickering. Every lawyer's dream was pulling off a definitive "Perry Mason" closing argument. Mr. Wright had just carried this out using his impressive credentials. I suspected his job was secure.

I was next, and I saw no way to top the last performance. While I awaited my introduction, the stage crew rolled an ornate, four-paneled, seven-foot-tall screen onto the stage. The design label read *Ordner's Exotic Furniture.* It looked like the dressing room divider actors use when changing clothes. Before I could give this much thought, Bill whispered, "Laurel, no matter what happens, focus on your speech. Promise?" I nodded as the crew placed a comfortable chair next to the podium.

Dr. Collier introduced me. "Ladies and gentlemen, our next speaker is Laurel Montgomery. Miss Montgomery, will you please come up?"

I climbed the stairs, focusing on keeping an upright posture. The crowd was silent, anticipating what they had come to see. Reaching the podium, I could see only the first few rows of the audience. I felt the crowd's presence, but being unable to see them was a relief.

When Dr. Collier shook my hand, she asked if the board could address me by my first name. I granted permission and she whispered, "Go get 'em, Laurel; I'm right behind you." Her words bolstered my confidence and infused me with courage.

I continued standing straight and keeping eye contact as I recalled Mr. Landsford's advice. Now I needed to remember my speech. "Members of the board, citizens of Sutter, and distinguished Sergeant Major Wright, my name is Laurel Montgomery. I stand before you in defense of my presentation in history class. Despite recent headlines, I wish to state I have done nothing wrong. Contrary to media reports, I will not leave school on a voluntary basis. If a long, drawn-out fight becomes necessary, I am prepared for the battle. I hope that won't occur, but I will not bow to false accusations and school officials who cannot judge me fairly."

The audience murmured, as board members Capellan, Simpson, and Bond were clearly caught off guard. The trustees quickly sifted through their notes to prepare a cross-examination. The crowd sensed that the gladiatorial games were about to begin.

Picking up where I'd left off, I said, "The issues I will address are freedom of speech and Mr. Martin's accusation that I participated in the cheating ring." The trustees shook their heads in agreement. "I want to emphasize that my mother makes me attend school; I have no choice in the matter. I don't work for the school, but I'm on student council to try to improve academic life. Like every American citizen, I have the right to free speech. If my words offend someone, they have the right to leave or confront me. The government cannot censor my words or deport me for what I say."

I paused briefly and then said, "Mr. Wright asked us to answer this question: why do wise men see God in many different ways? I used the same person to portray God in three different scenarios. That person stood in front of a spotlight so that a shadow would project onto sheets hung across the classroom. My goal was to highlight that most people never directly view God, but rather, everyone feels God's presence in different ways. The reasonable conclusion was that God becomes what He must become in order to provide comfort for every individual person. I was wrong to insult Elle Dutton, and publicly, I want to tell Elle again how sorry I am for my behavior."

Allison Bond responded first. "Miss Montgomery, did a person behind the sheets portray God and answer students' questions as if they were God? Tell us who portrayed God and what special knowledge they possessed to answer questions on God's behalf?"

"Ms. Bond," I replied, remembering that she might hold the deciding vote, "I won't reveal who represented God. Doing so would bring undeserved attention to that person. However, without reservations, I'll say this person is one of the wisest I know. I've already addressed the second part of your question. The person depicting God had the right to speak their mind. Assuming God can be anything to anyone, the person answering questions used God's guidance to provide understandable answers. Ms. Bond, is it your belief that only a religious leader can answer God's questions? If so, what makes their answers better than yours or mine?"

Tibor Kirschbaum asked, "Laurel, my son Avram witnessed your skit and felt it offered an outstanding answer. To clarify Ms. Bond's inquiry, usually when people ask God a question, they do it in prayer. Whenever God chooses to answer, it often comes as non-spoken communication. Your position suggests that God meets each person's needs. Don't you think it's unlikely God's answer applied to all twenty-four students?

"When a person portraying God gives a specific answer to a general audience," he continued, "it gives the impression no other right answer exists. People believe it's the only correct answer and, therefore, approved by the school district. Since this board's job is representing students of all faiths, we welcome free speech as long as others can argue its merits and feel free to express opposing views. Many parents felt their children were forced to accept your conclusion without hearing other opinions."

I replied, "Mr. Kirschbaum, I'm sorry for the confusion. Mr. Wright encourages us to debate the thoughts of historic figures. I thought students knew that my presentation was my viewpoint and open for debate."

Mr. Simpson jumped in. "Laurel, am I correct stating that you told the class God was whatever they needed Him to be?" I nodded, confirming his statement.

"So every student was advised to throw out their organized faith and accept a philosophy pulled from your ear? Your statement implies to atheist children that without God they won't have a happy life. Young lady, this hogwash isn't acceptable to the school board. We teach students facts based on knowledge that's withstood the test of time, not ideas dreamed up by teenagers. I'd like you to provide an argument that confirms the existence of God and shows Sutter's citizens why this board's skepticism is obsolete!"

"Ah, well, I, ah . . . "As I stumbled for an answer I knew had to be there, Mr. Simpson kept pressing.

"Miss Montgomery, you may think you're the next Martin Luther, but I can assure you, you're wrong. This board will not tolerate using our classrooms as a pulpit to promote blasphemy. The disgrace you've brought this town and its students will take years to mend. I have never seen any objective evidence supporting the existence of God and you have offered none here tonight. I will rise to your challenge and ensure your departure."

Mr. Simpson stopped, letting his words sink in. He caught his breath and prepared to pound the final nail in my coffin. But as he opened his mouth, Iris walked up behind me.

"That's enough, Mr. Simpson. Your treatment of Ms. Montgomery constitutes verbal child abuse, and I intend to make you understand the weight of your comments. Do not cross me in that tone, sir, or you will pay the price!"

Dumbfounded, I turned and stared at Iris Wimple. She was different—very different. Gone was the gray bun. Shoulder-length blond hair flowed to her shoulders. Her eyes were radiant blue, and she wore peach lipstick. Altogether, she looked forty years younger. The kaleidoscope of fashion familiar to all had given way to a knee-length milk-colored jacket with matching slacks and white two-inch heels. The final touches were a blue blouse complementing her eyes and three strands of natural pearls. When she took my hand and told me to have a seat, I felt a powerful force giving me comfort. "I'll take it from here, dear," Iris said.

The moment she spoke, I knew that the stately woman standing beside me was the sweet, elderly Iris Wimple who had always nurtured me.

Dr. Collier, unsure who this woman was, asked, "Mrs. Wimple, is that you?"

An authoritative voice replied, "Yes, sweetie. It's me. I think the makeup and color-coordinated clothes are what fooled you. We'll talk more when I finish, dear. Right now, I'm ready to give this talk, and my nerve tonic won't last forever."

Nerve tonic! Where the hell did she stash the nerve tonic? I'd searched that wagon high and low. Reaching to get my water, I noticed her purse sitting underneath the podium. That's where she had hidden the flask! I prayed that Iris, half plowed and giving the biggest speech of my life, could stay awake. If appearance counted for 80 percent, then maybe she'd dream up something memorable for the other 20 percent.

It would take only thirty minutes to realize that this thought was an earthshaking understatement.

I waited for an outline to appear; none did. In the most elegant voice I could imagine, Iris began, "Ladies and gentleman and members of the board. My name is Iris Wimple." She paused as the audience rose in a standing ovation. People trusted Iris like an extended family member—because often she was.

When the applause finished, Iris continued, "Laurel's mother, Marie, is overseas on an important business trip. In her mother's absence, Laurel asked me to comment on her character. Please bear with me. I've rarely delivered a message to a group this large. We've heard several versions of what happened in Mr. Wright's classroom. Which version should we believe, and who was the unknown person portraying God? I ask every-one here, how do we know Miss Montgomery's unique conclusion—one god for all people—isn't a new message God wants us to embrace?"

Murmurs rippled through the assembly. "Give this question thought as I continue; I'll return to it shortly. Mr. Simpson," Iris's right index fin-ger pointed to the vulture awaiting my death, "you claim no convincing evidence exists proving God is real. I contend you are wrong. Having lived here many years, I've enjoyed the soft touch of a baby, the taste of freshly picked tomatoes, and the sound of our community choir. Each day I behold the beauty of Mt. Hood while smelling the scent of my roses. Most importantly, I feel love from the people who've entrusted me with their children. Love is the only emotion God has reserved for humanity.

"There are reasons, Mr. Simpson, you cannot find sufficient evidence for God: you look but don't see. You hear but never listen, and you touch but never feel. These senses provide the evidence of God's existence, but unless you use them, you'll never find Him. Part of the purpose of Miss Montgomery's project was to point out that visual proof is not helpful in spiritual matters; it's rarely there. Would any of you recognize the Almighty if God stood here tonight? What would a divine being say to give you a hint? Would you believe Him if He told you? My guess is, you're not sure. Am I correct?"

Reluctantly, each board member, as well as Dr. Myers and Emmitt Pilcher, agreed.

"I propose that the reason you're unsure is because you lack faith in your own senses. Several weeks ago, God and Jimmy Dover produced a miracle to win a memorable football game. They found Jimmy's shoes driven into the ground under that huge pine tree, but his feet weren't in them. That is a fact unexplained by luck. God's existence depends on your willingness to seek, and He's easily found if you follow the signs. Depend only on your vision, and God rarely appears."

As Iris spoke, a crazy thought took hold in the recesses of my mind. Common sense said I was nuts, but intuition told me to keep listening and connect the dots.

Mr. Kirschbaum asked, "Iris, don't you think God delivering a message through a fourteen-year-old teenager is highly unlikely?"

"Tibor, you and I go way back, so I'll turn the question around. How do you propose God should deliver the message? Send it by post, broadcast it, or pass fliers around in synagogue? Any method He chooses will arouse suspicion. I'm certain Jesus didn't get people to board the Christianity bandwagon until time revealed the wisdom of His words."

Looking at me, Iris said, "Laurel hasn't planned to start a new religion or change an established one. If God finds her worthy to deliver a message, she's no less believable than other methods. Now I'd like to discuss the summary from the investigation. Before I do, I want the stage crew to place another chair next to your table, and Chip Martin should join us. It's only fair Ms. Montgomery faces all her accusers."

Looking at his wife, Mr. Martin seemed hesitant. Iris taunted him, "Come now, Chip. Surely you stand behind your words. I can't see Laurel frightening a man with integrity."

Chip Martin had no plans to admit defeat to me or Iris. I didn't frighten Chip one bit, but Iris was about to swing the ax. As he took his seat on stage, Iris said, "Being an administrator, you can undoubtedly explain several small details."

Addressing the audience, Iris said, "The evidence you're about to see favors Ms. Montgomery. Some scenes, while upsetting, are necessary to prove the truth. Other clips provide evidence of young women going above and beyond what anyone would expect. Please remain silent until I'm finished. This should only take ten minutes."

The stage lights dimmed, and seconds later, a movie began showing on the screen. I watched several minutes before realizing the film focused on my school locker from eighth grade. Iris described the scene in the clip, which showed a teacher walking the hall with a 1970–1971 school planning book. Iris stopped the film. "Everyone please note, the teacher's assignment book shows you're seeing a film taken last year. Continue to watch."

Who made this film was difficult to imagine, but several seconds later, two boys walked to locker forty-seven. The door had a glittery red sign that read "Laurel Montgomery." They opened the door, rummaged through my stuff, and took a file labeled "Math Tests."

The film stopped. Iris summarized, "From this video we see soon-to-be eighth graders removing Miss Montgomery's math tests without her knowledge."

Iris then turned attention to Dr. Dutton and his family. Abandoning formality, she lifted her right index finger, and waving it side to side, she scolded the Duttons. "Norman, Amelia, Elle, I'm ashamed of all of you. Norman, you have wonderful dental skills, which you've used to your very best. Yet with the money you've earned, the reason your family's been charitable is to elevate your own glory. No matter how big or small the project, your name had to be attached to it. The Dutton family made self-promotion an art form."

Looking at the audience, I saw Dr. Dutton stand and prepare to leave. Obviously, Iris noticed as well. "Norman," she bellowed, "sit down! You will not accuse Miss Montgomery of ruining your daughter's life and then run and hide."

Immediately, the auditorium went dark, and a film projected on the screen. In Technicolor, Norman Dutton sat in his burning car. I was in front placing a glove over his head wound, while Joann was trying to recline the driver's seat. We pulled him into the backseat and onto the trunk. Fortunately, the film didn't show us dropping him on the ground. The final scene showed Dr. Dutton lying in the truck bed with us standing to the side. Mom's car never appeared. The last few frames showed the car exploding in flames.

The lights came up, and Iris now stood right next to Dr. Dutton. "Well, Norman, what do you say to the young ladies who saved your life? This happened one day after you filed the complaint we're debating tonight."

Gasps and catcalls echoed throughout the audience. Iris squatted down, leveling her eyes directly at Dr. Dutton's. "Somehow, Laurel Montgomery overcame her disdain because no matter how much she disliked you, she knew her life would be haunted forever if she stood aside and let you die. Norman, I propose to you and the board as well as this audience: only God-given unconditional love allows a young woman to risk sacrificing her life to save the man who accuses her of emotionally harming his daughter and threatening all Christianity. And just so you're aware, Norman, she wouldn't think of accepting your reward because Laurel will never be indebted to you. Always remember who owes whom," she pointed out.

Now five inches from his face, Iris became silent and focused her blazing stare on Dr. Dutton for thirty seconds. The auditorium became deathly quiet as her words sank in. Slowly breaking her trance, Iris returned to the podium, ready to continue. "Now, let's see a third film clip with more peculiar facts." The movie rolled, but I noticed no signs of a projector. The projection booth was dark, and no light beam radiated through the dust particles. The movie couldn't project from behind the screen because it hung only five feet from the theater's back wall.

My crazy thoughts gained momentum as I started recalling the last three weeks. Then the film showed five girls toilet-papering Chip Martin's tree. Oh God! My stomach sank as the camera zoomed into a mailbox stenciled with *Martin*, but I suspected my principal's stomach flip-flopped worse. The scene changed from the mailbox to the front door.

Moments later, the camera was indoors, focusing on Mr. Martin in his boxers and Amelia Dutton in a see-through teddy.

The picture followed them as they desperately tried opening doors and windows. While I worried about appearing on screen, a demure Mrs. Martin broke records reaching the stage and delivering Principal Martin a blow that would have made Mohammad Ali jealous. Caught off guard, Mr. Martin slid out of his chair as his wife left through the back stage door. I didn't hear every remark, but "bastard" and "divorce" echoed throughout the theater.

Iris filed her nails as Emmitt Pilcher and Devlin Myers helped Chip to his feet. He wasn't there long. Norman Dutton appeared from nowhere and delivered a solid right cross to his cheek. This time, Chip remained flat. Officers converged from every direction, slapping on handcuffs and hauling Dr. Dutton away.

Several minutes passed before smelling salts from the nurse's office aroused Mr. Martin from his stupor. Mr. Pilcher and Dr. Myers once again lifted my principal off the floor and took him backstage. Despite Iris's request for quiet, the change from board meeting to boxing match had brought out cheers from the audience. Crowds only behaved this way if they attended professional wrestling or *The Phil Donahue Show*. Iris finished her nails and waited for Dr. Collier's permission to continue.

Dr. Collier pounded her gavel and repeatedly called for order. Law officers removed guests who continued yelling. The aggressive sweep by the authorities calmed the chaos.

"Mrs. Wimple," Jacquelyn Collier said, "I understand you have more film evidence to show the board. During the commotion, I discussed the issue with my fellow board members. They agree that to preserve safety, we'll accept your description of the next film clip, if you feel this is a satisfactory compromise."

Iris said, "Yes, Dr. Collier, that's fine, if the board promises to take appropriate disciplinary action against Mr. Martin. If there's any hesitation, this film will play on every newscast from Portland to New York. Board members, please raise your hands so I know you understand." Five hands shot up.

Looking at her colleagues, Dr. Collier confirmed the vote. "Please continue, Mrs. Wimple."

Iris took a moment to consider how she would describe the next film segment. "Very well. The next film clip presents scenes and audios from the junior high conference room. It shows trustees Capellan, Simpson, and Ball agreeing to vote against Ms. Montgomery. The meeting occurred before the investigation concluded and was attended by lawyers from the ACLU. Tonight those lawyers are sitting in the second row."

Iris looked at Mel Corcoran, who slouched into his seat. "If you need confirmation, ask Mr. Corcoran. Tonight he's here to intimidate the board's decision to favor the ACLU's objectives. His organization threatened a lawsuit if the trustees didn't amend the school charter to enforce the separation of church and state. Chip Martin agreed to falsify the cheating evidence so the three board members would have solid grounds to explain their vote. Do the board members have any questions concerning my summary?"

I watched Dr. Collier lower her head and speak into the microphone. "Andrew. Allison. Webster. Is Iris Wimple correct? Did the three of you previously agree on your votes?" None of the three trustees answered. The silence was deafening.

Dr. Collier consulted her notes as the school secretary appeared and whispered in her ear. She nodded and, after several seconds, addressed Iris. "Mrs. Wimple, I expect Brett Moore's arrival in the next several minutes. Do you wish to begin your closing remarks or wait until we finish his presentation?"

Iris said, "I'm happy to wait. It allows me time to collect my thoughts, seek advice, and await an answer from our three upstanding board members. Make no mistake, Dr. Collier: Laurel Montgomery and this audience demand an answer, and we will not leave this meeting until one is rendered."

The audience gave Iris a standing ovation. It was nine thirty, and Dr. Collier announced a short break. Iris asked Bill to come onstage, and soon the three of us huddled together. "Well, you two, how am I doing?" she asked.

Bill jumped in, "Iris, where did you get those films? They're wonderful evidence that has shifted the popular vote in Laurel's favor. The privacy violations you've racked up, I can't imagine. When Emmitt Pilcher returns and hears what's happened, board members may file charges against you. Remember, if they arrest you, I'm your attorney."

Iris commented, "Before I'm finished, only Heaven can help!"

"Iris, what are you doing with the dressing room screen? Don't change your outfit, or your makeup. You look stunning," I said.

Iris answered, "I'm glad you approve, Laurel; it goes back so many years it's new again. The dressing room screen is for a demonstration I dreamed up myself. Laurel, if I ask for your help, follow my instructions precisely to avoid getting burned. OK, you two—back to your seats."

I took my seat, wondering what Iris had planned. Across the stage was a thin man in a wheelchair. I couldn't believe it was Brett Moore. A seven-inch semicircle of stitches arched over his right ear. His shaved head tilted toward his left shoulder, and his eyes held a distant stare. A breathing tube was attached to his lower neck, and an electric motor strapped on the wheelchair powered the ventilator, sustaining his life. Brett's parents, Barbara and Charles Moore, stood behind him as Dr. Collier rose to present the award.

I knew that wherever Brett was, he no longer occupied the shell where Iris claimed God's spirit resided within us. Brett's spirit had left when he hit the goalpost. I'd heard the term "living dead," but it had meant nothing until I saw the emaciated man.

Dr. Collier spoke to Brett's parents. "Mr. and Mrs. Moore, the students, faculty, and coaches who make our schools outstanding centers of learning present you with a plaque listing Brett's accomplishments. Furthermore, the trustees have resolved that Brett is a lifetime captain of the Sutter football team. Finally, I'm honored to present a check for $10,000. This money, collected through fund-raisers as well as donations, is to help with expenses. We support your family in this difficult time, and our hearts and prayers go with you and Brett every day."

The Moores thanked Dr. Collier and the audience, who once again were on their feet in a standing ovation. As they prepared to leave the stage, Iris came and spoke with them and Jacquelyn Collier. Dr. Collier signaled the stage crew to set up two more chairs, and soon the Moore family sat beside the school board.

The three accused board members started to fidget as Dr. Collier asked, "Mrs. Wimple, are you ready to finish your remarks? If so, please begin. When you're finished, the board will recess ten minutes and then return to vote."

"Thank you, dear," Iris responded. "Ladies and gentlemen, what Mr. Wright and Ms. Montgomery brought into the classroom was the truth. Their actions caused this controversy because they influenced many of us to reexamine long-held beliefs. No one wants to admit they must change their thinking. But no matter which faith you follow, major religions share common goals. Each philosophy preaches hope, compassion, and a sense of right and wrong.

"Kindness and forgiveness are important objectives for every faith. They all worship a higher power and concur that helping others is a primary goal, no matter how little you give. Finally, there's love. I return to this theme because if you don't believe in God, you probably still recognize love."

I listened as Iris reaffirmed my own conclusions from several weeks ago. Most people experienced love sometime during their lives. Every person owns the power to offer and receive love, which, I've realized, is the greatest of all gifts.

Iris went on. "It's as easy as that, folks: God is love. Practice it every day and your lives will experience blessings and happiness."

I knew my earlier absurd thoughts were my wandering imagination. Iris had pulled another rabbit from her hat and concluded a magnificent presentation. There was nothing to add—until she closed her eyes and bowed her head. In a distinct and beautifully angelic female voice, she spoke.

"There's one more issue I must address. I know what occurred in Mr. Wright's classroom because I stood behind the sheets."

The crowd starting rumbling, and Dr. Collier called for order. My idea was gaining rapid momentum with every second. Iris looked at Allison Bond and offered, "Allison, you asked what special knowledge I might hold to accurately answer questions on God's behalf. If I may borrow Mr. Ordner's check, I'll answer your question. Laurel, would you get the check and bring it over?"

I rose to retrieve a check for the largest amount of money I'd ever seen as Iris walked behind the dressing room screen. In the few seconds it took to return with the check, the dots connected: Iris's knowledge, her insight, the philosophy about the existence of God—all of it was completely unfolding, here and now, before my incredulous eyes.

I went behind the barrier, feeling frightened and anxious as I sensed great power. I handed Iris the check and said submissively, "Do you have any idea what you're doing? Nobody has any remaining questions, and even if the trustees dreamed one up, these people are adults. They couldn't help but hear your strong message. Iris, I'm happy with everything you've presented. Keep your truth a secret. I'm humbled you chose me, but compared to famine and natural disasters, my situation is insignificant and a poor reason to reveal yourself. If you do this, our relationship will change, and I don't want you to leave. I love you with all my heart."

I gave her a hug as she said in a comforting tone, "Have a seat and trust me, dear. Mankind's advances during the last century demand a revelation I hadn't planned. Religions have strayed from helping people find God. I plan to redirect them. The last few weeks with you convinced me: tonight is the right moment."

There was no reason to argue. Iris owned the bat, the ball, and the ballpark. Clearly, this was her game, and I had a small part as the bat girl. There was no doubt Iris had every intention of winning. I walked from behind the barrier and noticed a backlight projecting Iris's shadow against the screen. I must have missed where she had hidden the backlight; it wasn't obvious how she'd disguised it. The silhouette showed Iris from the side holding the check out in front of her. The shadow stood motionless. My body tingled as a staggering flash erupted behind the screen. Intense heat radiated across the stage. When the commotion died down, Iris wasn't visible. The backlit dressing screen revealed the black outline of a loaded wagon.

Beyond explanation, the wagon rolled out and stopped directly in front of Mr. Simpson. Fully loaded with gold bars, the red Radio Flier seemed ready to collapse. Milt Ordner's check sat on top. Next to the check rested a handwritten note that said: "Dr. Collier, use the gold to remodel the school. Five million should cover it. Save and invest the balance. Ask Milt to use his check for research on treating brain injuries." I hadn't seen the message, but knowledge of the note's content came to me unannounced. Miraculously, I knew its words and felt 100 percent sure of its intent. As I sat bewildered, Iris's voice said, "Laurel, be a dear and get Brett Moore, would you?"

I slowly rose and walked over to ask Brett's parents if I could take him. Brett's father said, "I'm not sure what just happened, and I trust Iris, but I can't let Brett go alone."

Somehow, I knew what to say. "Mr. Moore, the heat radiating from behind the screen will burn you. You must have faith and truly believe you're making the right decision for Brett," I encouraged.

Mrs. Moore spoke, "Charles, I don't know what will happen, but Brett's not going to improve. If Iris can help, what's to lose?"

Procrastinating, Mr. Moore paused before he released his grip on the wheelchair. He and Mrs. Moore sobbed as they kissed Brett on the cheek. I stood behind the wheelchair and, overcoming my fear, pushed Brett toward the screen. Arriving beside it, I saw only bright light. The temperature forced policemen standing in front of the audience to move back. But in the midst of an oven, Brett and I remained cool and unburned.

Still frightened, I was ready to push the chair into the radiance and run. As I hesitated, sunglasses came out of the light, and a hand pulled both of us behind the screen. Putting on the sunglasses, nothing appeared immediately, but overwhelmingly, I sensed the presence of God. I dropped to my knees, and an unimagined power entered my existence and lovingly surrounded me.

"Laurel," It said, "rise from your knees. You need not humble yourself. Saving a man's life while risking your own demonstrated humility in its highest form. Restoring life to a man who will never acknowledge you exhibits the purest form of acceptance and forgiveness. Your answer to Mr. Wright's question was correct, and I am confirming your message: Muhammad, Jesus, Buddha, Moses, and Ghandi were men I trusted to spread My message—men who showed their people different paths leading to me.

"However, you're the first person to solve the riddle of Me adapting to each person's needs. Laurel, like everyone, you have free will and may live your life as you wish, but I will be there whenever you need me. For all you will endure, I've rewarded your leap of philosophical thinking by giving you divine providence. There isn't time to explain because Brett must return to his parents before they get too worried."

I continued kneeling in the presence of all that was, all that is, and all that ever would be. I figured even Billy Graham would be lost for words. My limited biblical knowledge of the Lord's Prayer didn't offer much help, and Luke 12:19—"Eat, drink and be merry"—probably had more appropriate uses at other occasions.

I admitted my theological faults. "Iris—God—I'm not certain what to call you. I know nothing about religion, so I'm not really worthy to be here. Right now, I think you're the cause of Mr. and Mrs. Moore's worry. What do you want me to do? I've never met God face-to-face and I've got a thousand questions."

"Laurel, call me Iris. I haven't discussed faith with anyone since Martin Luther King, but every hundred years or so, I make a personal appearance. When we're done, leave the stage by the side entrance and make your way home using the back route. I'll meet you there. Your mother has a Holy Bible. When you reach home, look up Luke 17:21 and you'll know why I've picked you. More than most, Laurel, *the Kingdom of God lies within you.* Now, grasp one of Brett's hands with one of your own."

I lifted the young man's limp hand and cradled it in mine.

"Very well, Laurel. Pray for Brett to get better, and when you're ready, touch your remaining index finger to mine."

Briefly, I remembered seeing the ceiling of the Sistine Chapel when I was ten. Michelangelo's *The Creation of Adam* depicted God and Adam extending their index fingers to within an inch of each other so God could transfer the gift of life to man. I touched Iris's finger and experienced a connection to the universe that remains a part of me now. My worries were gone, and a life-sustaining force flowed through me, renewing my energy. The flaccid hand I held warmed and began squeezing my fingers. In moments, the fabric of life was rejuvenated in each of Brett Moore's muscles, allowing him to rise from his chair.

I've been told the audience saw only the shadow of Brett, sitting in his wheelchair—silhouettes of Iris and me never projected onto the screen. Joann recounted that in the blink of an eye, the wheelchair vanished and the shadow morphed to a man as Brett Moore walked from behind the screen. He stood tall as his parents rushed to hold him. He hugged them and reassured everyone he was fine. People seemed poised to rush the stage when a gentle voice came over the speakers.

"Dr. Collier and members of the board, I've presented the evidence I'd planned to offer. I encourage the board not to expel Mr. Wright or Ms. Montgomery. This meeting is a reminder that the power of justice equals the power of love. My love encourages Me to forgive, but it's best for the trustees, and all of humanity, to correct their wrongs—or I assure you: justice isn't blind and it will be carried out!"

The theater went dark. Grabbing my arm, Iris led me offstage, saying, "Here's the side door, leading into the high school. Turn left and follow the back hall. You'll see a door leading to the football field. Head home! I love you."

The door opened as a high-pitched scream echoed throughout the theater, "My God, my fingers have grown back!"

It sounded like Nubs Fritzmeyer.

CHAPTER 43

To Ask of God

Leaving the high school was easy. As I opened the exit door, the increased noise echoing down the hall told me the lights must have come back on. As I walked into the chilled autumn air, silence engulfed me. The calamity that had filled the last three weeks was finally over.

Whatever the board decided was outside my control. But my school problems were insignificant compared to the responsibility Iris had handed me. Assuming Iris was God—and five million dollars' worth of gold plus a healthy Brett Moore confirmed she was—I was the only human in modern times to meet Her in person. Yes, God was a woman! Perhaps becoming the first female president was setting my standards too low.

Walking across the football field, I remembered Iris saying wise men would seek my counsel. Now I understood the reason: within days, people would assume I was God's intermediary. It wasn't true, but compared with Muhammad and Buddha, my world had mass media. TV and papers loved inflating a story, and God appearing onstage was top news and great for sales.

When I reached home, Ed was sitting on the front steps. He must have left while Iris was speaking. Standing up and hugging me, Ed said, "Get out your key, honey—I need to get you indoors."

"Ed, why are you here?" I asked. "I'm fine, and Iris said she'd be home soon. There's nothing to worry about," I insisted.

As I unlocked the door, I noticed the sequoia was missing, but Ed didn't give me time to ask how a thousand-pound tree had disappeared. He opened the door and nudged me into the living room. Then he locked the door and circled the living room, carefully securing windows and closing curtains. Next he headed to the kitchen, returning with a flashlight, Otis, and the two beavers. Then he pulled a letter from his pocket labeled *Laurel* and handed it to me.

I asked, "Ed, are you afraid of an attack? You've got the house secured like Fort Knox, and there are no lights. Tonight's the quietest evening we've had in three weeks. Why worry?" I asked.

"Laurel, I'm just doing what Iris told me to do. I've been listenin' to my transistor radio." He patted his shirt. "After many years, I bought this radio for ma first luxury item. Cost $8.95. Iris said to head here as she went onstage. Said you'd need protection from the press. She's right. Accordin' to KSUT radio, all hell's broken loose at that high school.

"They're reportin' a bomb explodin', causin' the lights to go out. Clearly, you and Iris done disappeared, but seein' as I'm lookin' at ya, I think *displaced* is a better term. KSUT's announcer Fred Bennington keeps sayin' God showed up and give the school some gold and cured their quarterback. 'A damn miracle,' he keeps tellin' everybody.

"You know, Fred's had a few strokes, but until tonight, I didn't think he'd changed much. He's crazier 'an a loon. Apparently, the lights is on, since authorities cleared the theater and called the Portland bomb squad. Fred's reportin' the board's in executive session and protected by the police. Says the audience is damned pissed at three trustees; he ain't said which three. I'm hopin' Iris gets home or I'm sleepin' on the couch. I'm tired and got work tomorrow, but I promised I'd stay 'til she got here. Why'd you come home, dear? Shouldn't you be stayin' to hear the decision?"

"Ed, I'm so confused, I'm not sure why I'm home." I omitted the details since Ed would have more questions than I had answers. "I'm probably here because Iris didn't want me facing the press. She did great defending me, and I can honestly say it's miraculous how she gets people's attention. Do you know what's in this envelope?" I asked.

"Does that envelope look opened? I don't think so. I stopped breakin' into stuff years ago, so I ain't got a clue. Kill our suspense, Laurel, and open it."

It was a letter from Iris. The unparalleled penmanship of the writing graced cotton paper of the finest quality. Considering the source, it seemed fitting. These words originated from the Hand that had written the Ten Commandments. I was holding the world's most important document. I read:

Dearest Laurel,

By now, you have many questions. The burden I've given you isn't easy, but you're the only person I've considered worthy to

handle it. When I get home, I'll explain further. Call Bill Landsford and the Van Skoks. Tell them you're safe and you'll check in
tomorrow. Notify the police station that both of us left during the
blackout, attempting to avoid questions. Keep the houselights off
so your home looks empty.

I've fed Otis, Bobby, and Jean, so they're fine. I also transplanted the sequoia and restored the trees in the Murdocks' backyard. It took time removing the toilet paper from Chip Martin's
tree. My, you are a busy young woman. Home soon.

Love,
Iris

P.S. Don't drink and drive, dear. This would have been the
Eleventh Commandment, but at the time, I didn't see the automobile coming.

Jeez, living with God had drawbacks. Thinking about my first
orgasm, I started to blush. Did Iris know about that too? How embarrass-
ing to think she might have shared my most private moments. Millions
of women experienced orgasms every day—they were normal human
behavior—and with all the world's problems, masturbation should be
low on Iris's list. But before doing it again, I'd wait for the next disaster to
keep her busy. Thankfully, disasters happened daily.

I called Bill Landsford's office and got Kay Formby. He'd called from
a pay phone and said he'd been swamped by reporters but was finally
on his way back. She'd tell him I was safe and have him call the moment
he arrived. So that's why Iris had made me leave quickly. A sea lion had
a better chance of outswimming a great white than me spending an hour
with reporters.

Somehow, I didn't think reporters were the wise men Iris referred
to. If they were, humanity was worse off than I thought. I was the best
person to make sense of what had happened, but I needed to collect
my thoughts. I'd spent three weeks learning how people twisted words
to support their beliefs. What reporters would do with half-truths and
incomplete answers, I could only imagine.

Since Ed and I had nothing to do but wait, I went and got us some
ice cream. While I was in the kitchen, the phone rang. I heard Ed
answer, "Hello, this is Ed. Can I help ya? OK. Sure, she's right here. Just

a moment. Laurel, phone call." If this call wasn't Bill or Joann, I was hanging up.

"Hello," I said cautiously. "This is Laurel."

"Laurel, it's Bill. I'm glad to hear your voice and know you're safe. I'm not sure where Iris went. Whatever occurred, she succeeded and blamed God for the result. The school board voted five to nothing to keep you and Mr. Wright. Three board members then resigned: Simpson, Bond, and Capellan. I got a call saying Mr. Martin was fired, but that's the least of his problems. Do you know where Iris is or how she got those movies?"

Mr. Landsford's voice drifted away. The favorable decision instantly removed my burdens, and contentment embraced my soul. School would continue as before, but I hadn't realized that the fork in the road had more than the two paths I'd imagined. The board would let me continue hiking my comfortable path, but Iris had increased its slope. Fortunately, progress occurred one step at a time.

Storing my introspections, I said, "Bill, I don't know about the movies, but she'll be home soon. Trust me, she is safe. Based on her stories, she's faced far more dangerous crowds than tonight's. I wouldn't worry. Why did the board members resign? I thought that required a recall election."

"Laurel, what I'm revealing is between you, Iris, and me. During the darkness, a package was handed to Dr. Collier. It held an unsigned message and a film. The note directed the board to privately view the film before voting. Without describing details, the video contained information about a fact-finding trip taken by three board members. Saying all three filmed a scene with their pants down is an understatement. Dr. Collier sought their resignations in return for not releasing the tape. She also insisted they repay the district for the trip's expenses.

"Dr. Collier called after the decision. She cares about you, Laurel. Between her and Iris, I've met two very gifted women. Your mother fits in there as well. Drop by the office tomorrow and we'll review the details. We also need to talk about getting an agent for you."

"Why do I need an agent? I'm just returning to school, not giving a world tour. In a week, nobody will care what happened. Besides, Mom's a lawyer and should return soon. She'll help if I need legal advice," I insisted.

Bill's tone of voice turned serious. "Laurel, let me put the meeting in perspective. Tonight, an old lady takes a three-million-dollar check behind a screen that casts her silhouette before six hundred people. Her shadow vanishes, and five million dollars of gold appears in a wagon. Performing an encore, the woman restores a brain-injured man in a persistent vegetative state to perfect health.

"Dr. Collier said the heat from behind the screen scorched the podium. Beyond explanation, you tiptoed unsinged through this inferno, becoming the only witness to an undisputed supernatural event. I'm not sure how you define a miracle, but for me, that's precisely what happened.

"The press is begging for an interview, and whoever gets that honor will probably win the Pulitzer Prize. Only Iris boasts a bigger story, and her chronicles exist worldwide in multiple translations. To my knowledge, you're the only living person who's interviewed the author. That's the reason you need an agent."

Fitting his reputation, Mr. Landsford had used clear words to outline his case. He'd convinced me. "I see your point," I said. "We'll discuss it tomorrow when I see you. Do you want Iris as well?"

Silence. "Gosh, Laurel, I've never represented God. Do you really think She needs it?" he asked.

"Bill, if Iris speaks for herself, I don't have to tell her story. I'll just live my life and she can be famous; she's had plenty of practice. Yes, she needs an agent. I'll bring her along."

"All right, Laurel. Thanks for the information. I'll see you tomorrow."

Otis starting barking when I hung up the phone. I followed him toward the back door, where Iris stood fumbling with the lock. It seemed God couldn't find the keyhole. I turned on the porch light and flipped the dead bolt.

"Oh, thanks, dear. Your mother needs a gate since old ladies scaling the neighbor's fence is not a pleasant sight. I'm sure I ripped my girdle. What a costly misfortune; I paid $15 to flatten my tummy."

Iris hugged me, asking, "Is Ed in the living room?" I nodded.

"Before we talk, let's go send him home. He has work tomorrow."

Ed was sleeping on the couch. My conversation with Mr. Landsford had bored him to sleep. Iris woke him and thanked Ed for staying.

I told him the board's decision. Ed said, "Iris, you've been a big help. Without you, I wouldn't be in Laurel's life. Anytime ya need help, let me know." Ed hugged us and headed toward the back door. He turned, showing a big smile. "Every day, I'm grateful to God for both of ya."

"Thank you, Ed. You're so sweet," Iris replied. "We love you too!"

Iris poured a whiskey and I got a Coke. The time was eleven thirty, but there was no way I was going to sleep—the adrenaline was still pumping. We lit the fire, and our three pets snuggled with us on the couch.

Iris turned and said, "Laurel, Ed's a good man, and he deserves the opportunity to prove he's worthy. Considering the pain Ed's caused others, he's paid the price five times over. The integrity he enjoys today will never falter because it's tempered by heat from the forges of hell. He'll always help if you ask. Now, dear, I suspect there are issues you want to discuss. Am I correct?"

Walking home, I had pondered questions for Iris. The night's chill and silence had helped focus my mind in preparation for this moment.

"Iris—God—I'm not sure what's proper. When you first came over, I asked you what defines God. From everything we've discussed, I'm sure I know. Obviously, I don't have your skills. Even if I did, I'm not sure I'd want them. The world's problems are overwhelming. What should I do to make the world better?" I asked.

"Honey, call me Iris—it's more personal than *God*. Let me explain what I am and my wishes for you. Einstein was correct, even though he surprised me: $E=mc^2$. This equation is profound in truth and simplicity. When scientists finally decipher the truth, it's almost always that elegant and simple.

"Twenty years from now, physicists will postulate that the universe consists of more than what's seen or measured. They'll use terms such as *dark matter* and *dark energy.* In 2001, the Wilkinson Microwave Anisotropy Probe, or WIMP, will explore space. Data from this probe will challenge long-held beliefs about the makeup of the universe.

"Matter composed of atoms makes up only five percent of the universe. Twenty-three percent of the cosmos is dark matter with no perceivable particles. The remaining seventy-two percent consists of dark energy. My essence lies in what science knows is there but can't quantify. Like now, I occasionally take the form of baryonic, or atomic, matter. Should someone ask, don't try explaining it. You'll find yourself tending flowers in the Oregon State Hospital.

"The message to carry forward is as simple as Einstein's: love your fellow man. Regarding your life and the lives of others, avoid hidden motives and make decisions using honesty as your guide. If you need help, ask a person who has the experience you're looking for. Laurel, making correct decisions is tough. You've probably noticed that many difficult questions are dealt with by people with higher educations. Black-and-white choices are simple, but the difficult judgments often lie in shades of gray. That's it, dear—nothing complex. And as they say in synagogue, it came from God's mouth to your ears."

"But, Iris, look at every religion. Each faith tells its followers how to live properly. Isn't your message far too simple? Do you want it printed on cigar wrappers and placed in fortune cookies?" Iris looked pleased at my suggestion. I continued, "Every religious belief the leaders discussed had sacred writings taking up volumes. Why read this stuff if there's only one rule?"

Iris sipped her whiskey and said, "Men seeking power over other men has occurred throughout history. War and religion are common methods that use fear to grasp that power. War provides the more honest path because both sides know the winner takes power; it's never given. Religion is the precise opposite. Religion uses God's wrath to punish noncompliance. Parishioners gladly surrender whatever their spiritual leaders advise. Self-proclaimed men of God preach, 'God's justice for parishioners depends on fearing the Almighty.'

"Leaders suggest that monetary contributions and following church doctrine find favor with God, which often makes evangelists wealthy. Over time, church rules have expanded to the point where it's impossible for people not to violate multiple church doctrines. Resolution of wrong-doing usually compels a visit to see worship leaders, leaders who've taken vows of poverty and can grant God's forgiveness—provided there's satisfactory compensation.

"In the past, threatening church doctrine cost you your life. This is still true in uneducated parts of the world. Provided the writings of faith promote good, not evil; humility, not pride; and moral behavior, not crim-inal intent, they serve my purpose. When influential zealots get screwball ideas and say God uses them as His messenger, that's when I take offense.

"Even when people behave properly, if their actions result from false teachings, their ideology won't sell unless they promote it door-to-door. Nearly every educated person knows baloney when they hear it, so poorly grounded faiths keep searching for ignorant people to swallow their bait. People often confuse freedom of religion with freedom from reality. Germans abandoned My teachings to follow Hitler's propaganda.

"Laurel, science has discredited most of the false gods people have worshiped throughout history. Man stands on the brink of seeing my true nature more closely than ever before. This vision awaits only his willingness to look. When science someday unlocks every principle of nature, it won't make nature any less a miracle. If anything, understanding the finished design will bring increased awe for the architect.

"Don't get me wrong, dear. People must still learn right from wrong, which most religions are good at teaching. This doesn't excuse faiths from ignoring progress. Many countries, including this one, treat women as second-class citizens. Letting people use the Bible or the Quran to justify this practice was never my intent. All humans are equal until they distinguish themselves by committing unselfish actions. Royal ancestry and unfulfilled plans don't impress me.

"My dear, I'd love to answer more questions, but your mother just cleared customs at Portland International Airport. She's in a taxi and headed home. I plan to leave before she arrives."

"But, Iris, what brought Mom back? We still have three more weeks together. You can't go—you're part of the family. Who's going to look after Bobby and Jean?"

"Dear, your mother's back because she's finished her work and feels guilty about not supporting you. She left China sixteen hours ago and called here during her stopover in Hawaii. I can't stay because I'm needed elsewhere. Father Blevins will receive my material goods. What subject haven't we covered?"

"Iris, people will wonder what they're supposed to do when they make a mistake. How do they avoid going to hell?"

"Look, Laurel, hell is way overblown. Hell isn't a place people go— it's a horrible feeling they get from continuing to make bad choices. Ed used to live in hell. Finally, the pain got so bad he decided to stop what he was doing. The way you correct mistakes isn't a mystery. First, admit your mistake to others, and then do everything possible to correct it. Make sure those you've harmed are satisfied with your solution. Finally, learn from your error and don't repeat it."

By the time Iris finished, I was crying. She put her arms around me and pulled me closer. That old comfort she always gave me, linked with a commanding power, bound our spirits together. Inexplicably, my mind sensed its small integral part in the heavens. When my life ended, I knew the energy forming my soul would rejoin the forces uniting the cosmos.

Wherever I went, I would never be lost, just changed. For fourteen years I'd been changing, so it wouldn't be anything new.

Looking at Iris, I said, "Thank you for the love and advice. I'll never forget you."

Iris tapped me on the head, saying, "Laurel, you're incredibly special, and we will meet again. I've presented you with divine providence as a lasting gift. Whenever life brings you problems, use your gifts and remember love's lessons to Laurel."

The doorbell rang and I went to answer it. Looking through the view port, there stood Mom. As I opened the door, I glanced over my shoulder at the fading image of Iris Wimple, who quietly said, "I love you."

She was gone.

Mom grabbed me, and we embraced for several minutes. "Laurel, it's so good to be home. Tell me all the details. Nothing too life altering, I hope."

Fall 2015

Sutter, Oregon, isn't much different than it was thirty years ago. French's Fry is gone and the cars are smaller, but the town's personality hasn't changed. I graduated from Sutter High in 1975, and although tempted by home economics, I attended the Julliard School of Music. Currently, I live in New York City with my husband, Tom, and our three children. I play second violin for the New York Philharmonic. My name is Joann Smithfield.

This weekend is my fortieth high school reunion. I haven't seen Laurel for eighteen years. Her name is now Rita Jones, or R.J. for short. She emails often so I know she's still alive, but she's reclusive; wherever Laurel is, even her mother doesn't know. I've prayed to Iris for Laurel to show up this weekend. My husband of twenty-two years is dying of melanoma. Laurel's always supported me in difficult times, and I need her now.

People wonder why Laurel lives in mystery, but her close friends know the truth. In the fall of 1971, Iris Wimple exited her sweet cocoon, giving the world an updated version of God. Yes, She was God. As well as Brett Moore quarterbacking Sutter to a state championship and five million in gold appearing out of thin air, other unexplained events left no doubt. Iris's Radio Flyer wagon contained a new titanium alloy that currently strengthens the hulls of submarines, classified by the navy at the time.

Following the infamous school board meeting, Nubs Fritzmeyer's injured hand was restored, and overnight, her vision returned. Appearing younger and more energetic, she started her own driving school and eventually taught Laurel and me how to drive. She's been gone twenty years, but she died happy, at 111, after falling off a ladder while painting her house.

The mystery of the giant sequoia wasn't a mystery for long. When the football team took the field the day after the board meeting, a three-hundred-foot sequoia had replaced the tree that almost killed Jimmy Dover. The world's tallest tree is still there today, topping out at 382 feet. The tree is only three decades old, and *National Geographic* is planning to try to discover its secrets. I could save them time.

Several other less dramatic events occurred closer to Thanksgiving. Two anonymous donors provided funds to build a homeless shelter. No one knows who, but I suspect one was Milt Ordner. Over the last twenty years, I've concluded the second donor was Denny Jensen. I know an authenticator who's worked at Sotheby's many years. Finding out my hometown was Sutter, she asked if I recalled Opal Bernstein. When I admitted I knew Mrs. Bernstein, she told me about auctioning Opal's jewelry in 1973.

The jewelry was auctioned by Sotheby's in 1971, but because the pieces were so rare they took two years to authenticate. Many of the auctioned gems were previously unknown and netted nearly six million dollars—a record for the time. When she showed me the auction catalog, I knew these were the jewels I'd seen during our "threesome" in Denny's basement. Strangely enough, the half-inch circular diamond surrounded by sapphires was not listed in the catalog. It was Laurel's favorite piece.

My parents still live in Sutter, as do Ed and Laurel's mother, Marie. The four of them play canasta every Wednesday night. Ed worked as Milt Ordner's foreman for years before he raised enough money to buy the company. He and Marie never remarried but own homes next to each other. Since I wasn't around during their wedded years, I can't say for sure, but it's fair to state they've rekindled their love, understanding that marriage isn't for them.

Marie recently retired as senior partner at Montgomery & Landsford, a law firm boasting six hundred attorneys and offices throughout the world. Her knowledge of foreign policy still makes her a valued source for the Secretary of State. Unfortunately, in recent months, Mrs. Montgomery's rheumatic heart disease has become worse. Plagued by heart failure and scarred heart valves, she's at Stanford being evaluated for a heart transplant. Ed is with her, and I hope Laurel comes out of seclusion to help. Marie's health has declined, and if she takes a turn for the worse, Laurel will never forgive herself.

The class reunion starts in two hours, and I'm excited to see old friends. This year, Penfield Wright is saying a few words. He replaced Chip Martin as junior high principal, and when we graduated, he was our high school principal. During all those years, he taught an elective called "The History of Religion through the Eyes of the Modern World." Mr. Wright recorded the lessons on Betamax because the class was so popular that many students never got in.

Recently, Mr. Wright's wife died, and Father Moore presided over the service—yes, the same Brett Moore who became Notre Dame's star quarterback and then shocked everyone by shunning the NFL to become a priest. I shouldn't lust after a priest, but Father Moore is hotter today than he was in high school. Catholic Charities raffled off a private picnic with him and raised $30,000. If he's ever allowed to pose half-naked for the Catholic calendar, I'll be first in line.

Bill Arnold is a district court judge. He's supposed to be fair, but when Kevin Stone's pot plants surfaced behind the old tree house, Bill sentenced him to seven years. He also presided over Chip Martin's third divorce. Chip married Amelia after their divorces went through. He wanted to stay in Sutter to be near his kids, but Amelia liked San Francisco. They divorced six months later. Chip has his own shoe store and is single again.

Occasionally, Bill sees Mel Corcoran and Robin Grace. They followed the directive of the ACLU, but when the tape surfaced, the ACLU's image suffered, and Corcoran and Grace paid the price. The ACLU abandoned Sutter Junior High's case and began searching elsewhere for a landmark case. Mr. Corcoran and Ms. Grace are estate attorneys who occasionally dabble in DUIs.

One person who Bill doesn't see is Emmitt Pilcher. His advice to Chip and the three board members got him disbarred, so he currently grooms lawns at the golf course.

Sutter has three citizens who've distinguished themselves: Dr. Collier, Mr. Donnay, and Don Caster. Dr. Collier became chief of surgery at the University of Oregon, and Mr. Donnay was appointed French Ambassador to the United States. I haven't seen Dr. Collier lately, but she still lives in Sutter. Ambassador and Mrs. Donnay gave me a standing invitation to have dinner at the Washington, DC, French Embassy when I'm in town. Cateline grows more beautiful with age; if I look half as good when I'm seventy, I'll be happy.

When Mr. Olson died in 1981, his partner, Don, became a gay rights activist. Substantial legislation against hate crimes wouldn't exist without Don's work. He still owns The Roasted Pear, and it's still the best restaurant in Sutter.

Tonight, I'll see Tanice and Susan. Utannah may attend, but her plans are uncertain. Susan and her family still live in Sutter. She enjoys singing, and her beautiful voice graces many weddings and funerals. Her husband, Rodney, and his partner, Ralph, own R & R Demolition, which specializes in imploding large structures. No one guessed these guys would do more than occupy a penitentiary, but both have engineering degrees and are successful businessmen.

Tanice and Mitch have been together since junior high. They have six kids—all boys. Not surprisingly, Tanice taught them to play baseball and football. She was one of the first women to coach Little League, and she currently coaches the offensive line for Sutter High. Local gossip says she's starting a women's hockey league. Even though she's forty-eight, I'd never discourage her; I don't want a fat lip. Mitch is a successful cattle rancher but hates sports, except for rodeo. Together, they've provided each other with love and support during difficult times.

Utannah owns a modeling agency, which has developed three superstar models over the last fifteen years. In a finicky industry, her flair for fashion and beauty propelled her to the peak of the profession. She's never married and probably never will. Utannah has homes in New York, London, Paris, Rome, and Hong Kong. She's bisexual and enjoys companionship wherever she goes. I've often envied her free spirit. The French don't suffer the hang-ups about intimacy that exist in American culture.

Reunions kindle old memories and occasionally old romances. Inevitably, our reunions spark questions about Laurel and Denny. When we look back, it's easy to see why. When Iris exited Laurel's life, she left no tools to deal with the onslaught of publicity. Few fourteen-year-olds have experience handling the press, let alone religious fanatics. Some folks equated Laurel to the Virgin Mary, while others called her the devil. She received an honorary doctorate from Boston College at age fifteen for, as she called it, "doing absolutely nothing."

Several magazines offered Laurel $200,000 for exclusive rights to her story. To her credit, she declined them, and I know she's never profited from her story. This isn't to say Laurel is without means. Long ago, under trial by fire, life demanded she learn to deal with fame. The reason she changed her name is because of her job.

When Iris told Laurel she'd granted her divine providence, it took a week to discover what that meant. We were eating lunch in the cafeteria with Denny and Mark when Mark decided he needed more cheesecake. The lunch counter was close, and Mark stood behind Cindy Summers.

Mark had problems with allergies and suffered from a runny nose. After talking several minutes, Mark looked surprised when Cindy offered her handkerchief for his nose. Nodding affirmatively, he returned without his cheesecake. He seemed aloof as he excused himself, saying he had an upset stomach.

As Mark walked away, Laurel said, "Joann, Cindy handed Mark her panties and asked to meet him in the janitor's closet. I know for sure that's where he's gone."

Denny and I assumed Laurel was suffering the aftereffects from her onstage exploits. Catching our dubious stares, she said, "Let's go look." I felt sorry for Laurel, but I went along to offer support for a sick friend.

The custodian was on vacation and always locked his closet, but when we arrived, muffled groans penetrated the solid wood door. Denny turned the handle, silently opening the door. On a bed of soft toilet paper rolls, Mark had Cindy's feet behind her ears and was stroking faster than the Oxford rowing team.

I'd never seen people having sex, so I was momentarily astonished. It looked much harder than I imagined. Later, Laurel reminded me there was a reason most people enjoyed sex in their bedroom instead of the custodian's closet. While I hadn't dated Mark enough to become close, his chances of getting closer disappeared up Cindy's skirt. Though usually levelheaded, I yelled, "He's all yours, Cindy, and you'll have plenty of time to enjoy 'im." I borrowed six pennies from Denny and repeated a trick I'd recently learned.

When I finished swim team, I dropped by the closet and knocked. The pennies were still in place, but I knocked just to make sure. Yup, they were still there. Next morning, Tilley Baumgart threw up and Mrs. Quinby needed a mop. Besides finding the bucket and mop in the janitor's closet, she discovered two spent teenagers.

I wasn't worried about "pennying in" Cindy and Mark. They didn't want folks hearing my version so they said they'd entered the closet looking for cleaning supplies when the door accidentally closed, imprisoning them overnight. During PE, Mark bragged about banging Cindy. Their concocted story fell apart, hastening Cindy's unplanned transfer to Sister Sarah Agnes. Nevertheless, Mark and Cindy got together after graduation and eventually married. Living in California, they own a vineyard and produce adult movies.

Laurel's ability to reach astounding conclusions from seemingly unconnected facts developed overnight. She received her doctorate in forensic psychology and started profiling for the FBI. She was so accurate, the mob took out a ten-million-dollar contract on her. Laurel tried witness protection, but she couldn't stop communicating with her mother. She changed her witness protection name to Rita Jones because it was a common name.

Then, without notice, she left witness protection and now stays in seclusion. Whenever Laurel leaves home, she's protected by three ex-Navy SEALs.

Eventually, Laurel discovered that her talents were useful in financial markets and politics, so she started her own business. Potential clients send proposals over encrypted Internet portals. If Laurel accepts their case, she's only paid if her analysis yields valuable information. If profit or power is the client's goal, Laurel has a minimum fee of $300,000. Missing children and high-profile crimes she does pro bono. Only one businessman refused to pay. Someone leaked information to the Internal Revenue Service and the gentleman found a new home in San Quentin.

In 1972, Bill Landsford released the story of Laurel's close friendship with Iris. Publishers offered millions for the rights, and today, *God's in the Details* is still a bestseller. The publishers still pay Bill's legal fees for representing Laurel, and Laurel gives most of her profits to charity.

In the early days, after Iris left, Laurel granted several interviews. When TV networks broadcast the discussions, half the world's population tuned in. Only the first landing on the moon had attracted more viewers. In the interviews, Laurel recapped Iris's words to the school board. The board hadn't allowed filming, but Mr. Landsford had received the court's permission to record the dialogue. For the first time, a recording captured God's words.

Her message rallied different religions to work as a team, promoting peace.

People begged for more of God's wisdom and assumed that if it existed, Laurel knew its location. But over the decades, nothing more spectacular happened—and Laurel couldn't be found—so the clamor subsided.

Then, two years ago, Laurel sent me an email. She worried something might happen and asked for my help in case she died. Reluctantly, I agreed, and soon after being sworn to secrecy, a messenger delivered a hand-addressed letter.

In the letter, Laurel described what had happened when she cleaned Iris's room. Tucked under the pillow on the bed was a manila folder, addressed to Laurel. She opened it and found a three-page Latin document titled, *Conservationem Hominus Dei Verbum.* The document was original and superbly written. Since Laurel wouldn't take the text for translation, she deciphered it herself. She never told me the body of the text, but the English title translation is: "God's Word on the Preservation of Man."

Since I'm Catholic, I know what a papal encyclical is, but I'm guessing this one trumps even the Pope. Laurel hinted the message was penetrating and splendid in its simple directions. To my knowledge, only Laurel and I know this document exists. Iris told Laurel to release the text in 2016. I don't know the reason, but I've assured Laurel that if something happens to her, I will publish it immediately.

The weather's warm, so I've decided to walk to the reunion. Yesterday, I hiked around the lake, as we did thirty years ago. Remnants of the tree house are still there, as well as a beat-up waterwheel. The beavers lived out their days with Marie and occasionally slept at Ed's. Bobby and Jean never had kits, so we assume they were the same sex.

Yesterday, before finishing my hike, I stopped at the swimming hole. I sat on the rock where Laurel and I had shared our last childhood adventure. Twenty minutes after we'd dressed, Laurel had agreed to a date with her soul mate—and our relationship changed.

Now, as I walk past Laurel's home, I know my classmates will wonder about Denny. The honest answer is, I don't know.

Laurel and Denny dated during junior high and high school. Throughout all the demands on Laurel, Denny stood by her, offering comfort and support. Except for Laurel and me, Denny continued giving classmates the impression he'd never amount to much—that is, until he won the Westinghouse Science Talent competition.

Two weeks before graduation, it was announced that Denny had edged out Elle Dutton by three-tenths of a point to become the class valedictorian. The Duttons demanded the school recalculate the GPAs; Elle's graduation announcements had gone out saying she was giving the valedictory address. The school obliged, and when they finished, Elle was correct: the grades hadn't been accurately computed. Elle's GPA was lower, making Laurel the salutatorian!

Awarded a scholarship to MIT, Denny had to make a hard choice. Laurel wasn't ready for the East Coast, and Denny wasn't ready for marriage. He decided to attend MIT, so they packed a year into the summer of 1975. By coincidence, a week before Denny was leaving, his parents and Marie Montgomery both had business outside Sutter. Only Denny and Laurel knew both sets of parents had left town.

Denny got into the AT&T switching box and sent the Montgomery calls to his home. On Friday, Laurel announced she was visiting friends in Seattle. No one knew that during that weekend, they'd lived every teen's fantasy. Denny found his parents' book *The Joy of Sex,* and the two of them tried seventeen positions over forty-eight hours. Three days later, Laurel described a pleasure machine Denny had invented. She told me the vivid details—and I thought she was joking. She wasn't. Science majors might be geeks, but innovation has inspired moments. During the seventies, their behavior seemed scandalous, but today, couples have sex on the first date. Waiting five years was a miracle.

Over the next three summers, they dated, and Laurel visited Denny twice during his senior year. Denny studied bioengineering and graduated summa cum laude. He planned to attend medical school and continue research in artificial organ development. He returned to Sutter before starting medical school at Johns Hopkins. Laurel and I expected Denny to propose, but at summer's end, there was no ring or even a promise. Without discussing her plans, Laurel surprised Denny when she suddenly ended their relationship. That day was the saddest Laurel and I ever endured. She wanted Denny as her husband, and I wanted happiness for my best friend.

Denny worked hard to have Laurel take him back, but she wouldn't communicate with him. She was the reason Denny had achieved his astounding goals. He said that when Laurel was in his corner, he couldn't lose. September came, and he left for medical school. Laurel and I watched from a distance as his parents loaded him into the car for Portland International Airport. Laurel cried when the door closed. Although she never admitted her plan, I think she wanted Denny to say she was more important than science.

Denny kept trying, but, not progressing, he abandoned further effort. Laurel never saw him again. Mr. Jensen's job transferred him to Northern California, so Denny had no reason to return. Sadly, two years later, I heard Oregon committed Denny to a state hospital for mentally disabled patients. I never confirmed the details, but his loss of Laurel probably played a critical role. Laurel still loves Denny, but we've stopped discussing it. The past can't be changed and life rarely offers second chances.

Mr. and Mrs. Jensen died in an auto accident, and a reliable source updated me about Denny, but I'll keep quiet until I verify the details.

Long ago, I enjoyed spreading gossip, but not so much anymore. Laurel's suffered enough from false hope.

I've often wondered what a girl once tucked under the wings of God did to deserve her poignant life. There is no satisfactory answer, just as there's no answer to why my husband is dying. Yes, I'm mad at Iris. There's probably some wise explanation, but love doesn't listen to logic. If it did, opposites would never attract and inspired masterpieces wouldn't exist. Perhaps someday, I'll revisit these questions and accept that God will answer my queries whenever She wants.

I've reached the high school. The reunion is in the high school activity room where we attended our first dance, but first I'm going to visit the stage. It's dark, but the fire exit signs make objects visible. The podium stands stoically, so I'm hoping memories from my past will take on life—but they don't. God is a hard act to follow, so I'm lucky I saw the only performance in 1971.

Well, it's time to stop thinking "What if?" and attend the reunion. The next time I see my classmates again after this, I'll be fifty-eight. My life changes daily, and I'm missing the one person who's been a constant. Deep down, I know Laurel won't attend, so I'll find strength from the classmates who've come.

Turning to head offstage, a familiar voice echoes from behind the podium, "Gee, Joann, hold up, will ya?"

Laurel runs over, and a bond—often stretched, never broken—pulls us into each other's arms. After several minutes of embracing each other, Laurel whispers in my ear, "I'm here to help as long as you need me." Her voice sounds ecstatic, and as I pulled back to look into her eyes, I see they radiate love.

"Laurel, something's good. Have you found a hot young stud who's bangin' your bones?"

Laurel explains how she unexpectedly found Denny after her mother's heart surgery and that he will be attending the reunion. She is overjoyed they've rekindled a passion born in an age of innocence, more than forty years ago. How Denny rose from the depths of destitution to be a world-renowned cardiac surgeon and recapture Laurel's heart is a story all its own.

Laurel put her arm around my waist and as we headed to the reunion, she said, "Let me tell you a magnificent story of redemption."

About the Author

RITA JONES is the pen name of Dan Eicher, a retired OB-GYN who delivered thousands of babies during his career. Within each newborn, he saw an essence often quickly hidden by the need to deal with life's hurdles. Rediscovering that essence is the foundation of *Love's Lessons to Laurel*.

A recovering alcoholic, Dan helps others seeking a spiritual path. He enjoys music and history and lives in Denver with his wife, Jacque, and Boston Terriers Arturo and Petunia.